Ludwig climbed back into his carr ᵒ ᵤ ꜱeat opposite his wife.

"All went well?" asked Charlotte.

"If you mean did we help him, then yes. If you're asking if he was pleased, the answer would be no. Apparently, he still bears a grudge."

"Even after all this time?"

"So it would seem."

"But Alexandra married Lord Emmett."

"Which apparently makes little difference to Darrian. You would think I interfered with his destiny or some such nonsense."

"So what happens now?"

"Simple," said Ludwig. "We continue on to Harlingen. Unfortunately, we'll see them at court, but at least we can look forward to meeting up with Merrick and Gita."

"Don't forget Kenley. I'm sure he and Frederick will become the best of friends."

"Doubtless, they will, but let us hope the realm won't be so rife with petty jealousies by then."

Charlotte craned her neck to look out the back of the carriage, but they'd gone too far to see Darrian's people. "This won't cause problems for you down the road, will it?"

"I wouldn't have thought so, but then again, I hadn't expected to meet with such animosity. You would think the scoundrel would at least be thankful for the help. Why, he practically bit Sig's head off."

"I can't imagine that went down very well."

Ludwig grinned. "Sig was remarkably calm, even after the baron threatened to have him whipped."

"Whipped? Surely not?"

"Well, that would only be an option had he been one of Darrian's people."

"My, he's a hot-tempered man. I suggest you try not to further antagonize him at court."

"I wasn't trying to do so here, yet he still took offence. What else can I do—completely avoid the fellow?"

"That might be best, at least in the short term."

"Short term? It's been years since we almost duelled. Just how much longer must I avoid him?"

ALSO BY PAUL J BENNETT

WARRIOR PRINCE

POWER ASCENDING: BOOK SIX

PAUL J BENNETT

First Edition: December 2023

ePub ISBN: 978-1-990073-70-0
Mobi ISBN: 978-1-990073-71-7
Smashwords ISBN: 978-1-990073-72-4
Print ISBN: 978-1-990073-69-4

DEDICATION

To my wife, Carol, who gave me wings to let my imagination fly.

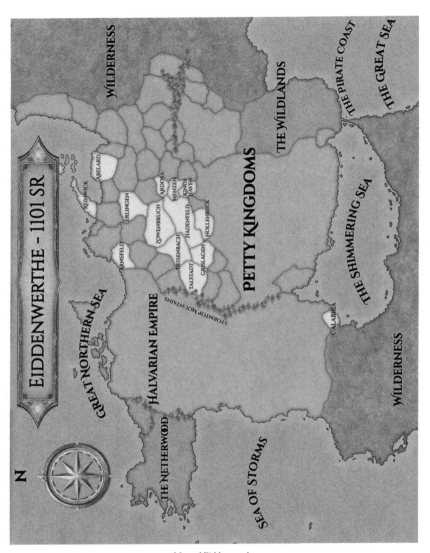

Map of Eiddenwerthe

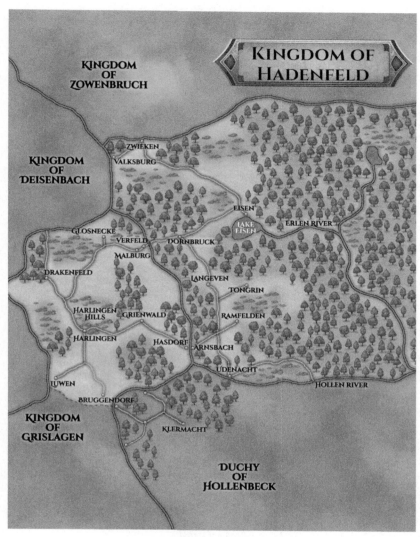

Kingdom of Hadenfeld

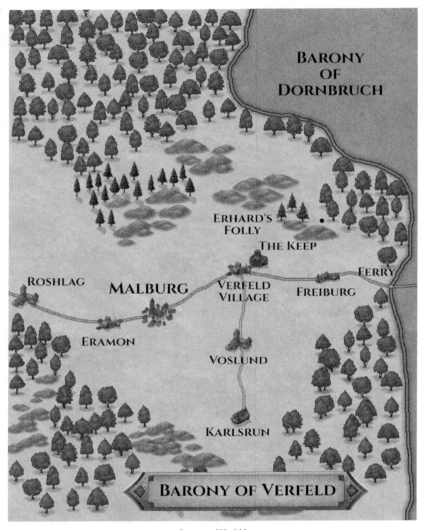

Barony of Verfeld

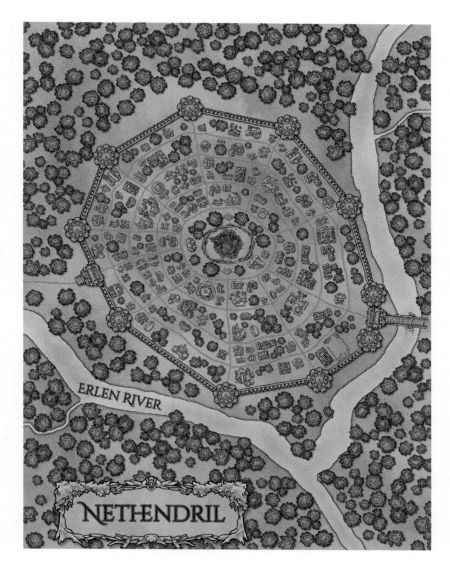

ERLEN RIVER

NETHENDRIL

1

AN UNEXPECTED ENCOUNTER
SPRING 1101 SR* (SAINTS RECKONING)

L udwig stared out the carriage window, absently watching the dark clouds hovering overhead. They'd been on the road most of the day, yet almost another week would pass before they arrived in Harlingen.

"Thinking about the coronation?" Charlotte's words interrupted his thoughts.

He switched his gaze to his wife, who was energetic today and had been since she awoke. He knew it wouldn't last, for she would eventually lapse into the melancholy her affliction brought on. Ludwig smiled, enjoying the moment. "I was wondering what kind of king Morgan will make."

"And your decision?"

"To be honest, I know very little of the man. I've met him but never spent much time in his company."

"Isn't he your cousin? I thought you would've seen him at family gatherings."

"Such things were never my father's favourite, and I fear I take after him in that regard." He looked at Frederick, sleeping peacefully beside his mother despite the uneven road. "I wonder if our son will turn out the same."

"Hard to say," replied Charlotte. "After all, Frederick has only just turned two."

At the mention of his name, the child stirred, looking around with bleary eyes. Realizing they were still travelling, he laid his head back on his mother's lap.

"At least it's not raining," said Ludwig. "I suppose we'd best make camp before it gets too dark to put the tents up."

The carriage slowed, causing him to look out the window once more. A rider appeared, and then a towering figure opened the door.

"Sorry," Sig said. "There's trouble ahead."

A look of alarm flashed across Charlotte's face. "Not bandits, I hope?"

"No. Only a carriage which appears to be in some sort of distress."

"Anyone we know, Sig?" asked Ludwig.

The northerner smiled back. "It bears the Baron of Glosnecke's Coat of Arms."

"Lord Darrian?"

"Well, it's his carriage. I've yet to see who's inside. Do you want me to enquire?"

"I'd best do that myself," said Ludwig. "The last thing we want is to upset the baron."

Charlotte grinned. "Wasn't it Lord Darrian who challenged you to a duel?"

He looked at Sigwulf. "You told her?"

"Cyn did," replied Charlotte, "although I fail to see why you didn't tell me yourself. Or is it you were ashamed it was over the affections of another woman?"

"That was before we were married," said Ludwig, "and as I've told you before, there was never any affection other than friendship."

"I'm only teasing. Still, you must remember to mind your manners. Lord Darrian is the baron now, and we are crossing through his lands."

"I'll remember." He rose from his seat and stepped out of the carriage door. The other carriage sat some hundred yards down the road, its horse team standing off to the side. A trio of guards milled around as servants examined something beyond Ludwig's view.

"Trouble?" he called out.

An older guard with a weather-beaten face put hand to hilt but then relaxed. "My Lord Ludwig, your arrival is most fortuitous. My master's carriage has suffered some damage."

"What sort of damage?"

"A wheel came loose as it hit a rut. Thankfully, it didn't come right off, but it frightened the horses, leading them to panic and charge off the road."

"And now it's stuck?"

"More or less, yes. We repaired the wheel, but I'm afraid it'll take more than our two horses to get that thing back on the road."

"I assume you are transporting Lord Darrian to the capital?"

"Indeed, Lord, along with a visiting knight, Sir Emril."

"Then I'd best pay my respects before we get to work. Where is His Lordship?"

"Still in the carriage."

"I would have thought it prudent to empty the thing to help free it from all those weeds."

The guard stared back, shrugging.

Ludwig turned, calling for Sigwulf. "Gather four men and bring them over. We'll try hauling this thing out by brute force." He moved closer to the stranded carriage and knocked on the door. Moments later, Darrian's scowling face appeared.

"Lord Ludwig? What are you doing here?"

"I'm on my way to Harlingen for the coronation, as are you, I assume."

Sir Emril leaned forward, his fashionable attire visible through the open door. "By the Saints, that was timely! Can you get us out of this mess?"

"It would be easier were you both not in it. It's the extra weight, you see. Makes it that much more difficult to extricate this carriage of yours."

"Very well," said Darrian, stepping out with a cane in hand.

"Are you injured?"

"Clearly," the baron spat back.

"He suffered a bad fall this last winter," offered Sir Emril. "The steps to the keep were icy, and he lost his footing." He followed his friend out and then helped Darrian back to the road.

Sigwulf returned with four men from their escort. Along with the baron's men, they took up stations and pushed, but the carriage refused to budge.

Cyn, who had wandered over, crouched to look beneath. "I see the problem," she announced. "There's a branch poking up from the ground, and it looks like it's wedged against a wheel."

"Can you cut it loose?" asked Ludwig.

"I'll certainly try, but I'll need an axe."

One of Ludwig's men, a Calabrian named Gustavo, produced his weapon. "Will this do?"

"It should." She crawled beneath and began hacking away. "This is likely to take some time."

Ludwig wandered over to Lord Darrian. "How long have you been here?"

"We left Glosnecke this afternoon."

"You're lucky. Had you left any later, we would've already passed by before your accident."

"I would hardly call our current predicament lucky." He glanced at Ludwig's carriage, sitting on the road. "Are you travelling with your family?"

"I am."

"My condolences."

"For what?"

"I'm led to understand your wife suffers from an affliction of the mind."

Ludwig tensed. Was the fellow offering insult or merely being rude? "Who told you that?"

"It's common knowledge. Still, at least she gave you an heir." Darrian paused for a moment. "Say, he's not afflicted as well, is he?"

"I have no complaints where my wife is concerned. Perhaps you should spend more time worrying about your own prospects than concentrating on idle gossip."

"My own prospects?"

"Yes," said Ludwig. "I'm led to believe you still lack a wife."

The Baron of Glosnecke puffed out his chest. "I hardly think that's any of your concern."

"Yes," added Sir Emril. "I know the story, as does everyone else in the kingdom. If you hadn't gotten in the way, Lord Darrian would be married to Lady Alexandra."

"That was six years ago!" replied Ludwig. "Can't we put that behind us?"

"You can make light of it," said Darrian, "but some things cannot be forgiven."

Upon hearing the exchange, Sigwulf moved closer. "With all due respect, Lord Darrian, you should watch your tongue."

The baron turned on the northerner in a fury. "How dare you speak to one of your betters in such a familiar manner? Why, if you were in my service, I would have you whipped."

"Then it's a good thing I serve Lord Ludwig."

Darrian stared at Ludwig. "Are you going to allow him to speak to me in that manner?"

"He's a northerner."

"Meaning?"

Ludwig shrugged. "He's used to speaking his mind. It's common up there."

Darrian stood there, his mouth agape.

Sir Emril stepped forward. "Let us not quibble over the ravings of a peasant. Can't we all act in a civilized manner?"

Darrian composed himself. "Yes, of course. My apologies, Lord Ludwig, if I offered insult. My present circumstances overwhelm me, and I am in great pain due to my injury."

"Apology accepted," said Ludwig. He noticed Cyn crawling out from beneath the carriage.

She nodded his way. "I removed the obstruction. Let's try to get you back on the road, shall we?"

The men took up positions and heaved. It worked this time, and the carriage was soon astride the road.

"There you are," said Ludwig. "Good as new. You'll pardon me if I don't wait around while you harness your team, but I must be on my way. I look forward to seeing you at court."

Darrian half bowed. "And you, Lord Ludwig," though he said it through gritted teeth.

Ludwig climbed back into his carriage, taking a seat opposite his wife.

"All went well?" asked Charlotte.

"If you mean did we help him, then yes. If you're asking if he was pleased, the answer would be no. Apparently, he still bears a grudge."

"Even after all this time?"

"So it would seem."

"But Alexandra married Lord Emmett."

"Which apparently makes little difference to Darrian. You would think I interfered with his destiny or some such nonsense."

"And his brother?"

"That wasn't his brother. It was a knight named Sir Emril, whom I've met before, although he spoke little."

"So what happens now?"

"Simple," said Ludwig. "We continue on to Harlingen. Unfortunately, we'll see them at court, but at least we can look forward to meeting up with Merrick and Gita."

"Don't forget Kenley. I'm sure he and Frederick will become the best of friends."

"Doubtless, they will, but let us hope the realm won't be so rife with petty jealousies by then."

Charlotte craned her neck to look out the back of the carriage, but they'd gone too far to see Darrian's people. "This won't cause problems for you down the road, will it?"

"I wouldn't have thought so, but then again, I hadn't expected to meet with such animosity. You would think the scoundrel would at least be thankful for the help. Why, he practically bit Sig's head off."

"I can't imagine that went down very well."

Ludwig grinned. "Sig was remarkably calm, even after the baron threatened to have him whipped."

"Whipped? Surely not?"

"Well, that would only be an option had he been one of Darrian's people."

"My, he's a hot-tempered man. I suggest you try not to further antagonize him at court."

"I wasn't trying to do so here, yet he still took offence. What else can I do—completely avoid the fellow?"

"That might be best, at least in the short term."

"Short term? It's been years since we almost duelled. Just how much longer must I avoid him?"

The way to Harlingen was bustling, for with news of a coronation, people of means were eager to witness the spectacle. Once they reached the Drakenfeld-Harlingen road, the number of wagons increased dramatically, and traffic slowed considerably. By noon on their fifth day of travel, they were hardly moving, for it appeared the entire kingdom was intent on heading to the capital.

Ludwig sighed. "At this rate, we'll miss the coronation entirely."

Charlotte's earlier joy at the excitement of travelling had shifted into melancholy. Her deeply entrenched sadness was beyond her control, so he sat beside her, holding her hand, doing his best to comfort her.

Frederick watched excitedly as they passed a group of horsemen. Ludwig didn't recognize their colours, but their air of professionalism was likely the result of being employed by a foreign lord. He thought of taking a horse and riding back to find out who this mysterious noble was, but that would mean abandoning his wife.

Instead, he concentrated on his son. The boy had come a long way in the last few months, now running all over the keep, though thankfully, the stairs still slowed him down. Frederick particularly liked horses, and Ludwig had taken his son riding several times. Strangely enough, of all the things in Verfeld to captivate him, the one that held the greatest allure proved to be Sigwulf.

He wasn't sure if it was just the northerner's size or his beard that drew his son's attention, but whenever Sig entered the room, Frederick would go silent, staring at the man. To make matters worse, whenever Cyn used the name 'Siggy', the child would break into outrageous fits of laughter.

Ludwig stared at his wife, fast asleep beside him. More than anything else in the world, he wanted to help her, but all his enquiries met with failure. He'd written to the best healers in all of Hadenfeld, even a few from beyond its borders, yet the result was always the same—there was no known cure for what ailed her.

A feeling of helplessness welled up inside him. To battle it, he dug out his Book of Saint Mathew, a gift from Rosalyn Haas, the Baron of Regnitz's daughter. In times such as this, it brought him comfort.

After reading a few passages, he felt revived. In his younger days, Ludwig never considered himself a religious man, yet now, at the ripe old age of thirty-three, his faith gave him strength when he needed it the most.

The words of the Saint turned his thoughts to Temple Knights and, quite naturally, to Charlaine deShandria. Now a Temple Captain in Reinwick, she'd attended his marriage to Charlotte, but that was over two years ago. Was she still there, or had the order seen fit to send her elsewhere?

He'd promised to write to her but had been negligent. His gaze wandered back to Charlotte, and guilt washed over him. A piece of him would always love Charlaine, yet his wife now held his heart. Was he being foolish? Was it even proper to harbour such thoughts? At first, he rebelled at the idea he could love two women, then when he looked at it closely, he realized it wasn't so much love with Charlaine as a sense of respect and friendship. He saw her as an equal when it came to their military positions, someone who understood the trials and tribulations of being in charge.

With this new-found revelation, he realized how deeply he loved his wife. When they first married, he'd promised to respect her, but never in his wildest dreams had he envisioned she would become so important to him. Was this the work of the Saints? Their teachings offered only advice on how to live, yet many saw them as a supernatural force, reaching out from beyond death to guide them when difficult decisions were necessary.

Centuries ago, the people of the Continent worshipped the Old Gods. Indeed, some still did. Were the Saints simply a replacement for these ancient beliefs? He found the thought disturbing to contemplate. Perhaps he was simply getting old?

He chuckled, causing Charlotte to open her eyes.

"What are you laughing at?" she asked.

"Just life in general."

"You need to do better than that."

"If you must know, I was pondering my mortality. Tell me; do you consider me old?"

She forced a smile. "Mature, perhaps, but you've still many years ahead of you."

"Do I? I sometimes wonder."

"I'm the one who ponders such maudlin matters. You're supposed to be full of energy and enthusiasm."

"And I am, generally," said Ludwig. "Especially when you're around."

"Then what brought about this mood?"

"I was contemplating religion."

"Then you should talk to Father Vernan. If anyone could answer your questions, it would be him. Why don't we pull over, and you can invite him to ride with us?"

"No. You need your rest. I can always chat with him later."

"Then perhaps you should turn your thoughts to something a little more pleasant?"

"Such as?"

"I don't know, the coming coronation?"

"I would feel a lot better about that if I had some idea of what kind of king Morgan will be."

"I doubt he knows himself."

"I hadn't considered that."

"You're also in the line of succession yourself, and with Morgan becoming king, you move one step closer to the Throne."

"I'm not sure that's entirely sunk in quite yet." He looked at her and smiled.

"What are you grinning at?"

"You! It's not every day I get to travel in a carriage with such a beautiful woman."

She shook her head. "I can hardly be called beautiful."

"But you are. Don't you see? To me, you are the most desirable woman in all of Eiddenwerthe. You are the queen of my heart." He made an elaborate bow, a difficult thing to do within the close confines of the carriage. Just as he reached the end of it, they hit an obstruction in the road, sending him tumbling into her lap.

She laughed, her mood lightening, if only for a moment. "If you wanted to be intimate, you need only say so!"

THE GATHERING
SPRING 1101 SR

Harlingen's narrow streets made the entire place feel like an immense maze. Ludwig had never been one for big cities, yet he had to admit the capital was much nicer than those he'd seen in the northern Petty Kingdoms. The feeling here was one he'd found nowhere else—the hope that a new king would usher in a time of peace and prosperity.

They rolled to a stop before the house of Lord Merrick and Lady Gita. Servants rushed out, one placing a footstool beside the carriage. Ludwig stepped down as his friends exited the building.

"There you are," said Merrick. "We were questioning if you'd make it here for the coronation."

"I'm afraid that's my fault," replied Ludwig. "I wasn't expecting the road to be so busy."

"Understandable. After all, it's not every day we crown a king."

Gita leaned to one side, peering behind Ludwig. "Is Charlotte not with you?"

"I'm here," came the reply, though it sounded exhausted. "Frederick is proving to be a handful."

Ludwig turned. "Let me," he said, reaching up and grabbing his son. With the child in hand, he swivelled back to his hosts. "You two are dressed very fine. Going somewhere?"

"Yes, as a matter of fact," said Merrick. "As you should be. The king invited all the nobles to the Royal Keep."

"The coronation is tomorrow, isn't it?"

"Yes, but Morgan wishes everyone to come and celebrate before all the official ceremonies commence. In truth, I think he wants the boost to his ego, but don't tell him I said that."

"Know Morgan well, do you?"

"Now, now," interrupted Gita. "You can talk about all that later. Let's get Master Frederick inside, shall we? Then you two must change into something more suitable for court."

"That soon?"

"My dear fellow," said Merrick. "We'd have gone there some time ago if we hadn't been waiting for your arrival."

"You could have left word for us to follow."

"And miss all the fun of going to the keep with you? I don't think so." They made their way into the house.

"Have you heard from the others?" asked Ludwig.

"Lord Emmett and Lady Alexandra send their regards. They arrived yesterday and are staying at Lord Meinhard's but promise to meet us at the keep. Of course, there's a host of others eager to welcome you. That's what comes from you being such a fine fellow."

"We ran into Lord Darrian on the way down here. He experienced some trouble with his carriage."

"I sense there's a bit more to this story," said Merrick. "He didn't cause problems, did he?"

"Nothing I couldn't handle, although I was surprised he still holds a grudge after all these years."

"So he didn't challenge you to another duel?"

"I doubt he'd be that foolish."

"It wouldn't be the first time a noble has done something foolish."

"True," said Ludwig, "but he's the baron now, and that sort of responsibility tends to mature a fellow."

"Just not enough to avoid insulting you?"

"Who says he insulted me?"

"You do, by your manner, if not your words."

Ludwig slowed, allowing the ladies to proceed, then lowered his voice. "He made some disparaging remarks about Charlotte."

"By the Saints! She didn't hear any of it, did she?"

"No, and I'd like to keep it that way."

"I understand completely. Have you heard anything about the ceremony?"

"Other than the date and time, no. Why? Is there something I should know?"

"Nothing in particular, although I would have thought that, as cousin to the king, you'd play a prominent role in it."

"If that were so, it would be a surprise to me. Perhaps Morgan wants the focus to remain on him. Not that I can blame him; he is about to be crowned king."

"Yes," said Merrick, "but I hope it ends there."

"What ever do you mean?"

"Let's just say Morgan can be a stubborn man, often at the most inopportune of moments. Do you recall the first time you met?"

"As you well know, it was at my induction as Baron of Verfeld."

"Oh yes, so it was. I should've remembered that."

"And yourself? When did you first meet him?"

"Years ago now, when my father was still around."

"And?"

"As I said, he can be stubborn sometimes, which served him well during the war, but court is a much different affair. I fear he still bears a grudge against the newer barons."

"And by newer," said Ludwig, "you mean those from the old Kingdom of Neuhafen?"

"Yes, though I believe the correct term these days would be the 'eastern baronies', which is a little less inflammatory."

"That doesn't bode well for Lord Emmett."

"Nor any of the others. Still, once Morgan's king, let's hope he'll adopt a more conciliatory approach."

"Has there been any news concerning a new queen?"

"None, I'm afraid," replied Merrick, "and there's very little indication he'll recognize any of those children he's sired outside of marriage. That's good news for you, I suppose... or bad, depending on your point of view."

"I'm far from being Morgan's direct heir."

Merrick grinned. "Then it's of no concern to you whatsoever."

Ludwig quickly dressed for court, then sat with Frederick, waiting for Charlotte. However, she succumbed to another bout of melancholy and insisted he attend without her. Thus, Ludwig entered the Royal Keep in the company of only Merrick and Gita.

A riot of colours filled the place, a stark difference from the sparsely decorated décor of King Otto, who'd reigned for over fifty years; some might even say Otto WAS Hadenfeld. Unfortunately, kings don't live forever, and although he would miss Otto, Ludwig knew change was inevitable. His own history was a great example of that. He looked forward to getting reacquainted with Morgan. Perhaps he wouldn't be as bad as Merrick suggested.

"There he is," came a familiar voice, cutting through the noise.

"Alexandra!" called out Gita. "Good to see you. I trust all is well?"

Ludwig noted the blonde hair pushing through the assembled guests, and then the rest of her came into view, revealing a swollen belly.

He grinned. "Congratulations. You never mentioned you were expecting." He lowered his voice. "You are expecting, aren't you?"

She laughed. "Of course, and as for not letting you know, I must apologize, but we've been busy of late, and I haven't had time to write." She looked over at the small group. "Is Charlotte not with you?"

"Unfortunately, no," replied Ludwig. "I'm afraid she's a little under the weather."

"Understood, but we shall keep her in mind going forward and offer our prayers for her recovery."

"Thank you. Where's Emmett?"

She stood on tiptoes, casting her gaze around the room. "He's here somewhere. The last I saw him, he was chatting with Lord Jonas, the Baron of Ramfelden."

"It's one of the eastern baronies, isn't it?"

"Yes, that's right. It lies up the road from Arnsbach. We were down that way ourselves. That's why we didn't pass through Verfeld on the way here."

"I trust all is well back home?"

"There's been some minor difficulties since the end of the war, but we're managing."

"Difficulties?" said Ludwig.

"Everything was fine when Otto was still alive, but since his demise, the Crown has grown more distant; one might even say punitive."

"I'm not sure I follow."

"Taxes have increased, though not for those barons who remained loyal to Otto."

"I wasn't aware of that."

"Nor I," said Alexandra. "If I hadn't run into my father, I would've assumed we were all suffering the same burden."

Ludwig shook his head. He'd convinced Otto to take a more conciliatory attitude towards the renegade barons at the Second Battle of Harlingen, but now it appeared that particular promise ended with his death. He wondered if this extra tax was Morgan's idea or the Royal Bureaucracy taking matters into their own hands. "I shall endeavour to bring it to my cousin's attention, though I daresay that won't happen till after the coronation."

"Thank you," said Alexandra. "I knew we could count on you."

Blaring trumpets announced the arrival of their future ruler, and they all turned, facing the front of the room as heralds entered, bearing the new king's Coat of Arms.

Everyone bowed and fell silent as Morgan swept in, draped in robes of ermine and mink. There was no crown upon his head, but there might as well have been, for everyone knew this was to be their new king.

Morgan made his way to the centre of the room, the crowd parting to allow him passage. There, he halted, taking in the nobles of his kingdom. Everyone held their breath, waiting for his words.

"My loyal subjects," he began. "It is with great pride I greet you here, in the Royal Keep, a building steeped in history. Tomorrow, I shall be crowned as your king in a ceremony passed down to us by our ancestors. Their spirit and passion built this glorious realm of ours, a passion I intend to reignite. Long ago, Hadenfeld was the mightiest of the Petty Kingdoms, with the largest army on all the Continent, save for Halvaria itself. I would see us rebuild that army and take our rightful place as the premier power in the region."

Polite applause greeted his remarks, but then he held up his hands to quiet them. After taking a measured breath, he continued, "I know we've had our differences. Under my predecessor's rule, the realm was fractured, its power split into two kingdoms. Through force of arms, we are once more one nation." He paused, meeting his subjects' rapt attention with great intensity. "No more will we be a broken people. We shall rise to be the pre-eminent power on the Continent!"

The crowd erupted into applause, this time more heartfelt, yet Ludwig couldn't help feeling worried. Morgan bowed, then made his way through his guests, accepting their congratulations.

"That was inspiring," said Merrick.

"Yes," agreed Ludwig, "but I can't help feeling a war is in our future."

"What makes you say that?"

"It's one thing to talk about becoming a great power, quite another to prove it. Unless I miss my guess, he's planning a military campaign."

"Against whom?"

"That remains to be seen."

"Perhaps it's only bluster?" suggested Merrick. "It wouldn't be the first time a king promised greatness only to fall back to idleness."

"Possibly, but as you mentioned earlier, Morgan can be stubborn. Considering that, I suspect he'll dig in his heels."

"He'd need the barons' support to launch a war, and after our recent losses, I'm not sure he'd find much enthusiasm. Perhaps he's talking in grander terms, say a few years down the road? In any case, the man hasn't even been crowned yet. Let's at least give him the benefit of the doubt."

Ludwig sighed. "Yes, you're right. Perhaps this is all bluster, as you said."

Alexandra tapped Ludwig on the shoulder. "You have an admirer."

He turned to see Sir Emril staring at him from across the room. The fellow was one of Otto's knights and had served in the recent war, but he and Ludwig had never seen eye to eye.

"He doesn't look happy," she noted. "Is there something you're not telling us?"

"During the war, we had an altercation of sorts."

"Of sorts? What in the name of the Saints does that mean?"

"When we first met, he took me for a commoner."

"And that annoyed you?"

"That he didn't recognize me, no. That he treated a common man with such disrespect, most definitely. I corrected him and thought no more of it, but I feel he still bears a grudge." He stopped for a moment. "Come to think of it, he was in amongst Lord Morgan's camp, and just this last week, I saw him in the company of Lord Darrian. Hmmm, that doesn't bode well. A few words in our new king's ear, and I could find myself on the outs."

She laughed. "What a strange thing to say. Did you pick that up in the north?"

"I suppose I did."

She sobered suddenly, drawing his attention.

"Something wrong?"

Alexandra nodded across the crowd. "Lord Darrian."

"You're married now. He's harmless."

"He still makes me feel uncomfortable. It's as if his eyes are undressing me."

"Shall I have words with him?"

She placed her hand on his forearm. "No, Ludwig. If anyone were to act on my behalf, it would be Emmett, but this is not the time or the place for such gallantry." She forced a smile. "Besides, this is meant to be a celebration."

"Speaking of your husband, here he comes now."

The Baron of Dornbruck grinned as he approached Ludwig. "I worried you wouldn't make it in time for the coronation. You certainly cut it close."

"It is quite a distance to travel. I imagine some of the eastern barons are in an even worse predicament."

"Yes." He lowered his voice. "If I'm being frank, I don't understand the rush. Morgan could just as easily be crowned next month. Which would have given us all plenty of travel time."

"It would," interrupted Gita, "but this puts the king firmly in control."

"How so?"

"We all rushed here at his bidding."

"Clever," said Emmett, "but I doubt it won him any platitudes."

"Oh, I don't know," replied Ludwig. "You could put forth the argument that it makes him look decisive."

"True, but he's got years to do that."

"Yes, but it sets everyone's expectations. I suspect Morgan will be more prone to making decisions without consensus."

"I think you have the right of it," replied Emmett, "though I'm not sure if that's good or bad. What about you, Merrick?"

"This is not the place for such discussions." He turned around as the king approached, then bowed. "Your Majesty."

Morgan smiled, although it looked a little forced. "That's Highness, at least until tomorrow, but I appreciate the effort. As for you, Ludwig, I shall expect to see you right after the coronation tomorrow."

"Me?" said Ludwig. "Whatever for?"

"If I am to be successful as king, my advisors must be fully informed of my plans, including you, Cousin. After all, whom can you trust if you can't trust blood relatives?"

"Surely you'll need time to settle in before worrying about that."

"We are but mortal men," said Morgan. "Thus, it behooves us to act with some haste, particularly when there is so much work to begin." He turned towards the women. "Lady Gita, Lady Alexandra, so nice to see you at court." His eyes flicked back to Ludwig. "Is Lady Charlotte not here with you?"

"I'm afraid she is under the weather," replied Gita. "But she will do her best to be present for tomorrow's ceremony."

"Make sure that she is. It's not every day someone has the opportunity to watch the crowning of a king." He nodded before continuing. "Lord Merrick, so glad to see you." He then turned to speak to Emmett but seemed to struggle.

"Lord Emmett," offered Ludwig. "Baron of Dornbruck and husband to Lady Alexandra."

"Of course," said the soon-to-be king. "I knew I recognized your face. If you will excuse me, I have many more guests to speak with." He pushed past them, his retinue crowding in behind him, amongst them Sir Emril, who looked at Ludwig briefly before shaking his head dismissively.

"That was rude," said Gita.

"The king is a busy man," replied Ludwig.

"I wasn't referring to the king, I meant Emril."

"You must take no notice," said Merrick. "He's nothing more than a sycophant, or perhaps parasite is a better description."

"Careful," warned Emmett. "Even the lowly tick can bring down a great beast."

"The beast being?"

"In this case, Ludwig, but we are both known associates of him, so either of us might find ourselves a target."

"Perhaps," said Merrick, "but what can he do? He's only a knight and not a particularly wealthy one at that."

"Yet he follows in the king's wake. That indicates his fortunes are on the rise."

"Enough of that kind of talk," admonished Alexandra. "On another note, my father asked me to invite you all down to Luwen once the coronation is complete."

"I'm sure the invitation would delight Charlotte," said Ludwig, "but I have no idea how long our new king requires my services."

"Then we shall take your wife and son with us," replied Gita, "and you can follow along once you're free."

"Yes," added Emmett, "although I suggest you keep those two mercenaries of yours nearby, just to be safe."

"You mean Cyn and Sig? Why? You don't think I'm in any danger, do you?"

"Danger, no, at least not directly, but with the wealthy of Hadenfeld fleeing back to their manors after the coronation, I imagine the lure of all that treasure on the road will only encourage banditry."

"Very well," said Ludwig. "I'll heed your advice."

3

THE CORONATION

SPRING 1101 SR

Six white horses pulled Morgan's carriage through the streets of Harlingen. Before him rode fifty knights, resplendent in their plate armour, while three companies of footmen followed, each wearing the blue surcoats of the Royal House of Hadenfeld.

They arrived at the Cathedral of Saint Mathew as the bells tolled noon. Ludwig watched Morgan enter the grand edifice, then duly followed along with the rest of the barons.

He spotted Father Vernan as he entered, for all the Holy Fathers had been summoned to witness the Royal Event. The Archprior of Saint Mathew would conduct the ceremony, while the Archprioress of Saint Agnes and the Archprior of Saint Cunar were in attendance.

He knew there were six different sects within the Church, but he'd only ever seen the three here. He sat down, his chains of office heavy upon his shoulders. The custom was to wear them to all official ceremonies, yet he hadn't had them when he was inducted as Baron of Verfeld. Truth be told, this was the first time he'd worn them, and the thick gold chain felt bulky and awkward, while his peers wore theirs with little sign of discomfort. He settled in, waiting for the ceremony to commence.

Upon entering, Morgan immediately went to a side chapel to pray privately before the crowning. Now that everyone was seated, the Archprior stepped onto the altar before turning to face the crowd. He commenced his speech with a blessing from Saint Mathew but soon turned to obedience and loyalty. He obviously referred to their about-to-be king, but Ludwig found it uninspiring.

His mind wandered, and he looked around, noting the overzealous displays of wealth. Towards the back of the Cathedral stood the poor, ushered in by soldiers to pay homage to their new overlord. Their gauntness haunted him, guilt overwhelming him as he realized he and the other nobles lived a life of luxury while they starved. Saint Mathew himself would be ashamed to see them treated in such a callous manner.

Lord Merrick nudged him back to the ceremony. The speech had finished, and the choir took up a hymn, their voices reaching high into the vaulted ceiling. Ludwig looked up at a giant mural depicting the first meeting of the Saints in the Holy City of Herani.

The six of them sat around a table, deep in discussion, a harmonious group of statesmen and one woman. Some believed the Saints had met out in the open rather than indoors, but that didn't suit the Church, which preferred to conduct its ceremonies within the shelter of its walls. Thus, the story evolved to become that which was now depicted above him.

Saint Mathew himself had called for humility and modesty, but looking at the Archprior bedecked in gold, the upper echelons of the Church apparently didn't take his words seriously.

Ludwig shook his head, then glanced down at his own chains of office. A sense of shame swept through him, and he knew, should he ever take the Throne himself, he would eschew the trappings of wealth and wear more modest attire.

The hymn ended, and the room fell silent as Morgan entered, followed by six knights. The soon-to-be king stopped before the altar while his loyal warriors turned to face the onlookers.

The Archprior stood silently as a page brought forth a pillow, upon which rested the Crown of Hadenfeld—a simple design, little more than a band of gold with six points, each symbolizing a Saint. No gems adorned it, nor any jewels to catch the light, yet merely looking at it took one's breath away, for each point was inlaid with scrollwork so fine only a master smith could have crafted such a thing.

The Archprior lifted the crown, calling on Saint Mathew to bless Morgan's rule before he placed it upon the sovereign's head, proclaiming him King Morgan the Second.

This surprised Ludwig, for though he held a fascination with military history, he knew nothing of the kings and queens of his homeland. That there had been another king named Morgan was unexpected, and he found himself wanting to read up on the first to bear that name. Would this new king live up to his predecessor?

Ludwig knew he was somewhere in line for the Throne, but seeing the crown upon Morgan's head somehow made it real, as if a mighty burden suddenly threatened to fall on his shoulders. He knew kings must make tough decisions, and his blood put him in that line. Would he fail as a cousin to a king? Would the weight of responsibility cause him to abandon all he held dear? He'd been cousin to Otto, yet now, with Morgan taking the Throne, it no longer felt like a distant and unlikely thing but something close and dangerous.

"Magnificent, isn't it?" asked Merrick.

The words brought Ludwig back to reality. All around him, people stood, their cheers drowning out the choir, once again singing the praises of the Saints.

"What happens now?" asked Ludwig.

"We follow him back to the Royal Keep. There, we'll each be expected to pledge our loyalty."

"And then?"

"Why, the feast! They say our new king has spared no expense to celebrate his ascension to the Throne."

"I would think there'd be better ways to spend his new-found wealth."

"And likely there are," replied Merrick, "but he's the king now, and the choice of how to spend it is his alone." He smiled as Morgan walked through the Cathedral, his knights following. "I daresay he cuts a much finer figure than his predecessor."

"It's a different time. Otto had to contend with a court half the size, and the shortage of funds was a constant problem for him."

"Was it? I hadn't realized. He still collected tithes from his barons."

"Yes, but since the reunification, the kingdom's income has more than doubled."

"I suppose it has, which is largely due to you."

"I am merely one man," replied Ludwig.

"Without your actions, we would've lost the battle and, with it, all hopes of a unified realm."

"Not true. Our king would just have been from Neuhafen."

"You make the entire war seem trivial."

"Do I?" said Ludwig. "That certainly wasn't my intention. Sorry, I'm just not in a celebratory mood."

"Worried about Charlotte?"

"Yes. Her mind will often shift between ecstasy and despondency without warning. I've tried everything to help her, but nothing seems to work."

"Surely you're not considering dissolving the marriage?"

"No, of course not. I love her. I'd never do anything of the kind, and to be clear, it's not myself I'm worried about; it's her. The struggle she goes through on a day-to-day basis seems insurmountable."

"Does it run in her family?" asked Merrick.

"Not that I know of, but I've only spent time with her father. I was introduced to her cousins at the wedding, but I doubt I spoke more than a dozen words to any of them."

"And she doesn't speak of them?"

"No, but then again, she lived an isolated childhood due to her moods."

"Did her father warn of this before you married?"

"He did, although I must confess I didn't know what I was getting into at the time."

"Would you still have married her had you known?"

Ludwig straightened. "Yes, I would. Aside from her bouts of melancholy, I find her demeanour both pleasant and engaging."

"Good," said Merrick. "Then all is as it should be." He glanced around the room as the other barons were leaving, indicating their new king had exited the Cathedral. "Now, let's find the others, shall we? There's a feast awaiting our appetites."

The Royal Keep's great hall was crowded, for somehow, they'd fit in tables enough for every baron, their wife, and any heirs who might be of age. It made for tight quarters, but no guests complained.

Not only was the room packed to capacity, but so were the tables. Morgan had gone to great lengths to ensure this was a feast of the ages, so much so the ovens were said to have been running for days.

Charlotte was in good spirits, while Frederick, being too young to attend, spent the day with Kenley back at Merrick's estate. Ludwig and his wife squeezed in between Gita and Emmett, who sat on Charlotte's left, which was handy, for they all knew of her illness.

After a quick toast from the king, everyone broke into their own discussions even as they plucked meat from overloaded plates. Servants scurried back and forth, filling goblets with wine and ale while various entertainers performed in the centre of the room.

The Lords of Hadenfeld gorged themselves, but Ludwig ate sparingly. Fat dripped off the meat while the sauces were thick with herbs, yet of all things, he craved barn bread. He'd become accustomed to it as a mercenary, for it was a standard meal when food was scarce. Even now, with the coffers of Verfeld Keep once more flowing with coins, he still found time to enjoy it.

The king called for silence as a familiar face, clothed in green and gold, stepped into the middle of the room and bowed deeply, lute in hand.

"Greetings, noble lords and ladies," he began. "My name is Rascalian, a troubadour of some repute. I came here today to sing the praises of your most noble king."

He strummed a few notes as he turned around, casting his gaze over the assembled guests, finally resting on Morgan, to whom he bowed. "With your permission, sire?"

The king nodded. "You may begin."

Ludwig buried his face in his hands. This bard had sung at his wedding, and while the tune had pleased Charlotte, he'd found it distasteful.

He felt a nudge from his wife. "Isn't that the same bard we saw in Korvoran?"

Ludwig forced a smile. "It is indeed."

"How marvellous. I wonder what he'll sing about this time?"

The fellow's voice launched into high notes, the first few words nonsense, until the song began.

Noble lords and ladies,
    And all knights, brave and strong,
    Gather round and heed my words,
    As I sing to you this song.

"It's the same song as he sang to us," said Ludwig, but Charlotte quickly hushed him.

A land of greatness, Hadenfeld,
    Had borders under siege,
    For rebels had, for many years,
    Fought hard 'gainst lawful liege

Rebellion raised, the armies marched,
    To punish rightful king,
    To take away the Throne of Gold,
    By sword and crossbow string.

An army strong did march to war,
    To fight for kingdom fair,
    Amongst them our Lord Morgan,

A master of warfare.

The battle raged for full a day,
  The casualties amounted,
  And more and more brave warriors fell,
  In numbers soon uncounted.

At last the kings of Hadenfeld,
  And rebel force contested,
  A duel of arms both face to face,
  To see who would be bested.

The rebel king struck hard and fast,
  His sword arm strong and mighty,
  And poor King Otto, old and weak,
  Put trust in Saints almighty.

Yet as the final blow was struck,
  Did Morgan come to save,
  His king from almost certain death,
  By deeds and words most brave.

His sword, the might of righteous Saint,
  Did strike usurper dead,
  And Morgan, future king of all,
  Had crown set on his head.

So noble lords and ladies,
  Heed my words of king most pure,
  Give prayers to he that rules the land,
  For Crown to long endure.

The crowd erupted into applause while Ludwig and his companions sat in stunned silence.

"Absurd," said Lord Emmett. "You slew Diedrich, not the king!"

"A fact of which I'm well aware," replied Ludwig, "but do not dwell on it. It's only a song."

"A song it may well be, but if it goes unchecked, we will soon see everyone believing it."

Morgan rose as the applause died down, the room falling into silence. "Thank you, Rascalian. By your words, you brought my spirit to the attention of all. His song paints me as a... What did he call me? Oh, yes. A 'king so pure'. Rest assured, I am not, but that doesn't mean I won't strive to be so. We are at the dawning of a new age here in Hadenfeld, an age of prosperity and progress that shall enrich the purses of you all."

He paused at their enthusiastic response before continuing. "I know some of you are nervous, and why wouldn't you be? To many of you, I am an unknown quantity. Yes, you've known me as a baron, but my circle of friends was always small, and I kept to myself. Those days are past us now, and I promise I will be a strong and decisive king who isn't afraid to make difficult decisions."

"Now, before I give up your attention, there is one more matter which I must address. As you know, I have not been blessed with an heir."

"I suppose," whispered Merrick, "that means he's not recognizing his bastards."

Morgan continued, "Now that I am king, I must announce that until I produce a male heir, my replacement in the line of succession shall be none other than Ludwig Altenburg, Baron of Verfeld."

The name caused a stir. Many assumed Morgan would declare one of his illegitimate children as his heir, even going so far as to marry one of his mistresses to make it legal.

Before the war, Ludwig had been seventeenth in line for the Throne, but all that changed at the Second Battle of Harlingen. He struggled to work out what happened to the other heirs. A few died in the war, but sixteen? It seemed highly unlikely.

"Come, Ludwig," said the king. "Rise and take your rightful place at my side."

He stood, unsure of how to respond. The assembled nobles clapped, particularly Merrick and Emmett. A few called out their congratulations, but Ludwig didn't miss the sneer on Lord Darrian's face or the look of contempt on that of Sir Emril.

He went through the crowd, accepting handshakes along the way, until he stood before King Morgan.

"Congratulations," said His Majesty. "I know this comes as a surprise, but surely you must have suspected it. After all, you are my cousin, and so many died since your own appointment as baron."

Ludwig bowed. "Thank you, Majesty. You humble me."

Morgan grinned. "Not at all, my dear fellow. Now sit, eat, and tell me how you've fared since the war's ending."

Ludwig took the proffered seat. "Thank you, Majesty. You're too kind."

"Well?"

"What would you like to know?"

"Let's start with your family, shall we? How's that wife of yours?"

"She is in good health, Majesty."

"I may be your king, but we're still family. Call me Morgan."

"Yes, of course, Maj... Morgan."

"There. That wasn't so hard, was it?"

"I'm afraid you've left me a little perplexed," said Ludwig. "How have I come to be next in line for the Crown? The last I heard, I was seventeenth."

"And I, fifth," replied Morgan, "yet between age and war, many died."

"But not all?"

The king shrugged. "What can I say? Some were merely unlucky in life. Cousin Kaspar injured himself falling from his horse. He survived, but I'm afraid his wits were scrambled. Then there was Cousin Luther, lost in a hunting accident."

"What kind of accident?"

"Trampled to death by a boar. A sad tale, to be sure, but one can't help but feel it was his own fault. I mean, who hunts boars in this day and age?"

"I still don't see how that puts me next in line for the Crown. Are you suggesting all of Otto's relatives before me were excluded?"

"I do, though admittedly, that was my doing. You see, unbeknownst to most of the realm, Otto suffered from an ailment of the mind. We couldn't risk that sort of thing appearing in another king, could we?"

"Otto wasn't mad," insisted Ludwig. "At least not the Otto I knew."

"You can't sit there and tell me he didn't have his quirks. The man was fixated on saving despite having full coffers."

Ludwig decided it was better not to argue, so he took a different approach, changing the subject. "I look forward to working with you. When would you like to start?"

Morgan smiled. "That's the spirit!"

4

LADIES OF THE COURT

SPRING 1101 SR

The sun reached through the leaves, dappling all below with freckles of light. Considering the season, it was an unusually warm day, but the ladies of the court turned out in full force for Lady Alexandra's gathering. She'd arranged to use her father's estate, the better to accommodate the large number of guests. As custom dictated, only the barons' wives were invited, their husbands relegated to more mundane activities. Even the servants were all women, setting a pleasant mood for the festivities.

Charlotte sat beneath an awning, squinting at the guests' brightly coloured attire while she, a northerner, dressed in more subdued tones.

"I'm surprised you're not more popular," said Gita. "Considering the circumstances, I expected they'd line up to gain your favour."

"That may yet come," added Alexandra, "but they don't know her like we do." She turned to Charlotte. "I'm afraid you'll have to put up with us."

Charlotte smiled. "I'm happy to do just that. You were my friends before I was… Well, whatever I am now."

"Your husband is next in line to the Crown," said Gita. "That makes him a prince, and if he's a prince…"

"Are you trying to suggest I'm a princess? I'm the daughter of a baron, not a royal."

"True, but you might as well be. If something happened to Morgan, you'd become queen."

"Queen? Or King's consort? There is a difference, you know. A queen is a ruler with the power to make laws or lead armies. A consort is simply the spouse of a king."

"Ultimately," said Alexandra, "it would be up to Ludwig whether or not you'd be a true queen. In any case, even as a consort, you would wield incredible influence." She glanced around at the guests. "Not that any of these women seem to be considering such things."

"Don't blame them," said Gita. "We've only just gotten a new king, so thoughts of succession at this time are rare. Morgan might still sire a legitimate child, so there's no guarantee Ludwig would succeed him."

"Also true. I suppose that's for the best. The last thing Charlotte wants is these sycophants toadying up to her for favours. It's one of the reasons I avoided court as much as I could when I was younger."

"Younger?" said Charlotte. "You make yourself sound old."

"Perhaps, but I'm an only child now, and my father felt it best to educate me in the ways of such things."

"You say you're an only child now. Does that mean you had a sibling?"

"I did," replied Alexandria. "My oldest brother died before I was born, but two years after my own birth, Amalric came along."

"What happened to him?"

"He died at the age of twelve, the victim of a fever—the same illness that took my mother."

"I'm sorry for your loss."

"Don't be," said Alexandra. "It was years ago, and the boy was a pest. I miss my mother, but I prefer to look to the future rather than the past." She held her belly and smiled. "Besides, I have my own family now, not to mention two aunts to spoil my children."

"Our children will grow up to be firm friends, I'm certain."

"That is my hope as well," added Gita. "Have you any names picked out, Alexandra?"

"Emmett and I have considered many but are yet to decide. I suppose it would be easier if I had a girl. Then we could name her after my mother."

"Would you name a son after Emmett's father?"

"That's certainly a possibility, but we've some time before we make a final decision."

Charlotte closed her eyes.

"Are you all right?" asked Alexandra.

"I'm feeling quite fatigued. Might there be somewhere I could lie down?"

"Of course."

"I can show her," offered Gita. "You stay here and look after the guests." She rose from her chair and took Charlotte's hand, helping her to her feet. "Come. Let's find you somewhere nice and quiet to lie down."

. . .

Charlotte awoke in a darkened room. The large, four-posted bed she lay in was soft, far more so than she was used to. Across the room, a servant girl sat beside the fireplace, watching flames dancing along a log. When Charlotte moved, the bed creaked, catching the girl's attention.

"My lady?"

"What time is it?"

"Late afternoon."

"And the gathering?"

"Over and done with. The guests all went home, milady, save for Ladies Gita and Alexandra. Shall I fetch them?"

"I don't want to be a bother."

"Nonsense. They left strict instructions to let them know when you awoke." The maid scurried from the room.

Charlotte lay in the bed, willing herself to rise, but an overwhelming desire to burrow into the sheets engulfed her.

Footsteps approached, and then Gita threw open the door. "You're awake!"

"Barely."

"You had us worried there for a while. We feared you might be having an episode."

Charlotte tried to fight off the lethargy, to leave the bed, but it was still too strong. She managed to push herself onto her pillows, using them as a backrest to elevate her slightly. "How went the party?"

"I don't think the term 'party' is the right word for it, more like a gathering."

"I sense you're unhappy with it."

"It was fine," said Gita, "at least for what it was. I suppose I shouldn't be surprised, all things considered."

"Meaning?"

"It was mostly gossip and innuendo."

"What is it you're not telling me?"

Gita remained silent.

"It's me, isn't it?" continued Charlotte. "They were all complaining about my suitability as a baroness."

"They don't know you like I do. Pay them no heed."

"What else did they say?" She waited, but Gita refused to answer. "Please, don't hold back. I'd prefer to hear it from you than in public."

"Very well, but I warn you, it's not very complimentary."

"Go on."

"They are of the belief Ludwig will one day make a great king."

"But not I, his queen?"

"That's about the gist of it, yes.

"Who did they see taking my place?"

"Alexandra, despite the fact she's happily married to Lord Emmett. In any case, it doesn't matter. She would never do something like that to you. All this talk is mean-spirited. I suspect they're trying to drive a wedge between you and Ludwig."

"To what end?"

"In a word—influence. Separating Ludwig from you leaves him susceptible to the suggestions of others. At least that's the general consensus."

Charlotte laughed. "Then they don't know Ludwig very well. He's surrounded by people he trusts."

"I know that, and you know that, but these women only think in terms of their own experiences. Most are so bored with life, all they can do to entertain themselves is to plot the misery of others."

Ludwig paused as the guard announced his arrival, then he swung the door open.

"Come in," said the king. "Would you care for something to drink?"

"No, thank you, Majesty."

"Are you sure? It's no inconvenience. After all, it's not as if I had to pour it myself."

"I'm not thirsty. I am curious, however, what plans you wished to discuss with me."

The king smiled. "There he is. The man who likes directness. Very well, come over here." He beckoned Ludwig towards a table where several parchments were scattered. "I've been looking through Otto's notes. Did you know he once commissioned a map of Hadenfeld? It was never completed, for the war saw to that, but it got me to thinking. Now that the kingdom is reunited, there is time for such things."

"You want an accurate map of Hadenfeld?"

"Not only a map, I want to take a full counting of our population, find out how many people live in this kingdom of mine. What do you think?"

"You could ask," replied Ludwig. "Any baron worth his salt knows how many people live on his lands."

"Perhaps, but that's a far cry from having accurate numbers. It's also not in their interest to report honest numbers, else they might end up paying extra taxes."

"Like they do in the east?"

Morgan stared back at him. "What are you suggesting?"

"Merely that the greater burden of supporting the Crown is on the shoulders of those barons formerly part of Neuhafen."

"But isn't that only fair? They haven't paid their dues for half a century. Why should they get off lightly now?"

"They paid taxes," said Ludwig. "It's not their fault the coins went to Eisen rather than Harlingen."

"They sided with a usurper. Are you suggesting that fact absolves them of their responsibilities?"

"They were not part of Hadenfeld at that time. Thus, they bore no duty to support its army. There is also the special tax they paid Otto after the war."

"You and I see things differently," said the king, "but I shan't argue it at this time. I brought you here to seek your advice, not for you to lecture me on taxes."

"Understood," said Ludwig. "My apologies if I overstepped."

"Now, where was I?"

"You were suggesting a census. Have you any other grand schemes in mind?"

"I do. It occurs to me that we know next to nothing about the eastern reaches of Hadenfeld. Why do you suppose that is?"

"It's covered in thick forest," said Ludwig. "I'm surprised you weren't aware of that."

"Oh, I've heard the rumours that say all manner of strange creatures dwell within those woods, but I'm of the opinion that, aside from animals, the only thing dangerous in that land is our expectations."

"I'm not sure I follow."

"As a people, we assign countless myths to unexplored regions. I propose we send expeditions into those woods to discover what's there."

"That's hundreds, maybe thousands of square miles."

"Agreed," said Morgan. "But think of how many more baronies we could create!"

"Your plan is based on the premise there are those willing to undertake such hardships. The truth is it was just such an idea that led to the creation of the eastern baronies in the first place. We'd be better off concentrating on helping them prosper rather than trying to establish even more towns."

"And they would have prospered had they not separated to form their own kingdom. Their failure in that regard is hardly my fault."

"Agreed," said Ludwig, "but the indifference of your predecessors led to civil war in the first place."

"What's that supposed to mean? The eastern expansion of Hadenfeld allowed us to become the largest realm in the Petty Kingdoms. I would hardly call an undertaking of that magnitude indifference."

"But it was, don't you see? Yes, the Crown got them off to a good start, adding nine baronies, but after the first few years, they were left to their own devices. It takes great strength and fortitude to build a barony from nothing, and from the very beginning, these new vassals were treated as lesser men."

"You can't blame me for the actions of those who came before."

"True, but you now have the chance to rectify that mistake."

The king stared back silently. Ludwig wondered if he had been wise to raise the subject, but then Morgan surprised him.

"What would you have me do?" said the king.

"For one thing, you can lower their taxes to the same level as the rest of us."

"I need those funds to build my army."

"And you'll get them in time. Building strong baronies will increase revenue, for the more the barons make, the greater the amount they'll pay you. It's a situation in which both sides prosper."

"And in the meantime, I am to let my coffers dwindle?"

"You inherited a kingdom with fifteen baronies, whereas Otto had only eight. By all accounts, you should have plenty of gold to pay a modest army."

"And what, pray tell, would you consider modest?"

Ludwig was fully aware of Morgan's ambitions regarding his army. As he now saw it, the trick was to present options in the best possible light. "We fielded over three thousand men at the last Battle of Harlingen. Against that, Neuhafen raised almost four thousand."

"You tell me what I already know," said the king. "How is that of any help to me?"

"With all due respect, Majesty, I'm not finished. Otto's own entourage consisted of some seven hundred souls, while the usurper, Diedrich, we now know, had about six hundred."

Morgan smiled. "So, you're suggesting I could maintain a combination of the two? Say, thirteen hundred men?"

"That was wartime, where other expenses become secondary to needs of the realm's defence, but I believe a thousand reasonable. Naturally, in times of war, you'd rely on the barons to provide more men. You know as well as I that during the war, we barons were required to supply four hundred men apiece, as were those of Neuhafen. Of course, Otto reduced the eastern barons to fifty men after their defeat. If you rescind that, it would ultimately give you a wartime army of over six thousand."

"I hadn't considered that. That would make us the largest army on the Continent, save for you-know-who."

"I caution against flexing your army's muscles too soon, Majesty. Half the men under the barons' control were ill-armed and under-trained."

"And in the east?"

"Their situation was a little different," replied Ludwig. "Diedrich planned his campaign for some time. As a result, he had better-equipped warriors."

Morgan nodded. "So he did. You have given me much to think about, my friend. If we are to take our place amongst the great powers of the Petty Kingdoms, we have work to do. How would you feel about overseeing the reorganizing of our army?"

"Reorganizing? What did you have in mind?"

"I shall lower the burden of taxes on the eastern barons, but in return, I expect each of them to maintain a competent, well-trained force of warriors."

"We already do that."

"Yes, but there is little in the way of uniformity. I want you to devise a reasonable balance of horse, foot, and bow that we can then pass on to all the barons."

"That would cost them more than the increased taxes."

The king waved it off. "It is a small price to pay in the grand scheme of things."

It wasn't a terrible idea, but Ludwig feared there'd be much resistance amongst the barons. "How much leeway would I have?"

"As much as you need," said Morgan. "After all, you're the one with the most battle experience. Consult others if you must, but by the end of summer, I want your thoughts on the matter." He hesitated for a moment. "Are you up to the challenge?"

"Most assuredly, Majesty, though I have a few questions."

"Then ask away."

"What do you intend to do with this great army you envision?"

"Keep the realm safe."

"We've done that for generations, save for our own internal struggles."

"True, but then again, we are living in a different age. How long, do you suppose, before the Halvarians push to expand their border even more? We cannot continue to sit back and ignore the threat, Cousin, or else we'll have nothing to leave our descendants."

Ludwig had received word from Charlaine that there had been a clash with the empire off the coast of Reinwick. Was Morgan aware of this, or was it mere speculation? The Halvarian Empire had threatened the Petty

Kingdoms for centuries, gobbling up smaller kingdoms in a relentless expansion many said was destined to occupy the entire Continent. How long until they came knocking at Hadenfeld's door?

"Well?" pressed the king. "Anything else you'd like to know?"

"Sorry. I was working out a few things in my head. Have you considered the effect a large army might have on our neighbours? Some could see the size as a potential threat."

"You raise a good point, but we shall take diplomatic steps to assure them such is not the case. We can even invite them here to come and see our army for themselves."

"I might remind you the Petty Kingdoms are a web of alliances and defence pacts."

"And it's time we changed that. Imagine this: a central power—us— surrounded by allied kingdoms, presenting a powerful deterrent to those seeking to enslave us."

"It is a glorious dream," said Ludwig, "but I fear there would be much disagreement over who'd be the central power in such an arrangement. No one wants to be subservient to another realm, particularly one with a large army. Are we to replace Halvaria with an empire of our own?"

"Of course not. I'm trying to make them allies, not vassal states. Now, will you oversee the reorganizing of the Army of Hadenfeld or not?"

"I will," said Ludwig, "though I pray we shall never have need of it."

5

LUWEN

SUMMER 1101 SR

S ummer was soon upon them, making it the perfect time to visit Lord Meinhard's estate in Luwen. Charlotte had gone ahead in the company of Merrick and Gita, along with the baron's daughter, Alexandra and her husband, Lord Emmett.

Finally free of his obligation to his king, Ludwig rode fast, putting Cyn and Siggy's horsemanship to the test. They reached Luwen in record time and were soon back amongst friends.

With the abundant fresh air and breathtaking landscape, Ludwig adopted the daily habit of racing over the rolling countryside with Merrick and Emmett. Sometimes, their host would accompany them, delighting them all with his knowledge of the area. Ludwig prided himself on his horsemanship and often rode ahead, forcing Cyn and Sigwulf to constantly play catch-up.

On this particular day, they were west of Lord Meinhard's manor, bringing them close to the border. Ludwig reined in his horse to take in the view while Sigwulf pulled up on his right. Moments later, Cyn joined them.

"Well," said Ludwig. "What do you think?"

"It's a grand place," replied Cyn, "but I prefer Verfeld."

"What I want to know," said Sigwulf, "is whose lands lie yonder?" He pointed westward.

"That," replied Ludwig, "is the kingdom of Grislagen."

"The name means nothing to me."

"I only recently learned about it myself, but I'm afraid I'm not sure where they stand in terms of politics."

"I suppose that will need to change," offered Cyn. "Now that you're named heir, I mean."

"Morgan has plenty of time to father a son."

"Does he, though? He's not a young man anymore; even if he did, he'd need someone to look after his child until the boy was of age. My guess is he'll be counting on you for that."

"Me? What do I know about raising children? I can barely manage my own."

"Frederick is a fine lad," said Sigwulf, "and you have servants aplenty to help. I'd say, overall, you've done well for yourself."

"I suppose I hadn't considered that. Still, looking after someone else's child feels wrong somehow."

"Nonsense. You promised to look after Henley if anything happened to his parents."

"That's different. He's the son of a baron, not a king."

"So it's not the child-rearing that's got you flustered, it's the training of a future king!"

"You must admit, I know little of court."

"All that will change now you're a prince. Should we call you Highness?"

"No. Please don't," said Ludwig. "That's the last thing I need. Even if I should one day become king, I want you two to promise you'll still call me Ludwig."

"That wouldn't be proper."

"I insist."

"Very well," said Sigwulf, "but only in private. For official gatherings, we'll call you Majesty."

"Or sire," added Cyn. "What else could we call him?"

"Your Eminence, perhaps?"

"Too stuffy. How about Your Magnificence?"

"And you called mine too stuffy?"

"Hey, now," said Ludwig. "Did you forget I'm right here? That's enough of that. Let's move on to something else, shall we?"

"Very well," said Sigwulf. "Have you given the king's idea any further thought?"

"Assuming you mean the changes to the army, yes."

"And..."

"The barons can't afford to raise more men, but perhaps they could be more uniform in their organization."

"What do you have in mind?"

"The vast majority of barons raised two companies of archers during the last war. I think that a suitable number, going forward."

"And the rest?"

"We learned from the war we lacked enough trained footmen. I propose each baron properly equip and train four companies of professionals."

"Saints alive," said Cyn. "Think of all that mail to armour them. That's likely to take a good chunk of coin."

"It wouldn't be immediately," said Ludwig. "Rather, I would see them slowly upgrade some of their lighter-equipped troops."

"And by slow, you mean?"

"Perhaps a year or two? That helps spread the cost out. Of course, once they're armoured, the bulk of the expense is taken care of."

"You talked about increasing the number of footmen," said Sigwulf. "What else are you considering?"

"Cavalry. Not fully armoured knights, they'd be far too expensive. No, I was thinking more in terms of mailed warriors."

"Like the Temple Knights of Saint Mathew?" asked Cyn. "They wear mail rather than plate."

"Yes. That's the idea," said Ludwig, "though they wouldn't have the same training as a Temple Knight. However, they'd be a professional company, not one raised for an emergency."

"Now that sounds expensive," said Sigwulf. "Any idea how much it would cost?"

"Not as much as you might think. Once again, we'd give them several years to raise these men, perhaps even contribute horses from the Royal Stables to get them started. Better yet, they could send the funds directly to the capital and let Morgan worry about training them."

"You're asking a lot of the new king, aren't you?"

"That's hardly my problem," said Ludwig. "Morgan wants a much bigger army, and someone has to fund it. The alternative is we have less cavalry than other Petty Kingdoms."

"So let me get this straight," said Cyn. "Each baron is responsible for eight companies, yes?"

"Yes."

"And two of these would be archers, four footmen and one cavalry?"

"Precisely."

"Then where does the last company come in?"

"For now, that would consist of a levy, but for the richer baronies, they could raise an elite company of foot."

"Elite?"

"Yes, veteran warriors with slightly better armour or more experience than their comrades. They would form a reserve, something to fall back on should disaster strike. They'd need to be paid a little more, but I don't see that being a problem down the road."

"Why is that?"

"The kingdom is finally at peace, which is the best time for growth. And growth means more people, and more people means more collected in taxes. Who knows? Perhaps each baron will supply even more men?"

"Assuming we don't get into a war somewhere along the way. Knowledge of politics was never your strongest asset."

"Point taken," said Ludwig. "Fortunately, we have the perfect source in the form of Lord Meinhard. He can tell us more about regional politics." He turned in the saddle. "Speaking of which, where did everyone go?"

"Back to the keep," said Cyn.

"And they didn't see fit to tell me?"

"Oh, they did," said Sigwulf. "That's why we're here, to tell you it's time to return."

"Why didn't you mention this earlier?"

The huge northerner shrugged. "I didn't want to interrupt you. You were too busy going on about... Well, all sorts of things."

"That's fair, but this conversation has run its course. Shall we join them?"

"I'd love to," said Sig, "but I'm not sure which way to go."

"Men," said Cyn. "You can't find your way out of the garderobe without a woman to help. It's this way." She turned her horse around, riding off to the east.

They entered the great hall as the sun was setting. Lord Meinhard had laid on a feast to celebrate his guests last evening with him, and most of those present had already eaten their fill.

"I see the hero of Hadenfeld returns," said Lord Meinhard. "We were just talking about you."

"Nothing untoward, I hope?" replied Ludwig.

"Not at all. We were discussing the battle that ended the insurrection."

"The Second Battle of Harlingen? That was a war, not an uprising."

"Yet one could consider it a continuation of the rebellion that led to the founding of Neuhafen, could they not?" He glanced around the room, his gaze resting on Emmett. "I mean no offence, my lord. I speak purely from an academic point of view."

"I'd be more worried about the neighbouring realms," replied the Baron of Dornbruck.

"Yes," added Ludwig. "What can you tell me of Grislagen?"

"You need have no worries on their account," said Lord Meinhard. "I know their king well."

"How well?"

"I dined with him shortly before the coronation of our new sovereign. I took his regards to the capital, although he's understandably nervous about Morgan."

"Why so?"

"Because he doesn't know the fellow. Doubtless, I shall see King Sagarus again, although I'm at a loss as to what I'll tell him concerning our new ruler."

"Why tell him anything?"

"Because he's an inquisitive fellow," said Meinhard, "and it will be the first thing out of his mouth, which is perfectly natural. After all, our kingdom is on his border. I'd want to know if one of my neighbours was enlarging his army."

"Perhaps he should bring his concerns to Morgan?"

"I'll suggest that the next time I see him. Shall I also tell him Morgan wants to raise the biggest army on the Continent? I'm sure that would sit well."

"My apologies," said Ludwig. "I thought it better for him to deal with Morgan directly."

"Perhaps it is I who should apologize. I prefer people to be plain-spoken, yet here I am, getting upset. Take your companions, for example. I'd be very interested to hear what they make of Morgan, them being northerners."

Ludwig turned to Sigwulf. "Well?"

"Don't look at me," the huge man replied. "If you want to discuss politics, you should talk to Cyn." They both looked at her.

"Oh, I see how it goes," she said. "You two are unwilling to say anything bad about the new king."

"And you aren't?"

"Oh, I have plenty to say."

"Then let's hear it," said Meinhard. "I'm sure no one here would hold anything against you."

"He's dangerous."

"In what way?"

"He wants to be a great king by building a large army, and in my experience, no one does that unless they intend to put it to use."

"You suspect he'll take us to war?"

"I do," replied Cyn, "although I don't know the politics of this region well enough to guess who he'd attack."

"I can help with that," said Meinhard. "Politics are a passion of mine."

He cleared his throat before continuing, "There are four major powers bordering Hadenfeld, eight if you count the east, but that area is mostly wilderness. Grislagen lies to the west, but, as I've already indicated, we can trust King Sagarus to keep the peace. It's also doubtful that Morgan covets his lands since they're not prosperous. Don't get me wrong, they do well enough, but they're hardly a kingdom of treasures."

"And to the south?" asked Cyn.

"A duchy known as Hollenbeck. They are weak in terms of an army, and their kingdom is, for the most part, thickly wooded. Politically, we have little to do with them. Otto tried making diplomatic overtures to them about twenty years ago, but their duke is an isolationist. Of course, that could work in Morgan's favour."

"In what way?"

"I know of no alliances on the part of Hollenbeck. If we attacked them, they'd be forced to stand alone."

"Morgan might see that as a quick victory," said Cyn.

"Then he's a fool," replied Ludwig. "That type of terrain would be easy to defend."

"A point on which we agree," said Meinhard. "Now, the north is an entirely different matter."

"Meaning?"

"North of your own lands lies Deisenbach, of which I'm sure you are familiar."

"Yes," said Ludwig. "I travelled through there when I returned from the north, although I wasn't paying much attention to their army. Have they a large one?"

Cyn chuckled. "That's a personal question, isn't it?"

Lord Emmett spat out a mouthful of wine.

"A quick wit," said Meinhard. "A quality I greatly admire. Would that the king had such a gift."

"Sorry," she added. "I didn't mean to interrupt. You were talking about Deisenbach's military prowess?"

"Though I don't know their army's strength, I know the tradition of jousting is popular there, implying a more martial society than ours. As far as the common soldiers go, they are armed and equipped much as us, and from what I've seen, their population is like ours, indicating an army of similar size to our own."

He sipped his wine before continuing, "Then there's Zowenbruch, which lies north of the eastern barons' lands. If we could consider anyone a military threat, it would be them."

"Why so?" asked Ludwig.

"As you are no doubt aware, the Petty Kingdoms are an odd assortment of alliances. Our traditional ally is Erlingen, which lies on Zowenbruch's northern border. Thus, they are, in essence, our enemy, at least from a political standpoint. They've never threatened us, but if war broke out in this part of the Continent, our alliance with Erlingen would put us on opposing sides."

"Do you think Morgan might be tempted to attack them?"

"If I'm being honest, no. It requires marching through the lands of our eastern barons, and I don't think our new king entirely trusts them."

"That leaves no potential enemies to attack unless you think he might march farther east?"

"With no roads? I doubt an army would even reach our eastern border. That area is nothing but ancient forests." He lowered his voice. "Some say those woods host all kinds of terrible creatures. You were in Eisen; you would know more than I."

Ludwig laughed. "I spent most of my time in Eisen imprisoned in a dungeon."

"So what you're saying is," offered Sigwulf, "there is no obvious enemy for Morgan to invade?"

"That seems to be the conclusion, I'm afraid," said Meinhard. "The problem is, if he wants to prove his military prowess, he needs to march to battle, which means he could attack anywhere."

"There is still time," said Ludwig. "I've yet to report my conclusions regarding reorganizing the army, and even then, it'll take several years to put them into effect."

"Does Morgan know that?"

"Not yet, but I'll emphasize that particular point when I tell him of my plans."

"Good, though I still harbour some reservations about him. I knew him as a lad, and he was never one to socialize and seldom took the advice of others. One might even call him headstrong. Of course, he's not the young man he once was, so perhaps he's mellowed with age. I wish I could say the same of my fellow barons."

"You don't trust them?"

"I trust those of you here, but there's still a lot of hard feelings concerning the war, particularly with the Baron of Hasdorf, and let's not forget Morgan's own lands were overrun during the war. He might be king now, but he's not likely to forgive that."

"We did not occupy them for long," said Emmett. "It was less than a week after we took Grienwald that we fought at Harlingen."

"The town was still sacked. I'm not blaming you, of course. It was war, and I daresay we weren't any more civilized than you."

"To what do you refer?" asked Ludwig. "I don't recall any tales of our men misbehaving."

"You were wounded, if you recall. We disarmed the enemy army after their surrender. You are likely unaware we removed not only their weapons but also their coins. Well, I say coins, but I mean anything of value. I daresay half the plunder of Grienwald ended up in the hands of our warriors." He glanced at Sigwulf and Cyn. "Not that I can blame them. It's not as if the average warrior receives much in the way of wages."

He went to take another sip of wine only to find his cup empty. He held it up, and a servant approached to refill it. "So there you have it—a brief description of all our neighbours. Unfortunately, it doesn't tell us which one the king will target, assuming he takes us to war. Who knows? Perhaps it'll all turn out to be bluster."

"I don't think so," said Ludwig. "Morgan wants to appear strong, and without a victory, that will be very difficult. Word of our recent civil war has likely spread to the four corners of the Continent by now, which won't help our reputation."

"But we won that war," said Cyn.

"Yes, we did, but we took significant losses in the process. To an outsider, it will look different. We'll likely be seen as a fractured realm, weakened by a recent rebellion and teetering on the edge of ruin."

6

WHISPERS

SUMMER 1101 SR

The first leg of the journey had them returning to Harlingen. Due to the relative proximity of their baronies, they would all continue north from there, Merrick and Gita leaving them as the road forked south of Drakenfeld. Emmett and Alexandra would travel through Verfeld, using the new ferry to cross the river east of Ludwig's domain.

The intent was to only stay at Merrick's house in the capital for a day or so, allowing Ludwig to make his report to King Morgan.

They sat down to eat on the evening of their return to the city. The meal looked sumptuous, and Ludwig's mouth watered as a servant entered.

"My apologies," the fellow said, directing his words to Merrick. "There are guards at the door, my lord."

"What do they want?" asked the Baron of Drakenfeld.

"They wish to talk to Lord Ludwig."

"About?"

"They wouldn't say."

Ludwig stood. "I'd best see what they want. Knowing my luck, the king has summoned me."

He followed the servant to find three soldiers waiting in the doorway, the eldest sporting a burgeoning black eye with cuts and scrapes across his face.

"Trouble, gentlemen?" asked Ludwig.

"Are you familiar with someone by the name of Sigwulf Marhaven?"

"Yes. He's one of my captains. Why? What's happened?"

"We've placed him under arrest, my lord."

"For what?"

"Causing a disturbance."

"That being?"

"Brawling," replied the guard. "Ordinarily, we would've left him behind bars, but the woman continued on about how you'd want to be informed."

"Ah. That would be Cyn." He noted the guard's puzzled look. "That's short for Cynthia. She's also in my employ. Where are they now?"

"Out front, shackled to our wagon."

Ludwig grinned. "I can't imagine that went over well."

"Nor did the arrest, my lord, but we did our duty."

"I'm sure you did. Very well, bring them inside."

He waited as the guard and his companions returned to the wagon. Together, they unchained Sigwulf while Cyn, sitting in the back, kept up a verbal diatribe that would turn a Holy Man crimson. She quieted as she met Ludwig's gaze.

"Here he is, my lord." The guard nodded to his men, who unshackled Sigwulf's hands.

"Thank you," said Ludwig, placing some coins in the man's hands. "And I apologize for any difficulties you endured at this fellow's hands."

One look at the coins, and the guard smiled. "You're welcome, my lord." He turned and left with his companions and the wagon.

Sigwulf rubbed his wrists. "I suppose you'd like an explanation?"

Ludwig shook his head, turning to Cyn instead.

"Don't look at me. I wasn't the one who started it."

"And I was?" said Sig.

"Let's not have an argument," said Ludwig. "How about we start at the beginning? You two were supposed to go to the local tavern for a meal. What happened?"

"Well," replied Cyn, "everything started just as you said. We arrived at the Cygnet and sat down to eat."

"And then?"

She cast her eyes down. "We may have overheard something."

"That something being?"

"Well, let's just say it wasn't nice."

"How about you tell me exactly what you heard?"

"As you know," said Sigwulf, "the Cygnet lies in the wealthier part of the city."

"I'm fully aware. What I don't understand is what that has to do with any of this. Surely you're not suggesting a fight broke out because of some form of snobbery?"

Cyn laughed. "Snobbery? Who do you take us for, fools?"

"Get to the point, will you?"

"Well," continued Sig, "there we were, waiting for our food, when someone started talking about Lady Charlotte."

"Yes," added Cyn, "and it wasn't very flattering. They said she was unfit."

"And that led you to start a fight?"

"Oh no. We remained calm at that point."

"Then what happened?"

"We heard several comments about you."

"What did they say?"

"That you were a scoundrel," replied Sigwulf.

"What he means is," added Cyn, "they implied you were a man of loose morals. In particular, they said you slept your way through half the women of Hadenfeld."

"And that's when you got into the fight?"

"Not precisely."

"Then what was the final straw?"

"They accused you of having a wandering eye."

"Look," said Sigwulf. "We all know that you were a bit of a womanizer in your youth, but suggesting you cheated on Charlotte was too much." He stopped for a moment. "You didn't cheat on her, did you?"

"No," said Ludwig. "Of course not. Who was responsible for these remarks?"

The great northerner reddened. "I didn't get his name."

"Nor did I," added Cyn, "but we found out he's a regular down at the Cygnet."

"What did he look like?"

"He was of average height," said Sigwulf, "but fairly muscular for someone of his size. I suspect he may be a captain or even a knight. Now that I mention it, there was something familiar about him."

"How was he dressed?" asked Ludwig.

"Like you."

"Not true," said Cyn. "He was much more fashionably attired. I would say expensively so."

"Was he pretentious?"

"Most definitely, and his voice was unusual, as if he were talking through his nose."

"That sounds like Sir Emril."

"Sir who?"

"Sir Emril, one of Otto's knights, although I suppose he belongs to Morgan now. He was at the king's pre-coronation celebration. You remember, surely? He was also in Lord Darrian's carriage when it ran off the road."

"Oh yes. I remember now. In any case, he clearly has it in for you."

"So it seems."

"What do you want us to do about it?"

"For now, nothing. It would only make things worse."

"Are you sure?" said Sigwulf. "I could always accost him on the street?"

"That might prove dangerous. Emril is a trained knight and likely to travel with similarly skilled individuals."

"But you can't let him get away with this. Something needs to be done."

"I thank you for bringing it to my attention, but this is my burden, not yours."

"And what's to happen to us?"

"Absolutely nothing," replied Ludwig, "though if anyone asks, you've been severely disciplined."

"Have we?" said Cyn.

"I said so, didn't I?" He lowered his voice. "I know you didn't intend to get into trouble, and you were attempting to end malicious gossip, but such talk has a life of its own. The best choice of action is to rise above it and ignore the remarks."

"What of Lady Charlotte?"

"She need hear nothing of this. It would only feed her anxiety."

"But if we do nothing, it will soon be the talk of the town. You are, after all, the king's successor until he fathers a son."

"We'll be returning to Verfeld shortly. I doubt such tales will travel that far. In the meantime, I'll have a word with Gita and Alexandra. They can help shield her from such remarks." He paused a moment. "As for you two, did you at least eat?"

Sig sighed. "Only a few bites. It all happened so fast."

"And by a few bites," added Cyn, "he means he only had two plates of food. Don't let him fool you; he's had plenty."

The next morning, Ludwig stood outside the doors to the Royal Audience chamber. He was one of three visitors awaiting the king's pleasure, though he was the only noble.

The door opened to a servant adorned in the king's colours. "Lord Ludwig," he said. "He will see you now."

"Thank you." He followed the servant in.

King Morgan sat at a table, picking away at his food. He looked up as Ludwig entered. "There you are. I wondered if you hadn't forgotten your little assignment."

"No, far from it. It has, in fact, consumed my thoughts for some time now."

"Then sit and tell me what you've come up with." The king turned to a servant. "Some wine for His Highness."

"Highness?" said Ludwig.

"Get used to it. You are my heir, after all." He waited while the servant filled his goblet. "Now, let's get to the point, shall we?"

"Where would you like me to start?"

"I suppose the first thing I should ask is if the idea is feasible."

"That's a hard question to answer. Historically, the barons kept only small garrisons that were enlarged in times of war. It's reasonable to require each baron to maintain a standing force, but your proposal might bankrupt them."

"Then what do you suggest?"

"They maintain two or three companies at most, committing to provide more were we to go to war."

"How many more?"

"The numbers fielded during the last war are quite reasonable. As we discussed before, each baron was responsible for four hundred men, and it was similar for the Neuhafen barons."

"Yes," said the king. "I'm aware of the numbers. What I want to know is, can we dictate the composition of these forces?"

"I believe we can. Most of the barons raised two companies of archers and six foot, although Lords Meinhard and Jurgen replaced one of theirs with cavalry."

"And in the east?"

"A remarkably similar number, but their foot was better equipped than ours, and all their cavalry was under the direct command of their king."

"You mean usurper," corrected Morgan. "I refuse to acknowledge his reign."

"Be that as it may, I think we could learn a valuable lesson from them."

"Lesson? But we beat them, Ludwig, even with their superior numbers."

"That was more through happenstance than planning. The terrain was also in our favour, but it was nearly a disaster."

"You don't need to tell me. I was there."

"Yes, of course," said Ludwig. "I believe, however, there is an important lesson to be learned from the conflict."

"Which is?"

"We need more cavalry, specifically, men in mail mounted on warhorses."

"Not knights?"

"Knights are valuable, Majesty, but lack the discipline and manoeuvrability of mounted warriors."

"But they'd be commoners. Can we truly trust them with warhorses?"

"Do you not trust in your footmen to protect the realm? Or the archers to do the same?"

"How many of these horsemen do you propose we raise?"

"I suggest each baron provide the funds to equip one company."

"Saints alive," said the king. "There are fifteen barons. That makes over seven hundred men!"

"Indeed, yet I would go further. You'll note I suggested they provide the funds, but I would place them under your command rather than the barons."

Morgan chuckled. "I doubt they'd like that. I am curious, though, how you came up with that idea."

"Using horsemen piecemeal will do little to win a battle. If they are to be truly effective, they need to be grouped together, and who but the king could be trusted to use them wisely?"

"Are you suggesting a baron might use them against me?"

"You yourself raised the issue of trust. If you don't trust commoners with horses, what better way to ensure they remain loyal than command them yourself?"

"I like your thinking. When can we put this into effect?"

Ludwig sat back. The king was obviously in a hurry to implement the changes. Did this mean he was already planning a war? "I'm afraid there's more to consider, sire."

"Are you suggesting the barons lack funds?"

"No, but we need time for this to work. Armourers must make the mail, and we can't wave a magic wand and instantly create over eight hundred horses. And there's another problem."

"Which is?"

"If we buy too many horses at once, the prices will be driven up, costing us even more."

"Have you a solution?"

"I do, but it will take time."

"Go on, then. Tell me how we accomplish this."

"We undertake a breeding program. My understanding is the fields in the south are well suited to such a thing, and I'm sure the barons of Luwen and Bruggendorf would be eager to increase their breeding programs, considering the funds that would flow their way as a result."

"And in the east?"

"I have only limited knowledge of the terrain in those parts, but I'm led to believe it's mostly forest, hardly the sort of land suitable for such things.

There are hills in those parts, so they might be a source of iron. Saints know we'll need lots of it to equip all these warriors."

"I'm impressed," said the king. "You've given this much more thought than I would have. Now tell me, what are your suggestions on the Royal Troops? You mentioned some time ago that a thousand men was reasonable. Are you still of that opinion?"

"I am, although the bulk of those would be foot."

"And knights?"

"Two hundred, along with a similar number of archers."

"Is that all? I expected at least double that number."

"Horses are expensive, sire, and with the barons supplying eight hundred cavalry, you can afford to cut down on the number of knights."

"I see it now," said Morgan. "The barons will now bear the cost."

"Precisely. It would also allow you to outnumber any two barons combined, thus making it more difficult for history to repeat itself."

The king held up his goblet. "I raise my cup to you, Cousin. This plan of yours is most excellent, although you still haven't given me an actual date when such measures might be completed."

"That's where things get difficult. The barons can raise and equip the foot within two years, but I fear the cavalry will take significantly longer. We could speed that up by sending buyers into neighbouring realms, but that risks our neighbours getting wind of our plans. Would that be something you'd consider?"

"I shall certainly look into it. Where do you suggest we start?"

"With a Royal Proclamation calling on all barons to equip and train two full companies of mailed warriors by year's end. We will then increase this number to four next year. In addition, each baron is to train two companies of archers, which won't be much of an issue since most already meet that goal."

"And the horses?"

"The first step is for you to meet with Lords Meinhard and Jurgen to propose expanding their breeding programs. You'll need to explain the plan to them so they understand the importance of it, but I doubt that will meet with much resistance."

"And yourself?" asked the king.

"I'm not sure I understand the question."

"You are a baron; is this proposal something you can accomplish within your own lands?"

"It will certainly be a challenge, but I believe, given enough time, I can see it through to completion. My question, as I'm sure the other barons will ask, is what you intend to do with this new army once it's in place?"

"The future is uncertain," replied Morgan, "but if there's one thing I've learned over the years, nobody attacks when they are outnumbered. I intend to make Hadenfeld so strong that none dare cross our borders."

"And how do we demonstrate that our army is superior?"

Morgan smiled. "There are conflicts all over the Petty Kingdoms and a complex web of alliances. Sooner or later, an ally will call for help, and when that happens, we'll march our troops to assist."

"There's more to winning a battle than simple numbers."

"Ah, but we possess something no one else has."

"Which is?"

"You, of course. You made a name for yourself in the north, then returned to Hadenfeld and played an important role in reuniting the kingdom. Ludwig, you shall be my marshal, leading our army to victory!"

That evening, as Ludwig sat staring into the fireplace, Charlotte entered the room and joined him.

"Troubled?" she asked.

"The king is mad. He wants to wage war across the Continent."

"Why would he want that?"

"He believes it will restore Hadenfeld to its rightful place as the pre-eminent power in the Petty Kingdoms."

"With all due respect," she replied, "was it ever thus? I've read quite a bit, but I don't recall ever hearing of Hadenfeld being the power you suggest."

"Nor do I, come to think of it, but the king wants what the king wants. Who are we to oppose it?"

"Did he speak specifically of who we'd be fighting?"

"No, but he seemed to believe all the alliances would eventually lead to conflict."

"And?"

"What makes you think there's more?"

"I think I know you by now. You grow reflective when burdened and were deep in thought when I came in. So tell me, what else vexes you?"

"When the time comes, he expects me to lead the army."

"You commanded before."

"Yes, but only the men of Verfeld, which amounts to little more than a few hundred."

"It was four hundred," replied Charlotte, "and I might remind you Lord Merrick's men were under your control as well."

"That was different. Sig commanded them."

"Just as a Royal Army would have others to command. A general does not lead individual companies; they command the captains."

"General? I've heard Cyn use that term."

"It's commonly used for those who command in the king's absence, or perhaps I should say ruler since many northern realms are duchies."

"We prefer the term marshal in these parts, although it amounts to the same thing."

"That's because you follow the Thalemites' example."

"I beg your pardon?"

"The term marshal comes from Thalemia, whereas general originated with the Old Kingdom, and thus is more common in the north."

"I had no idea. I saw nothing of this in the books I've read."

"Of course not. Texts concerning the Old Kingdom are often destroyed on sight."

"Yet you've read some," said Ludwig.

"I have. My father delighted in collecting ancient texts, although he read very few. I think he saw it as a way of connecting with the past."

"And do northern generals know of their connection to the Old Kingdom?"

"I doubt it, or they'd change the name. Generally speaking, the rulers of the Petty Kingdoms don't like anything that sounds even remotely Therengian."

"Which makes their ignorance all the more interesting."

"Want to know something even more intriguing?" asked Charlotte.

"Most certainly."

"According to some sources, the Temple Knights have a little-used rank called Temple General. I find that particularly strange, considering their efforts to stamp out any signs of the Old Kingdom."

"You're talking about the Cunars," said Ludwig. "They form the Holy Army."

"Actually, all the orders have the title, though it's seldom, if ever, invoked."

"It's fascinating to consider how much we, as a society, owe to the Old Kingdom. We even organize our men into companies like they did. I wonder how the armies of the Old Kingdom would fare against those of the Petty Kingdoms."

"But they did," said Charlotte. "That's what led to their collapse five hundred years ago."

He smiled. "You truly are an amazing person," said Ludwig. "You're both beautiful and well-read."

7

THE RAID

SUMMER 1101 SR

After many days of planning, King Morgan finally permitted Ludwig to return home. They'd spent most of their time discussing military matters, and Ludwig came to the conclusion his new king wasn't the most strategic of thinkers. His Majesty was more interested in numbers than anything else, convinced having more men was preferable to a well-trained army. In the end, Morgan finally accepted Ludwig's arguments, but the process had been exhausting and had worn him to the bone.

The sight of Verfeld was comforting, but as soon as Ludwig stepped from the carriage, Pelton Wakefield, his castellan, rushed to meet him.

"I'm sorry to disturb you, my lord, but we have a problem."

"Can't it wait?" said Ludwig.

"I'm afraid not. It concerns one of your tenants, my lord."

"Let me guess: someone not paying their rent?"

"Much worse, I'm afraid. Someone stole his livestock."

"Bandits?"

"Doubtful," said Pelton. "Such folk would be hard-pressed to take an entire herd."

"An entire herd? Now you have my attention. Who was robbed?"

"Dolf Macken, from Eramon, Lord. You remember him?"

"Of course. Half the cows in his care were mine."

"He is in the keep, my lord."

"Are you suggesting this just happened?"

"Indeed. In fact, he arrived right before you did."

"Where is he?" asked Ludwig.

"In the great hall. I was going to get a guard to talk to him, but then you arrived."

"Thank you, Pelton. I'll be there directly." He turned to his wife. "You'll have to excuse me, Charlotte. It appears I am needed."

"You'd best get to it. I am more than capable of looking after Frederick and myself."

He kissed his wife, then nodded at Cyn and Sig, who followed him up the steps to the keep. They were soon inside and making their way to the great hall.

"Trouble?" asked Cyn.

"Someone raided one of our tenants. You remember Dolf Macken?"

"Yes. His wife's name is Marjorie, if I recall."

"It is."

"All this over a stolen cow?" asked Sigwulf. "Could wolves have chased it off?"

"Wolves wouldn't take an entire herd," replied Ludwig.

"How many are we talking about?"

"If memory serves, there were a dozen last fall. I needn't remind you it represents a significant investment on my part."

"Someone has it in for you."

Ludwig halted. "What makes you say that?"

"Stealing that many cows sends a message, and I doubt it has anything to do with the Mackens. It's more of a slap in your face, a challenge, if you will."

"How would they know they belonged to me?"

"They didn't need to. As baron, a theft from one of your tenants is the same thing as stealing from you."

"I hadn't considered it that way."

"What do you want us to do?"

"Let's get the story from Dolf first, then you two take some men and see what you can discover." Ludwig resumed walking, entering the great hall as a servant opened the door.

Dolf Macken looked scared at the baron's arrival, for a tenant who loses his lord's cattle could expect little sympathy.

"Dolf," Ludwig said in greeting, "I'm glad to see you in good health. I hope Marjorie is well?"

"She is, Lord," the fellow replied. "But I'm afraid I bear bad news."

"So I've been told. How many cattle were stolen?"

"All of them, Lord."

"That being?"

"Fourteen, including several calves. I would have tried to stop them, but they were armed."

"You saw them?"

"I did. There were eight, with two mounted, and all bore swords."

"Did they wear any identifying colours?"

"The mounted men wore fine clothes. Both had beards, but the younger fellow's was neatly trimmed and only covered his chin."

"Did you recognize any of the others?"

"No, Lord," replied Dolf. "And I know everyone in the area."

"When did this happen?"

"Late yesterday afternoon. We set out at first light to bring word to you."

"You made good time."

"We were lucky enough to come across a trader heading to Malburg who let us ride in his wagon."

"You said us? Where's Marjorie?"

"She and the babe are in Malburg with relatives, Lord. I felt it best to keep her safe."

"That's good to hear," said Ludwig. "It's important you're all safe, but let's go back to yesterday, shall we? Can you describe what happened?"

"Aye. We were out behind the farm weeding the turnips when we saw them coming from the west."

"Along the road?"

"No, across the fields. They must have come from the woods."

"Go on."

"When we first saw them, we took them for travellers, but as they got closer, we noticed sunlight glinting off armour. They drew weapons as they came within hailing distance, so we rushed into the house, barring the door." He released a deep, shuddering breath. "I thought they were going to kill us."

"What happened next?"

"We heard noises as they broke the fence and drove the cattle from their pen."

"And nothing else?"

"Oh yes, now that you mention it. One called out that if we wanted to live, we shouldn't interfere."

"And you didn't recognize the voice?"

"No, Lord, but then again, I don't spend my time in such company."

"I'm not sure I understand."

"His manner was much like yours, Lord: well-spoken."

Ludwig directed his next words to Cyn and Sigwulf. "Take ten men and ride out to Eramon. If you're lucky, you might be able to follow their trail."

"And if we find who's responsible?" asked Cyn.

"Then you're to bring them back here."

"Alive?"

"If you can, but don't take unnecessary chances."

"What of me and Marjorie?" asked Dolf.

"I'll have someone take you back to Malburg. You wait there with Marjorie until we determine it's safe to return." Ludwig put a hand on the man's shoulder. "Don't blame yourself, Dolf. There's nothing you could have done to stop this. We'll find out who did this, and when we do, we'll make sure they pay for their crimes."

"Thank you, Lord."

"Don't thank me just yet; there's still much to be done."

Cyn, Siggy, and ten men escorted Dolf back to his family in Malburg in the morning, then continued on to Eramon. As they approached the Macken farm, the sun was nearly at its height in the cloudless sky. Though they had a good description of where the theft had occurred, it was hardly necessary, for it was easy enough to follow the exit of the cows through the broken fence.

"I expected this to be difficult," said Sigwulf, "but they left a trail so obvious, even a Holy Father could follow."

"You shouldn't speak so ill of the Church, Siggy. They're educated men."

"And you think they'd be able to follow a trail?"

"Considering your previous remark, then yes. Anything you'd like to add?"

"The horses are shod, not that it should surprise us."

"I'm more worried about those men. They must have ridden past Roshlag on their way here. You don't suppose they stole anything there, do you?"

"We'll find out soon enough," said Sigwulf. "What I'm more interested in is who's behind this theft. It's one thing to steal a cow for food, quite another to take an entire herd, calves included. That seems to indicate someone wants them for breeding."

"Then they should have stolen a bull. Clearly, they're not the brightest of thieves."

"Or are they? They wouldn't need a bull if they already had one."

"So you're suggesting another farmer stole them?"

"How else would you hide that many cows?" Sig turned to the men who'd accompanied them. "Rikal, you're from this area, aren't you?"

"Aye," replied the archer. "I was raised in Roshlag. I've travelled through here many a time on my way to Malburg. Why do you ask?"

"If you were going to hide a dozen cows, where would you take them?"

"That's easy. The edge of the Greenwood lies southwest of here."

"Look," said Cyn. "That's precisely where the tracks lead."

"True," replied the archer, "but these tracks are more than a day old. I doubt they're still amongst the trees."

"Why?"

"Wolves, mostly, but many other predators like the taste of meat."

"True, but these cows had men with them."

"Were any farmers?"

"Doubtful," added Sig. "They sounded more like a group of warriors."

"How about archers?"

"Not according to Dolf's description. Why?"

The archer shrugged. "Archers like me are generally of rural stock. Soldiers typically lack any skill when it comes to livestock."

"They might just be raiders?"

"If they were raiders, why didn't they sack the farmhouse? There's far more likely to be valuables in there."

"You make a good point," said Cyn. "But if not raiders, then who?"

"Aside from Lord Ludwig, only one person around here has his own warriors."

"Surely you're not suggesting Lord Darrian of Glosnecke?"

"I'm not accusing anyone," said Rikal, holding up his hands, "especially not a noble, but it takes coins to hire warriors. Who else could it be?"

"A rich merchant?" offered Sigwulf.

"No," said Cyn. "He has the right of it. A merchant would not want to herd cattle. The woods might be a good place to hide stolen goods for the short term, but it's not the healthiest of places for animals like cows."

"Oh? Are you a farmer now?"

"No, but the fact they were stolen and not killed indicates the value of keeping them alive. I suspect if we follow this trail, it'll lead us to Glosnecke."

"Then let's be on our way."

The trail led west, then south, as the archer predicted, towards the edge of the Greenwood, within which they found evidence of a fire, along with fresher tracks heading north. These they followed, crossing the road that led back to Eramon late in the afternoon. Once they entered the hills, tracking became more difficult.

The rocky ground in this part of the countryside made footprints scarce, and were it not for occasional droppings of cow manure, they might have lost the tracks completely. The path veered more west than north, and by the time the sun had nearly set, they were forced to temporarily halt their expedition.

Sitting by the fire that evening, they pondered their next moves.

"What if it's the baron himself?" asked Sigwulf. "Do we arrest him?"

"I doubt we could," said Cyn. "It's not as if we can ride up and tell him he's under arrest. Even if we tried, he would order his men to arrest us, and then where would we be?"

"So then, what's our next choice?"

"I think observation is our best option."

"We should just watch them?"

"What other choice do we have?"

"I suppose you're right, but what would be the point of it? If we can't arrest him, why are we even here?"

"So we can give Ludwig a full report," said Cyn. "Who knows? Perhaps we'll get lucky and find one of those men alone somewhere so we can chat with him."

"Talk? To someone who stole our cattle?"

"You mean Dolf's cattle, don't you?"

"I mean ours," said Sig. "That meat was destined for my belly, not the Baron of Glosnecke's."

"And there he is, the endless stomach."

"Say, do you think some of the baron's men got a little carried away?"

"Carried away? It took foresight and planning, not to mention commitment, to ride all the way to Eramon."

"Just out of curiosity, how do we tell Dolf's cows from those belonging in Glosnecke?"

"That's just it," said Cyn. "We don't. These are not temple mounts with tattoos on their ears—they're cows."

"It seems to me such a practice would prevent this sort of thing."

"I'm sure it would, but how often do you think thefts of this type occur?"

"I have no idea, nor am I eager to find out. Hey, what was it Dolf mentioned about those two riders?"

"That one kept a well-trimmed beard," replied Cyn.

"What exactly does that even mean?"

"It's only on his chin, Siggy. You've seen that sort of thing before. Remember Willy Stoltz?"

"Remember? I could hardly forget. He told your father I was in your tent."

"And?"

He grinned. "It was still worth it!"

"Of course it was, Siggy, but do you remember his face?"

"Naturally. He had that smirky beard he kept fussing over."

"Smirky?"

"Yes. He always had a smug attitude, like he was better than the rest of us; the carefully trimmed facial hair was all part of it." She waited as he finally put all the pieces together. "Oh, I see. The man here has the same beard!"

Cyn chuckled. "I knew you'd understand, eventually."

"Well, if that's the case, he shouldn't be too hard to spot, assuming he's outdoors. It's not as if we can wander through the baron's keep, looking for him."

"It's more likely he'd take them to the local village. He couldn't house cows within the confines of the keep."

"Hold on," said Sigwulf. "Lord Darrian doesn't have any facial hair."

"I'm not suggesting he does, but like Ludwig, he'll have people working for him. I imagine our unknown villain is one of those."

"Then we'll have to lie in wait for him to make himself known."

"How do you suggest we do that?"

Sigwulf looked across to the other fire. "Hey, Rikal. How good are you at hiding?"

"Don't look at me," the archer answered. "You want Kalen for that sort of thing."

All eyes turned to his companion. "What is it you're proposing?"

"We need to locate a distinctive-looking fellow once we reach the village."

"What village?" asked Kalen.

"The one sitting outside Lord Darrian's keep. I assume it's called Glosnecke, but I'm only guessing."

"Shouldn't be a problem. Rikal and I will wander into the village and look around."

"Won't they notice you?"

"Possibly, but we'll go in without weapons, and if we act like common labourers, I doubt anyone would take notice. Of course, you could provide us with some coins which might loosen a few tongues at whatever passes for the local tavern."

"I knew there'd be a catch," said Sigwulf.

"Hush now," insisted Cyn. "You know Ludwig will reimburse you."

. . .

They topped a rise the next morning to see Glosnecke off in the distance. The baron's keep sat atop a small hill, giving it a commanding view of the area, while the local village was nearby to the south. From their current vantage point, they noticed cows in a pasture, but they had no way of telling if any belonged to Dolf Macken.

Kalen and Rikal headed into the village, leaving the rest to wait amongst the hills to the east. The men took turns watching for their return, but the two archers didn't show their faces until well into the afternoon. They were wandering down the road at a sedate pace, then with a quick look to ensure they weren't being followed, they ran up into the hills to join their comrades.

"Well?" said Sigwulf. "Did you find him?"

"We did," replied Kalen. "He's at the Badger."

"That's not funny."

"It's not meant to be. It's the name of the local tavern."

"Time to get into position," said Cyn.

"Position?" replied Kalen.

"Unless I miss my guess, he's a guest of the baron."

"What makes you say that?"

"He was well-dressed, wasn't he?"

"He was."

"Well, I don't see any buildings in the village that suggest someone wealthy, do you?"

"No," said Sigwulf.

"So it stands to reason he's a guest of the baron, which means he'll eventually return to the keep."

"Smart thinking."

"Of course," said Cyn. "That's why you keep me around."

"Oh, I keep you around for much more than that."

"Keep that thought for later, Siggy. We've work to do."

The path from the village to the keep wound past a small copse of trees. The keep had obviously never experienced a siege, for such a hiding place so close to the baron's fortified home would make a surprise attack far too easy. As it was, the copse was enough to conceal Cyn, Siggy, and all of their men.

They settled in for what they expected to be a long wait, but almost as soon as they'd taken up their positions, their target came into sight, muttering something. As he drew closer, it turned out he was singing, or at least attempting to.

Sigwulf nodded to a footman, Paran, who stepped out into the light.

The well-dressed man slowed. "What's this, now?" he asked, his voice slurring.

"Someone wants to talk to you," the warrior replied.

"Does he? Well, you tell him I'm not interested." The fellow waved his hand. "Out of the way, cur, before I make it my business to teach you a lesson."

Paran took a step towards him, drawing his sword. "I'm afraid I must insist."

To his credit, the well-dressed man didn't back down. He fumbled for his own sword, his eyes glued to the person blocking his way.

"This has gone on long enough," said Sigwulf, coming out from the trees. "You're under arrest in the name of His Highness, Lord Ludwig Altenburg, Prince of Hadenfeld, and Baron of Verfeld."

The fellow turned to face him, clearly struggling to make sense of his words. It was a wonder he remained upright, for he stank so much of stale ale, he might as well have bathed in it.

"Will you surrender?" asked Sigwulf.

"I will not yield."

The big northerner stepped forward, striking out with his fist. Cyn didn't see the hit, for Sig's back blocked her view, but she definitely heard it. After the briefest of moments came a dull thud, and then the one responsible for the theft of the cows fell to the ground, blood pouring from his nose. She rushed forward, peering down at the poor excuse for a man.

"Did I kill him?" asked Sig.

"No," said Cyn. "He's still breathing."

"Good. Let's tie him up and get out of here before someone misses him."

8

PRISONER

SUMMER 1101 SR

L udwig jolted awake from his slumber. It was still dark outside, yet something was up, for the noises from below couldn't be missed. Father Vernan opened the door, lantern in hand.

"Sorry to disturb you, Highness, but Sigwulf and Cynthia have returned, along with a prisoner."

Ludwig wiped the sleep from his eyes. "I'll be down directly. Have them meet me in the great hall."

The Holy Father turned to leave, but the Prince of Hadenfeld wasn't done.

"And one more thing," Ludwig said. "Stop calling me Highness."

"But it's the proper form of address."

"In court, perhaps, but here, in private, you must call me Ludwig. Think of it as a way of keeping me humble."

"As you wish... Ludwig. Sorry, it doesn't naturally roll off the tongue, but I shall endeavour to do so."

Ludwig laughed. "Finally, someone who listens." He moved to a small table, picked up a pitcher, poured some water into a bowl, and then hurriedly splashed it over his face, desperate to wash away his fatigue.

He wandered over to the window and threw open the shutters, but it was too dark to see much more than shadows. At least the warm summer breeze was refreshing. Ludwig turned and dressed before heading downstairs. Halfway there, he ran across Carson.

The manservant wore a look of surprise. "You're up early, Lord... I mean, Highness—"

Ludwig cut him off. "Lord will do fine. See if you can find me some food, will you? I have business to attend to."

"In the great hall?"

"Yes. Cyn and Sig will be there, too, so we'll need something to drink." He hesitated, looking at his faithful servant. "I don't often say it, Carson, but thank you."

"For what? I'm only doing my job."

"A job you do very well, and I am truly grateful for your service."

Carson stood there, unable to speak. Ludwig placed his hand on the man's shoulder. "Now, you must excuse me. As I said, I have things to attend to." He left his servant, smiling to himself as he descended the steps.

Sigwulf stood by the fire, warming his hands, while Cyn sat sideways on a bench, wiggling her toes with her legs stretched out along the seat. She looked up as the lord of the manor entered, then lifted her feet, intending to put her boots back on.

"Don't rise on my account," said Ludwig.

"Sorry. It was a long night."

"And it's not over yet," added Sigwulf.

Ludwig's friends looked exhausted, but there was something in their eyes, a look of triumph, perhaps? "I assume you were successful?"

The northerner grinned. "Aye, we were. We locked the culprit up in the dungeon."

"Yes," added Cyn, "and better yet, no one saw us take him."

Ludwig dropped into a chair. "What do we know of him?"

"Not much, I'm afraid. He refused to answer any questions, wouldn't even give us his name."

"I suppose that's to be expected, considering what he's done. Tell me about him."

"He's well-spoken and wears finely made clothes. I suspect he's a wealthy merchant or even a lesser noble. Saints know you barons have enough cousins to field an army."

"What makes you think he's a cousin to a noble?"

"He was returning to the keep when we waylaid him."

"Does he know who you are?"

"We didn't tell him who we were but arrested him in your name."

"Did he resist?"

Cyn fell silent, looking at her partner.

"Well?" pressed Ludwig.

Sigwulf cleared his throat. "He resisted being arrested."

"What did you do?"

"I might have needed to subdue him."

"Subdue him?"

"What he means," said Cyn, "is he punched the fellow in the face. After that, there was no resistance."

"Are you suggesting you beat him?"

"No," said Sigwulf, shaking his head. "One punch was all it took. Knocked him out cold, though I think his tooth may have cut my knuckle."

"He didn't wake up till we were well out of Glosnecke," added Cyn. "Even then, he wasn't very talkative, other than to curse at us. Did you want to go and see him yourself?"

"No, let him stew for a bit. Let's have something to eat first. I need to think about this."

"What's there to think about? He stole your cattle!"

"True, yet what am I to do about it? I can't execute him, particularly if he's a noble, as you suspect."

"A minor noble," corrected Sigwulf. "I doubt anyone would miss him."

"On the contrary, even villains have friends; sooner or later, they'll realize he's missing."

"And you fear retribution? You're a Prince of the Realm, Ludwig. Who would dare move against you?"

"I'm not so enamoured with the title that I think it can shield me against all. Even princes are mortal, and those who believe otherwise are doomed to fail."

Charlotte opened the door, interrupting their conversation. "Sorry," she said. "I couldn't help but overhear."

Ludwig rose, taking her hand and guiding her to a seat close to the fire. "You should have stayed in bed."

"And miss all the excitement? Ludwig, you know as well as I that I must act while I have the strength. Tell me what you're thinking?"

"You heard about the prisoner?"

"I did," she replied. "Who do you think he is?"

"A sell-sword? To be honest, I don't really know."

"Did I hear his clothes described as finely made?"

Ludwig grinned. "You stood outside that door for some time."

"Naturally. It would have been impertinent to enter too soon. How else can I live up to my reputation as being all-wise?"

"As to your question, yes, he was well-dressed."

"Then I doubt he's a sell-sword. In the north, they are common, but even the most successful of that ilk prefer to dress as warriors. It's how they reinforce their reputations. And to a man like that, reputation is everything."

"Then who else could he be?"

"Did he have a foreign accent?"

"No," said Sigwulf. "He sounded a lot like Ludwig."

"Then he is likely from Hadenfeld, which narrows the field."

Ludwig's stomach lurched, and he abruptly sat down.

"Is something wrong?" asked Charlotte.

"I hate to say it, but I think I know who this man is."

"Go on."

He turned to Cyn. "Would you describe him as a young man?"

"He was full grown, if that's what you mean."

"What would you estimate his age to be?"

"Somewhere in his early twenties? Why?"

Carson entered, bearing a tray filled with cups and a pitcher full of wine. All remained silent as he filled them before handing them out. Ludwig downed his in one breath, waiting as the others took sips.

"What is it?" said Charlotte. "You're making me nervous."

"Cyn, you come with me. It's time we had a little chat with this fellow."

"And me?" said Sigwulf.

"Remain here with Charlotte, if you would be so kind."

"You don't want me there with you?"

"No. Don't take this the wrong way, Sig, but you're intimidating, and right now, I'd like to go with a more conciliatory approach. Look on the bright side. You'll be here when the food finally arrives."

"Now"—grinned the giant of a man—"that's more to my liking!"

The dungeon was barely large enough for someone to lie down. Ludwig half expected the prisoner to be doing just that, but as they descended into the lower recesses of the keep, they heard feet shuffling. Cyn led, a lantern held high to illuminate the area, forcing the man to shield his eyes.

Ludwig slowed, coming to a halt before the iron bars. "Well, well, well. Look who we have here." He turned to Cyn. "Oh, that's right. I don't think you've been introduced. This is Lord Gowan Forst, younger brother of Lord Darrian, Baron of Glosnecke."

"I demand my release!" said Gowan. "You have no right to keep me here."

"Don't I?" replied Ludwig. "You stole my tenant's cattle. Don't bother denying it. I have witnesses."

"Witnesses? You trust the word of peasants over me?"

"Do you deny the accusation?"

They stared at each other, but Gowan couldn't maintain his bravado and shifted his gaze to the floor. "No. I don't."

"Tell me, was your brother behind this?"

"No. It was my idea. He knew nothing until I showed up with them."

"Did he suggest returning them?"

"He said it was too late for regrets."

"That's it? No apology or attempt at reconciliation?"

"What would you have him do? Throw himself at your mercy? You know he would never do such a thing."

"You've placed me in a difficult position," said Ludwig. "You stole my property. Perhaps I should cut off your hand? That is, I believe, the punishment for theft?"

Gowan visibly paled. "Please, no. I beg of you."

"Then what do you suggest?"

"My brother is a wealthy man. I'm sure you and he can come to some arrangement."

"Are you suggesting he buy your freedom?"

"Think of it as ransom, if you will. I, in return, promise never to enter your lands again or covet what is yours."

"How do I know you'll keep your word?"

"Bring forth your Holy Father, and I will swear on the Book of Saint Mathew."

"That's no guarantee. You know as well as I the Saints don't punish oath-breakers. I need something more substantial."

"He will fill your coffers to gain my release. What more could you want?"

"I can think of a great many things, but now is not the time for such discussions. I will send word of your imprisonment to your brother and offer to meet. Perhaps, between us, we can come up with a suitable solution."

A look of relief flooded over Gowan's face. "Thank the Saints."

"If I were you, I would consider praying. From what I know of your brother, he's not the forgiving type. A ransom might pay off your debt to me, but it will only put you further into his."

"I am a second son, and it is my destiny to be beholden to my brother. Send word to him of my plight, and he will pay handsomely to secure my release."

"And my cattle?"

"I have no say over the baron's property."

"You're the one who stole them."

"I did what I thought my brother wished."

"What makes you think he wanted you to steal livestock?"

"He's hated you ever since... Well, you know when."

"When I refused his offer to duel? Lord Meinhard refused to sanction it; you were there."

"Yet your actions turned the Lady Alexandra against my brother."

"What madness is this? She was never on his side!"

"Their marriage would have cemented the power of the Forst family. Instead, my brother is a minor baron, forced to live in the shadow of your greatness." The words were complimentary, but the tone mocked.

"I understand your brother's disappointment, but Lady Alexandra was never going to marry him. Her heart was always with Lord Emmett."

"He is a traitor, while Darrian is from Hadenfeld!"

"Watch your words, Gowan. Lord Emmett is a loyal baron of Hadenfeld now, just as your brother and I are. An attitude like that won't do you any favours at court."

Gowan closed his eyes, letting his breath out slowly.

"I know you and I will not agree on the matter," continued Ludwig, "but life moves on. Your brother should as well."

"Easy for you to say. You have the king's ear."

"Who told you that?"

"You met with him on numerous occasions."

"Only in my duty as the prince. His Majesty sought my opinions on military matters. That is all."

"He named you his heir."

"Because I am his closest relation by blood."

"And you think that coincidence?"

Ludwig was taken aback. What was this man insinuating?

"Tell me," said Gowan. "Did the king confide in you about how you became prince?"

"Those in line before me died, while others lost their minds."

"Lost their minds? What manner of nonsense is that? Morgan had them locked up because they disagreed with him."

"Why would you even suggest such a thing?"

"Because I know it for a fact. Open your eyes, Ludwig. Morgan is not the man you think him to be."

"Then what is he?"

"Conniving, power-hungry, with delusions of grandeur. He removed those heirs because they stood in opposition to his dream. Were you to do likewise, I harbour no doubt he would also turn on you."

Ludwig shook his head. "You're lying, and in any case, it has nothing to do with your crimes. I will send word to your brother concerning your incarceration, but don't think for one moment your words will turn me against my king." He turned his back on Gowan. "We're done here."

"Do we feed him?" asked Cyn.

"Yes. He is a noble, although I draw the line at giving him the freedom of the keep. He'll remain in his cell for now, but let's see about getting him a decent bed."

He strode off, forcing her to catch up to him. They returned to the great hall to find Father Vernan had joined the others, along with Pelton, the castellan.

Ludwig threw himself into a chair while the rest, sensing his mood, remained quiet. Was Gowan correct in his assessment of their new king? He wanted to believe Morgan was looking out for the realm's best interests, but Gowan's words somehow rang true. There was no denying his cousin was trying to raise the kingdom's reputation, but was it an honest desire or a dangerous obsession? The thought made him remember the king's speech before his coronation. How far would the man go to achieve his aims?

A hand grasped Ludwig's shoulder, and he looked up to see Charlotte with a look of concern on her face.

"What ails you, husband?"

"It is as I feared. The prisoner is none other than Gowan Forst, brother to Lord Darrian."

"This is ill news indeed. It could lead to a war of barons."

"No," insisted Ludwig. "I saw that happen in Erlingen. I refuse to be a party to it here."

"You may have no choice, especially if he comes with an army."

"She's right," added Cyn. "You remember that mess in Regnitz? It almost cost us the war."

"True," replied Ludwig, "but Hadenfeld is not at war, nor would I wish it to be. I'll try to reason with Lord Darrian, but if it doesn't work, I shall take the issue up with the king."

"How can we help?"

"I need someone to bear a message to Lord Darrian."

"I'll go," offered Sigwulf.

"No," said Father Vernan. "I think it best I be the one to carry it. The baron bears a grudge, Ludwig, and there's a good chance he might imprison whomever you send. As a member of the Church, if he imprisons me, he'll have to deal with Temple Knights."

"What you say is true," replied Ludwig, "but I'll provide you with a carriage and guards to keep you safe on the road. The last thing I want to hear about is so-called bandits killing a man of the Church."

"You think they would be so bold?"

"They were bold enough to steal cattle in broad daylight," said Ludwig. "After that, I hardly think murder would trouble them."

"There is a big difference between murder and theft."

"To an ordinary man, yes, but Darrian doesn't impress me as the sort who'd have qualms about such things."

"Very well," said Father Vernan. "I accept your offer. Do you wish to write a letter, or will my word suffice when dealing with His Lordship?"

"I'll leave it to you. I fear my own words would only lead to misunderstanding where he's concerned. He's resented me for years and will likely twist what I say to his advantage."

"I shall set out as soon as can be arranged."

"Thank you, Father."

"Now, if you'll excuse me, I must prepare for the trip."

Ludwig watched him leave, unease building within him. Father Vernan would be safe, of that he was sure, but he had a growing fear Darrian would refuse the offer of a meeting.

"He'll succeed," said Charlotte, pulling him from his thoughts. "If there's anyone who can make Lord Darrian see reason, it's Father Vernan."

Ludwig nodded. "Yes, but now I must put some thought to how that meeting should address the issue at hand. By his own brother's admission, they stole those cows. Do I demand retribution or forget the whole affair to keep the peace?"

"That is a question I cannot answer, but I know, in my heart, you will do what you think is best. One can hardly ask for more."

9

DARRIAN

SUMMER 1101 SR

It was reckoned close to forty miles to reach Glosnecke, a journey of two days by carriage. Father Vernan, however, didn't return for almost an entire week, during which time Ludwig fretted. Would Darrian agree to meet, or would he show up at the head of an army?

Ludwig met the father as he disembarked, descending the keep's stairs before the carriage even stopped moving. "We were worried that Lord Darrian had locked you up."

"My apologies," replied Father Vernan. "I stopped off in Malburg to make arrangements."

"For what?"

"Why, for your meeting."

"I assume that means Darrian is willing to discuss things in a civilized manner?"

"He is, though whether he remains so has yet to be seen. He was not happy to learn of his brother's imprisonment but was glad to learn he was still alive. So complete was the mystery of his disappearance, Darrian believed his brother had met an unfortunate end."

"Did he admit to stealing the cattle?"

"He did not, but thankfully, still agreed to meet in person. That alone took a bit of convincing and was, I confess, only made under great duress. He wanted you to come to him, but I suggested the location of a neutral third party."

"Where?"

"The Temple of Saint Mathew in Malburg. I can think of no other place that might be considered unbiased."

"A good choice, although I fear we may still come to blows."

"Yes," admitted Father Vernan. "Prior Yannick feared that as well. He would have insisted on having Temple Knights present had they been nearby, but I fear this difference between you and Darrian can't wait that long. I told him as much, and he agreed, but there are limits on how many men may accompany you."

"A fair and equitable solution. When is this meeting to take place?"

"One week from today. The negotiations will commence at noon. How long do you think it will take to reach a consensus?"

"That's difficult to say," replied Ludwig. "Darrian dislikes me, so I doubt he'll be reasonable. However, his brother is in my care, which means I have all the bargaining power."

"You must try not to lord that over him. It will only cause further conflict."

"My apologies," said Ludwig. "Here you are, only just returned, and I'm bombarding you with questions. Let's get you inside and find you something to eat, shall we?"

They ascended the steps, entered the keep, and were soon before the fire, mead in hand, while servants went to fetch some food.

"You must tell me more about Lord Darrian," said Ludwig. "My few encounters with the man haven't been the most cordial."

"When I first arrived, I was met with some suspicion. The entire place was in a bit of an uproar due to Lord Gowan's presumed disappearance. I took it upon myself to assure His Lordship his brother was in good health, but it did little to soothe his ire."

"He blamed you?"

"Not at all. As a representative of the Church, he treated me with nothing but respect. However, that doesn't mean I was ignorant of his rantings."

"Rantings?"

"I was shown to some guest quarters," replied Father Vernan, "but sound carries easily in such a place, as I'm sure you're aware. His wrath was enough to make a Holy Brother blush, as was his choice of words. Once he calmed down, I offered my services to mediate the dispute."

"And you suggested Malburg?"

"Not initially. That came about because of our discussion. Although admittedly, when I say discussion, it was mostly him venting his spleen. Eventually, I realized no progress would happen without a face-to-face meeting, which is when I suggested a neutral third party host it. The natural choice was the Temple of Saint Mathew, so, armed with Lord Darrian's requirements, I set out for Malburg."

"And Prior Yannick?"

"The news of your feud disturbed him, but he agreed to host the meeting, hoping to resolve the matter quickly. He then asked me about your relationship with Lord Darrian."

"I'm guessing that's when he suggested getting Temple Knights."

"It was, but I assured him it wasn't necessary. Please don't give me a reason to regret my actions."

"I shan't," said Ludwig, "but I can't speak for Lord Darrian. I've tried to be civil with him, but he rebuffs my advances at every turn."

A servant entered and placed two plates of food on the table. They waited for him to leave before continuing their discussion.

"To assuage the prior's fears, I suggested we limit you and Lord Darrian to only six warriors each. I hope that wasn't too presumptuous of me?"

"Not at all, but I'm curious about Darrian's response. Surely you won't ride all the way back to Glosnecke for his approval?"

"I don't have to, for his castellan accompanied me to Malburg to arrange the details."

"Good," said Ludwig. "You've done a much better job of arranging this than I ever could."

"Don't sell yourself short, Highness."

"That's Ludwig, remember?"

"Of course. Now, having made the arrangements, we should ensure you're ready."

"Ready, how?"

"If you are to argue before Prior Yannick, you must prepare what you are to say."

"The facts speak for themselves."

"Facts," said Father Vernan, "are subject to interpretation. We would do well to scrutinize your side of the story so you know what to expect."

"Meaning?"

"Lord Darrian will take every opportunity to discredit you, Ludwig. You must be prepared to counter."

"I have no wish to impugn the honour of Lord Darrian."

"And I'm not suggesting you do that, merely that you be prepared for his arguments."

"You've made your point. How do we proceed?"

"I suggest you lay out your arguments to me. I, in turn, will offer counter-arguments in the spirit of Lord Darrian. You must promise me, however, that you won't think it a personal attack. I seek to emulate the baron's tactics, not upset you."

. . .

One week later, Ludwig sat in his carriage, accompanied by Father Vernan, while Cyn and Sigwulf escorted them on horses, along with a trio of guards.

"Do you think I'm ready?" asked Ludwig.

"As ready as you'll ever be," replied the Holy Father. "It is essential you keep a level head. The last thing you want to do in front of Prior Yannick is lose your temper."

"Perhaps I should convince Lord Darrian to lose his?"

"You are trying to negotiate an acceptable arrangement for both of you, not start a baron's war. At least that's what I assume you want."

"It is," said Ludwig. "I was merely trying to lighten the mood a little."

Father Vernan leaned to one side, peering out the window at the city. "We're getting close now. It won't be much longer before we arrive at the temple."

"I hope we don't run into Darrian before we enter."

"We will enter on the south side whereas he will come in from the north. Considering the animosity between you two, I thought it best to take precautions."

"The animosity is all on his side," said Ludwig, "not mine."

"Yet you speak of him in disparaging ways. I'm not saying he's perfect, merely that we are all imperfect, you included. That's why the Saints guide us."

"Are you lecturing me?"

"No, only reminding you that you are a living, breathing person, the same as Darrian. Today's objective is to let you both walk away from this meeting as winners. Any other result will prolong this antipathy and cause further hard feelings."

"Your time in Eidenburg was well-spent," said Ludwig. "Or were you always naturally this wise?"

"I would like to think a little of both."

The wheels rattled as they hit the city's cobblestones.

"It won't be long now," said Father Vernan."

Ludwig looked out the window. They were close to the artisan's quarter, the view making him think of Tomas deShandria.

"You're thinking of Charlaine, aren't you?"

"Actually, I was thinking of her father. He's a city elector now."

"And what of her?"

"The last time I saw her in person was at my wedding. We've corresponded, but I fear I've been a little lax in replying to her letters."

"So she knows nothing of you becoming the prince?"

"It's not the type of thing one casually mentions. I suppose I haven't written because I don't feel like explaining our complex succession laws."

"Then do so without reference to them."

"You surprise me. I would think a Holy Father the last one to suggest I write to a woman other than my wife."

"She is a Temple Captain and therefore beyond reproach. As a valued member of the Church, she deserves your respect, which seems to be lacking from your absence of correspondence." He smiled to lessen the blow. "I'm not saying you need to tell her your life story, but you owe her the decency of informing her of recent events. Hadenfeld is her home, too, and I'm sure she'd be pleased to know it's recently been reunited."

"You're right. I shall see to it once this business with Lord Darrian is handled."

"Good, because we've arrived."

The carriage rolled to a stop.

Other than the chairs and a single table in the room that Prior Yannick had chosen for them to meet, the only thing of interest was the candles, and even then, they were dwarfed by the giant windows bathing the room in sunlight. Lord Darrian was already present, sitting on one side of the table.

At Ludwig's entrance, Prior Yannick stood, offering a bow. "Your Highness, welcome."

Ludwig nodded a greeting. "Your Grace. Thank you for hosting this meeting. I trust it hasn't been too much of an inconvenience?"

"Not at all. I am merely doing the Saint's bidding."

Ludwig approached the table opposite Lord Darrian and nodded again, this time without offering words. The prior waited until he sat before taking a seat himself.

"I understand there is some animosity between the two of you," Yannick began. "Let us put that aside for the moment and attempt to get to the facts, shall we? Ludwig, why don't you go first?"

"One of my farms was raided, and all the cattle stolen. I sent men to track down the culprits, and they apprehended Gowan Forst, Lord Darrian's brother. He now sits in my dungeon awaiting trial."

"Trial?" said Darrian. "You can't put him on trial? Such things need a tribunal composed of nobles, not the judgement of a single baron."

"He makes a good point," offered the prior.

"I am happy to release him," replied Ludwig. "All it would take is for Lord Darrian to apologize and return the cows."

"Return the cows?" said Darrian. "How in the name of the Saints am I to tell yours from mine?"

"Are you suggesting you don't know how many cows your people are said to possess?"

"How do I know you're not exaggerating your losses? You could be fabricating this whole thing."

"Your brother indicates otherwise. He's already confessed to the crime. I can offer you written statements, if you wish."

"I should very much like to see them," replied Yannick, "but let us concentrate on what is to be done with Lord Gowan."

"I propose you release him," said Darrian. "Call it an act of good faith, if you like."

"Why, so you can keep him without compensating me for my loss? He's not going anywhere until I see some coins or my cows."

"Holding one of our realm's nobles in a dungeon is unconscionable. Such punishment is reserved for traitors, not minor infractions of the law."

"Minor infractions? Do you even hear yourself? He robbed one of my tenants of his livelihood. A price must be paid for such an act."

"I'm not arguing that," said Darrian. "I am pointing out that the man accused, my brother, is a noble and by rights is innocent until guilt can be proven."

"What he says is true," offered Yannick. "The laws of Hadenfeld are very clear on this matter."

Ludwig cleared his throat. "Yet the law was still broken when the cattle were taken."

"You are no farmer," said Darrian.

"True, but my tenants are, and my coins paid for half those cows."

Prior Yannick held up his hands. "You both have valid concerns, but rather than concentrate on the past, the best thing would be to consider possible remedies. Lord Ludwig, what is it you seek?"

"The return of my lawful property."

"And Lord Darrian?"

"The release of my brother."

"Then it seems," continued the prior, "that there is little to discuss. I suggest Lord Gowan be remanded into the Church's custody until arrangements can be made to return the cattle."

"I will not," said Darrian. "Nor will I pay a single coin to Lord Ludwig. His actions are not only reprehensible, but they are also blatantly illegal."

"Let's be clear about this," replied Ludwig. "My men did not know Lord Gowan's identity when they apprehended him."

"That doesn't make his arrest legal. If anything, it only demonstrates your lack of diplomacy. If your cattle were stolen, as you claim, you should have brought it to my immediate attention. Instead, you sent spies into my lands and abducted my brother. Are these the actions of a law-abiding baron? I think not!"

"You argue your brother's arrest was illegal, yet you won't take responsibility for the theft in the first place."

"I know nothing of this theft," replied Darrian. "As far as I'm concerned, you're making the entire thing up."

"Then let us examine your accounts. It shouldn't take much to count your herd and establish the truth."

"I will not submit to such an examination. My accounts are none of your concern."

"I beg to differ. They would establish your guilt."

"Let us pause a moment," said Prior Yannick. "You are both passionate men, an admirable trait but one which, I fear, leaves us unable to resolve the issue. Since you don't wish to move forward with my suggestion, the only remaining option is Royal Intervention."

"I agree," said Ludwig. "Let us take this matter to the king."

"No," said Darrian. "King Morgan is Ludwig's cousin. How can I expect a fair hearing, especially against the Prince of Hadenfeld and heir to the Crown?"

"You have little choice," said the prior. "Matters of this nature can only be adjudicated by someone superior in social status, and since barons are the only nobles in Hadenfeld, that leaves the king."

"Very well," said Darrian. "When do you propose we do this?"

Yannick forced a smile. "I shall bring the matter to him at once. Bearing in mind His Majesty is new to his position, it may take some time before he's prepared to offer judgement. I will send word once he sets a date."

"How do we know you'll offer the king an unbiased opinion?"

"I'll not be judging the merits of this case, merely alerting King Morgan to the necessity of a tribunal. It will be up to you to present your arguments to him directly." He stopped, looking at each in turn. "I suggest, in the meantime, you learn how to control your respective tempers. I doubt His Majesty cares to host a yelling match."

Both barons fell silent.

"Are we all clear on how I will proceed?"

Both nodded, though neither looked pleased.

"Good. Then it's settled. Now, I ask that Lord Gowan be escorted to Malburg. We shall keep him here until his fate can be determined. Is that suitable to you, Lord Darrian?"

"It is."

"And you, Lord Ludwig?"

"I agree with your decision. I shall arrange for him to be delivered tomorrow."

"There is one more thing you must both agree on. Until the king calls you to the tribunal, you must refrain from entering each other's lands. Do I make myself clear?"

"Yes," said Ludwig.

Lord Darrian had other ideas. "What if I want to take the road to Dornbruck?"

Yannick was no one's fool. "Why would you need to go to Dornbruck?"

"I am merely trying to make allowance for a baron's obligations. It is not my place to question the orders of my king."

"Should you receive orders to that effect, you may pass through Verfeld. Otherwise, you are to avoid it at all costs."

"I accept the restrictions."

"Then I must bid you a good day, my lords. I have much to write before I ride for the capital."

10

ARBITRATION

AUTUMN 1101 SR

The leaves fell, announcing the changing of seasons, and Ludwig wondered when they might hear from the king. He sent Father Vernan into Malburg to talk to the prior, but His Grace remained in the capital.

Weeks dragged on, and then months. A Royal Messenger finally arrived as the wintry winds blew in, but he bore only the king's orders regarding reorganizing their forces. Ludwig knew what was coming, for the king had adopted his plan, yet it stung, as the changes required a substantial investment, one made even more difficult because of the expense of buying new cattle.

He sent letters back with the messenger to both the prior and the king, but still there was no response. In desperation, he wrote to Lord Meinhard, asking him to intercede on his behalf. Alexandra's father agreed to speak with Morgan, but three weeks later, he sent word back that His Majesty refused to talk of such things. It looked more and more like Morgan was upset with his feuding barons.

Ludwig set to work carrying out the king's wishes. During the last war, he'd fielded four hundred men, but the bulk were little more than unarmoured militia, with two hundred of those raised by Malburg and thus, technically, not his. He had a core of decent archers and a company of veteran footmen, but that was a far cry from these new requirements.

He put aside his feud with Darrian to concentrate on doing his duty. A trip to Malburg enlisted the guilds' help in equipping this new force, for raising his own men meant the city no longer needed to supply warriors. Pleased to be free of such commitments, they offered substantial savings for their services and allowed him to pay them over months instead of in advance.

Under Sigwulf's tutelage, the two companies of foot learned to work together, while Cyn undertook the training of an additional company of archers. However, the increase in Ludwig's retinue resulted in another problem. Verfeld Keep was a decent size but far too small to house everyone, so he invested in constructing buildings in the village of Verfeld. Thankfully, they were completed well before the ground froze, thus freeing up space in the keep.

Winter that year was bitter, and traffic to and from the capital became scarce. It wasn't until spring that word finally arrived the king was ready to pass judgement.

Ludwig prepared to set out at once. Not wanting to endure the long ride, Charlotte chose to remain in Verfeld, along with Cyn and Sigwulf, who were needed to continue the men's training.

The trip itself was uneventful, and before long, Ludwig and Father Vernan were riding through the streets of the capital. They stopped briefly at an inn to clean themselves up before proceeding to the Royal Keep, only to find Sir Emril waiting for them.

The corner of the knight's lips raised slightly while his eyes remained cold. "Your Highness, I'm so glad you could make it. I trust your trip was pleasant?"

"It was," replied Ludwig. "You know Father Vernan?"

The knight nodded at the Holy Man. "A pleasure, Father." He waved a couple of servants forward to take the horses. "If you'll follow me, I'll conduct you to His Majesty."

"I assume Lord Darrian has already arrived?"

"Indeed. He's been in Harlingen for some days now. Unlike some, he makes it a point to be on time."

"Now, now," said Vernan. "Let's not be churlish. I might remind you the king wanted us here at noon, and the Cathedral's bells have yet to ring."

"My pardon," said Emril. "I meant no disrespect."

They continued in silence, arriving at a sitting room with several chairs arranged around a fireplace. A servant placed another log on the fire and then backed out.

"If you'll wait here," said the knight, "I shall inform His Majesty of your arrival." He left them without any further word.

"Well," said Father Vernan. "I can't say that sounds promising. If Lord Darrian has been here for days, he's likely been spreading his version of events throughout the city."

"It's not like you to sound so pessimistic," said Ludwig. "Aren't you usually the one who gives people the benefit of the doubt?"

"It's true. I'll not deny it, but we can't overlook the fact Sir Emril greeted us. You and he had words, did you not?"

"That was ages ago."

"Not so long ago, he couldn't resist a jab at your expense. This bodes ill if he has the ear of the king."

"Let's not rush to any conclusions."

A servant opened the door and bowed. "Highness, His Majesty will see you now."

They were led into a long room with an immense table placed in the middle. At first, Ludwig assumed it was a dining hall, yet one look at the bookshelf-lined walls suggested otherwise. King Morgan sat silently at the head of the table, with Darrian off to one side. The servant pulled the opposite seat out for Ludwig.

He sat while Father Vernan stood behind him, for to sit in the king's presence uninvited was considered bad manners. Sir Emril entered, moving to stand to the king's right, a statement of how he was favoured. Ludwig wondered if Father Vernan's speculation might prove true. The king nodded at the knight.

"We are here today," began Sir Emril, "to resolve the issue standing between Lord Darrian Forst, Baron of Glosnecke, and Lord Ludwig Altenburg, Baron of Verfeld."

"That's Prince Ludwig," said Vernan. "And you should address him as His Highness, not lord."

The knight opened his mouth, but Morgan held up his hand, forestalling him. "Let's dispense with all the pleasantries, shall we? I'd like to get to the heart of the matter." He glanced down at some papers sitting before him. "According to this report, you arrested Lord Gowan Horst. Is that correct, Ludwig?"

"It is, Majesty."

"And you claim he stole cattle from one of your tenants?"

"Indeed."

"And you, Lord Darrian, claim that, as a noble, such an arrest is illegal. Is that it?"

Darrian cleared his throat. "That is correct, Majesty."

"Where is Lord Gowan presently?"

Sir Emril supplied the answer. "At the Temple of Saint Mathew in Malburg, sire. The prior there offered it as a compromise."

"Ah, yes. I remember reading the good prior's report." He shuffled through the papers, withdrawing one and holding it up close to read. "It says here you two acted most disgracefully despite being in a Holy Place. Have you no reverence for such things?"

He stared at each in turn, and neither so much as blinked, but he was not expecting a reply, for he soon continued.

"I will not tolerate this kind of behaviour in my kingdom. You are nobles of Hadenfeld, and as such, I expect you to behave in a civil and polite manner. We are trying to unite the realm, not split it up again!"

"With all due respect," said Darrian, "this is not a matter that threatens the kingdom's security; it is an attempt by one person, Lord Ludwig, to force reparations where none are warranted."

"Are you suggesting," said the king, "your brother was not responsible for this theft?"

"I maintain his innocence, Majesty. In fact, the very idea Gowan would ever consider such a thing is ludicrous."

"Then how do you explain the missing cows?"

"That's just it, I don't. We only have Lord Ludwig's word that anything was stolen. For all we know, his farmer sold off all the cattle."

"That's not true!" shouted Ludwig. "Your brother confessed to the theft."

"A man under duress will admit to anything."

Ludwig stared back. Darrian had gone from arguing his point of view to denying everything. Where did this idea come from? He met Sir Emril's smirking gaze and instantly understood. How, then, could Ludwig counter?

"Lord Darrian makes an interesting point," said the king. "What have you to say for yourself, Ludwig?"

"I have witnesses placing Lord Gowan at the scene of the theft, sire, and one of my captains witnessed his confession."

"Prior Yannick notes none of this."

Darrian wasn't done. "The only evidence His Highness has is from his own people, Majesty. How do we know he didn't order to make these statements?"

"Can a captain in service to the realm not be trusted to tell the truth?" replied Ludwig.

"And who is this captain?" asked the king.

"Captain Cynthia Hoffman, sire."

"Hah," said Darrian. "The woman is a mercenary. She'll say anything given sufficient coins."

"I might remind you," said Ludwig, "that particular mercenary helped restore the Throne of Hadenfeld."

The king waved away his comment. "It matters not. The crux of the matter is all these witnesses are bound to you in service. It therefore comes down to the word of one baron against another. Before you argue the point, consider this: prince you may be, Ludwig, but this concerns your barony, not your title, and thus you can claim no special circumstances."

Morgan made a show of gathering the papers before him, then continued. "I find the behaviour of both of you to be abhorrent. You come here like a pair of children, squabbling over a parent's affections. As your king, I refuse to put any further effort into this. Lord Ludwig, you will see that Lord Gowan is released from custody. As for you, Lord Darrian, I suggest you keep to your own lands from now on, the better to avoid future conflict."

"What of the theft?" asked Ludwig.

"You mean the purported theft," snapped Morgan. "That is hardly my concern. I am a king, gentlemen, not a magistrate. I have far more important things to consider than your petty squabble. From now on, if you have a problem with each other, I suggest you discuss it in a civilized manner, like adults. We are done here." He stood, prompting the others to do likewise.

Morgan strode from the table, but as he got to the door, he paused, turning to face them one last time. "If either of you tries to bring this to me again, I shall strip you of your title. Do you understand?"

They nodded in response, and then the king was gone.

"Well," said Sir Emril, "it appears the meeting is over, my lords. If you'll follow me, Lord Darrian, I'll escort you out. I believe the prince is needed elsewhere."

"I am?" said Ludwig.

"Yes. Lord Egan, the Baron of Hasdorf, wishes to speak with you."

"Concerning?"

"That is none of my business. I suggest if you truly want to know, go and see him."

"Where is he?"

"In the great hall. I presume you remember the way?"

"I do," said Ludwig.

"Good. Then I'll leave you to it. Come, Lord Darrian. Let us be on our way."

Father Vernan waited until the door closed before he let out a breath of air. "What did you make of that?"

"That depends," replied Ludwig. "Do you refer to the behaviour of Sir Emril or the king?"

"Both, but let's start with His Majesty, shall we? It surprised me how easily he lost his temper."

"I can't say it surprised me. I assume Sir Emril had something to do with that."

"You suspect him of poisoning the king towards you?"

"It certainly appears that way. At least he didn't strip me of my place in the line of succession, although I'm still undecided whether that's a good thing or not."

"What do you suppose Lord Egan wants?"

"I have no idea," said Ludwig. "Truth is, I hardly know the man."

"Could it be something to do with all the proposed changes you suggested concerning the raising of men?"

"Possibly, though I can't see why he'd want to speak with me. After all, the king commanded it, not me."

"But you were the architect."

"I was, but who would know that other than the king?"

"You know as well as I the Royal Keep has paper-thin walls when it comes to rumours."

"Well, we shan't find out sitting here. Let's go visit him."

Lord Egan Kohl, the Baron of Hasdorf, was a full ten years younger than King Otto had been on his death, yet Egan looked far older with his snow-white hair and beard thin with age. Even his eyebrows had succumbed to the aging process, for not only were they of a similar colour, they were thick with long hairs poking out. That, combined with his pale complexion, made him look like death was coming for him.

Ludwig and Father Vernan entered the great hall to find him sitting, cup in hand, staring off into nothing. At first, Ludwig feared the old man had passed on to the Afterlife, but as they drew closer, the baron's keen eyes focused on him.

"Ludwig," the fellow said. "I wondered when you'd deign to show up."

"Sorry. I had a meeting with the king. I trust you haven't been waiting long?"

Egan looked into his cup. "Only long enough to drink half of this. Shall I fetch you some?"

"No. I'm fine, thank you. I understand you wished to see me?"

The baron lowered his voice. "I did. I wanted to ask you about something."

"Let me guess, the changes to our warriors?"

"Not at all. I was curious if you'd heard anything about Jurgen."

"The Baron of Bruggendorf? What about him?"

"I hear he's gone and found himself a mage."

"That's news to me."

"Curious. Being the prince, I expected you'd be better informed."

"I've spent the last few months in Verfeld, away from court. Why? Is there something wrong with hiring a mage?"

"In theory, no, but it's unusual for a mere baron to employ one."

"And what type of mage do these rumours suggest?"

"A Fire Mage, if you can believe it." Lord Egan took a sip of his ale. "It's all a bit suspicious if you ask me. I mean, I'd understand if he'd hired on a Life Mage, but a Pyromancer? What good is a Fire Mage to a kingdom at peace?"

"Perhaps it's nothing more than a false rumour. Saints know it wouldn't be the first time such a thing happened."

"You're probably right." Egan took a long draught, emptying his cup. "And what about that other matter?"

"What other matter?"

"You're a man in his prime. Can you honestly tell me you haven't been sampling?"

"Sampling what? What in the name of the Saints are you talking about?"

"Your affair, of course."

"What affair?"

"The one you're having with Lady Alexandra. We all know you spend a lot of time in her company; it's not hard to believe you'd carry on a dalliance."

"I'm not dallying with anyone except my wife!"

"That's not what the rumours purport."

"Who spoke of such things?"

"I can't say."

"Can't?" said Ludwig. "Or won't?"

"If you must know, the rumours started last summer when you visited Luwen, and they've only grown in your absence."

"What else do they say?"

"That you are tired of your wife and wish to remarry."

"I shall never leave Charlotte, and I'll challenge any who say otherwise."

Egan held up his hands. "I am not your enemy, my dear fellow, merely the bearer of bad news."

"How widespread are these rumours?"

"They are the talk of the town, or at least they were. They've died down a bit now spring is upon us, but you know how the court is. Without any actual news, they'll invent their own."

"Where did you first hear these stories?"

"From my wife, if you can believe it. She heard it at last year's party celebrating the king's coronation."

"I should very much like to know who started these lies."

Egan nodded. "I can see now that you are gravely offended, and I owe you an apology. I do think, however, it's better to be aware of such stories than not. If I hear anything further on the subject, I shall be pleased to pass them on to you."

"Thank you," said Ludwig. "I appreciate the offer."

"How are things with your lovely wife? Getting any better, is she?"

"She is well."

"Shall we expect more children in your future? After all, you're a prince now. One day, you'll be king, and it'll be important to have heirs."

"Frederick is more than sufficient at present," said Ludwig. "Any further discussion on that subject is a private matter between me and my wife."

"Understood." Lord Egan unsteadily rose to his feet. "It was good to see you, Ludwig, but I doubt we'll meet again."

"Lord?"

"I am dying and haven't much time left. My physician expected me to pass this last winter, but my body had other ideas. When I finally pass on to the Afterlife, my eldest son will take up his rightful place as baron. I trust I can count on you to help him with the adjustment?"

"Of course."

"Thank you. You've soothed an aching heart."

11

THE SEASONS PASS

SUMMER 1102 SR

The seasons passed, as they were wont to do, keeping Ludwig busy with his baronial duties. By the summer of 1102, he'd accumulated enough armour and weapons to equip the required four companies of foot and two of archers. Of these, only half would be in service at any given time, the rest being called up only in time of war. Determined to ensure no more thefts of his property occurred, he had them carry out regular patrols of the barony.

With the onset of the winter snow, and little news from the capital, he believed Morgan had forgotten about his disagreement with Lord Darrian.

It wasn't until the spring of 1103 that he received word of Lord Egan's demise. The Barony of Hasdorf passed to his eldest son, Wilbur, who was well into his thirties. Remembering Egan's wishes, Ludwig intended to visit the new baron, but his own duties delayed him.

As summer finally arrived, so did visitors, in the form of Lord Emmett and Lady Alexandra, returning to Dornbruck after visiting Harlingen. This, by itself, was not an unusual occurrence since the road through Verfeld provided the quickest route home, but it was the first time they had seen them since the birth of their daughter Evangeline.

They settled in the great hall, catching up with what was happening in the capital. After the usual pleasantries, they turned to the business of politics.

"So," said Ludwig, "how is our king?"

"Distant, if I'm being honest," replied Emmett. "I only saw him once, and even that was a little strained. I don't think he's ever forgiven us eastern barons."

"He'll need to get over it if he wants the kingdom to prosper."

"Don't I know it, but I can do only so much."

Ludwig sensed a hesitation. "What is it you're not telling me?"

"Alexandra had best explain. She heard of it first."

"Not more rumours of my infidelity, surely?"

"No," she replied. "Those have been firmly put to rest. No, this is something I heard from my father, and for once, it doesn't concern you."

"Then why bring it to my attention?"

She chuckled. "What I meant to say is it's not about you, but I have no doubt you should be made aware of it."

"Go on," urged Ludwig.

"It seems there is a new alliance of sorts."

"Alliance? With whom?"

"It is an internal grouping, if you prefer, of like-minded barons."

"It's not unusual for barons to have friends. You and your husband are prime examples of that."

"This is different. It's not precisely friendship, but a shared objective— that of war."

"War? Has someone threatened us?"

"Not as far as I know," replied Alexandra, "but now that the barons have reorganized their companies, they're eager to see them put to use."

"Against whom?"

"The Duchy of Hollenbeck."

"I remember your father mentioning them some time ago. If I recall, they have a small army, but the terrain is said to be thickly wooded. Even so, it is a place we thought the king might attempt to conquer."

"And that seems to be what the barons are pushing for."

"Which barons?" asked Ludwig.

"Those in the south. Bruggendorf was the first to suggest there were problems on the border, but Hasdorf quickly followed. It appears our newest baron is eager to make a name for himself."

"I daresay it would take more than two barons to be considered an alliance."

"And so it would," replied Alexandra. "But shortly after these rumours started, word reached my father that the barons of Arnsbach and Udenacht were travelling to Bruggendorf to discuss the matter. All four of those baronies border Hollenbeck."

"Where does your father stand on the issue?"

"He was invited to attend the same meeting with Lord Jurgen but declined, as he has no wish to go to war."

"Was this brought to the king's attention?"

"Emmett tried, but as he indicated earlier, the king never gave him a chance. In fact, whenever he attempted to bring up anything in the way of news, His Majesty changed topics."

"He still bears a grudge against the eastern barons."

"Does that mean we are heading to war?"

Ludwig thought it over. King Morgan was keen to prove the might of Hadenfeld, yet his new army was not complete. The original plan called for all the barons to fund horsemen for the Crown, but that still depended on enough mounts. Could their king be so eager to prove himself that he would risk defeat by moving without proper cavalry support? It seemed unlikely.

"Well?" pressed Alexandra.

"I wish I could tell you such was not the case, but I cannot assure you with any certainty. Have there been any incidents in the south?"

"Such as?"

"I don't know," said Ludwig, thinking fast. "Bandits or raids against livestock?"

"None I'm aware of, although my father would know more. Why? What is it you're thinking?"

"The king is eager for war, but I doubt even he'd attack without reason. If these barons wish to go to war, they'll need to create some sort of provocation."

"And what would that look like?"

Ludwig shrugged. "I suppose the most obvious would be soldiers of Hollenbeck raiding one of the baron's lands, but that seems unlikely."

"There is another option," piped in Charlotte, who'd remained silent for most of the night. So much so that Ludwig was ashamed to admit he'd forgotten she was even there.

"Go on," he urged.

"What you speak of is common enough in the north. The kingdoms there constantly argue over borders, and on several occasions, it has led to all-out war."

"Interesting," said Ludwig. "How do they justify war?"

"There are several tactics, chief amongst them the idea people are being oppressed."

"I'm not sure I follow."

"It's simple. They arrange for people to flee the territory in question, then claim they were being persecuted."

"So you're suggesting refugees of Hadenfeld descent would make this sort of claim?"

"In this instance, yes. Of course, it's not the only way to engineer a war.

There's also rumour and innuendo, which are the most powerful persuaders."

"I find that hard to believe," said Ludwig.

"Do you? It wasn't so long ago false rumours of your infidelity inflamed you. Imagine how fervent the desire for revenge would be if someone suggested we were about to be invaded?"

"She makes a good point," said Emmett. "And Saints know there are plenty of rumours at court. The entire capital thrives on such things."

"The more important question," said Alexandra, "is what we can do about it."

"I shall go to the capital," replied Ludwig. "Hopefully, I can convince the king to put an end to this scheming."

"And if not?"

"Then we may have no choice but to go to war. Hadenfeld has already suffered a civil war; the last thing I want to see is another. If push comes to shove, though, we must obey our king, and if that means a war, then so be it."

"Let's hope it doesn't come to that," said Charlotte. "Shall I travel to Harlingen with you?"

"Much as I'd appreciate the company, I feel better knowing you're safe here, in Verfeld."

"What if she came with us?" asked Alexandra. "She and Frederick could come and visit us in Dornbruck? I'm sure Evangeline would love to spend more time with her auntie."

"I would love to," replied Charlotte, "providing Ludwig has no objection?"

"I think it a marvellous idea," replied Ludwig. "I would sleep better knowing she's amongst friends."

"Then it's settled," said Emmett. "We'll head out on the morrow."

With the training of the Verfeld companies complete, Cyn and Sigwulf were available to accompany him to Harlingen. They elected to forego the use of a carriage, riding horses instead, the better to travel swiftly, for the fate of a kingdom might very well hang in the balance.

Even so, a week passed before they arrived in Harlingen. Ludwig initially thought of going directly to the king, but he visited Merrick and Gita's house first, for they often spent their summers in Harlingen. They were ushered into a waiting room, and then Lord Merrick arrived, looking none too pleased.

"I hope we haven't caught you at an inconvenient time," said Ludwig. "I don't mean to be a bother."

"It's not you," replied Merrick, "it's the king, or rather my inability to speak with him."

"Is he not here in Harlingen?"

"Oh, he's here, but that parasite, Sir Emril, decides who's worthy enough to be in His Majesty's presence."

"Perhaps I can be of some help? What did you want to see him about?"

"Drakenfeld has had problems of late; a plague of insects forced us to burn our crops. If we are to survive next winter, we need wheat."

"I'll send you some from Verfeld," said Ludwig. "In addition, I'll write to Lord Emmett on your behalf. I'm sure he can spare some. Don't worry. We won't let your people starve."

"Thank you," said Merrick, "though I daresay you wouldn't need to if the king released some of his stores."

"Tell me more of your issues with Sir Emril?"

"He's wormed his way into the king's confidence. In effect, he's become the voice of the king and knows full well the influence that gives him."

"I assume he outright refused your request for an audience?"

"He did, though I have it on good authority Lord Jurgen suffered no such slight."

"Lord Jurgen is here?"

"He is. Why?"

Ludwig smiled. "It just so happens I need to speak with him about something. It sounds like I can accomplish my objective without seeing the king after all."

"Now you're sounding mysterious. What is it you have in mind?"

"I've heard rumours of discord in the south, and Lord Jurgen appears to be in the middle of them."

"You're referring to the raids?"

"What raids?"

Merrick smiled. "For once, I know more than you. Just yesterday, I heard about a band of raiders who crossed the border south of Udenacht, making off with more than a score of cattle and leaving three dead in their wake. What do you know of the area?"

"It's an eastern barony run by Lord Nikolaus Wendt. I've only ever met the man in passing but have heard rumours he's part of a new southern alliance."

"That doesn't sound good."

"I agree," said Ludwig. "That's why I'm here in Harlingen. I suspect those involved are pressing the king to invade Hollenbeck. I only hope I'm not too late to stop it."

"What can I do to help?"

"Could you arrange an introduction to Lord Jurgen? Do you know him?"

"I do. Shall I tell him of your concerns?"

"No. If something is amiss, I don't want to risk you being accused of anything untoward. On second thought, I'll visit him without an introduction."

"Be careful, Ludwig. If he's involved in a conspiracy, it could be your head on the chopping block."

"I'll take care. I promise. Now, where is his house?"

"Surely you're not going there right now? You've only just arrived."

"I realize that, but time is of the essence. If I am to act, I must do so before they consolidate their plans."

The Harlingen manor of Lord Jurgen Voltz, Baron of Bruggendorf, was immense, taking up almost an entire block. The attentive guards scattered around the estate added an air of strength. Ludwig halted across the street and dismounted, handing Cyn his reins.

"I don't like this," said Sigwulf. "It could be a trap."

"Lord Jurgen would have to be aware I was coming to do that."

"And what, precisely, do you hope to achieve?"

"I need to know what's happening in Bruggendorf."

"How do you propose to learn that?"

"By pretending to be of a similar mind."

"You're playing a dangerous game, Ludwig."

"How else am I to get to the bottom of this?"

"Yes," said Cyn, "but you need him to trust you to do that."

"I'm the Prince of Hadenfeld. I can offer them access to the king."

"In theory, but what if they already have that?"

"Then I'll convince them my military experience would benefit them."

"Now, that," added Sigwulf, "is an excellent idea."

"Glad you approve," said Ludwig. "You two wait here while I see if the baron is in."

He walked across the street, pausing at the gates. His approach had been noted, for a pair of guards met him on the other side.

"Can I help you?"

"Is the baron in?"

"He is."

"Then please inform him Prince Ludwig wishes to speak with him, and don't dawdle. I haven't got all day."

The guard's eyes nearly fell out of his sockets. "Of course, Highness, at once." He punched his companion in the shoulder. "Go on, then. Tell His Lordship who's here!"

The second one rushed off, his armour jingling as he ran.

"My apologies, Highness. We weren't informed of your visit today."

"It was unplanned," said Ludwig, adopting an indifferent attitude. "But if His Lordship is too busy, perhaps I shouldn't bother?"

A look of panic crossed the guard's face. "I'm sure he'll see you, Highness, and I know for a fact the others won't mind."

"Others?"

"Yes, Highness. He is in the company of other barons."

"Let me guess, Hasdorf and Udenacht?"

"Indeed, and the Baron of Arnsbach as well."

The familiar jingle returned, along with the now out-of-breath second guard. "His Lordship will see you, Highness. Shall I take you to him?"

Ludwig forced a smile. "If you would be so kind."

The guard escorted him to the rear of the house, where a stone patio overlooked a lush garden. He recognized Lord Jurgen immediately, along with Lord Heiden Bohm, the Baron of Arnsbach and Lord Nikolaus Wendt, Baron of Udenacht. He couldn't place the third individual's face, although there was something familiar about it.

"Highness," said Jurgen, with a bow. "To what do we owe the pleasure?"

Ludwig looked at each in turn, nodding slightly in greeting. "I am here to discuss the border," he said at last. "I hear there's been some trouble of late."

"There has indeed," agreed Lord Nikolaus. "My lands were raided."

"And what, may I ask, did you do in response?"

"My men followed the raiders to the border with Hollenbeck, but without Royal Approval, they dare not cross."

"Had it been me, I would exact revenge."

"What is it you're suggesting, Highness?"

"Merely that we must sometimes take extraordinary measures to protect what is ours. Have you taken this matter to the king?"

Lord Nikolaus looked at his host.

"As we all know," replied Jurgen, "His Majesty is a busy man."

"Have there been any other issues in the south? Sightings of an enemy massing, for example?"

"Nothing substantive, Highness, although rumours persist they're preparing for war."

"Rumours?" said Ludwig. "Is that the only thing you have? You must strive to learn more if you are to convince the king to act."

The third baron cleared his throat. "Excuse me, Highness, but might it prove advantageous for you to see what we're up against, in person?"

Ludwig stared at the man, trying to place him, but his memory failed him. He raised an eyebrow. "And you are?"

"My pardon for speaking out of turn, Highness. I am Lord Wilbur Kohl, Baron of Hasdorf."

"I see it now. You bear a striking similarity to your father, the late Lord Egan. Pray continue, you have me intrigued."

"I merely suggested you visit the south and see the problems we face, firsthand."

"An excellent idea," said Lord Jurgen. "If it pleases, Your Highness, would you do me the honour of staying in Bruggendorf during your visit? I assure you we will make it worth your while."

Ludwig considered his offer. It might lead him to the centre of this conspiracy, but he could also be placing himself in great danger.

"I shall consider it," he said at last, "but I would, as prince, insist on my bodyguards accompanying me."

Lord Jurgen let out a sigh of relief. "Of course, Highness. When would you deign to visit us?"

"I can be on the road first thing tomorrow morning, providing that does not inconvenience you?"

"That would be most acceptable, Highness. Shall I make the appropriate arrangements?"

"What arrangements would those be?"

"Why, a carriage, along with an escort."

"I'll need neither as I intend to ride. Shall we say the south gate tomorrow at first light?"

Lord Jurgen bowed. "Most certainly, Highness."

"Then I'll see you there. If you will excuse me, gentlemen, I have a few things to attend to before tomorrow."

He let a guard escort him back to the front gate, where Cyn and Sigwulf waited.

"Well?" said Cyn as Ludwig climbed into his saddle. "Learn anything interesting?"

"It's not a matter of what I learned so much as what I accomplished."

"Meaning?"

"I got us an invitation to Bruggendorf."

"Is that a good thing or bad?"

"You know," said Ludwig, "I have no idea."

12

BRUGGENDORF

SUMMER 1103 SR

U nlike most of the other baronies in the kingdom, Bruggendorf had no keep. Instead, Lord Jurgen owned a sprawling manor house over-looking a green valley where horses roamed at will. It was a picturesque sight, and Ludwig couldn't help but admire the view.

A servant appeared, tray in hand. "Would you like a drink, Highness?"

Ludwig took it, his gaze still glued on the distant horses. "Your herd is thriving, Lord Jurgen."

The baron moved closer, absently holding a chalice of wine. "Those are my destriers, bred to take knights into battle, but not much use for these new mailed cavalrymen we're expected to fund. For those, you need coursers."

"And have you bred any of those?"

"Quite a few. Most are still young, but I have high hopes for the future. Perhaps you'd like to see them?"

"I would, although I know little about horse breeding."

"It's the destriers which are the most profitable. A well-trained warhorse can fetch hundreds of crowns, but there are only so many knights in the kingdom. However, coursers cost much less to train. Ordinarily, the profit margin would also be lower, but the king's new requirements increased demand significantly."

"How long do you estimate it will take to breed enough to meet what's needed?"

"A few years yet. Of course, seeking them from outside our borders is always possible, but that would be expensive. It's all about demand; the more horses desired, the higher the price."

"In other words," said Ludwig, "you stand to make a substantial amount at the Crown's expense."

"Not the Crown's—the barons. If you recall, the plan called for us each to pay the cost to equip one company of mailed horsemen."

"I stand corrected."

"I own a few horses besides the breeding stock. Perhaps I can entice you to take a ride with me?"

"I'd be delighted, although I must insist my guards accompany me."

Lord Jurgen grinned. "I would have it no other way." He glanced at Cyn standing off to one side. "Pardon my asking, but I know you've been in the north. Is dressing one's mistress as a warrior common up there?"

"She's one of my captains, not a mistress, and I wouldn't suggest you call her otherwise, especially not within the hearing of her larger companion." He nodded towards Sigwulf. "He's likely to take offence."

"Perhaps, but it's not like he'd strike a noble."

"I wouldn't bet on that," said Ludwig. "He's a northerner, and the rules of etiquette concerning such things are far different from ours."

"How curious. It appears I must mind my manners. Shall I show you to my stables?"

"By all means."

A tour of the baron's personal stables proved brief, and before long, Ludwig was mounted on a fine courser, Cyn and Sigwulf trotting along at a respectful distance on their own mounts.

Lord Jurgen, being the polite host, described the scenery as they rode. His extensive lands stretched for miles, far larger than Verfeld. Ludwig's home was mainly hills and forest, while the land here was full of meadows and streams. It was most idyllic, something his guide pointed out many times.

They rode for half the afternoon, crossing the valley to the top of a rise, gazing out over a large river.

"That," said Jurgen, slowing to a halt, "marks the border of Hadenfeld. Beyond lies Hollenbeck."

"What do you know about them?" asked Ludwig.

"They are a small duchy, less than half our size."

"Yes, but a good portion of our kingdom is wilderness."

"That is true of Hollenbeck as well. Their towns are scattered, with the roads all leading to their capital. It wouldn't take much to march an army in and seize it."

Ludwig saw his chance. "You've given this some thought. Tell me, what do you estimate their numbers to be? I speak only of their army, of course."

"Interesting you should mention this, as we were discussing that very matter when you showed up at my Harlingen estate."

"And your conclusion?"

"Our best guess is their army will number less than fifteen hundred. Of course, that largely depends on how long they have to prepare. If we struck quickly, we might be in their capital before they can raise half of that, but we'd need the king's cavalry to do that."

"You haven't supplied the necessary horses."

"Well," said Lord Jurgen, "we may not have enough to equip them all, but if you recall, Lord Meinhard and I each fielded one company during the war."

"I remember," said Ludwig. "They were placed under my command."

"So they were, and what a magnificent job you did of leading them. We might have lost the battle if it hadn't been for your actions that day."

"I learned much during my time in the north."

"Then would you allow me to ask your opinion?"

"What did you have in mind?"

"I have maps of that," said Jurgen, nodding towards the distant fields of Hollenbeck. "I even have a good idea of which roads go where. What I don't have is an assessment of our king's new army or the experience to command it effectively. A man such as yourself would be of immense value in leading it."

"It is the king's right to decide who commands."

"True, but who better than the Prince of the Realm? I can think of no one more suited to the task."

"You humble me," said Ludwig. "I shall consider it should the king think me a good fit. In the meantime, I'll gladly look at your maps and offer my opinion."

"Then let us return with all haste. With a bit of luck, we could be poring over them before the sun sets."

In their absence, Lord Jurgen's wife had organized a feast in honour of the prince. Ludwig was disappointed, for he wished to get to the bottom of this conspiracy, but such things couldn't be rushed, or else he would appear suspicious.

The guests arrived promptly, including the barons of Hasdorf, Udenacht, and Arnsbach. He'd met them all before when he'd visited

Jurgen's house in the capital, but they had travelled here separately, and now he knew why, for their wives were also present.

Of more interest to Ludwig, however, was the presence of another individual whom he'd never met. Based upon the fellow's above-average height and long, flowing blond hair, Ludwig assumed he was an Elf, for the woodland folk were said to be thin of frame, but as soon as he stood in profile, his ears marked him as Human.

"Greetings, Highness," the man said, bowing before the head of the table. "My name is Koldan Sartellian, a Fire Mage of some renown."

"A Fire Mage, you say?" replied Ludwig. "How very interesting. From whence do you hail?"

"I was born in Ruzhina but learned the arcane arts at the academy in Korascajan."

"Ruzhina? Why does that name sound familiar?"

"It is an eastern kingdom, Highness, on the coast of the Great Northern Sea. You may be familiar with the Volstrum, an academy for Water Mages."

"Ah, yes. If I recall, the Stormwinds train there."

"You are familiar with it?"

"I had the pleasure of making the acquaintance of Mina Stormwind, though she no longer resides in Hadenfeld."

"A pity," said Koldan. "It would've been interesting to compare notes."

"I'm curious. You hail from Ruzhina, a place famous for producing Water Mages, yet here you are, a Pyromancer. How did that come about?"

"Those of us with magical potential are tested once we come of age. As is typical in my family, I favoured the element of fire."

"So you're related to the Stormwinds?"

"We are. In fact, you might consider us cousins of a sort."

Ludwig let that sink in. Charlaine warned him about the Stormwinds, which prevented him from falling under Mina's spell. She'd attempted to manipulate Hadenfeld for her own purposes—was Koldan any different? He realized he'd fallen silent. "My apologies. I was trying to remember something Mina told me."

"Nothing important, I hope?"

He waved it away. "It was trivial if I recall, but amusing, nonetheless. How is it you came to be in Bruggendorf? I would think the capital more to your tastes."

"That's where I found him," said Lord Jurgen. "He revealed to me he sought employment, and I've always fancied the idea of having a mage in my service."

"I wouldn't think there's much for a Fire Mage to do in a small town like Bruggendorf."

"I'm more than just a mage," said Koldan. "We Sartellians, like our cousins the Stormwinds, are trained in various disciplines, including history, etiquette, politics, even military strategy."

"See?" said Jurgen. "A fellow like that would prove most useful, don't you think?"

"Undoubtedly," replied Ludwig, "but it's the Fire Magic everyone wants to see. Perhaps we might organize a little demonstration of your skill?"

"I would be delighted, Highness, but this room is far too combustible for such a thing. After all, I wouldn't want him to set the place aflame."

"Perhaps tomorrow?"

"An excellent idea," said Lord Jurgen. "What do you think, Koldan? Up to it?"

The mage bowed. "It would be my greatest pleasure, my lord."

"What would you require for such a thing?"

"Some archery targets would suffice, although if you wish further entertainment, we could use cups, bottles, or other targets. I once demonstrated my skill in Zowenbruch by melting a suit of mail."

"Melting? The heat was that intense?"

"Most assuredly," replied Koldan. "Of course, it took some time; even magical flames don't instantly melt steel."

"I wonder," said Ludwig, "are you a powerful Fire Mage as such things go?"

The mage straightened his back. "Were I not, I would scarcely offer my service to Lord Jurgen."

"My apologies. I did not mean to insult, but I find the entire concept of Fire Magic most fascinating. How long have you wielded this power?"

"I first manifested my power at the age of fourteen, Highness. I was tested and then sent to Korascajan, where I learned to control it. Fire Magic is particularly dangerous, as you can well imagine. Had my potential not been properly identified, I could have immolated myself. Thankfully, I learned to harness the most volatile of all the elements."

"I once worked with an Earth Mage, but the poor fellow died during a siege. Have you seen any battle?"

"Alas, no, though I've always aspired to, as it was part of my training as a battle mage."

"Now that," said Ludwig, "is something I'm not acquainted with. What's a battle mage?"

"A mage who's been trained to use magic in battle."

"Aren't all mages capable of that?"

"They are, but a battle mage is taught how best to employ their magic to guarantee victory."

"You sound awfully certain of your abilities."

"We are taught not to doubt ourselves," said Koldan. "To do so in battle limits our effectiveness. Some might see us as haughty or proud, but it's just the awareness of how impactful we can be on a battlefield." He bowed one more time. "Now, if you will excuse me, Highness, I should like to retire to my room."

"Retire?" said Ludwig. "You only just arrived."

"Indeed, but if I am to present you with a demonstration of my power, then it behooves me to make it worthy of a prince."

Ludwig waited until the man left before turning to Lord Jurgen. "He's impressive, I'll grant you that, but is he as proficient as he claims?"

Jurgen grinned. "You shall see on the morrow, Highness."

Everyone assembled in the nearest field early the next day. They'd set up three archery targets, along with a table holding six bottles, a scarecrow, and a bust with a helmet placed atop it. Koldan Sartellian strode to the front of the group, then turned to address the crowd.

He started with a bow. "Greetings, my lords, most noble Highness. At the request of Prince Ludwig, I prepared a demonstration that will display several spells. As you know, Fire Magic can create flames, but many people don't realize it can also manipulate heat."

Turning unexpectedly, he flung out his hands, sending a streak of fire hurtling towards an archery target. It struck with a popping sound, and then the straw burst into flames. Those watching clapped, but Ludwig noted the spell almost missed. Perhaps this mage was a little more show than skill.

"That," said Koldan, "is what we call a fire streak, one of the first offensive spells we learn. Another is produce fire, which has its uses, although it's seldom employed in battle." He waved his hand towards a lantern held by a servant, and a flame sprang to life within.

"Most impressive," said Lord Jurgen. "What else can you show our guests?"

"How about this?" Koldan moved his hands around once more. Ludwig heard the words tumbling out of his mouth this time, yet he could make no sense of them. The air sparkled, and then a curtain of flame descended as if held in place by a rod.

"There is also the ability to conjure forth creatures that burn." The Fire Mage pointed dramatically, and a snake made entirely of flames erupted from the ground and spat fire, but then he quickly dispelled it before it could ignite something important.

"The fire snake is but one creature," continued Koldan.

"Useful for a duel," countered Ludwig, "but I doubt it would be helpful in battle."

"You are correct, Highness. That spell is primarily of use when fighting a single opponent. On the battlefield, using something that can affect multiple targets is wiser. Behold, the phoenix!"

Ludwig watched as more words poured forth. This time, the hand movements were different, and Koldan stared upward as if reading something. Flames leaped from the mage's fingers, taking the form of a large bird that screamed as it flew overhead, its fire so bright it appeared white.

Ludwig's first thought was how to counter such a spell. He risked a glance at Sig and Cyn, who appeared to be thinking the same thing. It would be interesting to compare notes later this evening. He clapped as the Fire Mage dispelled the creature. "Fascinating. From where does such a creature come?"

"It is a conjuration," replied Koldan. "That is to say, it has no mind of its own."

"Then how does it pick its targets?"

"Both it and the fire snake require the concentration of the casting mage."

"And if your attention was diverted?"

"The creatures would continue their last action."

"I imagine a Water Mage would be able to extinguish them."

"Only if they were powerful enough, Highness. A caster uses a portion of their energy to create such a creature. To dispel that creature, another mage must use an equal amount of magical energy to counter it. That's always assuming the person in question knows how the spell works."

"It's very impressive," said Ludwig, "although I am curious why you've got bottles lined up on that table?"

"That's to show off my spell of burning embers. With your permission?"

"Of course. Please proceed."

Koldan quickly cast another spell, and when he finished, a small, acorn-sized object flew from his hands, landing in front of the bottles. Everyone held their breath, and after a count of five, something exploded, sending out a ring of fire that knocked over the bottles.

"My apologies," said Koldan. "The spell is usually much more powerful, but I didn't want to risk flying glass hitting anyone."

Lord Jurgen appeared at Ludwig's side, offering a cup. "Well, Highness? What did you think? Useful, entertaining, or a waste of time?"

"Honestly, my mind is still grappling with what I've witnessed. It's most impressive; I'm just unsure how such power could be utilized in battle."

"I felt the same way when I first met him. Don't worry. By tomorrow, your mind will make sense of it all."

"And is his knowledge of strategy as impressive as his use of magic?"

"That's the best part," said the baron. "It's even more magnificent."

"Then why do you want my opinion?"

Lord Jurgen lowered his voice. "You are a fellow noble of Hadenfeld, Highness, whereas this mage, despite his skill, is still a foreigner. He claims to be a good strategist; from what I've seen, he knows his stuff, but I'm not a military man. For all I know, he could be bluffing."

"And so you want me to verify he's as skilled as he claims?"

"There. You understand perfectly."

13

CONSPIRACY

SUMMER 1103 SR

B efore them lay a map purported to be Hollenbeck, but Ludwig doubted its accuracy. There was no mention of rivers, and very few roads were marked, two things that could easily make the difference between victory and defeat.

"Well?" prompted Lord Jurgen. "What do you think?"

"It is a most curious strategy," replied Ludwig. "Your Fire Mage appears to favour splitting the army. I hardly think that a good thing."

"That's the genius of it, don't you see? One column advances from Bruggendorf, the other from Hasdorf. The duke will have no option but to split his own forces."

"Or he can take on each army one at a time and destroy both with superior numbers."

"Koldan is a trained battle mage. I'm sure he knows what he's doing."

"Does he?" said Ludwig. "Because to me, it looks as though he's trying to engineer our defeat."

"Based on what we know, we outnumber the duke's army almost two to one."

"And by splitting our forces, we lose that advantage. It might be a different matter were there more than one way to march on their capital, Klermacht, but according to this map, there is but one road leading from Bruggendorf to their capital, and that's easily defended."

"Which is the beauty of his plan. The army moving out of Hasdorf will take this route." Jurgen traced a line with his finger.

"That would involve marching through a forest."

"Yes, which is the last thing they'd expect. We'd catch them by surprise."

"And how do you propose to feed this army as it advances? They can't live off the land while marching, and you won't be able to get any wagons through terrain like that."

"The men will march carrying their own supplies."

Ludwig shook his head. Did the man understand nothing when it came to war? "Have you any idea how much food one can carry when encumbered by weapons and armour?"

The baron waved away the matter. "I'm sure Koldan has already taken that into account."

"Then let me ask you a different question. How long will it take for that army to reach its target?"

"The plan is to be at their capital's door within a week and a half."

"A reasonable assumption based on distance, but how can your army find its way in unfamiliar territory?"

"By navigating using the sun. I'm surprised you, of all people, didn't think of that."

"And how can one use the sun when they can't even see it? There is also the matter of rivers and streams."

"What of them?"

"There are none marked, save those serving as the border between our two realms."

"Your point?"

"This army of yours could be halfway through the forest and discover a river that can't be crossed, or even hills, for that matter. How accurate is this map?"

"What kind of question is that?" replied Lord Jurgen.

"A pretty obvious one, if you ask me. Where did it come from?"

"Koldan supplied it. He has people in the duke's court."

Ludwig stared back. Did this fool not understand the implications? "Do you realize what that means?"

"It means he has spies. What else could it mean?"

"A great many things," said Ludwig. "For example, maybe he's leading you into a trap."

"And why would he do that?"

"It wouldn't be the first time a mage secretly worked for someone else."

"What in the name of the Saints are you talking about?"

"I was sent to Eisen right before the war broke out."

"Yes, I'm aware," said the baron. "You were imprisoned, if I recall."

"I was, but there was a Water Mage there called Mina Stormwind."

"Hardly surprising. Having a Stormwind at court is considered a mark of success."

"Perhaps, but the Stormwind family harboured its own agenda, and were it not for her interference, the war would likely have been avoided."

"Then it's a good thing she was there," said the baron, "else we never would have seen Hadenfeld reunited."

"That war very nearly ended in defeat."

"Perhaps, but that's all in the past. We have a golden opportunity, Ludwig. We can increase our lands significantly by brushing aside the Army of Hollenbeck and adding their lands to our own."

"There is plenty of land to the east that we haven't even explored."

"True, but that's wilderness. The land to the south is fertile and, more importantly, ripe for conquest. I might also remind you King Morgan wishes to display our military strength to the rest of the Petty Kingdoms. And why not? You yourself reorganized our army. Would you now have it sit by and do nothing?"

"I did that to keep our kingdom safe, not go on a rampage of conquering."

"Then let me ask you this," said Jurgen. "If your king ordered it, would you do your duty?"

"Of course, but there's no way he would agree to something like this. The entire campaign is predicated on a weak strategy and questionable tactics."

"Then what would you suggest?"

Ludwig shook his head. "We're not currently at war,"

"True, but things can change." Lord Jurgen smiled.

"What are you implying?"

"Merely that sometimes events work in our favour, especially if given a little nudge."

"Are you suggesting we create an incident?"

"Why not? There's already been trouble in Udenacht." He stopped as they locked eyes. "Let's assume, for the moment, His Majesty wished you to carry out this campaign. How would you suggest we proceed?"

Ludwig examined the map. It was difficult to plan without accurate information, but some things were obvious. "Well, for a start, I'd mass the army here, at Bruggendorf, with the intent to cross the river in force, then march on their capital."

"But what if they counterattacked to the east?"

"A small force there is more than sufficient to repel any river crossing, and I doubt the duke would even try."

"Why is that?"

"For the same reason it's impractical for us to attack from there"—he stabbed his finger onto the map—"miles of forest."

"So that's it? Just march the army up the road and take their capital?"

"There would be more details, of course. A cavalry screen, for example, but that's the gist of it, yes. When you face an enemy in battle, it's wise to group together as many warriors as possible. As was said earlier, we have an estimated two-to-one advantage. It, therefore, benefits us to pin the enemy down and force a battle."

"But that would leave no possibility of a flank attack."

"We wouldn't need a flank attack. We'd already possess superior numbers."

"This plan of yours sounds far simpler than what Koldan suggested." Jurgen hesitated, then nodded. "I think yours is the one we'll go with."

"This is only an idea," said Ludwig. "An actual campaign requires far more planning."

"Which we'll have plenty of time for. We can't even mass the troops until the king agrees, and he's not likely to do that until we've arranged our little incident."

"What kind of incident?"

"Something that will further inflame the other barons. One can hardly announce a war without getting them on our side."

"What, specifically, did you have in mind?"

"An enemy incursion. One word that warriors of Hollenbeck crossed our borders and killed innocent folk is all it'll take."

"I beg your pardon?"

"You heard me. They won't be actual men of Hollenbeck, merely a select group of our men dressed in their colours, but the outcome will be the same."

"And you would have them kill our countrymen?"

"We must all make sacrifices for the greater good."

Ludwig bit back his response. He wanted to put an end to this immediately but knew the only way to do so was to go to King Morgan and reveal the plot before Jurgen dragged the kingdom into war!

That evening, Ludwig stood in Sig and Cyn's room, momentarily peeking out the window before closing the curtain to hide his presence.

"That's fiendish," said Cyn. "We need to get word to the king."

"Precisely my thought," replied Ludwig, "but we must act carefully. If we tip them off to our plans, it could well mean the death of us."

"What can we do to help?"

"We'll need our horses saddled."

"When do you want us to leave?"

"Tonight."

"That'll be difficult," warned Sigwulf. "The stable hands sleep above the horses. One whinny, and they'll know something's up."

"Still," said Ludwig, "we must do what we can."

"What about this mage of theirs? You don't suppose he's secretly a Stormwind, do you?"

"No. They're all Water Mages, although that doesn't rule out the possibility he's in league with them."

"I don't see the connection," said Cyn. "Even if that were the case, what does he hope to accomplish here?"

"A good question," replied Ludwig. "Thanks to Charlaine, I know the Stormwinds are in bed with Halvaria, and if this fellow is connected, it could be an attempt to weaken us. After all, his strategy was to split the army of Hadenfeld."

"Perhaps he's not a strategist?"

"Then why suggest that plan in the first place?"

Sigwulf smiled. "He didn't know you'd be here to second-guess him."

"So we run," said Cyn. "I assume the intent is to reach the king?"

"Not all of us," said Ludwig. "Sig, I want you to travel to Hollenbeck. Let the duke know what we've discovered. If he's smart, he'll send a small force to oppose the crossing. I doubt the plan will go forward if Lord Jurgen can't get south of the river. Cyn, you and I will head for Harlingen, but we'll split up if necessary. No matter what happens, one of us must reach the capital and warn the king."

The door burst open, and guards rushed into the room, weapons drawn. Ludwig grabbed the hilt of his sword, but it was too late. Naked steel pointed at his throat, as it did his two companions.

Those guards nearest the door parted, allowing Koldan Sartellian entry. He paused after stepping into the room, taking in the scene. "It appears I was wise to keep my eye on you, Lord Ludwig. Or should I say, Your Highness? The customs of the Petty Kingdoms are so challenging to stay current with."

"I am the Prince of Hadenfeld," said Ludwig. "To imprison me is an act of treason."

"Agreed. At least it would be if I were from this miserable realm of yours. As I indicated previously, I'm from Ruzhina, and as a Sartellian, your laws don't apply to me." He nodded at the guards, who removed Ludwig's sword, tossing it to the floor alongside Cyn and Sigwulf's weapons. "Now," he continued, "if you'll follow me, we'll see you safely locked up in the dungeon. Well, I call it a dungeon, but really, it's more of a storeroom."

"You won't get away with this."

"My dear fellow, I already have!"

Sigwulf paced as much as he could in their prison—a room hewn from the dirt, less than five paces wide, with a single door occupying one wall. The room would've been completely dark if not for the lantern light bleeding through the cracks in the door. As it was, it illuminated just enough to make out everyone's outline.

"Could be worse," said Cyn.

"Worse? How?" asked Sig. "We're locked up and surrounded by traitors. What could possibly be worse?"

"We could be dead?"

"I suppose there is that." He turned to Ludwig, lowering his voice. "What do we do?"

"To begin with, we break out of here."

"And how do we go about that?"

"By overpowering whoever is the first to open that door."

"And if no one comes?"

"Oh, they'll come," said Ludwig. "That Fire Mage impresses me as somebody who likes to show his superiority. Either he'll come to gloat over us or send someone to feed us."

"Why should he feed us?"

"Because if he wanted us eliminated, we'd already be dead."

"Supposing we overpower the guard, what then?"

"We head down the corridor to the left," said Cyn. "When they brought us down here, I noticed another way out. I think it heads towards the stables."

"Wouldn't it be better to escape on foot?" asked Sigwulf.

"Horses would allow us to cover more ground. Anything less, and they'll outride us, and who knows what story they'll tell the king."

"But Ludwig is the prince!" insisted Sig.

"Do you think that matters once he's dead? In any case, I doubt his body would ever be found. He'd just be considered missing, a mystery of the ages."

"You make a point," said Ludwig, "but I hope it won't come to that. Once we're on the road, it'll become a race to the king's court, and if we're lucky, we'll have a head start. Of course, that's still dependent on someone coming here to visit us."

"What do you think our captors will do now?" asked Sig.

"They'll need to accelerate their plans. Jurgen wanted to create an incident to motivate the barons into calling for war, but now we've discovered his plans, he can't afford to dither."

"He could still decide to kill us," said Cyn.

"He could, but even that isn't without risk. People know I came down here. Should I fail to return, questions will be asked. His only option is to act now and hope the threat of war overshadows my disappearance."

"So you're saying we made matters worse by coming here?"

"Yes. I believe that would be an accurate assessment of the situation."

"All right," said Sigwulf. "What's the plan? If we all rush the door the next time it's opened, we'll only get in each other's way."

"You stand back a bit," said Ludwig. "It swings outward, meaning whoever opens it must step back slightly to avoid it hitting him. As soon as you see it swinging, I want you to rush forward and knock it into whoever opened it. You're nimble, Cyn, so it'll be your job to hop over him and grab whatever weapon you can."

"Hop over Siggy? He's too tall!"

"I am," said Sig, "but I'll likely be prone after shouldering that door, especially if someone is in the midst of pulling it open."

"I'll follow your lead," said Ludwig. He looked around the room, but it was impossible to see much of anything in the dim light. Desperate, he threw his arms out, feeling along the wall. The guards had cleaned out the room in some haste, and though they'd removed everything they thought might serve as a weapon, they neglected to take away a shelf that used to hold bottles and jars. It felt solidly built, yet Ludwig suspected it wouldn't hold up to Sigwulf.

"Over here, Sig," he said.

The huge northerner moved beside him, reaching out to not collide with the wall.

"Think you can remove that shelf?" Ludwig asked.

"I'll give it a try."

Ludwig stepped back into the darkness. Moments later, he heard a crash and wood splintering as Sig kicked out. Two more kicks and the shelf hit the floor.

"It broke in half," said Sigwulf.

The sound of scrambling feet drifted in under the door as the guards came to investigate the noise. Sigwulf pressed a board into Ludwig's hand, then prepared to attack.

They tensed at the sound of a key rattling in the lock. As the door opened, light flooded in, causing Ludwig to squint, and then a large shape hurtled past, filling the doorway with his bulk.

Sigwulf barrelled into the door, knocking it wide open and sending the guards to the floor. He tripped over them as he exited the room and landed sprawling across the two bodies.

Cyn acted quickly, darting out into the torch-lit corridor, her fist slamming into a third, who staggered back, blood gushing from his nose.

Not to be outdone, Ludwig advanced, the half shelf held firmly in his grasp. As he stepped across the threshold, one of the downed men reached up to grab his leg. Ludwig struck out with a jab, jamming the board into the fellow's teeth and silencing him.

Sigwulf climbed to his feet, using his meaty fist to silence the second guard. Cyn, meanwhile, kicked the third one in the groin, and he doubled over in pain, his battered face leaking onto the floor even as he clutched his manhood. She reached down, removed the fellow's sword and strapped it around her waist.

"Not a mace," she said, "but we must make do with what we have."

Sigwulf retrieved the other guards' weapons, handing one to Ludwig. "We'd best move quickly," he said. "It won't be long before someone misses these guards."

Ludwig buckled on the sword. "Lead on, Cyn. You know the way."

They rushed down the hallway, soon finding the door that led out back. Here, they paused while she opened it a crack, peering outside.

"It's all clear," she whispered, "though I don't expect that to last."

They cut across a grassy field, passing a row of hedges, and the stables came into view, but then shouts erupted in their wake, indicating the bodies had been found.

"Run!" screamed Ludwig.

14

FLIGHT

SUMMER 1103 SR

With the sounding of the alarm, reaching the stables proved impossible, so they now huddled beneath the trees, letting the dense thicket hide their location.

Cyn was closest to the edge of the woods, peering out occasionally for any sight of pursuit. Off in the distance, the rising sun threw a golden hue across the land. Soldiers milled around Lord Jurgen's manor while horsemen rode off in all directions.

"See anything interesting?" asked Sigwulf.

"That depends," she answered. "What do you mean by interesting?"

"Something that might risk our discovery?"

"Not as yet. As far as I can tell, they're sticking to roads, but we can't see everything."

"It's to be expected," said Ludwig. "The most logical route is up the road to Harlingen. I imagine they'll set up sentries to watch for us."

"How long do we stay here?"

"Until we come up with a better option."

"Well," said Cyn, "at least I can see the surrounding area now the sun is up."

"And?"

"To be honest, there's not much there."

Ludwig crawled up beside her. The small forest where they'd hid lay northeast of the baron's manor house. The road to Harlingen was easy to see, along with a trail leading eastward towards the border with Hollenbeck. He smiled, noticing the terrain.

"What are you grinning at?" said Cyn.

"I may have just found us that option we're looking for."

Sigwulf squeezed in between them. "What are we looking at?"

Ludwig pointed. "You'll note the ground gets quite hilly over there to the east, but the road cuts through it, following what looks like a dried-up riverbed."

"And?"

"The terrain is littered with rocks. If we managed to get above that sunken road, we could conceal ourselves, not to mention it would give us an advantageous position."

"Are you suggesting that we ambush them?"

"You think we'd be that lucky?"

"Actually," said Cyn, "if you watch closely, you'll note they send their riders out in pairs. Think we can take out two riders, Siggy?"

He grinned. "Most assuredly."

"Good," said Ludwig. "Then that's how we'll acquire ourselves some horses."

"We need to get there without being seen first."

"Leave that to me," said Cyn.

"Why?"

"Because I'm the sneaky one, remember?" She silently made her way out of the trees and began heading east.

The area they'd observed earlier proved flatter than they needed, so they moved farther east, paralleling the road until they found what they were looking for—a place where a slight overhang of rock gave them a clear view of the road and the perfect place from which to strike. There, they waited, crouched in amongst the rocks to conceal their position.

With the sun at its height and nothing to cover their heads, they soon found the heat unbearable. They were about to abandon their location to find water when they heard the distinctive clip-clop of horseshoes.

All three moved closer to the ledge, ready to drop on their victims as they rode past. They had drawn swords, and the element of surprise was on their side, but it could well spell the end of their ambush if they failed to take these riders out quickly.

They agreed Cyn should act first, her being able to creep closer to the edge due to her smaller stature. Ludwig and Sig, meanwhile, would hold back, rushing forward only when they saw her prepare to jump. As the horses drew closer, the men's voices wafted towards them.

"And then," one said, "he turned around, and there she was."

His companion laughed, and at that point, Cyn stood. Sigwulf rose next, fast despite his size, rushing forward and jumping as Cyn did. The cliff edge was about ten feet above the dried riverbed, and to hit their targets, they needed to jump down and out three or four feet.

Cyn struck her target, landing on the horse's rump. She kept her head, using her legs to hold herself in place while she half pushed, half pulled the rider from the saddle. The fellow fell to the dirt with a cry of alarm. Sigwulf missed but landed on his feet, shy of his target, who'd been riding beside his comrade.

Ludwig was right behind Sig, but the second horseman urged his mount forward just as he jumped. Ludwig, not used to such acrobatics, landed solidly on his posterior, eliciting a yelp of pain. Someone lunged at him before he could stand, and he rolled to one side, desperate to avoid the tip of a sword.

He looked up at the fellow standing over him just as Sigwulf's sword tip emerged from the man's chest. Without a word, his eyes rolled up in his head, and he slumped to the ground. Sigwulf grunted, then placed one foot on the body and hauled his blade free.

"Where did he come from?" asked Ludwig.

"Cyn's horse, where else?" Sig glanced westward, but the lone survivor was already too distant to chase after. "Well, it seems we have a partial success. What do we do now?"

"We follow through with the plan. Sig, you take the horse and ride for Hollenbeck."

"Surely it's wiser for you to take it, Ludwig. That way, you can warn the king."

"A horse will only make me a target."

"And it won't me?"

"No, it won't. They're expecting us to make a run for Harlingen, remember? That's north; you're riding east to bypass Bruggendorf, then south to cross the border."

"And how do I know when I'm safe?"

"Simple," said Cyn. "You'll have crossed that great big river. Don't worry," she added. "You can't miss it." She dismounted, passing the reins to him.

Sigwulf hesitated, wrapping one arm around her and pulling her close. "Be careful," he said, then kissed her.

Ludwig looked away, granting them some privacy. The sky was clear, the sun out, and a long trip to the capital awaited them.

"We're done," said Cyn.

Ludwig turned back towards them, but Sigwulf had already ridden away.

Cyn wiped her eyes. "Look at me, crying like a maid who's lost her virtue."

"It's quite natural," said Ludwig. "You're worried, and rightly so. His path is treacherous, but he knows how to handle himself. We, on the other hand, have a more difficult route."

She turned to face him, her eyes still red, but her face held a look of determination. "About that. I have an idea."

"I'm all ears."

She leaned to one side, looking at his head. "No. You only have the two."

"Very funny."

"You can't blame a girl for trying. Now, on to more serious matters. We can't take the road north—too many people are looking for us. That means our best chance to avoid them is to travel across the countryside, but how do we find our way?"

"It's not as difficult as you might think," said Ludwig. "When planning the army's reorganization, I spent a lot of time looking over maps of the region."

"Why?"

"The idea was if we build an army capable of defending our land, we need to understand the terrain. That's what led me to suggest raising more horsemen. If I recall, the road to Harlingen heads north, then curves to the northwest."

"How does that help us?"

"If we head due north, we'll soon be out of sight of their patrols."

"Assuming they don't spread out and search for us off the road."

"The farther we get from Bruggendorf, the larger the area they'd need to search."

"So north, it is," said Cyn. "But there's a lot of wilderness out there. How do we locate the capital?"

"Simple. We keep heading north until we hit the Harlingen-Hasdorf road. The problem is what we do for food and water."

"I doubt water will be a problem. There are likely to be plenty of streams hereabouts."

"Really?" said Ludwig. "We didn't cross any on the way here."

"True, but then again, we were heading into the hills. Over there"—she nodded to the north—"you can see the tops of trees, and they don't grow without some sort of water."

"And food?"

"Did you forget who you're with? I spent my life as a mercenary; scavenging for food is second nature to me."

"Glad to hear it, although I wonder why you didn't teach me those skills when I was with the Grim Defenders."

"I didn't need to," said Cyn. "If you recall, we were under contract then, which meant we could purchase provisions. After that, you went and got yourself captured. Hmmm. I sense a pattern."

"Whatever do you mean?"

"You were captured at Regnitz, then again when you travelled to Eisen before the war. I'm beginning to think you may be bad luck."

"Perhaps," said Ludwig, "but I might remind you I still ended up on top, even after all that."

"And I'll remind you, only Siggy gets to be on top."

His cheeks burned. "My apologies, I didn't mean—"

"Relax. I'm pulling your leg. I expected that you, of all people, would understand my twisted sense of humour by now."

Ludwig cleared his throat and changed the topic of the conversation. "We should get going before that one who escaped raises the alarm."

They were in amongst the trees by mid-afternoon, and it didn't take Cyn long to find a stream. They slaked their thirst, then rested in the shade of the forest, conserving their strength for the journey north.

Eventually, they got to their feet and resumed their trek, keeping an eye out for anything that might prove edible. Blackberries and blueberries were both common in this region of the country, so they at least had some sustenance. Their progress was slow, for their need to forage consumed much of their time. As the day wore on, Ludwig worried their trip would take too long.

Cyn was eternally optimistic despite the danger, giving him the strength to continue. That evening, they risked a fire, and as they sat watching the flames, the topic of Sigwulf soon cropped up.

"I know you two served in your father's mercenary company," said Ludwig, "but how is it Sig came to join the Crossed Swords?"

"As you know, he was a refugee, fleeing persecution for his father's crimes. Of course, we didn't know that when he first sought employment."

"And your father just hired him on?"

"I wasn't privy to the conversation, but something about Siggy caught my eye. I saw him enter my father's tent, and they spoke at some length. When he came out, my father shook his hand and welcomed him to the company."

"If you don't mind me asking, when did you two become serious about each other?"

"There was always a mutual attraction. We were relatively young, and it was purely physical at first, but the more time we spent in each other's company, the closer we became. It seems like ages since we met, and now I can't imagine my life without him."

"I'm sure he feels the same way."

"I have to thank you, Ludwig. You gave us a home."

"Nonsense. You and Sig had a home in the Grim Defenders."

"True, but the life of a mercenary is not an easy one. Had we stayed on, we'd likely be dead by now."

"I doubt that, but it's nice that you consider Verfeld your home. You know, I never had friends when I was growing up."

"None?"

"I had acquaintances, but I was the baron's son. Most were paid servants or hangers-on intent on taking advantage of my wealth."

"And then you met Charlaine, and everything changed."

"It did, although it took me a long time to acknowledge it was for the better."

"If you could do it all over again, would you make the same choices?"

"My choices, good or bad, all led me to where I am today. Had I not fallen out with my father, I never would've met you and Sig."

"But you still would have become the baron."

"True, but I suspect I would've turned out a completely different man. I like to think of myself as an enlightened, fair person, but I doubt that would've been the result had I stayed. Instead, I'd be bitter and lash out at those who only have my best interests on their minds."

"Like Lord Darrian?"

He grinned. "A perfect example. Thank the Saints that's not how everything turned out."

Cyn stared into the fire. "What do you suppose will happen when we bring this news to the king?"

"I'll not lie; it has the potential to lead to another civil war. Those barons are conspiring to cause a war between Hadenfeld and Hollenbeck, all while we're rebuilding our army."

"But it's what the king wants, isn't it? You did say he wanted to show how strong Hadenfeld was."

"I did, but Morgan is a headstrong individual. He'll want war on his terms, not through the actions of others."

"So he'll send his new army to Bruggendorf to arrest the baron?"

"That's certainly possible, although he might summon Lord Jurgen to Harlingen and strip him of his lands. Either way, it won't end well. There's also the matter of his co-conspirators. He wasn't in this alone, and I suspect his allies will now share the same fate."

"They'd only be getting what they deserve. What do you think will happen when Siggy reaches the Duke of Hollenbeck?"

"I'm hoping he's taken seriously, but there's no guarantee they'll even let him see His Grace, the duke. They might turn him away at the gate."

"No," said Cyn. "This is important. Siggy will find a way in. I know it. I only hope he doesn't go and get himself arrested."

"For what? All he's doing is carrying a warning of a possible attack. That's a far cry from causing a war. If the duke is smart, he'll send some men to the border to investigate, thus ruining Jurgen's chance at a surprise invasion. If anything, Sig should receive a friendly welcome and thanks for preventing a war."

"I agree, but I can't help worrying about him when he's not by my side."

"You and he make quite the pair," said Ludwig. "And I mean that in only the best possible way. It's like you're two sides of the same coin."

"It wasn't always like that. Things were awkward in the early days, especially after my father caught Siggy in my tent." She laughed. "I've never seen my father more furious."

"How did Sig take it?"

"He blushed furiously, and when I say blush, I mean all over; he wasn't wearing any clothes. Now, understand that if you mention anything of this to him, I'll deny it. As far as he knows, only he and I know the details."

"I give you my word. Now, get some sleep. It's going to be a long day tomorrow."

They resumed their journey at first light. The terrain cleared, and although trees cropped up occasionally, the land was mostly open fields and gently rolling hills. They ate sparingly, taking time to gather food whenever they found it. Ludwig would have tried hunting if they had a bow, for they saw plenty of game in the area. Unfortunately, it all ran off before they got close enough to do anything about it, but it gave them something to occupy their time.

They found the Harlingen-Hasdorf road three days later and turned west, heading for the capital. Towards evening, they came across a trades' camp consisting of a trio of wagons and their owners. Ludwig told them nothing of who they were, but they were welcomed nonetheless, and for the first time since their escape, they fell asleep with full bellies.

They were invited to ride along in the wagons the following day, making the trip west much faster. They headed into the Harlingen Hills, arriving at the gates of the capital as the sun set.

The guards paid them little attention, merely watching as they passed, and then Ludwig and Cyn bid goodbye to their new friends with a promise to someday repay the kindness.

"So," said Cyn. "What do we do now? Go straight to the Royal Keep?"

"I doubt we'd gain entry dressed as we are. You may not have noticed, but our clothes are in a frightful state."

"Don't you have a house here in Harlingen?"

"You know I don't. We always stay at Lord Merrick's when we visit."

"Then that's where we should go." She made an exaggerated bow. "Lead on, my prince, and I shall follow in your humble footsteps."

"Why, thank you," he replied. "Though I think it more fitting we walk side by side, considering we look like commoners."

"In that case, let us be on our way."

15

RECKONING

SUMMER 1103 SR

B y the time he'd cleaned up at Lord Merrick's estate, it was too late, so he waited until morning to visit the king. Cyn, adamant she remain nearby if only to corroborate his story, stayed in Merrick's borrowed carriage while Ludwig sought an audience.

The streets of Harlingen were quiet as Ludwig stepped from the carriage. He walked up to the gatehouse and stopped before the guards. They recognized him and ushered him through with no fanfare.

At this early hour, no visitors were in the great hall. All he saw were servants, scurrying this way and that, bearing trays of food and even clothes. It wasn't until a herald walked past that anyone noticed him.

"Your Highness," the fellow remarked. "I was not aware you had an appointment with His Majesty."

"I don't," said Ludwig, "though I fear I must talk to him on a matter of great importance."

"Indeed? If you told me what it was, I could let him know why you're here."

"I'm afraid it's not something I can discuss with others."

The herald's face fell, for court was a place of subterfuge and treachery, where any little bit of knowledge could be wielded as a powerful tool.

"Is the king busy?" pressed Ludwig.

"His Majesty is always busy," said the herald. "I can inform him of your arrival, but unless you give me some idea of what this involves, I can do little to assure you an audience."

"Tell him it's a matter concerning the army."

The fellow bowed reverentially. "I shall see what I can do, Highness." He then disappeared into the bowels of the keep.

Ludwig wandered the great hall. Morgan had gone to the trouble of displaying the Coat of Arms of all the barons, even those formerly under the dominion of Neuhafen. Did that indicate the king was in a conciliatory mood?

Footsteps echoed on the stone floor, and he turned to see Sir Emril staring back at him.

"Lord Ludwig," the knight replied. "To what do we owe the pleasure?"

"I'm here to speak with the king."

"For what purpose, precisely?"

"I have news. I've recently returned from the south."

"Can you be more specific?"

"No. This is for the king's ears only."

"You speak in riddles," said Emril, "but you'll have to do better than that if you want to get past me."

"I am a Prince of the Realm. If I wish to see the king, it's your duty to make that possible."

"Is it? I was under the impression my duty was to serve His Majesty, and right now, he doesn't wish to speak with you."

"Why not?"

"He's indisposed."

"Is he ill?" asked Ludwig.

"No. Merely busy."

"Then I'll wait."

"He may be a while yet."

"It matters not. I have nowhere else to be."

"Might I suggest I schedule a meeting for later in the week? Surely that's preferable to waiting here all day?"

"The business on which I must engage him cannot wait."

"It will have to," snapped Emril. "As I said, His Majesty is indisposed."

Ludwig was on the verge of exploding. He fought hard to keep calm, but the edge to his voice betrayed him. "Listen to me, Emril. The reason I'm here is the entire realm is in peril. If I don't see him this very day, there's a good chance he'll lose his Crown."

"Is that a threat?"

"No, you fool, a warning. There are forces at work here with their own agenda. The king needs to know what's happening around him, or it may end in disaster."

"Disaster, you say?"

Ludwig nodded.

The man stared back in a moment of indecision. "Very well. I shall take this to His Majesty. I'm sure, once he's heard of your warning, he'll be more than amenable to meet with you."

"Thank you."

Emril strode off, leaving Ludwig wondering whether the knight was friend or foe. A knot grew in his stomach as the idea struck him that Sir Emril was part of this conspiracy. Lord Jurgen had significant influence; had he corrupted this very knight? The impulse to run threatened to overwhelm Ludwig. He fought to keep the panic at bay while he scanned the room, looking for an exit. He was almost ready to flee when Sir Emril returned.

"Sorry for the delay," said the knight, "but His Majesty was in the middle of a meeting. If you come with me, I'll conduct you to him."

King Morgan stood, staring at a portrait of his predecessor, but turned as the door opened.

"Your Majesty," said Sir Emril. "Prince Ludwig is here."

"What is this about?"

"My apologies, sire. He wouldn't tell me."

"I was talking to him," snapped the king, his eyes boring into Ludwig. "Well? What have you got to say for yourself?"

"I uncovered a plot, Majesty. One that could lead us into a war."

"Go on."

"I heard rumours that certain barons were up to something in the south. I took it upon myself to investigate further and arranged a visit to Bruggendorf."

"And you didn't see fit to inform me of your plans? How do I know you weren't part of this conspiracy yourself? Perhaps you and they had a falling out, and now you've come to cry about it?"

"I assure you I did no such thing, Your Majesty. I have only the best interests of the realm at heart."

"I shall be the judge of that. Continue. I'm eager to hear what you've uncovered."

"Lord Jurgen, the Baron of Bruggendorf, conspired with other barons to orchestrate an incident that would ultimately lead to war with Hollenbeck."

"And have you unmasked his co-conspirators?"

"I have. The barons of Udenacht, Hasdorf, and Arnsbach. There may be others involved as well."

"Talk is one thing, actions quite another. Have you any proof of this conspiracy?"

"I saw their plans myself," replied Ludwig. "They've already mapped the entire campaign out, though I fear it ill-conceived; either that or the man planning it wishes us to suffer a loss."

"It wasn't Jurgen's plan?"

"I suspect the idea of invading was his, but the plan was the work of a Fire Mage named Koldan Sartellian."

"Sartellian, you say? How curious. Tell me, what was the gist of their plan?"

"For our armies to cross the border at two points. The first would cross at Bruggendorf while the second would march from Hasdorf."

"A strategy no doubt designed to force the enemy to split their forces."

"I believe the idea was for the first army to tie down Hollenbeck's army while the second marched on the capital."

"It seems a sound enough strategy."

"But they did it behind your back, Your Majesty."

"I admire your loyalty, Ludwig, but planning is a far cry from moving forward with such a campaign."

Ludwig tried to reason out the king's response. Did he really see nothing wrong with such treason? He thought through his recent experiences, but to his mind, there was no doubt about Jurgen's ultimate objective. "There's more."

"I'm listening."

"Lord Jurgen told me of a plan to kill innocents."

"How would that lead to war?"

"He intended for men dressed as Hollenbeck soldiers to massacre some commoners."

"Ingenious," said the king. "But tell me, what would be the point of such a thing?"

"It would inflame the other barons of the realm, Majesty, and they, in turn, would pressure you into starting a war of retribution."

"It seems you have uncovered all their secrets. The question now is, what do you expect me to do about it?"

"Majesty?"

"You've unearthed this plot, Ludwig. Surely you must have given some consideration to what punishment I should mete out?"

"I assumed you'd want to make some arrests or, at the very least, call the barons to the capital to explain their actions."

"There it is, at last, the great mind at work." Morgan turned to the portrait of the late King Otto once more. "Do you know how Otto kept the peace for so long?"

"No," replied Ludwig.

"He was a cautious man who never took risks."

"That's a good thing, surely?"

"Is it? Timidity is not a quality that best suits the ruler of a kingdom like Hadenfeld. We are strong, Ludwig, and sometimes our neighbours forget that. Therefore, a show of force is occasionally necessary to remind them of our military prowess."

A feeling of dread grew in the pit of his stomach. The king should be outraged, yet here he was, defending the actions of these men. He started to get the feeling he had missed something.

"Tell me," said the king. "What actions did you take once you discovered this plot?"

"I sent someone to warn the Duke of Hollenbeck and then came here to warn you."

"You sent someone to Hollenbeck? Why would you even consider such a thing?"

"To prevent a war," replied Ludwig. "It would only take a relatively small force to repel a river crossing."

"So you sabotaged us?"

"Us?" Ludwig let the words sink in. "This was your plan all along."

"It was," admitted Morgan. "And now you've ruined any chance we had of success. By all rights, I should have you hanged as a traitor."

"I don't understand. You are the king. Why go to all this trouble when you could simply declare war?"

"You said it yourself—to inflame the barons into supporting it." He turned to meet Ludwig's gaze. "While it's true, I can declare a war whenever I like, but without the support of my barons, it would soon fail."

"But why go to war at all? Especially now when we're reorganizing our army?"

"Three years ago, we narrowly averted disaster by defeating Neuhafen. That war might have reunited the realm but revealed our vulnerability to our neighbours. We must show them our strength."

"And you feel attacking one of our neighbours is the best way to do that?"

"Naturally. How else do we project power? Did you think we could send delegates out to all the other realms and tell them how strong our army is? Rulers respect strength, Ludwig, and the only effective means of proving our might is by exercising it."

"War with Hollenbeck would prove nothing."

"Wouldn't it?" said the king. "The duke has no allies and fewer men under arms than us. To my mind, they present a perfect opportunity. You, however, have spoiled my plans."

Ludwig kept silent. Morgan paced back and forth, occasionally stopping and staring at him. Was His Majesty considering something drastic?

"I'm of two minds," continued Morgan. "I would be within my rights to remove you from the line of succession."

"Then why don't you?"

"Because, despite my best efforts to cut you down to size, you've cultivated friendships amongst the barons. To remove you now would only make it harder to gain their support for a future war."

"You still mean to invade a neighbouring realm?"

"Of course, but thanks to your efforts, Hollenbeck is no longer an option. Instead, I must punish you in a different manner, one which will make it appear as though you were still in my good graces."

"What are you suggesting?"

"Suggesting?" roared Morgan. "I'm king. I don't suggest, I command!"

"Your pardon, Majesty."

"Emril?"

The knight, who thus far had stood in silence, moved a step closer and bowed. "Your Majesty?"

"Escort His Highness to another room while I ponder his fate."

"With great pleasure, Majesty." The knight looked amused as he waved his hand to indicate the door. "This way, Highness."

Ludwig followed him into a small room holding naught but a fireplace and a candle.

"Wait here," said Sir Emril. "I shall return once the king decides your future."

"You're enjoying this."

"I am. It's nice to see you finally put in your place."

"What is it you hold against me?" asked Ludwig.

"Shall I speak frankly?"

"I wouldn't have it any other way."

"You are a pestilence, a rot gnawing away at the nobility of this great realm."

"How so?"

"You were born the son of a baron," continued Sir Emril, "yet you have the manners of a cur. You associate with commoners and wed a poor excuse for a baroness."

"I might remind you our marriage was arranged by King Otto, but even if it wasn't, Charlotte is more worthy of the title than any wife of yours could be!"

"Your life was handed to you on a silver platter, but you ran away instead of embracing the role of a baron's son. Your father would be ashamed were he still with us."

"Are you done?"

"Why?" said Emril. "Have you had enough?"

"Your words fall on deaf ears. I am at peace where my father is concerned, and as to your accusation that I ran away, I returned. Not only that, but I helped save this wretched kingdom from almost certain destruction!"

"There it is, your disdain for the very realm which you stand to inherit."

Ludwig struggled to contain his anger. It would do no good to rant about the shortcomings of King Morgan, especially when his future hung in the balance. "What is it you're after?"

"Who says I'm after anything?"

"You wormed your way into the king's confidence. It only stands to reason you expect something in return for your devotion. Let me guess, an elevation to baron?"

There it was, a flicker in the man's eye. He'd hit the mark.

"We are not here to discuss my future," said Emril. "Rather, to determine yours."

"We will be doing nothing of the sort. That is the king's decision, not yours."

"True, yet I am the sword of the king. You would do well to remember that."

"You are an advisor, but I think you overestimate your influence regarding the Crown."

"I don't care what you think."

"But you do, and that's why you're here. You want to gloat over my perceived failure."

"Perceived? You quite literally ruined the king's plans. That's not perception, it's fact. We'd be marching to war if it wasn't for you."

"A war we would ultimately lose. I know the king wants to show us off as a powerful kingdom, but that was not how to do it."

"Wherever did you get the impression the choice was yours to decide when and where we go to war? You are a prince, Ludwig, not a king."

"I swore an oath to defend the kingdom with honour and justice, but that doesn't include blind obedience."

"Doesn't it?"

"What are you implying?"

"I'm familiar with a baron's oath. You swore fealty to the rightful king of Hadenfeld. To my mind, fealty is loyalty, which includes following the king's commands. Or are you intimating Morgan isn't the true ruler of Hadenfeld?"

"I make no such claim."

Sir Emril stared back. He looked like he had more to say, but a king's guard opened the door. "My pardon, Your Highness. His Majesty commands your presence."

They returned to the king, who was in discussion with another noble, and it wasn't until the fellow turned around that Ludwig recognized Lord Jurgen.

"I have come to a decision," declared Morgan. "You're going to Eisen."

"To what end, Majesty?"

"I'm giving you one more chance. Do not fail me again."

Ludwig bowed. "What is it you want me to do?"

"You will be my representative in the east. You shall oversee the former province of Neuhafen and ensure any disloyalty is dealt with using whatever force necessary."

"Yes, Majesty. Is that all?"

"All? I haven't even started. You value your standing amongst your fellow barons, but I will make them loathe you. Once you take up residence in Eisen, you will command the barons to begin clearing the great forest."

"To what end?"

"Within a decade, I want to increase the number of baronies within Hadenfeld. Who knows, I may even elevate some to higher ranks." He glanced at Lord Jurgen. "You see, I reward my allies, Ludwig. My enemies, however..." He paused, letting the threat linger. "Well, let's not get into unpleasant details. In any event, I will send further instructions once I work out the details. For now, I order you back to Verfeld to prepare for your trip to Eisen. It will be some time before you return home. Do I make myself clear?"

"Yes, Majesty."

King Morgan kept his gaze locked on him. "Play your part over the next few months, and you may yet be restored to my favour. Cross me again, and it will be the end of you."

"Understood," said Ludwig.

"Good. Now, be about your business. I have things to attend to. Sir Emril will see you out." He paused but for a moment. "One more thing, Ludwig."

"Yes?"

"I shall have people watching you closely. One false move, and you will return to me in chains!"

16

DEPARTURE

AUTUMN 1103 SR

Ludwig paused at the carriage door, looking at the two companies of footmen and one of bow waiting to accompany him to Eisen, the former capital of the now extinct Kingdom of Neuhafen. King Morgan was treating it as a form of exile, but Ludwig wondered if it wasn't something more sinister.

"Are you sure this is wise, Highness?" Pelton's question interrupted his musings. "The king might take offence at you bringing your own men."

"My family is accompanying me. I'll not risk their safety in the hands of others."

"Have you any idea when you shall return?"

"That," replied Ludwig, "is entirely up to His Majesty."

"But that could mean months, even years."

"What would you have me do? Act against my king?"

Pelton cast his gaze down. "No. Of course not, Highness."

"I promise I shall eventually return, although I can't honestly say when. In my absence, you'll see to the running of the barony. I've called up an extra company of foot to garrison it, but you must keep an eye on them. They're still green."

"You shall be missed," said Pelton. "The halls of the keep will seem empty without Master Frederick running around."

Ludwig smiled. "I shall be sure to keep you abreast of his progress."

"Goodbye, Highness." Pelton bowed once more before heading into the keep.

Ludwig turned, ready to climb into the carriage, but noticed Sigwulf riding towards him, so he waved him over. "I was wondering when you'd see fit to return to us."

"I couldn't help it," replied the northerner. "His Grace, the duke, was a most accommodating fellow."

"Care to explain?"

"First, he insisted I march to the border with his men."

"He probably suspected a trap."

"Seeing the warriors massed on the other side reassured him I spoke the truth."

"Truly?" said Ludwig. "I expected Lord Jurgen would cancel the entire affair once I spoke to the king."

"He probably did, but you had to travel to Harlingen first, and then the king had to send word south. In any event, it didn't matter. His Grace acted quickly, dispatching cavalry to oppose any crossing."

"Did Jurgen's army attempt to cross?"

"No. They saw the futility of it."

"And then?"

"Why do you think there's a 'then'?"

"The fact you've only just returned to us now."

Sigwulf sighed. "Ah. That's a little more complicated. We stuck around the border for a while, and then he insisted I return to his court for a reward. Which reminds me..." He reached behind him, withdrew a sizable purse, and tossed it. "This is for you."

Ludwig caught it, feeling the weight. "What's this now?"

"Your share of the reward. A significant sum, if I do say so myself."

"This is yours, surely?"

"I told the duke it was your idea to warn him—that's his thanks. Don't worry. I got my own reward. By the way, His Grace, Lord Ulfric Sternhassen, wanted me to tell you he is forever in your debt. If you should ever require help, you need only send word."

"Sternhassen? That's Merrick's family name, isn't it?"

"Indeed. They are cousins, although several generations removed."

"What a small world," said Ludwig. "Does that mean Merrick could potentially inherit a duchy?"

"Not unless a major catastrophe wipes out Ulfric's family. I saw them all at the duke's court. The man has seven children, and four of them are boys." Sigwulf looked around. "I assume we're marching for Eisen?"

"You heard?"

"When I travelled through the capital, your new assignment was the talk of the town. I half expected I'd be too late to find you still here at Verfeld. Where's Cyn?"

"With the archers," said Ludwig. "Why don't you and her remain at Verfeld tonight? You can catch up to us tomorrow. It's not as if we'll move fast with all these men."

Sigwulf grinned. "Aye, I'd like that. Give my regards to Her Highness." He turned his horse around and trotted towards the archers.

Ludwig gave Verfeld a final glance before stepping into the carriage. Frederick kneeled on the seat beside his mother, his attention focused on the keep. As they rolled forward, Ludwig sat opposite them next to Father Vernan.

The march to the river would be brief, but then the laborious process of using the ferry would slow their progress. It wouldn't have been too bad if it were only the carriage, but a hundred and fifty men would not get across any time soon.

"I sense you're troubled," said the Holy Father.

"Only by the unknown," replied Ludwig. "When I was last in Eisen, they threw me into the dungeon."

"Ah, but this time, your allies, not to mention your own men, will keep you safe."

"What do you know about Eisen?" asked Charlotte.

"Not much," said Ludwig. "It's the easternmost city of Hadenfeld, lying astride a lake bearing its name. As for the keep itself, I saw little, save for the guest rooms and the great hall."

"I know more," offered Vernan. "I took it upon myself to learn all I could once I heard of the king's decision. The city is large, though not as expansive as Harlingen. The keep there is more of a castle, with outer works. They say the kings of Neuhafen were convinced Hadenfeld would eventually attack, so they endeavoured to increase its defences."

"How did you learn all this?"

"I wrote to the prior in Eisen, and he was most informative."

"Did you, perchance, warn him I was coming?"

"As a matter of fact, I did. He was most eager to meet you. It seems their last king, Diedrich, was not the most religious of men."

"Anything else you'd care to share?"

"Oh yes," replied Vernan. "Since the war, the place has become a Royal Keep of Hadenfeld, although no king of ours has ever set foot in it. A company of the king's men was sent to garrison it after Morgan's coronation, and sometime later, a warden was appointed to oversee its day-to-day running."

"A warden? Not a castellan?"

"King Morgan felt the name more fitting."

"Because he thought of Eisen more as a prison than a palace?"

"I cannot speak to His Majesty's state of mind, merely his decrees. Berath Yorrian currently occupies the position, but I'm afraid I know little about him."

"The king appointed him," said Ludwig. "That's enough to tell me I likely won't be overflowing with friendship. It appears I will be a prisoner once more."

"Nonsense," said Charlotte. "You are travelling to Eisen with your own men. Banished from court you may well be, but you're far from being thrown in the dungeon."

"Am I? I would have thought so before that debacle in the south, but now I'm not so sure. If I had a few less friends, Morgan might have executed me for treason."

"Then that is how you survive," she replied. "You make more friends."

"If only it were that easy."

"It is, don't you see? Emmett and Alexandra will introduce you to the other barons. All you need is to give them a sympathetic ear."

"That's easy to say," said Ludwig, "but Morgan has given me strict instructions. He wants the eastern barons brought into line."

"And what does that mean, precisely? Did his letter specify how you should accomplish this objective?"

"No."

"Then you must find your own way to bring them into the fold. I know you," she added, "and if there's one thing you're good at, it's listening to the concerns of others. You brought together the feuding barons of Erlingen and helped heal this realm after a bloody war. If anyone can bring these two groups together, it's you."

"You humble me."

"I speak only the truth."

"She's right," added Vernan. "Few men could've convinced Otto to spare the rebellious barons' lives. Without you, the aftermath of the Battle of Harlingen would have become a blood-bath."

"You're right," said Ludwig. "I've been looking at this all wrong. This isn't a punishment; it's an opportunity to make Hadenfeld all the stronger."

"There. Now that's settled, I shall contemplate my eyelids. I find such mental exercise exhausting."

As the crow flies, Dornbruck was a bit over thirty miles from Verfeld, yet the distance was deceiving, for they must cross the river by ferry. Added to that was the nature of the road, little more than a woodland pass wandering through thick forest.

Sigwulf and Cyn caught up to them on the morning of the second day. They arrived at Lord Emmett's keep to discover joyful news awaiting, for Lady Alexandra had given birth to their second child, a sister for young Evangeline.

After the ladies went to bed that night, Emmett and Ludwig sat discussing their hopes for their children. It wasn't until the wee hours of the morning the subject finally came around to Ludwig's intentions.

"The barons are nervous," said Lord Emmett. "There is a fear the king sent you to punish us rather than help."

"I think that's what Morgan intended," replied Ludwig, "but that's not the approach I'm taking."

"Go on."

"The problems in the east have long been ignored by those in Harlingen, leading to rebellion in the first place. I intend to discover what those issues are and address them head-on."

"And if the king objects?"

"Provided we keep his coffers full, he should be happy. My objective is to encourage growth, thereby increasing the barons' wealth, which provides more coins flowing into the king's treasury."

"You make it sound so simple," replied Emmett.

"Perhaps, but I'm earnest about my desire to help. Exactly how I'll accomplish this growth has yet to be seen, but I'm willing to do whatever it takes to improve your lives. For Hadenfeld to survive as a kingdom, all barons must be equal, and if that means convincing Morgan of the error of his ways, then that's what I'll do."

"Any ideas how you'll start?"

"Once I'm settled in, I'll invite the eastern barons to come for a visit. I must establish trust with them if we are to make any progress, and I can't do that by issuing orders."

"Do you mean to say you'll actively seek their advice?"

"Of course. They know more about this region than I do."

"Not so long ago, you were on the other side."

"Yes," said Ludwig, "but that's no longer true. To my mind, there are no sides, merely barons with different priorities. My task is to determine which ones we address first. What can you tell me about the eastern barons? I met them at the coronation but had no opportunity to speak with them at length."

"Where would you like me to start?"

"How about in the north?"

"Very well," said Emmett. "Let's begin with the Barony of Zwieken. Lord

Anson Meier rules there, and though he has a son and heir, he likes to look after the day-to-day running of his barony himself."

"Where does he stand, politically?"

"I'm afraid he strongly supported an independent Neuhafen."

"Meaning he won't like the idea of me being here."

"That's to be assumed. Still, the man's not stupid. Show him you care, and you might get him on-board."

"Zwieken is on the border with Zowenbruch, isn't it?"

"It is," said Emmett. "Even though they trade across the border, I wouldn't say there's much friendship."

"Why's that?"

"It goes back to when Diedrich's father, King Ruger, tried to make an ally of Zowenbruch. He didn't take kindly to their rejection and made threats, which, in all probability, led to the invasion of eighty-five. There's been little contact ever since."

"And it's likely to remain so," said Ludwig. "One of our allies is Erlingen, the northern neighbour of Zowenbruch. That alone speaks volumes."

"Ah, yes. The ever-shifting alliances of the Petty Kingdoms. Still, can you not negotiate more peaceful terms now that Neuhafen no longer exists?"

"I doubt it, not with our current alliances, but I'll definitely try. Who's next on your list?"

"Lord Rikart Schreiner, the Baron of Valksburg. He trades a lot with Deisenbach, so he favours peace, regardless of the cost. I imagine he'll do anything to avoid war since his trade tariffs make up much of his wealth."

"He's our age, isn't he?"

"Yes," said Emmett. "When he took over from his father five years ago, he spoke against invading Hadenfeld. Still sent his troops, though."

"I'll keep that in mind."

"Then there's the Baron of Langeven, Lord Merten Boesch. He's another old-timer, having become baron over thirty years ago. He has a daughter, Esmerelda, whom you likely saw at court."

"Let me guess; she's seeking a husband?"

"She is. Not that there are many available here in the east."

"Would she be amenable to a foreign match?"

"I couldn't say. While I know of her, I cannot claim to know her mind."

"Still, she might prove to be a valuable ally. How old is she?"

"Close to thirty, I imagine. Why?"

"I have some friends in Erlingen. Perhaps I'll suggest she go and visit them at the duke's court?"

"You would do that?" asked Emmett.

"I could certainly try. I was in a similar situation when I returned from the north—either I married Alexandra or found a bride elsewhere."

"Well, I, for one, am thankful you went to Reinwick."

Ludwig grinned. "As am I. Now, who's next?"

"Let's see. That would be Lord Werner Zimmer, the Baron of Tongrin. He's about ten years older than me and the poorest baron this side of the river."

"Why is that?"

"It's a newer barony with little to offer, save for wood, and we've all got plenty of that."

"I assume he has tenants?"

"Enough to keep him fed, but his contributions to the Army of Neuhafen cleaned out his reserves. There was talk about mining the hills south of him, but nothing ever came of it."

"Mining, you say. What for?"

"Iron, I believe. Why?"

"That could be a valuable commodity, considering the army's recent expansion, and they can also export it. You say nothing came of it. Is that due to the cost of getting started?"

"You'd have to ask Lord Werner. I'm not familiar with the particulars."

"I'll be sure to add that to my list of possibilities," said Ludwig.

"Ramfelden is next, and you'll never find a more cantankerous individual than Lord Jonas Goswald."

"He's contrary?"

Emmett laughed. "Contrary? That's a polite way of putting it. He'll argue till he's blue in the face to prove his point."

"Aside from his prickly personality, is there anything else worth knowing about the fellow?"

"Yes. He has a firm friendship with Lord Werner, but aside from that, he visits none of his other neighbours. That brings us to the barons of Arnsbach and Udenacht, whom I believe you already know."

"Yes. They conspired with Lord Jurgen of Bruggendorf," said Ludwig.

"Since then, they've turned their backs on the rest of us easterners. I doubt they'd come to Eisen, even if summoned."

"Truly?"

"They were the first eastern barons and are more economically developed, rivalling those to the west. If I were you, I wouldn't count on them for much of anything."

"So that gives me only five barons to deal with?"

"Six, if you include me, and each of us has our own problems."

"There's a lot of work to be done."

"You've already taken the first step by learning about everyone."

"One step on a very long road," replied Ludwig. "But I thank you all the same."

"Any more questions?"

"Yes. When can you and Alexandra be ready to travel?"

"You want us to go with you to Eisen?"

"Does that surprise you? You already demonstrated you know more about these barons than I do. How can I not have you at my side?"

"You flatter me."

"Nonsense. I'm merely telling the truth."

"Will you give me two days? I'll need to make arrangements for Dornbruck during my absence. You're welcome to stay here while I see to everything."

"Thank you," said Ludwig. "And while I'm here, my warriors can lend a hand with clearing your land. I imagine the extra manpower would come in handy to cut down more trees."

"I shall be pleased to take you up on that offer."

17

EISEN

AUTUMN 1103 SR

The sky remained clear throughout their journey to Eisen, the lack of rain allowing them to make steady progress on what was, even on a good day, a poor road. They were forced to halt several times while Ludwig's men cleared obstructions, usually nothing more than branches, but at one point, a stream had washed away a segment of the road. These delays made Ludwig think he needed people to patrol the roads and report any problems.

As the sun set in the west again, they came upon a farmer returning to his homestead from Eisen. Buoyed by the city's proximity, they continued, hoping to spend the night in a comfortable bed.

Lanterns hanging on the gatehouse were a welcoming sight in the darkness. Unlike his last visit, the guards waved the carriage on without any interrogation. They rolled through the streets with Lord Emmett's carriage in the lead.

To Ludwig, the journey to the keep took much longer than the first time he'd come here. When the carriage finally slowed, and a guard issued a challenge, he knew they'd arrived at his new home. Once they rolled to a stop, Ludwig touched Charlotte's arm, waking her gently.

"We've arrived, my dear," he said.

The door opened to a grinning Cyn. "We're here, boss."

"I was just telling Charlotte the same thing."

"I'll help with Frederick. There's someone here who wants to speak with you." She waited for Ludwig to exit the carriage before she climbed inside to assist.

They'd stopped in a large courtyard, cobblestones spreading from wall to wall. With lanterns few and far between, the keep was hard to distinguish in the shadows. He did, however, note the approach of a man in fine clothes, followed by a group of soldiers.

"Highness," the fellow said. "We weren't expecting you to arrive so late." He glanced at the carriages. "And with so much luggage."

Charlotte stepped out of the door, and the fellow's gaping mouth belied his shock. "You brought your family?"

"I did," said Ludwig. "Is that a problem?"

The man bit back a retort. "Of course not, Highness. It has merely caught us by surprise. We assumed you would be alone." He paused, taking a breath. "Where are my manners?" He bowed. "My name is Berath Yorrian, and I have the honour of being the Warden of Eisen Keep. If you come this way, I'll show you to your rooms."

"In a moment. I must attend to a few things first."

"That being?"

Cyn stepped from the carriage, carrying a now sleeping Frederick.

"You brought a child? This just won't do."

"I beg your pardon?" said Ludwig.

"We are not equipped to handle children, Highness. None of our servants are trained in such things."

"Then you had best find someone who is."

Sigwulf rode into the courtyard, leading the first company of footmen.

The warden gasped. "W-w-what's this, now?"

"Those," replied Ludwig, "are my troops. They will form the garrison here for the duration of my stay."

"The king has provided Royal Troops to protect the keep. Yours are not required."

"And yet here they are. From this point forward, my men will guard the inner keep, while yours guard the courtyard and the outer wall."

Berath appeared ready to object, but he could do little in the presence of a Royal Prince. "Of course, Highness."

"Sig," called out Ludwig. "Have the first company take position in the keep; the second should set up their billets. Cyn, your archers head to the barracks for the time being. We'll see to their disposition first thing in the morning." He turned back to the warden. "If you'll kindly show us to our rooms, the rest can wait."

"Yes, Highness. I'll take you there directly."

He waited as Ludwig took Frederick from Cyn, and then they followed him inside. The inner keep was much larger than Verfeld, being twice the width and depth. Added to that was the outer wall, which stretched around the courtyard, including round towers on its four corners.

Multiple doorways branched off the keep's entranceway, with the double doors to the great hall directly opposite the front door. Inside the massive room lay a long, wide table with an assortment of chairs, making an ideal location for nobles to gather, yet the layer of dust indicated no one had used it for some time.

The warden ignored the room's unkempt state, taking them up a grand staircase leading to a corridor stretching left and right. Here, he paused, turning to face his guests.

"Lady Altenburg will be housed down there"—he pointed to their left—"while His Highness's quarters are at the other end."

"No," said Ludwig. "That won't do."

"Pardon, Highness?"

"Lady Charlotte shares a room with me."

"That is most irregular. You are a prince after all."

"One who prefers to share a bed with his wife. Have you an objection to that?"

Berath started to nod but then wisely stopped. "Might I enquire why, Highness?"

"Why do you think?"

"I'm afraid I couldn't say. The custom of royalty is to reside in separate rooms, the better to ensure privacy."

"Are you suggesting I might want privacy for a mistress?"

"You wouldn't be the first, Highness."

"I assure you, I have no need for one. My wife will share my bed, and I shall brook no arguments from you."

The warden bowed. "As you wish, Highness."

Charlotte's fingers entwined with his. "Thank you," she whispered. He gave her hand a gentle squeeze before looking at the warden. "Show us to our quarters, Master Berath."

Their guide led them down the hallway to the door, opening it into a room where the floor was nearly covered with rugs, no doubt to reduce the uncomfortable chill of the stone beneath. They had also gone to the trouble of putting up wooden walls to hide the keep's rough stone. Whoever completed the work showed remarkable skill, but Ludwig wondered whether they built secret viewing alcoves into the panels, for the wood carvings were excessively ornate.

It didn't look much like a prison, but he couldn't forget the king had banished him here and threatened that the people here would keep a close eye on him. Did that include the servants? He wondered if he could trust any of them.

"Thank you, Master Berath. That will be all."

"My pleasure, Highness. If you or the good lady require anything, you need only call out." The warden turned to leave, almost running into Sigwulf. He quickly sidestepped, then fled, leaving a very bewildered northerner.

"What was that all about?" asked Sigwulf.

"I've upset the Warden of the Royal Keep."

"How?"

"By insisting my husband and I share a bed," offered Charlotte. "I think he found it hard to accept my husband loves me."

"I suppose that's to be expected," said Sigwulf. "Most Royal Marriages are arranged."

"As was ours, yet we are happy."

"We are indeed," agreed Ludwig. He lay a sleeping Frederick on the bed. "We need to arrange some rooms for Emmett and Alexandra."

"Not necessary," said Sigwulf. "They're staying at Emmett's cousin's tonight. They'll catch up with you tomorrow."

"And the men?"

"We've expelled the Royal Guards from the inner keep, and ours are now in control."

"Expelled?"

"I could say invited them to leave, if that sounds more charitable?"

"Any problems?"

"Plenty," said Sigwulf, "but nothing I couldn't handle. I'll need to make some adjustments over the next few days, but you can sleep knowing you're safe."

"Thank you, Sig. Now, get some sleep yourself. It's going to be a busy day tomorrow."

"Good night, Ludwig, Charlotte." He left, closing the door behind him.

"He's a good man," said Charlotte. "You're lucky to have someone you can trust. Most others in his position would let it go to their head."

"I'm not sure I understand what you mean?"

"Those in positions of influence tend to get an over-inflated ego and throw their weight around."

"Sig would never do that. If he did, Cyn would quickly put him in his place. Suffice it to say, I have no worries where they are concerned."

"Can you say the same for the rest of your retinue? We are in a dangerous position, politically, and some here may be willing to change loyalties for the right incentive. You must remain vigilant."

"I hadn't considered that. Then again, aside from you and Father Vernan, who else do I confide in?"

"Servants. We didn't bring any from Verfeld, which means those in the king's service will be waiting on us. We must guard our words while in their presence, lest His Majesty find some way to twist them to his advantage."

"I shall bear that in mind. Anything else you'd care to discuss?"

"Not at the moment, but I know where to find you if I think of anything," she said with a grin.

A knock at the door awakened them, and then a bevy of women entered bearing washbasins, jugs of water, and an assortment of trays full of food. Ludwig took one look at the wide-eyed Charlotte and stood up.

"Out," he snapped. "All of you." He shooed them into the hallway, closing the door behind him. "You are not to enter our chambers unless invited. Do you understand?"

A younger servant took exception. "But we have the mistress's breakfast, Highness."

He relieved the servant of the tray. "I shall take that. As for the rest of you, you can leave your trays here for now and return later to reclaim them."

They scurried off, wearing looks of confusion. He considered explaining Charlotte's condition to the warden but was concerned it would find its way back to the king.

He carried the tray inside, set it beside the bed, and then shook Frederick awake. With blurry eyes, the child saw his father holding a slice of bacon. As he lunged for the meat, Ludwig picked him up and carried him from the room, then down the hallway, where he ran into Kandam.

The fellow, one of his men of Kurathian descent gifted in the healing arts, stood guard on the balcony overlooking the great hall but turned at Ludwig's approach.

"Your Highness."

"Just the man I wanted to see. I need you to stand watch over Lady Charlotte's door. No one is to enter without her say or mine, understood?"

"Yes, Highness."

"Good. I'll let Sigwulf know I've moved you. Expect someone to relieve you sometime before noon." He set down Frederick, who sprinted over to the stairs and slowly descended them. Ludwig followed, noticing Cyn was waiting, as were Lord Emmett and Lady Alexandra.

"Please," said Ludwig. "Take a seat. Let's not stand on ceremony."

"How are you finding the keep?" asked Alexandra.

"I can't really say. I've only seen this room and our bedchambers. Cyn would know more." They all looked at the mercenary.

"It's pretty standard fare," she replied. "We've taken over some guest rooms to house the men, but that's a temporary solution. I'm told the garrison here is billeted in houses spread throughout the city, but I see no reason why we can't set up a barracks here."

"Don't we have barracks?"

"We do, but it only houses thirty men; that's barely half a company, and we brought three."

"I'll leave that in your capable hands. Let me know if there's anything you need."

Sigwulf entered, taking a seat beside Cyn. "Sorry I'm late."

"Problems?" asked Ludwig.

"Nothing major. Merely a disagreement that needed dealing with."

"What kind of disagreement?"

"When we reallocated the Royal Garrison last night, they neglected to inform their morning replacements we were here, so they arrived to find us standing guard and thought they'd been invaded."

"I assume it's all sorted now?"

"It is, but I've told our men to inform me if they encounter any more trouble."

"Good," said Ludwig.

"Is Charlotte not joining us?" asked Alexandra.

"I'm afraid not. She's indisposed."

"Understood. Please give her our best wishes."

"Thank you. Now, it's time to get started."

"That was fast," said Emmett. "Not that I have a problem with fast. How can we help?"

"I want to send a note to each baron asking them to come to Eisen."

"I'll draft letters if you like, then you can read them over and add your seal."

"That would be most appreciated."

"When do you want the barons to come?"

"That's the complicated part," replied Ludwig. "I'm not familiar enough with the area to know how long it takes them all to get here. What's your recommendation?"

"Winter will soon be upon us, which is a slow time for us barons. Might I suggest inviting them for the Midwinter Feast?"

"That's months away," said Sigwulf.

"I agree," said Ludwig.

"Perhaps the Feast of Saint Mathew?" offered Alexandra. "It marks the official start of winter. I understand it's not a customary time to gather the nobles of the land, but you could make it a family affair by inviting all the wives and their children."

Frederick climbed onto a chair and tried to reach for something on the table. "Not so fast there, young Master Frederick." Alexandra picked him up and put him on her lap, where he immediately settled.

"That gives us a month," said Emmett, "which is more than sufficient time to receive replies. Am I to make this a request or a demand?"

"A request. I'm not trying to force anything; merely get to know them better."

"I can arrange things here," said Alexandra, "providing Charlotte has no objections. I will consult with her, of course."

"Very well. The Feast of Saint Mathew, it is. Who knows, perhaps this will become an annual event?"

"Speaking of Saint Mathew," said Sigwulf, "where's Father Vernan?"

"He's gone to the Cathedral to meet the local prior," said Cyn. "I understand that's the custom for Church folk in these parts."

"I would think a city the size of Eisen would warrant an archprior."

"And it did when this was Neuhafen," said Emmett, "but Hadenfeld is now a united kingdom, which warrants but a single archprior, meaning Harlingen gets him."

"Are there any Temple Knights in the city?" asked Ludwig.

"Only a handful, and they're busy guarding the Cathedral. Why?"

"Just trying to get the lay of the land. Anything else local I should know about?"

"You tell me," said Emmett. "What is it you're looking for?"

"Let's see... Is there a smith nearby?"

"This is Eisen; there are plenty."

"Are any of them guild members?"

"Haven't a clue. Is that important?"

"It could be." Ludwig thought of Charlaine. She'd sent letters by way of the smiths guild on several occasions. Would they still reach him here? He must make time to inform her of his new residence.

He quickly changed the topic. "What's the market like for horses?"

"The prices were rising the last time I was here, which was bound to happen since the king wants to raise so many horsemen."

"Which reminds me; I need to look into how the barons are coping with the changes to the army."

"I've had no problem," said Emmett, "but I've heard others aren't faring as well."

"Let me guess—Lord Werner? You mentioned his barony was struggling."

"He's one, certainly, but Lord Jonas of Ramfelden is in the same situation. Those to the north have enough trade to fill their coffers, but Tongrin and Ramfelden are stuck in the middle of nowhere."

"Surely the same could be said of the rest of them?"

"Not so. Valksburg, Zwieken, and Udenacht are all on the border, not to mention major rivers. In essence, they are the gateways to the markets of Hadenfeld. Even Arnsbach has river trade, which encourages growth."

"Then we must find something to spur growth in Tongrin and Ramfelden. Do you think Lords Werner and Jonas will come to Eisen?"

"That's hard to tell. Jonas can be stubborn, and Saints know the King of Neuhafen gave him little help. On the other hand, he has nothing to lose and everything to gain."

"Is that your way of saying he'll accept or refuse the invitation?"

Emmett laughed. "I suppose it's my way of saying I have no idea."

18

SETTLING IN

WINTER 1103 SR

The fire crackled, sending sparks shooting up the chimney. Ludwig rubbed his hands together, then held them out, seeking warmth. Two servants entered, bearing tankards of hot mulled wine, and he returned to his seat at the head of the table.

Winter had finally arrived, and with it, the realization that the Royal Keep of Eisen was one of the coldest places Ludwig had ever been in. He picked up his tankard, cradling it in his fingers, its warmth slowly seeping into his hands.

"Well, my lords," he started, "shall we get down to business?" Around the table sat the six eastern barons who'd accepted his invitation. While they and their families had enjoyed the Royal Keep's hospitality, they now needed to discuss more serious subjects. With Alexandra's help, Charlotte entertained the women and children, freeing up the lords to speak of more worldly matters.

"Where would you like to start, Highness?" asked Lord Emmett.

"I'd appreciate an accounting of where you all stand regarding the king's proclamation for raising troops?"

All, save for Lord Emmett, were reluctant to meet his gaze.

"Come now," he soothed. "I am not here to berate you. Rather, I want to know where we stand regarding the king's requirements. Let's start with you, Lord Anson. How many men are presently under your command?"

Anson cleared his throat. "I'd be lying if I said we'd complied fully with His Majesty's requests, Highness. What he asks is no small feat; many of us drained our treasuries during the war."

"I am a baron myself," said Ludwig. "I understand the burden the king's requirement places on your coffers. The plan to expand our army was mine, but perhaps I should've spread it over a longer period to lessen the financial blow. How many can you call on in time of war?"

"Three companies."

"And their composition?"

"A company of bow, and two of foot."

"Are your footmen armed and trained according to His Majesty's requirements?"

"They are."

Ludwig shifted his gaze to Lord Rikart. "And how many men does Valksburg have available?"

The baron fidgeted in his seat. "Five companies, but only two possess armour, Highness."

"And how many archers?"

"Two."

"Is it manpower you lack or the funds to raise and equip them?"

"Funds, Highness."

"I'll try to arrange something to ease the burden. Lord Emmett, your own progress?"

"I possess the required footmen and archers to meet the king's request. I also transferred funds to the Crown for the Royal Cavalry, but I'm told there are no mounts for horsemen."

"I'm in a similar situation," added Lord Merten. "Langeven has been most loyal in terms of preparation, yet we send coins to the capital without a word to their employment. I was under the impression this new cavalry force was intended to help keep the kingdom secure, but all we've witnessed so far is the draining of our coffers."

Ludwig considered the situation. These barons were trying to do their duty, but he was beginning to suspect the cavalry force was just an excuse to enrich King Morgan's treasury. He needed to address the situation, and soon, else the barons might see fit to withhold their coins. If that were to happen, he harboured no doubt Morgan would march an army to force the issue.

"What if I offered an alternative?" he asked.

"You have our attention," said Lord Merten. "What is it you're proposing?"

"What if we undertook training some of that cavalry here?"

"There's still the problem of mounts," said Emmett. "The price of horse-flesh in these parts was always high, and His Majesty's recent demands only worsened it."

"Then we shall seek them elsewhere."

"We could get some from Deisenbach," offered Lord Rikart, "but I doubt Zowenbruch would be so inclined. How many are we looking at?"

"Enough for two companies to begin with," replied Ludwig.

"And when do you want them by?"

"I had hoped to begin training them in the spring."

"Then I shall reach out to my contacts in Deisenbach."

"Hold on," said Lord Merten. "How do we know His Majesty will agree to your plan, Highness?"

"We don't," replied Ludwig, "but it doesn't matter. Morgan can't have his army unless he agrees, and I don't intend to inform him of our plans until everything is in place."

"You play a dangerous game."

"We live in dangerous times. Make no mistake, gentlemen. These companies will be part of the Royal Army, but Harlingen isn't large enough to host that many permanently. If anything, I'm furthering his cause."

"You impress me," said Lord Jonas. "And I'll be the first to admit that's not easily done. However, what I'm more interested in is how I'm expected to raise additional men when I can barely afford to pay the one company I have now. The war drained my coffers dry."

"I'm in a similar situation," added Lord Werner. "What does King Morgan expect us to do? Hire mercenaries?"

"Mercenaries aren't a long-term solution," replied Ludwig, "and are almost as expensive as raising your own companies. For the present, we need to concentrate on building your economy. Once more coins are flowing into Tongrin and Ramfelden, the rest will be taken care of."

"Surely you jest? Even were the coins there, the population is not!"

"Eisen is a large city, as is Harlingen. With enough encouragement, people will migrate, but we need something to convince them it's worth their while."

"What are you suggesting?"

"Well, you could offer incentives to newcomers: land grants, for example, or lowering taxes for a year or two while they get settled."

Werner smashed his fist on the table. "So you would have me lose income, now?"

"The aim," replied Ludwig, "is to encourage people to settle in your lands. Think of it as short-term pain to achieve a long-term gain."

"I'll consider it, but I'm not making any decisions until I've consulted my castellan."

"Good. Then let's consider the matter closed, at least for today."

"You mentioned the funds for raising cavalry," said Lord Merten. "What if we forwarded all our taxes to Eisen instead of directly to Harlingen? We each escort strongboxes all the way to the capital, thus incurring further expenses, not to mention stripping us of part of our garrison. Eisen is a shorter trip, and you'd still be collecting on the Crown's behalf."

"An excellent idea," said Ludwig. "I would then send the collected funds to Harlingen on your behalf. The savings would be substantial, and the Royal Garrison from Eisen can deliver the coins to the king."

"But wouldn't that strip you of your own defences?"

"Not at all. I brought my own companies to Eisen. As far as I'm concerned, the Royal Troops here are added manpower."

"You're taking an incredible risk," said Lord Anson. "The king may not look kindly upon you taking matters into your own hands."

"What would you have me do—demand you fulfill your obligation to your king, regardless of cost? There is an opportunity here to bring our realm closer together rather than drive it apart."

"If the king disagrees, this could all be for naught."

"I cannot live my life in fear of making mistakes. I must do what I believe is best for Hadenfeld. If you barons don't see the merit of these ideas, you only need to say so. I shall not hold your differing opinion against you."

"You surprise me once again," said Lord Jonas. "After the Battle of Harlingen, I had to stand by and watch your men rob me blind, yet here you are, standing up for our rights. I admire your character, but how do we know you won't turn on us?"

"I'll vouch for him," said Lord Emmett. "I knew Lord Ludwig before the war, and he's never gone back on his word. He is also not your typical noble."

"What's that supposed to mean?"

"It means," said Sigwulf, "he can be trusted." He moved from where he stood near the door to the end of the table opposite Ludwig. "I fought beside him, repelling the invasion of Erlingen. He is a man of honour as well as a master tactician. If he tells you he'll do something, then, by thunder, he'll move the Saints themselves to keep his promise."

"And who are you to speak thus to the barons of Hadenfeld?"

"I am Sigwulf Marhaven, a captain in service to His Highness Prince Ludwig."

Lord Jonas grimaced. "That hardly makes you qualified to speak of such matters; you're in his pay."

"Then would you take the word of a man of the cloth?" Father Vernan stepped into the room. "It appears I arrived at the right moment."

"Another interruption?" said Jonas. "Is there to be no end to this?"

"My apologies. I am here on an entirely separate matter." He looked at Ludwig. "The prior wishes to meet with you, Highness."

"When?" asked Ludwig.

"He is waiting just outside and hoped you'd be available now. Shall I have him meet you in the chapel?"

"If you would be so kind, thank you."

Vernan left, closing the door behind him.

"Impressive," said Lord Jonas. "I'm willing to give this a try, but if you don't deliver something tangible by the summer, I shall report this to the king."

"As is your right," said Ludwig. "Now, I suggest you rejoin the ladies while I speak with the prior."

The Royal Chapel was a small affair meant to serve a king and his confessor's spiritual needs. The stained-glass window on the outside wall opposite the entrance depicted Saint Mathew, with the other Saints in the distance. As things often go, the likeness was crude, for whoever created it gave the Saint a bushy beard. However, those who studied his writings knew he was fastidious about his appearance. Indeed, the Temple Knights of Saint Mathew kept neatly trimmed beards and went to great lengths to maintain them.

Ludwig entered to find Father Vernan and the prior waiting for him. Prior Hieronymus bore a striking resemblance to his Saint, except for his hair, which was black with a liberal sprinkling of grey instead of the brown of Saint Mathew.

"Highness," the prior began, "may I say what a great honour it is meeting you."

"I could easily say the same," replied Ludwig. "My pardon if I sound abrupt, but to what do I owe the pleasure?"

"I am here on behalf of the good people of Eisen." The prior hesitated. "May I speak frankly?"

"Of course."

"The people here are worried. Rumours have been circulating since the war, and your arrival only heightened fears of reprisals."

"I assure you I have no wish to do anything of the sort. Yes, I'm here at King Morgan's behest, but my duty is helping the people of Eisen, not subjugating them."

"And what would that involve? Under your predecessor, things didn't exactly go smoothly."

"My predecessor? I wasn't aware anyone else was here."

"Did you not meet Master Berath, the warden?"

"I did," said Ludwig, "but my impression was his only responsibility was the care and maintenance of the Royal Keep."

"Would that it were so simple. Since his arrival, he has aggressively made demands of the citizens of this fair city."

"What type of demands?"

"Coins, in the form of special taxes."

"I've seen no record of these collections."

The prior shrugged. "If you were to line your own purse, would you provide incriminating evidence of it?"

"No. I suppose not," said Ludwig. "Trust me, Prior. This ends immediately. Please inform your congregation there will be no more special taxes."

"And if someone shows up, trying to collect?"

"Bring the matter to Father Vernan's attention. I shall make it his responsibility to investigate and bring me the details." He turned to the Holy Father. "Providing that meets with your approval?"

"I would be delighted. Have I permission to take action against the perpetrators?"

"To arrest them, yes, but punishment will only be after a suitable hearing. I don't want people making accusations merely to settle differences. I will provide you with a Royal Writ in case anyone seeks to obstruct you."

"We have a few Temple Knights here," said the prior. "Might I offer their services for an arrest of this nature, should it prove necessary?"

"That is most gracious of you. Thank you."

"It is my pleasure, Highness. Father Vernan tells me you are a devout worshipper of Saint Mathew. Might we expect to see you and your lady wife at our services?"

"I cannot promise to attend every week," said Ludwig, "but I'll endeavour to make it a priority."

"I shall make the arrangements when His Highness requests it," said Father Vernan. "That will free him up for affairs of state."

"In that case, I bid you a good day." Prior Hieronymus bowed. "It was an honour to meet you, Highness. I look forward to our next visit."

"As do I," replied Ludwig.

"Come, Your Grace," said Father Vernan. "I shall show you out."

Ludwig sat in reflection as they left. It appeared the Warden of Eisen was filling his own coffers. He wondered if the king knew or even cared. Upon stepping out of the chapel, he spotted one of his guards.

"Gustavo, go find Sigwulf, will you? Tell him to meet me in the drawing room."

"Yes, Highness." The fellow ran off.

Ludwig wandered through the keep, his mind racing. He knew he was taking chances here, but they all served the Crown's best interests. Would exposing the warden as a thief help or hinder his relationship with Morgan? He rounded a corner and spotted Sigwulf heading towards him.

"Trouble?" asked the northerner. "I heard you met with the prior."

"I did, and he brought to my attention that someone's been collecting extra taxes from the populous."

"Anyone we know?"

"Master Berath, the warden."

Sigwulf rubbed his hands together. "Want me to show him the error of his ways?"

"I was going to say yes, but I think a more diplomatic approach is better. Don't use any physical violence, but ensure he understands we know what he's up to, and he'll either make restitution or suffer the consequences."

"And if he doesn't agree to that?"

"Then threaten him with treason. He is, theoretically, stealing from the Crown. If that doesn't bother him, we'll consider something more drastic."

"What if he writes to the king?"

"I hadn't considered that," said Ludwig. "Have Cyn talk to some servants. She's good at that sort of thing."

"What's she looking for?"

"I'm interested in knowing who delivers Berath's correspondence to the king."

"Hah," said Sigwulf. "I know what you're up to. You want to know what's in those letters. That could get you into further trouble."

"Not if he doesn't know."

"Say, you're good at this ruling thing. You sure you don't want to be king?"

Ludwig shook his head. "I'm not plotting a rebellion, Sig, merely watching my back to ensure someone doesn't plant a dagger in it."

"No one's going to stab you while I'm around, or Cyn, for that matter."

"That's comforting."

"I'll be off, then. Let me know if you change your mind about leading a rebellion. I have some knowledge on the topic."

"Your father's rebellion failed."

"Precisely, which means I know what not to do!"

Ludwig continued to the drawing room to find Lady Alexandra waiting for him.

"Something wrong?" he asked.

"I have some concerns regarding the servants here."

"What kind of concerns?"

"Those who serve Charlotte don't understand her condition. It would have been better if you'd brought servants from Verfeld."

"I could send for some," said Ludwig, "but they're not likely to want to travel this time of year."

"Then perhaps we could find someone more empathetic."

"And how do you propose we do that?"

"I understand the last time you were here in Eisen, you met Emmett's cousin, Liesel?"

"I did. She helped me escape. Are you suggesting she'd be willing to look after Charlotte's needs?"

"I think so, providing we confide in her and tell her the truth."

"Excellent. I approve, as long as Charlotte agrees."

"Good," said Alexandra, "because she already has."

Ludwig chuckled. "If you already decided, then why ask me?"

"To keep up appearances, of course. After all, you are the prince!"

19

WARNING

SPRING 1104 SR

The frigid winter winds made way for the spring thaw, and with the warmer weather, Ludwig's thoughts turned to putting his plans in motion. Lord Rikart returned from Deisenbach with the news that he'd purchased enough horses to raise not two but three entire companies of cavalry. They cleared a field east of the city, building some temporary stables while they worked on a more permanent solution.

Ludwig was there for their arrival but was too busy with other matters to oversee their training personally. With the horses in place, the next step was to recruit riders. To this end, he returned to the Royal Keep to consult his notes. Since coming to Eisen, he'd gathered information on every conceivable subject, and these papers now littered his desk, demanding his attention. Even the servants had gotten into the habit of tossing new letters atop the pile. He desperately needed the time to sort through them all.

A knock on the office door interrupted him. "Come in," he said, ignoring whoever entered as he plucked another note from the pile, expecting a list of cavalry candidates only to discover it contained a request for more barracks space.

A cleared throat reminded him of his visitor, and he looked up to see a short individual with a bushy beard. A Dwarf stood before him, but Ludwig saw no reason why one would be one here of all places.

"You don't remember me, do you?" the Dwarf asked.

"No. Should I?"

"Aye, the name's Rurlan. I'm a courier for the smiths guild."

This individual's presence meant only one thing. "You brought a letter to me from Temple Captain Charlaine?"

"No." The Dwarf waited while Ludwig's face fell, then continued, "I have a letter from Temple COMMANDER Charlaine."

"Commander? Now, that is news." Ludwig waited for the letter, but Rurlan refused to hand it over.

"Not so fast. I must use my phoenix ring to open it, or all you'll get is ashes." The Dwarf momentarily placed his ring on the seal, breaking it, then unfolded the envelope. Inside was another letter sealed with the three distinctive waves of Saint Agnes. This he handed over. "Shall I await a reply?"

"If you would be so kind, though it won't be till tomorrow. I'll have someone fetch you something to eat, shall I?"

"Aye. That would be grand."

Ludwig rose, moving to the doorway to peer into the hall. "Gustavo, take Master Rurlan to the great hall and ensure he's fed, would you? And once he's done, he'll need a room."

"Yes, Highness."

The Dwarf bowed. "Highness, is it? Last I heard, you were a baron."

"A lot has changed since last we met."

"More than you know, but that letter will fill you in."

"You are aware of its contents?"

"The Temple Commander herself placed it into my hands."

"That's highly unusual, isn't it?"

"It is," said Rurlan, "but these are unusual times."

"And how was the commander?"

"In good health, but I'll let her letter do the talking, if you don't mind. After you've read it, feel free to send for me if you have any further questions."

"Thank you. I will."

"This way," said Gustavo, leading the Dwarf away.

Ludwig sat and stared at the letter. What did Rurlan mean by unusual times? He broke the seal of Saint Agnes and unfolded the letter. It consisted of two sheets, one folded inside the other, but there was no mistaking Charlaine's strong hand.

He read it over, devouring the words. Its contents set his heart racing, not over the thought of Charlaine herself but of the implications of what she'd written. Not only was there danger in the north, Hadenfeld itself was now threatened.

They gathered in the great hall. Cyn and Sigwulf were there, as was Father Vernan, but at Ludwig's insistence, Charlotte joined them, along with the

Dwarf, Rurlan. Rounding out the group were Emmett and Alexandra, who'd extended their stay in Eisen. The arrival of Prior Hieronymus surprised the others.

"Please. Sit," offered Ludwig. "I know this meeting wasn't planned, but Master Rurlan brought unexpected news from the north."

He took a breath to steady his nerves before continuing. "The Empire of Halvaria attempted to invade the northern kingdom of Arnsfeld."

"Attempted?" said Sigwulf. "Does that mean it failed?"

"It does. Temple Commander Charlaine pulled together enough troops to stop it."

"That's marvellous news," said Charlotte.

"There's more, much more. While Charlaine's group held off the Halvarian army, Admiral Danica defeated their fleet, sending the enemy scurrying back across the border."

"Scurrying?" said Sigwulf. "That doesn't sound like the Charlaine we met in Reinwick."

"My pardon," said Ludwig. "That's my interpretation of her words."

"One moment," said the prior. "You say this Temple Commander led the battle herself?"

"I did."

"Are you certain you did not misinterpret her words? The Church is forbidden to interfere in such matters."

"She spoke plainly, with no doubt about her involvement. The era of Temple Knights sitting on the fence instead of fighting is at an end. By the way, Temple Knights of Saint Mathew were also present at the battle."

"When did this happen?"

"Last summer."

Rurlan cleared his throat. "I was dispatched within a fortnight to carry word to you."

"How did you know I was here?" asked Ludwig.

"I didn't. I first travelled to Verfeld, but a man named Pelton informed me you were here in Eisen."

"All this is fascinating," said the prior, "but I'm at a loss to understand why I wasn't notified?"

"I might be able to explain that," said Ludwig. "This letter suggests there may be some corruption within the Church. It specifically mentions that the Temple Knights of Saint Cunar tried to prevent the sisters from reinforcing Arnsbach."

"Saints alive!"

"There's more, though it doesn't pertain to the Church as much as it does Hadenfeld. We've been aware for some time a family known as the

Stormwinds has been gaining prominence at courts across the Petty Kingdoms."

"Of course," said the prior. "What of it?"

"There is good reason to believe they are working in conjunction with the Halvarians."

"We knew that already," said Sigwulf. "What is it you're not telling us?"

"There is another group equally complicit, the Sartellians."

"No!" said Cyn. "Tell me it's not true."

"What is she talking about?" asked Charlotte.

"There's no easy way to put this," said Ludwig. "When we uncovered the plot to invade Hollenbeck, Koldan Sartellian was the man behind it. I later learned he worked on behalf of King Morgan."

"I see what you mean when you say it affects Hadenfeld. What do we do about it?"

"There's little we can do, save being vigilant." He looked at each in turn. "We must keep this to ourselves, at least for now. If word got out that we knew, we might find our lives in jeopardy."

"So that's it?" said Emmett. "We pretend the danger doesn't exist? We just reunited the kingdom; we can't let the whole thing rot from within."

"Then we shall begin working to discredit this Sartellian and anyone else of his ilk."

"How?"

"I have no idea."

"Perhaps I do," offered Prior Hieronymus.

"I'm listening."

"You are preparing to train this new cavalry of yours here in Eisen, yes?"

"That was certainly the intention. Why?"

"Might I ask who will train them? Your mercenary friends?"

"No," said Ludwig. "Neither is skilled in mounted combat. Nor am I, for that matter."

"What if I provided you with the necessary expertise?"

"I'm not sure what you're offering."

"It's simple," replied the prior. "You intend for these men to wear mail?"

"Correct."

"And you wish them taught how to charge and fight in battle?"

"Yes."

"Then who better to train them than Temple Knights?"

Ludwig couldn't believe his ears. "Are you suggesting the Temple Knights of Saint Mathew train our cavalry?"

"They are armoured like your men would be and mounted on similar-sized horses."

"Isn't the Church opposed to interfering in secular matters?"

"We were," said the prior, "but that has changed. Our brothers stood shoulder to shoulder with their sister knights and vanquished the Army of Halvaria. What more proof do we need?"

"Wait a moment," said Emmett. "I don't mean to cast aspersions, but there is only the word of this woman to verify the contents held within. How do we know she's telling the truth?"

"She is a Temple Commander," said Father Vernan. "If you can't trust her, then who can you?"

"I agree," said Ludwig. "I've known Charlaine for years and have no reason to doubt her now."

"Nor do I," added Charlotte. "She looked after me during our wedding and impressed me as an honest and straightforward woman."

"Then I withdraw my objection," said Emmett. "I meant no disrespect."

"As for me," said the prior, "I will speak with the Temple Knights guarding the Cathedral in Eisen to find out if they can get permission to assist you in your training."

Emmett knitted his brow. "They are not yours to command?"

"No. Without a commandery, they answer to their regional commander in Deisenbach. It may take some time, but if word from the north reached them as it has us, I doubt they would object."

"Let me sweeten the deal," said Ludwig. "Tell them I offer them land to build a commandery here in Eisen."

"That is most generous, Highness."

"It benefits us all in the end. If Halvaria launches another attack, as I suspect they will eventually do, we shall need all the help we can muster to keep them at bay."

"How much time do we have?"

"A few years, at most," replied Ludwig. "I'm of the opinion that Koldan Sartellian is in Hadenfeld to lure us into a war that will decimate our army. Morgan may have his faults, but his desire to make us stronger works to our advantage, for when the empire does strike, we shall possess the numbers to deal with it."

"Not alone, though," said Sigwulf. "We'll need allies."

"Hadenfeld has many," said Lord Emmett. "Do you not know about the complex alliances throughout the Petty Kingdoms?"

"Oh, I know about them. I'm also aware it's one thing to raise an army, quite another to march it to help an ally, thereby depriving your own countrymen of their protection. Hadenfeld would have difficulty marching to Erlingen without leaving ourselves defenceless."

"Well said," said Ludwig. "This underscores the urgency for the king's reforms and the need to make all our baronies profitable if only to pay for the added men."

Charlotte rose. "The time for talk is at an end. Let us do what we can to prepare for the coming war."

Father Vernan informed Ludwig a messenger had been sent to the capital of Deisenbach immediately after their fateful meeting, yet weeks had passed, and still no word from the Temple Knights of Saint Mathew.

The first crop of mounted warriors began training, limiting themselves to simple horsemanship, but Ludwig had high hopes his prayers would soon be answered. In the meantime, he busied himself with affairs of state, including setting aside time once a week to deal with civil complaints in the great hall.

This day, he was trying to settle a disagreement between two smiths, each claiming the exclusive right to equip the Royal Troops. He listened to each in turn, but neither could produce anything in writing, and the person they'd made the agreement with was nowhere to be found. He ruled that each would receive a contract for half the needed equipment and repairs. If either of them complained, they would forfeit their share of the work and the profits. He dismissed them, turning to speak with Father Vernan while Cyn escorted them from the room.

"Who's next?"

"Lady Erisella Zimmer, Baroness of Tongrin."

"Lord Werner's wife? Why's she here? This court is for commoners."

"She arrived unexpectedly, Highness."

"Then, by all means, send her in."

Father Vernan nodded to Cyn, who, having removed the smiths, had taken a position by the door. She, in turn, left the room, returning with Lady Erisella.

"My lady," said Ludwig. "What brings you to court this day?"

She bowed. "Highness, I bring greetings from my husband, Lord Werner. He would have come himself, but he's trying to deal with... well, we're not sure what it is."

Ludwig waved her closer before turning to Father Vernan. "You can dismiss the other attendees, Father. I suspect this is not for the ears of commoners."

"Of course." He waved at the guards, who escorted the townsfolk from the room.

Ludwig waited until the doors were once more closed before continuing. "Pray continue," he said. "What has happened?"

"That's just it," she replied. "We're not entirely sure. It all started a few weeks ago with reports of people amongst the trees north of town. At first, we assumed them to be hunters or possibly townsfolk mistaken for outsiders, but the sightings continued. My husband then suspected someone was spying out the area, most likely in preparation for a war."

"Tongrin is a long way from the border."

"Agreed, yet what other alternative is there?"

"Have you considered the possibility they might be bandits?"

"Most certainly, but Tongrin is a poor town with nothing worth stealing. My husband rode off to Harlingen to bring this to the king's notice, but I thought you, being closer, better equipped to investigate."

"I shall certainly do my best to discover who these people are. What else can you tell me about them?"

"Just before I left Tongrin, I sent a patrol into the forest to investigate. What they found was disturbing."

"That being?"

"The tracks of iron-shod horses indicated mounted warriors in the area."

"Most interesting," said Ludwig. "How many prints were there?"

"My master of the hunt estimates a dozen, possibly more. He tried tracking them back to their lair, but I'm afraid they somehow obscured their route."

She seemed hesitant to continue, so he pressed her on the matter. "What is it you're not telling me?"

"It is likely no more than superstition," replied Lady Erisella, "but it is rumoured those woods are haunted."

"By whom?" Cyn, enthralled by the possibility, moved closer.

"We don't know," replied the baroness. "Perhaps there was another settlement in the area centuries past, possibly a forgotten outpost of the Old Kingdom."

"And how long ago did people start seeing these ghosts?"

"Ever since Tongrin's founding." She turned back to Ludwig. "I know what you're thinking—it's all superstitious nonsense, but the people there have seen things that can't be explained."

Ludwig nodded at Cyn, allowing her to continue the interrogation.

"How are these ghosts described?"

"As pale figures, dressed in white and silver."

"Could it be that people see shapes in the mist, and their fears make them imagine ghosts?"

"Had it been only a few, I would say yes, but there are too many accounts to dismiss the matter so easily. Will you help us, Highness?"

Ludwig doubted the existence of ghosts, yet there was no denying something strange was happening in Tongrin. He ignored the baroness, concentrating instead on Cyn. "What do you think?"

"It's worth investigating. With your permission, I'll take some men down there and look into it."

"How many?"

"Ten footmen and three archers."

"Those three wouldn't happen to be my best trackers, now, would they?"

"Naturally," replied Cyn.

"I'm curious why you need the footmen."

"If these ghosts turn out to be bandits, I'll want someone to help me teach them a lesson."

"Very well. The command is yours." He turned back to Lady Erisella. "Will that suffice, my lady?"

"It is most generous of you, Highness. Thank you."

Cyn escorted the baroness out.

"Ghosts." Father Vernan shook his head. "Can you believe it?"

"I can," offered a guard.

The Holy Father turned on the fellow. "It is not your place to speak out of turn."

"No," said Ludwig. "Let him speak. Come here, Edwig."

The grey-eyed foot soldier approached.

"What did you mean by your remark?"

"Only that stories of ghosts are everywhere, even here in Eisen. Why, they say the woods to the east are crawling with them."

"Who are they?"

"The townsfolk, mostly," replied Edwig.

"And who do they say these ghosts are?"

"Spirits who haunt the forest."

"There are no such things," insisted Father Vernan.

"I'm only repeating what I heard."

Ludwig sat quietly for a moment. "I have new orders for you, Edwig. Take two others with you and head into town. I want you to collect as much information about these ghosts as possible. Can you write?"

"A little."

"Then keep a record of what you discover, or return here and have someone record your findings. I want everything you can find—rumours, eyewitness accounts, even children's bedtime stories, if necessary. Understood?"

"Yes, Highness. When do you want me to start?"

"This very evening. You'll find people more willing to open up over an ale or two, so I'll provide you with some coins. This is not, however, an excuse for you to get drunk!"

The fellow bowed. "Yes, Highness."

"Good. Now go round up two men you trust, and plan out how you're going to proceed."

Edwig left the room quickly, eager to prove himself.

Father Vernan gave Ludwig a stern look. "Are you certain it's wise to encourage this sort of thing? Once that floodgate opens, you'll be up to your neck in all sorts of ridiculous stories."

"True," said Ludwig. "But somewhere amongst all those tales, we might find a kernel of truth."

20

TRACKS

SPRING 1104 SR

L udwig splashed water over his face, then towelled it off.

"What happens now?" asked Charlotte, rising from the bed while Liesel placed a robe over her shoulders.

"We wait," he replied. "It'll be at least a week before we hear back from Cyn, and I'm beginning to wonder if Edwig will find anything useful. Places like Eisen always have their stories, but very few can face the cold reality of day."

"But even fairy tales have some basis in fact, surely?"

"Perhaps, but I'm not ready to start believing in ghosts just yet."

"Ghosts?" said Liesel. "My pardon, Highness, but you aren't talking about the Greywood, are you?"

"The Greywood?" replied Ludwig. "What's that?"

"It's what the locals call the forest to the east of the city."

"Then yes, that's exactly what I'm talking about. Why do you ask?"

"I'm just naturally curious. I suppose it comes from living in Eisen my entire life."

"And how do you explain these rumours of ghosts?"

"I imagine they come from the ruins."

"What ruins?" said Charlotte.

"My apologies. I assumed you knew our history. They built Eisen on the site of an ancient ruin, a village. Of course, that was long before I was born."

"A village, you say?"

"Yes. Just like the others."

"What others?" said Ludwig. "Are you suggesting there are more in the area?"

"Several," replied Liesel. "Though most have long since been picked clean."

"But not the one in the Greywood?"

"That's my understanding. People don't venture that far into the woods without good reason."

"But you have?"

"In recent years, no, but in my youth, it was considered a rite of passage, at least amongst us younger folk."

"Could you show us this place?"

"I think so, though it's been a few years."

"Good. I'll assemble an escort."

"I want to go as well," said Charlotte.

"Are you sure you're up to it?"

"I am feeling strong today, and an outing would be just what I need."

"Then it's settled," said Ludwig. "We'll eat something, and then be on our way."

Sigwulf stood waiting, reins in hand. They planned to ride to the edge of the Greywood, leaving a few of Ludwig's men to guard the horses, then proceed on foot due to the thick undergrowth.

The exploration team consisted of Ludwig, Charlotte, Liesel, and Sigwulf, accompanied by six footmen to dissuade any animals from attacking them. Finding the trail from Liesel's childhood memories took half the morning.

The forest proved challenging to traverse, forcing them to cut away the underbrush with axes. Eventually, they reached a clearing where bits of stone jutted out from the ground, evidence that a building had once stood there.

"Here it is," said Liesel. "We used to call it the haunted village."

Sigwulf moved up, stooping to scrape away some moss and examine what lay beneath. "These are cut stones," he said, "and very old, if I'm not mistaken."

"Likely from the Old Kingdom of Therengia," said Charlotte. "I've read there are many such ruins in Erlingen. It was said to be the heart of the Old Kingdom."

"I don't know about that. I've seen the ruins of a Therengian village, and they don't use stone like this." He used his dagger, digging around the base of the stone. "See here?" he said, looking at Ludwig. "These stones are smooth and fit together without any sign of mortar."

"Could it be Dwarven construction?" asked Ludwig.

Charlotte moved closer, kneeling to get a better view. "This is no Dwarven stone."

"How can you tell?"

"It's too thin. There are several Dwarven-built homes in Blunden, and their structures consist of an outer and inner wall built back to back."

"Maybe that's a regional design, made to keep the northern winds at bay."

"Perhaps, but their buildings are generally more robust. I know this wall lasted for centuries, but I can't see it as built by the mountain folk. And even if, by some miracle, it were, why in the name of the Saints would we find it in the middle of a forest?"

"An excellent question," replied Ludwig, "but if Dwarves didn't make it, then who?"

Sigwulf grunted. "Not Therengian, not Dwarf, and certainly older than Hadenfeld. Could it be Elvish? It is amongst the trees after all."

"Elves have not trod in the Petty Kingdoms for centuries," said Liesel. "They're extinct, or so the great scholars believe."

Ludwig grinned. "What if I told you they weren't?"

"Have you proof?"

"I do. It just so happens a group of Elves helped the Temple Knights up in Arnsbach."

"Truly?"

"So wrote Charlaine, and if she claimed it, I'm inclined to believe her."

"That may well be," said Charlotte, "but there aren't any tales of the woodland folk in these parts, are there?" She looked at Liesel.

"Not that I've heard," the woman replied. "I'm sure if there were, we'd know about it by now."

"Would we, though?" said Ludwig. "Think of it. Over half the land we call Hadenfeld is wild forest. You could hide an entire kingdom in all those trees, and we wouldn't have a clue."

"This is all wonderful speculation," said Sigwulf, "but I suggest we take a more pragmatic approach and look for signs of tracks."

"A good idea. Spread out, everyone, and remain vigilant."

The thick underbrush impeded their progress, slowing them, so it took half the afternoon to search the area. They found further traces of stone, likely the remains of walls, yet no clues as to who'd built such a place. Ludwig was ready to give up and head home when one of his guards, Paran, called out.

"Highness. I found something over here."

Ludwig moved closer, as did Sigwulf.

"It's a hoofprint," Paran continued, "though the horseshoe is unlike any I've seen. You?"

"It's not one of ours," said Ludwig, "and it appears to lead farther east."

"Should we follow it, Highness?"

Ludwig looked skyward. They were still far from home, and he needed to allow for travel time. The last thing he wanted was to lose their way in the forest, especially as nighttime approached.

"We shall," he finally said, "but not too far. We need to return to the keep before darkness descends."

"This is exciting," said Charlotte. "It's like being on an adventure. Frederick would love this."

"Frederick would hardly be able to move amongst all these plants."

Her laughter brought joy to Ludwig's heart. He didn't often see this side of his wife, but when he did, he enjoyed every moment.

Ludwig let Paran take the lead, following along a few steps behind. "How old do you reckon that print is?"

"Within the last few days, I would think."

"What makes you say that?"

"The horse crushed a leaf and pushed aside some moss, which hasn't grown back yet."

"And here I thought you were a footman, not an archer."

"I know how to follow a trail," replied Paran, "but a bow is a bit too much for me. It's the coordination, you see, or rather my lack of it."

"Have you ever tried a crossbow?"

"No. Do we have any?"

"I'm afraid not," said Ludwig, "but I'll see if we can rustle you one up."

"For hunting trips?"

"As you know, I don't hunt. I leave that sort of thing to those who are good at it."

"Then what do you do for sport, Highness? If you don't mind my asking?"

"I like to ride when I get a chance, but opportunities for that are few and far between these days."

"You two are awfully chatty up there," called out Sigwulf.

"Yes, we are." Ludwig was about to say more, but Paran halted and then crouched, examining the ground.

"More prints," said the foot soldier. "And not only horses this time." He moved forward slowly, pushing aside some weeds.

"Any idea what they were doing here?"

"I can't be certain, Highness, but I think they met someone on foot here."

Ludwig moved to where the soldier pointed. "If you look here," continued Paran, "you can see a footprint."

"What does it tell you?"

"I can't rightly say, Highness. The sole is smooth, likely soft leather, but there's no sign of nails or stitches. They also had a light step."

"Could it be a youth?"

"With a foot that size? I doubt it. No, the length indicates a full-grown man, just not a heavy one."

"How about a woman or young maiden?"

"Aye. Could be, but why would they be wandering around this deep in the woods?"

"It could be anyone," said Ludwig. "Perhaps we've stumbled across a hunter. A little farther, and we might find he's built a hut for shelter."

"What if it's an Orc?"

"It's not an Orc," said Ludwig. "I've seen Orc prints back in Verfeld, and their feet are broader."

"You saw Orc prints before?" said Sigwulf, coming up behind them. "When was this?"

"Years ago. I was up near the standing stones north of Verfeld. Mind you, we never saw any Orcs, only boot prints, but it was enough for me to warn my father."

"What happened?"

"He sent out riders to investigate, but whoever left those tracks was long gone."

"It appears we're looking for a hunter, then," said Paran, "or possibly a trapper. I hear all sorts of creatures live along the shore of the lake."

"Where are we, relative to the lake?" asked Ludwig.

"Just north of it, Highness. Is that important?"

"I couldn't really say. In any event, we've gone far enough for today. If we don't start heading back now, we'll be stumbling around in the dark."

"Do you want me to return tomorrow?" asked Sigwulf. "Paran and I can continue looking for more tracks?"

"No, not until we've made more sense of this. Hopefully, Edwig will find something of value to help us explain these so-called ghosts."

"And if he doesn't?"

"Then we're no worse off than we are now."

"There should be archives in Eisen," said Liesel. "The last King of Neuhafen didn't contribute to them, but his predecessor certainly did. Perhaps there's something of value to be found there?"

"It's definitely worth a try."

. . .

That evening, Ludwig sat in the great hall, books and scrolls cluttering the table. He'd found them in the keep's archives, but they were poorly organized, and it was impossible to date any documents accurately. In desperation, he'd brought forth a dozen books and an assortment of scrolls to peruse in more comfortable surroundings, thus leading to the current mess before him.

He almost fell asleep twice, so boring were the great tomes, yet something drove him on, urging him to seek answers to unknown questions.

A servant placed a tankard on the table, and Ludwig pushed away several scrolls to avoid spilling his drink on them. When one unrolled slightly, he noticed it was a map. He grabbed it, spread it before him and anchored one corner with his tankard.

It took him a bit to make sense of it, for the paper was worn and stained with something dark, perhaps blood, although it could also be wine. He recognized the outline of a lake, and then everything fell into place. This was a map of Eisen, drawn when it was still little more than a village.

It was a curiosity, to be sure, and he was about to discard it as such when he noticed a short annotation. To the east, along the lakeshore, was a small dot with the word Thorncraft beside it. Did this denote the existence of another village, or was it a man's name? He was suddenly struck with the desire to discover which it was.

"Find Father Vernan," he called out. "I seek his counsel."

A servant's footsteps receded deeper into the keep. Ludwig picked up the map and moved closer to the fireplace for more light. He was possibly missing something obvious, but by the firelight, there was no mistaking the text. Who or what was Thorncraft?

The sandalled feet of Father Vernan slapped their way down the stairs. "You sent for me, Highness?"

"I did. What do you make of this?" He offered him the map.

The Holy Father held it up, squinting at the markings. "Where did you find this?"

"In the archives. What do you make of it?"

"It's a very old map by the look of it. What area does it show?"

"To my mind, it looks like Eisen," replied Ludwig.

"So it is. It's even labelled."

"Is it? I hadn't noticed."

"Yes," said Father Vernan. "Down here at the bottom, but this stain partially obscures it."

"Look to the east. What do you see?"

"There's something written there. Thorncraft, is it?"

"I believe so," replied Ludwig. "What do you think it means?"

"It could be just about anything. A village, the name of a boat, a hunting cabin?"

"Why would someone place a boat on a map? Or a simple hunting cabin, for that matter?"

"I suppose that makes it a village. You don't think it's the one you found earlier today, do you?"

"No. According to that map, Thorncraft is on the edge of the lake."

"Why do I get the impression I'm being roped into a trip along the lakeshore?"

Ludwig smiled mischievously. "You like a mystery as much as the next man. Are you telling me you aren't a little bit curious about what this means?"

"Oh, I most assuredly am, but before we go gallivanting off into the woods, shouldn't we try to find out as much as we can about the name Thorncraft?"

"What do you suggest?"

"Well, for a start, you should have some people comb through the archives, looking for any mention of that name. Meanwhile, I'll go and visit the prior."

"Do you think he might have some idea what it means?"

"Not at all," said Father Vernan, "but the Temple of Saint Mathew keeps very accurate records, and I was told the Cathedral was one of the first buildings constructed in Eisen. If a village bearing the name Thorncraft existed, there ought to be records of births from there."

"But wouldn't they be kept in a local temple?"

"Doubtless they would, but the Church has a strict hierarchy, and a copy of those records would be forwarded to the prior at the time. But you needn't concern yourself with that; that's my domain, and I'm happy to assist. You will, however, require assistance if you're to search the entire archive. Could Charlotte help you? I know she's well-read."

"I'd prefer not to overburden her unnecessarily."

"I understand. Might I suggest Sigwulf lend a hand? It'll give him something to occupy his mind while Cyn is absent. Speaking of Cyn, when can we expect her to return from Tongrin?"

"Not for some time yet, I fear. Knowing her, she'll conduct a detailed search of the area, which will take another week or two."

"It appears you've found plenty to keep us busy while she's gone."

The banging of a door woke Ludwig. He was head down on the table, having fallen asleep while reading or attempting to. He arched his neck before seeing Charlotte looking down at him. She looked exhausted, and he could only imagine the effort it took for her to drag herself out of bed.

"I was worried about you," she said. "You never came to bed." She glanced at the papers still littering the table. "Did you find something?"

"I'm not sure. Amongst all these notes, I found an old map of the region. I believe they made it when Eisen was first starting out."

"And?"

"It may be nothing, but it appeared to show a village to the east, or rather southeast, along the shores of the lake. A place called Thorncraft. You haven't heard of it, have you?"

"No, but then again, I spent my childhood in the north, not Hadenfeld. I can ask Liesel, if you like. At least she's from the area."

"We'll hold off on that until Father Vernan returns. He thinks if this place were a village, the Cathedral in Eisen would retain copies of its births."

"And how does that help us solve the mystery of these ghosts?"

"That's just it. I'm not sure it does."

"Then why pursue it?"

"I've asked myself the same question."

"And your answer is..."

"Well," said Ludwig, "if a village was there, what happened to it? Villages don't disappear for no reason."

"Perhaps a plague devastated their population, or they gave up because conditions were too extreme?"

"Possibly, but I can't shake the suspicion someone intentionally wiped them out."

"But who would do such a thing?"

"That," said Ludwig, "is what worries me."

21

HISTORY

SPRING 1104 SR

"Ah, Edwig," said Ludwig, looking up from his papers. "I wondered when you were going to return to us. What did you learn?"

"Sorry, Highness, but there's little to add. There've been rumours of ghosts for generations, but no one has much in the way of details, save for figures in white."

"On foot or on horse?"

"Both, it would seem. How did you know?"

"We took Paran into the forest east of town, and he found some tracks. Nothing we could follow, but it tells us there's more to this story than ghosts, unless you're suggesting spirits leave behind prints?"

"No, of course not, Highness."

"Did you find any stories about people exploring the woods?"

Edwig hesitated. "Not quite."

"Care to explain?"

"I didn't come across anyone who went looking for ghosts, at least not in recent history. However, I learned an expedition was recently lost on the river."

"What river?"

"Lake Eisen drains to the east. Some speculate it leads into the Hollen River that forms our southern border. A scholar named Jochen Frei took it upon himself to explore downstream."

"Why in the name of the Saints would he do that?"

"If he navigated his way to the Hollen, then ships could follow, bearing trade goods."

"You seem to know a lot about trade," said Ludwig.

"Only what I've learned these last few days. It has nothing to do with those ghosts, though."

"Don't be so quick to dismiss the possibility. What else can you tell me about his expedition?"

"He took three men with him, and two were veterans of the recent war. They set out towards the Erlen River last fall."

"I assume no one's heard anything since?"

"You're correct," said Edwig. "They intended to sail along the Erlen—the river Lake Eisen drains into—then continue downstream."

"You say there were four men. Who was the last one?"

"A hunter, though I couldn't find out his name. Most of the information I got was from the merchant who sold them their supplies."

"Who paid for this expedition?"

"Jochen Frei himself," replied Edwig. "I'm told he was a man of means. He still has family here in Eisen."

"Did you visit them?"

"I did, but they added little to the story. Frei lived alone and was a secretive fellow."

"And his family?"

"A brother and sister, both adults who no longer live under his roof."

"His roof?"

"Yes. He was the eldest child and inherited the house upon the death of his parents. That was years ago, of course."

"How old was this scholar?"

"Forty-two at the time of his disappearance."

"And did you identify the other two members of his expedition?"

"His family knew nothing of them. I got a rough description from their supplier—no names, though. Is that important?"

"Not at the moment," said Ludwig, "but you can never tell when such things might be beneficial."

"Do you think their disappearance has something to do with these ghosts?"

Ludwig mulled over the idea. The ghosts were reported to be east of the city, and if Edwig's information was accurate, the Erlen River ran through the same area. It was becoming more likely that something sinister was behind all these stories.

"We cannot dismiss the possibility," he finally replied. "Take a couple of men and search the house of Jochen Frei. I doubt you'll discover any mention of ghosts, but hopefully, we can get a better idea of what he expected to find on his expedition. Who knows? With some luck, you might discover the identity of his companions."

"You think that important, Highness?"

"Ghost stories are certainly interesting, but the fact four citizens of Eisen vanished is of more immediate concern."

"Are we to look for them?"

"Eventually, but we must gather all the facts before we do. For all we know, this Frei might be running away from a gambling debt. I also need to hear what Captain Hoffman found down in Tongrin before I commit men to a rescue operation."

"I'll see to it at once, Highness."

"Good man. Let me know if you find anything."

Edwig gave a nod, then turned, opening the office door to see a startled Father Vernan.

"Saints alive!" said the Holy Father. "I very nearly ran right into you."

"My apologies, Father," replied Edwig.

"No need to apologize, my son." Vernan stood to one side, allowing the foot soldier to pass. "I assume he's in a bit of a hurry. What did you ask of him?"

"To look into another mystery," said Ludwig.

"Another one? Eisen seems to be crawling with them."

"How went your search of the Cathedral's records?"

"Quite well, although there's a lot to relate. Perhaps a drink might soften the blow to my already parched throat?"

Ludwig laughed. "I can accommodate you in that regard, but let us find somewhere more comfortable to sit. This office has its uses, yet the furniture is hardly what I'd call comfortable." He rose, leading Father Vernan to his drawing room. "Did you discover any more about Thorncraft?"

"I did, but if anything, it only adds to the mystery."

"But you found records of the place?"

"Yes, but the last entry was back in eighty-five."

"Nineteen years ago? Is that date significant?"

"It is if you're familiar with local history."

"Hold on," said Ludwig. He opened a door, then indicated Father Vernan should sit while he, as host, poured them both some wine. "Sorry, I didn't mean to interrupt. Please continue."

"Where was I? Oh yes, I was talking about the year 1085. As you are aware, Neuhafen won its independence back in 1050, but the war cost them dearly. Their victory gained them their own kingdom, but the loss of life weakened them for decades. By eighty-five, Zowenbruch started casting their eyes south, to Neuhafen's lands."

"I recall reading something along those lines," said Ludwig, "but I don't remember the details."

"Let me enlighten you." Father Vernan took a sip of wine. "They crossed the river, capturing Zwieken and Valksburg with ease. They planned to travel directly to Eisen, which was the capital of Neuhafen, but were unprepared for the march. I've read the Army of Zowenbruch neglected to consider the sparseness of the terrain."

"I assume they relied on plunder to feed their army?"

"They did, but at that time, Zwieken and Valksburg were little more than villages, incapable of feeding an entire army. They advanced down the road, expecting to find other villages to plunder, only to discover nothing but wilderness. Their advance soon ground to a halt, and they stopped halfway to Eisen, the King of Zowenbruch struggling to get supplies to his men."

"Yet the invasion ultimately failed, else we wouldn't be here now."

"It did," said Father Vernan. "In an unexpected turn of events, Neuhafen attacked at night, defeating the invaders and scattering their army. They even captured the King of Zowenbruch and forced him to pay reparations. That victory gave Neuhafen a sense of legitimacy, not to mention filling its coffers."

"All very interesting, but what has this to do with Thorncraft?"

"As I mentioned earlier, the last entry for Thorncraft coincides with the attack from Zowenbruch."

"You just said the invaders only made it halfway to Eisen. Are you now suggesting that wasn't the case?"

"I'm afraid it's much more complicated than that. In the weeks leading up to the invasion, reports flowed in from Thorncraft detailing all sorts of strange phenomena. The king swore to send troops, but then word of the invasion reached him."

"And so he left the village on their own?"

"Precisely. Once the battle was over, the king dispatched men to investigate, but that only deepened the mystery."

"In what way?"

"They found it empty, and when I say empty, I mean completely devoid of life: no people, no cattle, not even chickens, if you can believe it."

"But there were bodies, surely?"

"That's just it. They were simply gone, vanished as if the Saints themselves took them to the Afterlife."

"Did they search for survivors?" asked Ludwig.

"Naturally, but they found none, nor any tracks indicating where they'd been taken. Bear in mind these were the king's soldiers, not men skilled in tracking, but still, how do that many people disappear without a trace? It's been almost twenty years, and we still have no idea what happened."

"And you're sure this wasn't some raid by Zowenbruch?"

"To what end? If a raid was meant to instill fear, wouldn't they leave the bodies behind? And even if they didn't, why didn't they torch the buildings?"

"Have you a theory about what happened?"

"I wish I did," said Father Vernan. "I find the entire thing most perplexing. It seems the deeper we investigate, the stranger the story becomes. I can think of nothing that would explain these strange disappearances, can you?"

"No," replied Ludwig, "though everything strange seems to be in the east. I'm beginning to suspect the answer lies deep within those woods. The truth is, we know very little of the area. In fact, we only have those lands because the kingdoms to the far east—Ardosa, Menzen, and Kingshaven—are, from what Lord Meinhard told me, technically our allies."

"I'm afraid I don't see the relevance."

"Those three kingdoms argued over their borders for years. The only way to stop the constant bickering was for them to agree the territory belonged to Hadenfeld."

"So they'd rather us have it than their arch-enemies?"

"That was the general gist. Of course, that happened decades ago. I believe they all get along now, but we never settled the region. As far as we know, it's forest from here to Ardosa."

"So the question, now," said Father Vernan, "is what we do about all this?"

"Unfortunately, it's too late to help the people of Thorncraft, but I recently learned a small group of explorers went missing in the area. My intention is to go looking for them."

"And when is this rescue to begin?"

"Not till I hear back from Cyn. The last thing I want is Tongrin suffering the same fate as Thorncraft."

"You think it that widespread?"

"Don't you? Both places have stories of figures in white. Surely you're not suggesting that's mere coincidence?"

"How large is this expedition to be?"

"I haven't decided, though there'd need to be enough to counter any threats we might encounter."

"But how many is that? How can you guard against an unknown threat?"

"That's an excellent question. I wish I had an answer."

"I would still like to go with you," said Father Vernan. "There are many questions that need answering."

"And I'd like you to accompany us, I'm just not sure your superiors would want you to go. I doubt they would view it as Church business."

"Ah, but it is. Don't you see? The welfare of all is a basic tenant of Saint Mathew. I might also remind you I can wield an axe if necessary."

"Very well. You're in, although I've yet to decide who else will make up this expedition."

The days dragged on. Ludwig wanted to be on his way but was reluctant to leave until Cyn returned. In the meantime, he arranged for a pair of boats, each capable of carrying fifteen men. Since the voyage could conceivably take them hundreds of miles downriver, he reduced the complement, allowing extra storage space for food, water, and camping supplies. He wasn't sure what they'd find on their journey eastward but was determined they would be safe. To that end, he chose to take both footmen and archers on the trip.

The next step involved deciding who those individuals would be. He knew his men well, particularly those who'd served with him during the war, but the problem wasn't so much who to take as who to leave behind, so enthusiastic was the response.

He was pondering this very matter in the great hall when Cyn entered.

"I'm back," she announced. "Did you miss me?"

Ludwig looked up and smiled. "I was beginning to think we'd lost you. Was your trip a success?"

"That depends on your definition of success. We scoured the woods north and east of Tongrin but found no sign of intruders. What we did find, however, were lots of stories concerning riders in white."

"An interesting discovery. Do you mean riders white in colour or wearing white?"

"That's quite the distinction, and I'm glad you picked up on it. When I first arrived, all anyone spoke about was the mysterious white strangers, but once I got them talking, they confessed they meant their clothing was white or very near to it. Most were only momentary glances at figures deep within the forest, so I suppose it's not surprising they didn't have much to offer in the way of details." She looked at the pile of papers spread out on the great hall table. "What's all this?"

"I'm preparing an expedition. Care to join us?"

"Who's going?"

"Father Vernan, myself, and a few warriors. Sig, too, if—"

"I'm in," she said, not letting him finish.

"You don't even know where we're going."

"If you think I'm going to let Siggy go off exploring without me, you're mad."

"Good," said Ludwig. "Would you like to know what we're looking for?" He indicated she should join him.

She sat, leaning her elbows on the table. "Go ahead."

"Last autumn, a scholar named Jochen Frei undertook an expedition down the Erlen River to discover if it met up with the Hollen, which forms our southern border, but he was never heard from again."

"You believe he met his demise?"

"I think he may have found whoever is responsible for these tales of ghosts."

"Just not actual spirits, I assume?"

"That's my belief. I'm not certain, but I suspect these sightings are a carefully arranged spectacle to keep people away from the area. Most country folk are superstitious, and this ruse plays into those fears."

"Hmmm," said Cyn. "Why go to all that trouble in the first place? Wouldn't it be better to withdraw deeper into the forest?"

"What if they can't?"

"Why couldn't they?"

"What if they have villages or even cities at risk of discovery? You can't move a city without leaving a trace, and trust me, treasure hunters would like nothing better than to learn of such things."

"What kind of people are we talking about?"

"That, I don't know," said Ludwig. "I hoped you might have some ideas?"

"It can't be Dwarves. From what I've heard, they live in the mountains. The only other race I can think of is Orcs, but wouldn't they take a more active role in raiding our lands if that were the case?"

"Not necessarily. I've never met an Orc in person, but I discovered their tracks in Verfeld. At least, I assume that's what I found. In any case, we never experienced any trouble with them."

"Perhaps," said Cyn, "but they're seen as more of a threat in the north. However, it's said they are savage brutes, so if there are Orcs in those woods, we must take proper precautions."

"How do we do that?"

"By arming ourselves to the teeth. They are also supposed to be masters of the hunt, so we can expect them to strike from places of concealment. I suggest each member of the expedition be armed and armoured."

"That was my intent," said Ludwig, "although I hadn't considered Orcs could be responsible. If that's true, there might be hope our people are safe."

"What makes you say that? We don't even know if Orcs speak our language."

"If you remember the stories of the Saints, you'll recall they negotiated a treaty with them over the Holy City of Herani. Of course, that could be nothing more than a myth."

"Aside from seeing tracks, have you ever heard of Orcs raiding in Hadenfeld?"

"No, but most eastern barons have worked the land for over a century. If any Orcs were in the area, they would've driven them out long ago."

Cyn remained silent, but she was clearly thinking things over.

"Having second thoughts?" asked Ludwig.

"No, but if we expect to run into Orcs, it might be an idea to dig up whatever information we can about them."

"Any suggestion on how we do that?"

"By combing through the Royal Archives, and the Brothers of Saint Mathew might also have some information on the subject. Have you considered sending word to King Morgan?"

"I'm a bit hesitant to do that. In all likelihood, he'd ban me from pursuing the matter."

"Why would he do that?"

"Morgan is only interested in showing the rest of the Petty Kingdoms the power of our army. Getting involved with a hunt for Orcs makes us look weak."

"Because they're in our lands?"

"Precisely," said Ludwig. "Also, picking a war with an enemy who can disappear into a dense forest would be mad."

"If you feel that way, why are we even going?"

"Because I have a duty to the people of this region, no matter their position or title. In any case, I go seeking knowledge, not a war."

"So you're saying, if we encounter Orcs, you won't fight?"

"I'll fight if I must, but I'll do everything possible to avoid a war."

22

EXPLORATION

SPRING 1104 SR

The boat rocked slightly as Ludwig stepped into it. His men were aboard, five on each side, manning the oars, with Father Vernan sitting in the bow, watching the way ahead. Ludwig intended to man the starboard-side tiller, so he sat at the stern, craning his neck to look at the boat behind them. Cyn waved back, indicating all was ready.

"Push off," he called out, and the men on the port side shoved their oars against the dock, sending them farther into the water. Then all ten men dipped their oars, and the boat moved forward.

Ludwig sat back, leaning against the stern, his right hand loosely gripping the tiller. The boat could take a sail, but for the purposes of this expedition, they'd removed the mast, making space for the barrels of fresh water and supplies to feed them for the next few weeks. Each man brought armour but didn't wear it for the first day since the lake offered little in the way of danger. Once they reached the Erlen River, however, they would be more cautious.

Father Vernan guided them along the lake's edge, leaving plenty of room to manoeuvre. The oarsmen, eager to be on their way, put their backs into their strokes until, under the good Father's encouragement, they settled into a steady rhythm designed to conserve their strength.

Ludwig had sailed the Great Northern Sea on the Temple Ship *Valiant*, a warship designed to cleave through the rough waters of the north. The lake here was relatively smooth, with the occasional wave rocking the boat. He glanced aft at Eisen as it disappeared into the distance.

They planned to follow the coast to the abandoned village of Thorncraft, camping there for the night, and then search the area the next day before setting out for the mouth of the river. The journey would not be difficult or long, for the Erlen was estimated to be some twenty miles from Eisen. The idea was to pace the rowers and get them used to their work.

Ludwig thought about the abandoned village. He had no doubt something unusual had occurred there, yet it was difficult to sort fact from fiction. An abandoned village was one thing, but the complete lack of bodies was unsettling. To him, it suggested they'd been marched into captivity; only, if that were true, why hadn't they found any tracks? He knew rain could wash away some, but an entire village's worth?

There was also the matter of animals. Whoever brought about the ruin of Thorncraft saw fit to remove all signs of life, livestock included. Was something more sinister going on? Could this be the result of dark magic?

Ludwig had witnessed Earth Magic in person, and while Koldan Sartellian's Fire Magic demonstration impressed him, that was a long way from completely depopulating an entire village.

Almost twenty years had passed since the inhabitants disappeared. What did he expect to find? Surely, if anything was worth knowing, someone would have discovered it long ago. His fascination both intrigued and nagged at him.

The oarsmen kept up a modest pace as the day wore on. They took breaks occasionally to rest and slake their thirst, but by late afternoon, the village of Thorncraft came into view. It sat astride the lake, its houses like any others in the Petty Kingdoms. It wasn't until they closed the range that the passage of time became more evident.

Despite the village's crumbling roofs, weed-covered fences, and deteriorating dock, Ludwig was impressed by its overall condition. The place seemed frozen in time, waiting for its inhabitants to return. The rowers slowed, letting the boat glide until the hull bumped against the dock. Gustavo hopped out to tie them off.

Ludwig stood, then climbed onto the dock to look around. "Gustavo, you stay here and mind the boat. The rest of you can come ashore and stretch your legs, but don't wander off. We don't know what danger lurks here."

He looked lakeward at the second boat gliding into position behind his own. Cyn deftly leaped onto the dock, rope in hand, tying it off to a post. Sigwulf soon joined her, and they made their way towards Ludwig.

"What now, boss?" asked Cyn.

Ludwig looked skyward. "We'll take a quick look around while we still have light. The men will remain here and set up camp."

"I'll take care of that," offered Father Vernan. "One of these buildings should do nicely."

"Make sure nothing's in them. It's been a long time since any Humans were hereabouts. I shudder to think what creatures took up residence in their absence." He turned to Sigwulf. "Let's start by walking the village's perimeter, shall we?"

"Drawn weapons?" asked Cyn.

"I suppose it wouldn't hurt."

Thorncraft should have been referred to as a hamlet due to its lack of large buildings. The biggest was a storehouse that must have doubled as a meeting hall, for although it contained no sleeping quarters, a few rough wooden chairs were lined up in the middle. Crates stacked along one wall had all been pried open and deprived of their contents. They quickly examined the rest of the building before moving on.

Three small boats pulled up beside the storehouse which had long ago succumbed to the elements, now being little more than warped boards and iron fittings. Ludwig thought they might be fishing vessels, but if that were the case, there was no sign of any nets.

Seven small huts encircled a clearing on the landward side of the storehouse. At first glance, they appeared to be more storage, but then Sigwulf opened a door to reveal a firepit for cooking, tables, chairs, and even straw mattresses, although the latter had mostly rotted away. Though narrow, the tables were littered with assorted plates, bowls, and knives, as if someone had gathered things of value.

"Interesting," said Cyn, pushing in behind him. "Why do you suppose all this stuff is laid out here?"

"I doubt the original inhabitants did that," said Ludwig. "It's probably the result of those who came to investigate. My guess is they were trying to determine what was missing."

"I'm surprised someone didn't loot it," said Sigwulf. "Those plates alone are worth a few coins."

"More evidence that the king's men were here. Say what you will of the kings of Neuhafen, but it requires discipline to leave valuables behind."

"Still," said Cyn, "there's nothing here to suggest what happened to the inhabitants."

"And likely we'll find none. It's been abandoned for too long."

"I don't know about that. What if whoever was responsible comes back to visit every so often?"

"Why would they do that?"

"To ensure we didn't try to resettle the region?"

"She makes sense," said Sigwulf. "I'll get some men and scout out the surrounding area. Don't worry. We'll stay within sight of the village."

Ludwig and Cyn left to investigate the other houses while Sigwulf collected four men and scouted the woods.

It was dark by the time they finished their search. Father Vernan took charge of the storehouse in their absence, clearing away space for the men to sleep. He'd set up a campfire out front to keep the darkness and the growing chill of the evening at bay.

Ludwig sat and warmed his fingers. It was almost summer, yet a cool breeze blew across the lake. Some might call it an ill omen, but he didn't believe in such superstitions.

His thoughts turned to tomorrow's plans. They'd already conducted a search today, freeing up their morning to be on their way. The mouth of the Erlen lay a short distance away, and by his calculations, they should reach it no later than noon. The next thing to consider was whether to follow their plan and camp there or continue downstream.

If there were indeed Orcs living along the riverbanks, the going could become dangerous. He knew little about them but found it hard to believe civilized folk would raid a village and take everyone, leading him to consider alternatives.

He could think of only one reason people might be carted away—slavery. Could slavers be responsible for these tales? It certainly seemed plausible in the case of Thorncraft, but what would slavers possibly gain by convincing folks the forest was haunted? And would slavers operate in an area stretching all the way from Eisen to Tongrin? It seemed unlikely, yet what else explained these things?

Sigwulf returned, taking a seat beside Ludwig. "Well, that was a waste of time."

"You didn't find anything?"

"No, not that it surprises me much. Still, it was worth checking."

"Did you see any signs of life?"

"Some animal tracks, but nothing dangerous."

"That's good," said Ludwig. "I imagine something like ghosts would scare off the wildlife."

The northerner grinned. "I never thought of that. I suppose that means we'll sleep well tonight."

"Some of us might."

"You worry too much. We've a boatload of trained warriors... well, two boats. What could possibly go wrong?"

"That depends entirely on what lives in that forest. I've given it some thought, but for the life of me, I can't conceive of an explanation that makes sense."

"What about an animal of some type? Something rare, like a dragon or a gryphon?"

"Dragons died out centuries ago. Why, there hasn't been a sighting of a great wyrm in almost a thousand years."

"Says who?"

"Trust me. If there was proof of a dragon, it would be all over the Petty Kingdoms. Think of all the knights trying to hunt it down."

"I disagree," said Sigwulf. "I believe they do exist but live high in the mountains in the middle of nowhere."

"And what makes you say that?"

"It stands to reason, doesn't it? Where else can they live where we won't hunt them down? Though I haven't heard a story about a knight slaying a dragon, have you?"

"No, now that you mention it. Maybe they never existed in the first place?"

"I'd like to believe there's still magic left in the world."

"That's a funny thing to say," piped in Cyn, who'd wandered out to the fire with a trio of tankards. She handed one to both Sigwulf and Ludwig before taking a seat. "You talk of magic as if it doesn't exist, yet you've seen it with your own eyes."

"True," said Sigwulf, "but I'm not talking about spellcasters; I'm referring to creatures of legend, like dragons and gryphons, that sort of thing."

She giggled. "What about badgers?"

"Enough with the badgers all ready!"

"Still," she pressed, "you must admit, dragons and gryphons can't be the only thing you hope exists. What about a unicorn? Or perhaps a piecost."

Sigwulf looked confused. "What's a piecost?"

"About five pence." She burst out laughing.

"I think we can safely rule out dragons," said Ludwig. "There's no evidence anything was burned, and even if such creatures existed, wouldn't they leave behind signs of an attack?"

"It could still be gryphons," said Sigwulf.

"Don't they live in mountains?"

"Perhaps there's some to the east. That area is vast."

"You forget, there are kingdoms on our eastern border."

"Yes, but there must be two hundred miles or more between here and there. Plenty of room for some mountains, or at least some steep hills."

"True," replied Ludwig, "but if it were gryphons, the villagers could have retreated inside their homes and barred the doors. There is no sign of forced entry here."

"Interesting you should say that," said Cyn. "That seems to indicate there was no fight. I put it to you: whoever did this was initially friendly."

"Wait," said Sigwulf. "We're looking at this all wrong. These people weren't kidnapped or killed—they were lured away."

"By what?"

"There are all sorts of mystical creatures that might be responsible."

"Such as?"

"A spectre, nymph, even a witch?"

"Let's not get carried away," said Ludwig. "We may be making false assumptions. This village was abandoned long ago. There were likely clues as to what happened then, but the people coming to their aid missed them. They were soldiers, after all, not hunters or trackers."

Sigwulf sighed. "I suppose you're right. Not that it matters much. Whatever was out here has long since moved on."

"Cheer up, Siggy," said Cyn. "We'll find you your fantastical beast someday. In the meantime, I suggest we all get some sleep. Tomorrow will be a busy day."

They made good progress the next day, and by mid-morning, they arrived at where the lake fed the Erlen River. They approached cautiously, worried there might be rapids or a small waterfall, but the river water proved slow. The oarsmen lifted their oars, letting the mild current take the vessel.

It was peaceful here, with only the occasional ripple or chirping bird. It had a lulling effect, and before long, Ludwig started drifting off to sleep. He dipped his hand in the water and splashed some on his face.

The snap of a twig drew everyone's attention. Someone or something was moving along the riverbank, the abundance of weeds and bushes hiding its presence. Ludwig stood, trying to get a better view of the area, the tiller suddenly forgotten.

One of his men, a foot soldier named Kenmar, pointed to something ashore, and then an arrow blossomed from his back, its head burrowed deep. Blood splattered those nearby, and then Kenmar fell forward, pitching over the side of the boat.

As more arrows flew from the south, Ludwig had the presence of mind to order everyone down. Thankfully, no one else was hit, but the boat jarred to a halt when it struck something in the water.

"What's that?" he called out.

"A log," replied Father Vernan. "Someone laid it across the river to block our way."

A group of warriors appeared on the southern bank, their armour glistening in the noonday sun, helms obscuring their faces. Ludwig risked a glance rearward, but Sigwulf's boat was also trapped, for another log lay across the river behind them. Boxed in as they were, there was only one escape.

"Abandon ship," he called out, then jumped overboard, hoping the bulk of the boat would shield them from the hail of arrows.

The cold water took his breath away, but thankfully, the river was only chest-deep. He waded towards the northern bank, and those of his men still alive followed his example. An arrow hit his shoulder, but his armour deflected it.

The river grew shallower, but weeds and the mucky riverbed slowed him down. His men were yelling now, fear gripping them as yet more arrows rained down.

Gustavo took one to the shoulder and then fell, face-first, into the river. Ludwig waded over and grabbed his arm, trying to lift his head above the water.

The bulk of the boat blocked his view of whoever was loosing the arrows, but they knew what they were doing, for two more of his men fell. Ludwig despaired. He'd led his men into this mess, and now they were paying for it with their lives.

He halted, turning Gustavo onto his back to keep his head above water. Ludwig dragged the fellow onto the riverbank, then collapsed, his breath heaving. He attempted to get his bearings, but the underbrush was so thick he could see little of his surroundings. More screams came his way, and then a man ran past, blood pouring from his shoulder where an arrow had penetrated his mail shirt. He went two more steps before falling face-first to the forest floor.

Ludwig crawled towards him, intent on trying to help, but he came upon a set of mailed boots as he clawed through the underbrush. He looked up at a silver-clad warrior, then the butt of a spear took him in the head.

23

ELONIN

SPRING 1104 SR

L udwig opened his eyes to a sun-filled glade, the brightness sending pain coursing through his head. He quickly closed them, listening as sounds drifted into his consciousness and feeling returned to his limbs.

He was bound, both hand and foot, as he lay on the cold, hard ground. Voices came from all around, yet he made no sense of the words. He wondered if the blow to his head had done more damage than he thought, but then it dawned on him that these strangers spoke another language.

Ludwig squinted, trying to let his eyes adjust. Figures moved around him, and he spotted two others lying nearby, bound as he was. His head pounded, and his muscles were sore, yet he was determined to take stock of his situation. Now adjusted to the daylight, he opened his eyes wide.

Warriors, whoever they were, filled the clearing. Some warmed their hands by a small fire while others stood guard. Nearby lay five of his men. He couldn't see their faces but knew none were Cyn or Sigwulf, nor Father Vernan. The thought they might have perished nearly overwhelmed him.

He fought down the anguish and concentrated on his captors. They appeared to be of two types: warriors in strange fish-scale armour, wielding spears and shields. They also wore helmets, though conical and taller than those he'd seen in the north. The others were archers armed with strange bows as tall as them. They, too, wore the same armour, and though they bore short swords, they carried no shield.

The armour fascinated Ludwig, for he'd never seen anything like it. When a guard walked past him, he took the opportunity to observe it up close. It looked to be highly polished metal, slightly overlapping, similar to fish scales. He couldn't identify what it was made of, but it appeared light, for the guards manoeuvred around effortlessly.

One of his captors noticed he was awake and moved closer, kneeling beside him, saying something in their own language. Ludwig shook his head in response, an action that sent fresh waves of pain through his skull. He closed his eyes, trying to will the pain away, but his head continued throbbing.

He opened his eyes again, determined to discover who these people were. He thought them Orcs but then took note of the archers holding their bows with ungloved hands, revealing there was no green skin, merely pale flesh as you might expect of someone who lives beneath the boughs of trees.

The warrior before Ludwig grasped his chin with one hand and moved his head back and forth, checking for injuries. He poked and prodded until satisfied his prisoner was unhurt before moving to the next captive, who proved unresponsive. The warrior called over one of his comrades, and they lifted the body into a sitting position, placing something under the nose until the fellow gasped for air.

Obviously satisfied he was, in fact, alive, they hauled him to his feet and then half walked, half dragged him closer to the fire. Here, they forced him to kneel while a guard drew a knife.

Ludwig wanted to look away but couldn't. The knife sliced across the man's neck, and then the body slumped forward. The sight of it sickened Ludwig, and he fought down the bile threatening to spew from his stomach.

Hoofbeats echoed off the trees, and then a lone rider burst into the clearing, their armour similar to the others but more ornate, marking them as someone of distinction.

The camp exploded into action as the new arrival called out. The next thing Ludwig knew, they hauled him to his feet, then looped a rope around his wrist restraint before moving on and doing the same to the remaining prisoners until they formed a chain of sorts. He realized, with a shock, that only four others had survived. Another guard followed, untying their feet, and then spears prodded him forward.

Ludwig tripped frequently on the difficult path, but they lifted him to his feet each time, the march continuing without stopping. His head still throbbed, and he tried to keep his mind distracted to somehow avoid the pain.

Upon hearing water on his right, he reasoned they were moving parallel to the river. They continued like this for hours on end until they abruptly stopped, and the prisoners collapsed to the ground.

A guard moved amongst them, dropping a large, folded leaf into their hands. Ludwig stared down. A plant stem bound the leaf, but he couldn't fathom its use. He tore at the binding, breaking it to reveal a lump of brown paste.

The rider he'd seen earlier stood over him and removed their helmet, locking eyes with Ludwig. The features were feminine, but this was no Human woman, for the face was elongated as if stretched from top to bottom, framed by silver-white hair. But it was the ears that left no doubt about her race, for Ludwig stared into the face of an Elf.

She said something to him, but he didn't understand. Realizing this, she reached out, took a small amount of the brown paste, and placed it in her mouth.

An unpleasant smell assaulted his senses as he leaned his head towards the leaf. Steeling himself, he shoved it in his mouth, its bitter taste making him think of dirt, yet he picked up a hint of spearmint. After he swallowed, he noticed some of the soreness had left his limbs.

The Elf leader rose, moving back towards a knot of her soldiers and began issuing orders. Another Elf let Ludwig sip from a waterskin, then gestured for him to get back on his feet.

The trees flew by as their pace quickened. His fatigue vanished, his limbs once more full of energy, and even his head stopped pounding. On and on they went through an endless expanse of trees. At first, Ludwig tried to memorize landmarks, but the trees were so similar, this proved impossible.

As darkness fell, the column halted. The Elves led the prisoners into a small clearing and motioned for them to sit while they set sentries and built a fire.

The Elven leader rode into the clearing, waving her hands around in an intricate pattern as strange words issued from beneath her helmet. The surrounding air buzzed, then small lights, like fireflies, flew from her fingertips to the camp's outer perimeter, hovering as they illuminated the area with an eerie glow.

With her spell complete, she dismounted, handing her reins to one of her warriors. Once she removed her helmet, she looked around the clearing, sparing Ludwig only a momentary glance. With the pickets set, the others removed their helmets, revealing almost half were females.

A rattling noise drew Ludwig's attention. He spotted three Elves examining the armour they'd just dumped out of a sack. Their leader joined them, and a discussion ensued. When a warrior pointed at Ludwig, the leader walked over to him and knelt.

"Elonin," she said, tapping her chest.

"Ludwig," he replied, mimicking the action as best he could with his hands bound.

She nodded, then asked a question—at least that's what it sounded like—but he didn't understand a word. Elonin muttered something under her breath, then stood, backed up slightly, and uttered more strange words while her hands flowed around her in a graceful pattern. It was over in a thrice, and then she moved closer again, locking eyes with him.

"Who are you?" she asked.

Ludwig stared back, not quite believing his ears. "You speak my language?"

"With the aid of my magic, yes. Who are you?"

"Ludwig Altenburg, Prince of Hadenfeld and Baron of Verfeld." The absurdity of his claim suddenly struck him. Could he still claim to be a baron after being exiled from his barony? The very thought of it made him want to laugh, but he forced it down. This was no time to come across as arrogant.

"Why are you here?" she asked.

"I came seeking my countrymen. They disappeared while attempting to chart the river."

"You entered the Goldenwood. To do so without the High Lord's consent carries the sentence of death."

Ludwig thought fast. "How are we to follow your rules if we are ignorant of them?"

A wry smile escaped her lips. "You are wise. I see I was right to spare you."

"What of my men?"

"Those we captured were spared."

"Not true. I saw you execute one."

"We did, but we brought no healer with us, and his wounds were too severe to survive. We granted him eternal peace rather than force him to suffer needlessly."

"Who are you exactly?"

"We are the chosen of Tauril," said Elonin. "You Humans refer to us as Elves, though High Elves would be more fitting. We were the first race the Gods created. They gave us the solemn responsibility of safeguarding their creation."

"But the world is immense, and Humans are everywhere. What makes this forest worthy of such protection?"

"It has been our home for thousands of years." She paused, her unblinking eyes penetrating his soul. "I see you are full of questions, but I am a mere talon. It is not for me to decide your ultimate fate."

"A talon?"

"Yes. A leader of a group of warriors. Have you no similar rank amongst your own race?"

"We call them captains."

"Perhaps we are not so different as we appear."

"Where are you taking us?" asked Ludwig.

"Nethendril, the city from which our High Lord rules."

"You have more than one city?"

"Of course," replied Elonin. "Is it not so amongst your own kind?"

"Up until recently, I thought your race was confined to the north."

"A belief we sought to nurture, although I'm told our cousins there took a different approach."

"Meaning?"

"It is not unknown for those Elves to grace Human cities with their presence, although none from the Goldenwood would dare do such a thing."

"Why is that?"

"The secret of our presence guarantees our very existence."

"And now that you've told me, I suppose I must die?"

"Not necessarily," she replied. "The High Lord might let you live the rest of your natural life in Nethendril."

"If entering this forest carries the death sentence, why did you spare us?"

"I wonder that myself. On occasion, Humans have wandered into our lands, and in each case, we enforced the law. Your group, however, was larger than any other. We could have killed you all, but the loss of so many warriors might be noticed, leading to further incursions. I therefore concluded it served our interests to capture prisoners to learn more about you."

"But by your own words, we'd still be missed."

"I cannot argue with you there. I always believed Human encroachment on our lands was inevitable, so it makes sense we learn as much about you as possible. However, my good intentions may all come to naught once you are before the High Lord."

"Why is that?"

"He likes to follow tradition."

"Meaning, either way, we will never see our families again."

"Perhaps you will be the one who proves to our High Lord Humans can be trusted."

"I'm curious," said Ludwig. "You said you'd been here for thousands of years, but surely you weren't isolated from the rest of the world all that time?"

"You are correct. Before the coming of Humans, we were a mighty Elven realm, extending from the Stormtop Mountains to the far eastern reaches, but the Great War changed everything."

"What great war was that?"

"The war for dominance of the Continent. It saw us wage war on a scale unimaginable to you Humans."

"Who was it you fought?"

"Orcs," said Elonin.

There was no mistaking the distaste in her manner. It appeared much enmity between the two woodland races remained.

"If you don't mind me asking, how did it all come about?"

"The conflict was long in the making, although I know not what fanned the embers into the flames of war. A bitter struggle for survival saw cities razed to the ground and entire kingdoms turned to ash. The loss of life was so great, Elves withdrew deeper into our forest homes to survive."

"And the Orcs?"

"We destroyed them. Not completely, but by the war's end, they were reduced to a wandering people, struggling to survive in the Continent's most remote regions."

"And this pleases you?"

"No, but not for the reasons you might think. I harbour no love for Orcs, but their defeat proved to be our own downfall. Ever since, we have struggled to regain our position of dominance."

"I'm afraid I don't understand," said Ludwig. "This war ended before the coming of Humans, and we've been here for over a thousand years. Are you suggesting that, in all that time, you could not rebuild your population?"

Elonin seemed taken aback. Had he opened an old wound? Ludwig's strength had never been numbers, but even he spotted the flaw in her story. Or was there something she wasn't revealing? He wanted to ask her more but then reconsidered. She was a mere captain. Did she have access to such information?

"Get some sleep," said Elonin. "We have a long march ahead of us." She stood, walking away without another word.

Ludwig observed those sitting around the campfire. Someone had bandaged Gustavo's shoulder, while Kandam, the Kurathian, appeared uninjured. Next to him sat the archer, Rikal, whom he'd recruited in Roshlag. The last survivor's face was covered in blood from a scalp wound. He only noticed Edwig's distinctive grey eyes when the fellow looked at him.

He'd brought these men here and fought beside them, but now all he could do was weep at the knowledge his actions condemned them to death. He thought of Frederick, whom he'd never see grow up, and of Charlotte, whose warm embrace would no longer comfort him. Despair threatened to overwhelm him, and then the words of Saint Mathew came unbidden. *"Fear not the unknown,"* he had said, *"for in the discovery thereof lies the future."* A surge of comfort wiped away the fear. He would persevere and come out all the stronger for it.

They rose early the next day and continued on. Ludwig had no idea how far they'd travelled or where they were relative to their capture. All he knew was the forest seemed endless, and the river still ran nearby.

His mind wandered as he walked. If it was so close, why did they not use boats, for they'd be much more efficient? Could the water be too dangerous? Were there rapids or maybe a creature living there that made such a choice impossible?

He couldn't think of any animals that posed such a threat other than the stuff of childhood fantasies. That thought reminded him of Sigwulf's fascination with dragons and gryphons, and he wondered if the big northerner still lived. And what about Cyn, Father Vernan, and the others? Were they nothing more than rotting skin and bones, denied a proper burial by their brutal captors?

He tried not to dwell on the negative and instead set himself the task of remembering the prayers of Saint Mathew. It helped pass the time, giving him strength.

After a brief rest at noon, Ludwig chanted a hymn to ease his mind. He hadn't meant it to be loud, but Gustavo soon picked it up, and before long, all five were singing. Their guards appeared unbothered by it, and why not? It wasn't as if their captors understood the tongue of Humans.

As they camped that evening, Ludwig half expected Elonin to rebuke him for his temerity in singing, but her interest in the Humans appeared to have dissipated. As they lay down to sleep, he led his men in prayer, calling on Saint Mathew to watch over them and help them survive their captivity.

He saw a marked improvement in their morale the next day. No longer did they complain of their treatment or despair; instead they endured, as their Saint did over eleven hundred years ago.

24

NETHENDRIL

SPRING 1104 SR

The Elven city of Nethendril sat beside the Erlen River at the point it joined up with another coming from the north. A high wall surrounded it, with towers spaced strategically for protection from all fronts. A massive tree stood on a hill in the very centre of the city, its golden boughs reaching out in all directions. Apart from the tree, though, it looked like any walled city on the Continent.

As they approached, Ludwig noted the presence of a typical gatehouse, but a surprise awaited once they passed through. Wooden planks covered the streets, no doubt designed to keep the mud at bay. However, the deep, almost black colour, revealed it to be shadowbark. In Human lands, this rare wood was a highly prized substance. This one street alone would be worth a king's ransom anywhere in the Petty Kingdoms. He wondered if the Elves realized the wealth they had at their disposal.

The buildings were similar to those found in Harlingen or Eisen, with thatched roofs, although others bore wooden shingles of the same wood as the road. Ludwig was struck by the signs identifying each business, for they had Elvish script accompanied by a painting, making their identification a simple matter.

He noted bakers, cobblers, smiths, and even a dress shop as they passed through the city streets. Aside from their Elven features, the city's residents were similar to people found elsewhere, making it easy to distinguish a working trade from whatever passed for the upper echelons of society.

It took four blocks for him to realize what was missing. Across the Petty Kingdoms, a person expected crowded streets in a city of this size, yet here, in Nethendril, the foot traffic was light. Ludwig wondered if the lack of population was due to different customs, but then he noticed more and more empty buildings.

Elonin and her warriors marched them in silence, winding through the city streets while bringing them ever closer to the great golden tree until they reached the base of the hill, whereupon stood an enormous wooden building.

Grander in scale than the Royal Keep in Harlingen, it lacked the upper floors of such a defensive structure. Instead, it was more akin to a manor house, with oak panels forming the walls with a shadowbark roof. Images depicting nature in all its glory were carved into the wood, while the doors were of a different wood that appeared to glow in the late afternoon sun. This building belonged here as if nature itself blessed the place.

They halted out front. Elonin dismounted, passing off her reins, then disappeared into the building without a word. The guards ushered them off the road, where they sat, watching the curious stares of passing townsfolk.

"What are they looking at?" asked Gustavo. "You'd think they never saw a Human before."

"They probably haven't," replied Ludwig. "We are unfamiliar with their customs; perhaps they see us as mere vermin?"

Edwig stared at the townsfolk. "Has anyone noticed anything odd?"

"Such as?"

"There are no children here."

"Hardly surprising," said Rikal. "They doubtlessly think Humans are dangerous. Would you allow your children to be exposed to people like us?"

"I don't have children."

"It's a bit late to start worrying about it now. In case you forgot, they intend to execute us."

"That's enough," chided Ludwig. "We will survive this. I promise you. Edwig will have plenty of opportunity to fill his woman's belly."

"He has no woman," said Gustavo.

"That will probably change, especially after we return to tell our tale."

"You think we'll survive?"

"I do," said Ludwig. "They've had plenty of opportunity to kill us, yet we live. They want something from us, else, why capture us in the first place?"

Elonin exited the building and walked over to a trio of her guards. They exchanged words, and then her warriors moved towards their captives and forced them apart.

The talon stood before Ludwig, casting a spell. The air buzzed as a warmth flowed into him. At first, he assumed it was healing magic, but then he heard the guards chatting nearby and understood them.

"*You cast your magic on me,*" he said, realizing he spoke in Elvish. "*May I ask why?*"

"*You are about to be taken inside to speak with High Lord Falandril. His closest advisors and influential council members will be present. It is more efficient for me to cast the spell of tongues on you than attempt the same on everyone else.*" She turned to one of her guards. "*Untie him.*"

She waited until his restraints were cut before speaking again. "*You are being brought before the High Lord. Promise me you will behave, and I guarantee the safety of your warriors.*"

"*I agree,*" said Ludwig.

She stared back at him, perhaps deciding on his character, then nodded. "*Follow me.*" Elonin led the way, guards opening the ornate double doors as they approached.

Inside, the doorway opened into an entrance area where another pair of warriors armed with swords and shields stood. Upon entering, the guards opened the inner doors to what could only be described as the great hall.

Roughly sword-shaped, the entrance formed the handle, with three steps leading to a sunken floor that filled the centre of the room. At the far end, three individuals sat upon a raised platform. On both sides of the floor, steps served as seating for the gathering of Elves. Ludwig had no idea if these people held any actual power or were merely observers, but they took a keen interest in his arrival.

There was no mistaking the High Lord sitting on a large throne carved from a tree trunk. To his right sat a female Elf bedecked in gold-and-green robes, while to his left was another male Elf, strikingly similar to the ruler of Nethendril.

Elonin placed a hand on Ludwig's chest, stopping him in the centre of the room while she took up a position four steps in front of him, bowing reverentially.

"*Your Eminence,*" she began. "*May I present the Human Ludwig Altenburg, Prince of Hadenfeld and Baron of Verfeld.*"

The High Lord nodded his head in acknowledgement. Elonin moved aside, allowing Ludwig to view those who would determine his fate.

"*This,*" said Elonin, "*is Falandril, High Lord of Nethendril.*"

"*Greetings,*" said Ludwig.

"*And these*"—she nodded to the right and left of the throne—"*are Lady Sindra and Lord Reylar, his most trusted advisors.*"

Ludwig bowed. "*The honour is mine.*"

Reylar grimaced. "*Honour? You dare speak to me of honour? Humans have no understanding of the word.*" He turned his anger on Elonin. "*What is the meaning of this? Do you not understand your duty?*"

Elonin glanced briefly at Sindra, then locked eyes with the High Lord. *"If Your Eminence would permit me to explain—"*

"Explain?" roared Reylar. *"The punishment for invading our land is death. And you should know better than to address the High Lord directly."*

"I am sure she meant well," said Sindra, turning to the High Lord. *"Please, Father. Allow her to speak."*

"I will permit it," said Falandril.

Reylar gripped the arms of his chair. *"To reward such insolence is a mockery of your position."*

"I warn you, Brother. I am the ruler here, not you. You would do well to remember that." The High Lord nodded at Elonin. *"Speak, Talon, but get to the point. I am in no mood for frivolities."*

Elonin cleared her throat. *"The Humans have encroached on our lands for years."*

"You are stating the obvious," said Reylar. *"Get on with it."*

"These encroachments are becoming more frequent. It is only a matter of time before they arrive in greater numbers."

"And how does that concern us? We shall kill them as all who came before."

"To what end?" said Sindra. *"As Elonin already stated, their numbers increase. How long before they arrive in such quantities that we can no longer resist them?"*

"That is not the issue here. This talon overstepped the bounds of her authority and acted contrary to our laws. For that, she must be punished!"

"Elonin has served Nethendril for centuries. You yourself recommended her to the position—a position, I might add, that encourages initiative."

Ludwig realized no love was lost between uncle and niece, but where did the High Lord sit on this? For that matter, what of Elonin? Did she share a familial connection with Falandril, or was she only a captain trying to do her duty?

"My lord," said Reylar, *"our laws must be upheld, or our entire realm will fall into chaos. Would you have us abandon our beliefs so frivolously?"*

"Let the prisoner speak," suggested Sindra. *"He might be able to enlighten us on this matter."*

Falandril ignored her, focusing instead on Elonin. *"You stated the Humans come more frequently, but what was your thinking on bringing them here?"*

"I was always told," she replied, *"to defeat an opponent, you need to under-stand them. How better to do that than speak with one directly?"*

"And you did not think to do that in the forest?"

"It is not my place to anticipate your questions, Eminence."

The High Lord sat back, surprised. *"A good answer. Did someone suggest that to you?"* He glanced quickly at his daughter, then back to Elonin.

"No, Eminence. The decision was entirely mine."

"This is treachery," said Reylar, "or at the very least, incompetence. This Human deserves death, Brother, or have you forgotten your oath to protect our people?"

Falandril ignored the remark, finally looking at Ludwig. "Tell me, Human. Why have you come to our lands?"

"To find those of my people who were lost, Eminence."

"There you have it," said Reylar. "It is clear he means to wage war on us."

"Does it?" replied Sindra. "It sounds more like he wishes to recover his people. Would you do any less for one of ours?"

"An Elf would never trespass on another realm's land."

"That's where you're wrong," said Ludwig. "Or do you deny your people wiped out the village of Thorncraft?"

"Outrageous," said Reylar. "Now this Human tries to blame us for enforcing our own laws."

"How long ago was this?" asked Falandril.

"Nineteen years, come autumn," replied Ludwig. "And we have more recent sightings of your people near Eisen and Tongrin: both lands held in the name of my king."

"Why are our warriors patrolling areas so close to the Humans, Reylar?"

"It is the only way to keep our eyes on them, Brother. How else would we have warning should they decide to attack?"

"These patrols have become more aggressive," said Elonin.

Reylar turned on her. "I do not remember asking for your opinion, Talon."

"Let her speak," said Sindra. "It is her right."

"I will allow it," said Falandril.

The talon paused, taking a deep breath before speaking. "Before us is a golden opportunity. Ludwig is a prince; sparing him would surely earn great favour at the Royal Court of Hadenfeld."

"Favour?" said Reylar. "Of what use are Human favours to Elves?"

"The Humans grow more numerous with each passing year. If we do not learn to live beside them, we risk them sweeping us aside."

The High Lord silently considered Elonin's words. "You have given me much to consider," he finally said, "but I will not rush a decision on such an important matter." He rose and stood before Ludwig. "What have you to say on the subject, Human?"

Ludwig locked eyes with him, realizing with a shock his words could condemn him and his men. "I am no warmonger," he insisted. "I came here to discover the fate of those missing men. If you wish to remain isolated in this forest, I shall petition my king to ban his subjects from entering. Had this been done years ago, we could have avoided all this bloodshed."

"You speak wisely, but how do we know your king would honour such a pledge?

And what about his successors? Humans have short lifespans, and we must ensure future generations honour an agreement of this nature."

"A man is only as good as his word, and the same could be said of an Elf. We are different people, Eminence, but to live in harmony, we must learn to trust each other."

"You speak with a silver tongue, yet your words ring true."

"Do not be misled, Brother," said Reylar. "He will say anything to save his miserable life. It is the way of Humans."

"And how would you know that?" asked Sindra. "By your own admission, no Human ever set foot in our land and lived to tell the tale. Are you now claiming otherwise?"

"Enough," said Falandril, letting his gaze sweep the room. "Remove the prisoner, but ensure he is kept safe. I may need further words with him."

Guards moved, taking positions on either side of Ludwig. Elonin spared a glance for Sindra before moving to stand before him. "Turn around," she said, "and let my warriors escort you."

He did as she bid, marching out of the room, his escorts keeping pace.

Once outside, Elonin called a halt. "It seems you impressed the High Lord, although whether that was enough to save you has yet to be determined."

"Why all this secrecy? Surely it is better to embrace the outside world than remain hidden."

"Is it? Tell me, Human, what does your race think of Elves?"

"I've heard of Elves living amongst Humans in the north. They even helped the Kingdom of Arnsfeld stave off invasion."

"When was this?"

"Last year."

"And how do you know this?"

"A good friend of mine serves as a Temple Knight. She fought in that battle and talked favourably of your people."

"Temple Knight?"

"Yes," said Ludwig. "They are a religious fighting order. Have you anything similar here?"

"We have sword dancers, but they do not serve the forest goddess; they dedicate their lives to mastering battle."

"They sound a lot like our regular knights who spend their life training for war but serve a lord."

Elonin nodded. "We have more in common than I thought."

"What happens now?"

"You will be caged until the High Lord decides your fate."

"And my companions?"

"Held alongside you. Why is their fate of concern to you?"

"Why wouldn't it be? Are you not concerned for the welfare of those under your command?"

"I am, though I was under the impression that was an Elven trait. What else have you not yet revealed?"

"Would it surprise you to know we have dealings with Dwarves? Do your people interact with them at all?"

"Not for thousands of years, unfortunately. Our tales reveal a close friendship with the mountain folk, but the Great War shattered that relationship."

"And you've had no contact with Dwarves since?"

"No," said Elonin. "At least not that I recall."

"Recall? Do you mean to suggest you were there?"

"I was, although I was barely a century old when the war began."

"But I thought you said that was thousands of years ago?"

"Two thousand, give or take a century."

"How is that possible?"

"We are immortal," said Elonin. "We can die from misadventure or battle, but there is no natural end to our lifespan."

"Is that why you have no children?"

Her face darkened. "We do not speak of such things."

"Why not?"

"It is forbidden."

"Then how do you replace those you lose?"

"We cannot replace those who pass from the world of the living."

"Isn't Sindra the High Lord's daughter?"

"She is, but like me, she was born before the war."

"And you've had no children since?"

She remained silent.

"Now I understand why your people took refuge in this forest."

"Do not breathe a word of this to the High Lord. It will only invite your execution, not to mention put me in great danger."

"I shall keep it to myself. I promise you."

25

IMPRISONED
SPRING 1104 SR

The cage was small, barely fitting the five of them. Ludwig was the last to be pushed into the wooden structure, then they hoisted it into the air and left it dangling before the great hall for all to see. Curious onlookers stopped to gawk, but none dared come too close.

"This is a mite uncomfortable," said Edwig. "Couldn't they put us in a place with room to stretch our legs?"

"Stop your complaining," replied Rikal. "We're still alive."

"And likely to remain so," added Kandam, "at least for the foreseeable future."

"What makes you say that?"

"They helped Gustavo, didn't they? Why bother if they intended to execute him?"

"He's right," said Ludwig, "but I'm afraid they might decide to keep us here the rest of our lives."

"Not in this cage, surely?" said Edwig. "Death is preferable to spending an eternity in this contraption. Why did they hang us up here?"

"I imagine the idea is to make escape more difficult. Not that we could get far if we broke out."

"You'll find us a way out, Highness. The same as you escaped from the dungeons of Eisen."

"Lord Emmett released me then. I doubt we'll be so lucky this time."

"Shush," said Kandam. "Someone's coming."

Elonin exited the building, her silver hair almost golden in the setting sun. She halted briefly, taking a deep breath of fresh air, her gaze drifting to the cage. A few words of magic escaped her lips, and then she pointed at Ludwig, and a familiar warmth spread over him.

"What's happening?" asked Ludwig, now using the Elvish tongue.

The Elf briefly glanced at the great hall door. "They are discussing your fate. I pleaded your case, but I fear the council members believe strongly in tradition."

"So we are to die?"

"I think the High Lord sees the advantage of keeping you alive for the present, but I doubt you will see your homes again."

"Why do your people hate Humans so much?"

"You are usurpers, claiming the land once under our dominion."

"A land your people abandoned to live here in isolation."

"Then perhaps it is simple jealousy? You spread out across the land with no fear, multiplying like vermin."

"How would you know how far we've spread? You said you have no contact with the outside world?"

"That is not entirely true."

"What's that supposed to mean?"

"As you no doubt witnessed, there are those amongst us who use magic. Some can communicate over great distances, even observing what our eyes cannot view directly."

"You're talking about scrying," said Ludwig. "I've read of such things."

"I am, though the magic employed varies depending on the caster. As an Enchanter, I cannot scry that which I have never seen before."

"And is this true of others?"

"It gets more complicated. A wielder of Earth Magic sees through the eyes of another, using birds or animals to observe an area. A Water Mage gazes into a body of water and sees a reflection from a distant pool."

"Magic is much rarer in Human society."

"Invariably due to your short lifespans."

"Yet certain families have gained renown for their magical power."

"In our experience, the mastery of magic takes centuries."

"So says someone who lives forever. We don't have that luxury."

"True," said Elonin, "but this may be the very reason your race has thrived. Humans are always in a rush to do things; in many ways, you are like the Orcs."

"I'm not familiar with their ways," said Ludwig. "My understanding is they still wander the Continent, though only in small groups."

"Doubtlessly to avoid us finding them."

"Does the hatred run that deep?"

"It does, though there is little logic to it. The Great War ended over two thousand years ago, yet if an Orc appeared in this forest, it would galvanize our people into action. They are the one thing that causes nightmares amongst us."

"But why? Didn't you say you reduced them to a wandering people?"

"I said that, but it is not the entire story. There were always rumours of another Orc city that escaped our gaze. Some believe it will one day emerge, bringing about our ultimate downfall."

"Then you should seek allies rather than creating more enemies."

"Allies?"

"As you said, Humans have spread across the entire Continent, forming ourselves into a collection of kingdoms. Alliances are how we resist the depredation of others."

"We were allied with other Elven realms in the past, but they fell from their days of glory."

"Then why not consider allying yourselves with Humans?"

"The High Lord spoke eloquently on the subject; in any case, the decision is not mine."

"And if it were," asked Ludwig, "would you consider it?"

"I cannot deny I would give it careful consideration. In all truth, we are unaware of your ways."

"Then you should send delegates to spend time amongst us. Then you might see the wisdom in the proposal."

"I shall pass your thoughts on to Lady Sindra, but I cannot guarantee she will introduce the idea to the High Lord."

"Is she your sister?"

Elonin's face flushed. "No. That would be most inappropriate, considering the nature of our relationship."

"I'm afraid I don't understand."

"Do you have a family?"

"I do," said Ludwig. "A wife and child."

"Remove the child, and you have what Sindra and I enjoy."

Ludwig fell silent.

"That disturbs you," she said.

"No. It merely surprised me. Saint Mathew teaches us acceptance, and this is an aspect of that. It is not my place to judge you."

"Yet here I am, doing precisely that to you, or at least my people are."

"You yourself said you have no say in the matter, but I believe you're wrong. A single voice can make a difference, especially when raised at the right moment."

"You have given me much to consider."

"That seems to be a common theme with you Elves."

"It cannot be helped," said Elonin. "When a race is as long-lived as ours, it naturally leads to being contemplative."

"I suppose I hadn't looked at it quite that way."

The door to the hall opened, flooding the now darkened street with light. Sindra stepped forth, seeking Elonin.

"There you are," she said. *"I was beginning to fear you had run out on me."*

"I would never do that," the talon replied. *"I came out for a breath of fresh air. Have they made a decision?"*

"Not as yet. Father is still discussing the matter with the other lords of the council."

"Yet you are now out here with me."

Sindra stepped closer, her gaze flicking to Ludwig for only a moment. *"I could not stand being in there one moment longer and desired your company."*

"Let me guess—your uncle and father are fighting again?"

"They are, but I fear it may come to blows this time. The arrival of the Humans has brought their long-simmering anger to the surface."

Elonin looked down, shaking her head. *"I should not have brought them here. It only made matters worse."*

Sindra reached out, gently raising her chin until their eyes met. *"You did what you believed best."*

"My actions could lead to bloodshed."

"If it does, then so be it. We can no longer ignore what has been brewing for centuries."

Elonin took a step back. *"Do you realize what you are saying?"*

"Do not mistake my intent," replied Sindra. *"I am not promoting violence, merely observing long-held disagreements are boiling to the surface, and we all know what happens when a pot is left unattended."*

"You should leave Nethendril before it escalates."

"And abandon my father in his greatest moment of need? I think not."

"Even at the risk of your own life?"

"I shall take care. I promise you. But I am needed here." Sindra turned, walking towards the great hall. She glanced back at Elonin one last time before entering the building. The door closed silently behind her, cutting off the light.

Ludwig let his eyes adjust to the darkness. *"Bringing us here has caused you trouble,"* he said. *"It would have been wiser to kill us while you had the chance."*

"We cannot change the past, only act in the best interests of the future." She looked up at him. *"I wish you well, Ludwig of Hadenfeld, but I fear this may be our last meeting. My actions were not well-received by the High Lord's court, and even if they decide to let you live, I shall likely be sent away."*

"To where?"

"Another city, though it matters not which one, for I fear it will part me from Sindra."

"How many other cities have you?"

"Are you afraid we are too numerous? That we might wage war against you?"

"I would be lying if I didn't say you posed a risk."

"You need not worry on that account. We are not a warlike people."

"By your own admission," said Ludwig, "you fought a war so massive, it almost wiped out your entire race."

"As I mentioned before, that was a long time ago." Elonin paused, deep in thought. "Tell me," she continued. "Did you mean what you said about gaining allies?"

"War is coming to the land of men," he warned, "and on such a scale, it could well mean the end of our way of life."

"Who threatens you so?"

"A great Human empire called Halvaria."

"You would war with your own race?"

"We have no choice."

"Then your people should prepare for it."

"A fact of which I'm well aware, but convincing others of the danger has thus far proved difficult."

"What proof have you this war is coming?"

"There's already trouble in the north," replied Ludwig, "both on the coast of the Great Northern Sea and our western frontier with the empire. It's only a question of time before they launch a full-scale invasion."

Elonin chuckled. "Here you are, your own life in danger, yet your primary concern is the safety of your countrymen. Are all Humans so concerned for others?"

"Very few, I'm afraid, which makes it all the more important we act now."

"Are you referring to your own people or mine?"

"Could it not be both? You realize your way of life is in peril, just as I do mine. This very same concern for others should unite us."

"So you are suggesting, what? That we help you defend your lands against this oppressor, and you, in turn, will help us defend our own lands?"

"Something like that, yes."

"You are not a king."

"Nor are you," said Ludwig. "Yet you have the ear of Lady Sindra, just as I have of my king. I cannot guarantee either leader would agree, but we'll never know if we don't ask."

"You speak wisely. I only hope it is not too late. I shall raise the idea with Lady Sindra."

With that, she headed back inside, leaving Ludwig to ponder the situation.

"What was that all about?" asked Edwig.

"Hope," replied Ludwig.

"And how long does her spell last?"

"I couldn't say."

They sat in silence, the only noise the chirping of crickets and wind blowing through the trees. Ludwig grew drowsy, then the door opened, and Lord Reylar stormed out of the building, followed by two others.

"*This is outrageous,*" shouted the Elven lord. "*This will only lead us to ruin. We must preserve the old ways, or we are doomed to extinction.*"

"*What would you have us do?*" asked one of his companions.

Reylar responded, but Ludwig no longer understood, for Elonin's spell had worn off.

"Oh, for Saint's sake," he muttered under his breath.

The Elves spared him a cursory glance before disappearing into the darkness.

Ludwig leaned against the cage, sweating as the night wore on.

Despite being spring, the Elven city felt humid, no doubt due to a combination of the river and trees in such close proximity.

Gustavo, meanwhile, snored loudly, leading to the occasional elbow from Kandam, who struggled to find sleep. The Kurathian was preparing to do so again when he suddenly froze. "Did you hear that?"

Ludwig scanned the area as best he could, given the cage bars surrounding them on all sides. He saw little in the glow of the moonlight, but then Kandam pointed somewhere behind him. Ludwig shifted to get a better view, seeing shadows moving down the street, hugging the walls of buildings, but without a doubt, they were heading towards the hall. Even more alarming was the presence of bared blades glinting in the moonlight. These Elves were intent on murder this night.

He turned his gaze to the great hall below. The door was closed, but a flicker of light illuminated the bottom, proof someone remained within.

The Elves positioned themselves on either side of the doors. One, a little taller than the rest, put out his hand and swung it down, signalling the assault's commencement. The rest pushed open the door, surging in, clashing steel echoing forth until all was quiet again.

Ludwig nudged Gustavo. "Wake up. All of you. Murder is afoot."

His men roused from their slumber as Kandam rattled the cage's bars. "How do we get out of this thing?" he shouted.

"Put your feet against this side," replied Ludwig, "and your backs against the other." He cajoled them into position, then gave the order to push. They all strained, and the wooden bars bent slightly.

"That's it," he said. "Now put your backs into it."

They pushed harder, the wood cracking with their efforts. Feeling the bar with his fingers, Ludwig discovered where it had split. "Again," he shouted.

With another push, the bar splintered. They caught their breath as Kandam reached out, grabbing the broken timber and twisting it loose.

"I've got it," he said at last. "Hold on." He used the split end to saw at the ropes holding the other bars. They collectively held their breath until the strands came loose, and another bar fell away. Kandam squeezed through the gap, landing safely on the ground, alert for any sign of danger. Edwig followed, and then, before long, they were all crouched beneath the cage.

"We're free," said Rikal. "Now what?"

"This way," said Ludwig, leading them towards the great hall. He paused at the open door, peeking in. Two guards lay dead in the entrance, the inner doors open enough for light to bleed into the entranceway.

Ludwig retrieved a weapon as he made his way to the second set of doors. Peering through the opening, he witnessed a scene he would never forget. The High Lord lay in a pool of blood, with Reylar standing over the body, sword in hand, his warriors spread out on either side. Elonin stood opposite them, protecting Sindra, a look of horror etched on both their faces.

Gustavo came up beside Ludwig, sword in hand. "We are armed and ready," he whispered. "The guards wore daggers as well as swords."

"Speak for yourself," added Rikal. "I still have nothing to fight with."

"Ignore him, Highness. Give the command, and we'll attack."

"Are you so eager to die?"

"Better to die fighting than at the hands of the executioner."

Ludwig shoved the door open wide, striding into the room. One of Reylar's men hissed a warning, and the Elven lord backed up slightly, turning to face this new threat.

Elonin cast a spell, and a tingling sensation encompassed his whole body, but he ignored it, charging the Elven lord, striking with his sword. Reylar was faster, his own weapon quickly deflecting the blow, then counterattacking in a blur of steel. Ludwig feared he'd lose his arm, but as the blade struck, an invisible force deflected the attack. Reylar cast a look of disgust at Elonin.

Rushing to the side, Gustavo intercepted an assassin attempting to flank Ludwig. The sound of steel on steel echoed throughout the hall as Ludwig found himself on the defensive. He considered himself a good swordsman, for his training master, Kurt Wasser, had spent years instructing him in the art of duelling, yet he was hard-pressed to defend himself, let alone contemplate an offence.

As the Elven lord drove him back, he tripped, crashing to the floor, his weapon knocked out of his hand. His opponent advanced, ready to end this. In a desperate move, Ludwig kicked out with all his strength, his boot connecting with the Elf's knee.

Reylar fell to one side, screaming in agony. Ludwig used the opportunity to grab his sword and launch himself onto the Elf's body. He sat up, attempting to ready his sword for a death blow, but Reylar suddenly reached up, wrapping his hands around Ludwig's neck, squeezing the life out of him.

Elonin leaped forward, her sword taking one traitorous warrior in the throat while Sindra uttered words of power. Her hands glowed as a tiny spark flew from her fingers, landing in amongst the attackers. The floor cracked, and vines sprang forth, spreading out like the tentacles of some creature from the Underworld. Bones snapped as they wrapped themselves around arms and legs, and then Elonin silenced the screams of the assassins forever.

Unable to breathe, Ludwig's vision blurred. He hammered away at Reylar's arms using the hilt of his blade. He wanted to strike out, to plunge the blade into the Elf's chest, but his strength failed him. He prepared to surrender to death, but then a sense of peace flowed through him. He stopped breathing, ignoring the protestations of his body and raised the sword, blade down, the tip resting against the Elven lord's chest, the metal breastplate preventing it from doing any damage.

Ludwig silently prayed, and in that moment, a resurgence of strength imbued him. He rose onto his legs as best he could, his neck still held in a vice-like grip, his body hovering over the hilt, surrendering himself, letting his weight drive the sword downward, scraping across the breastplate until it found Reynar's exposed throat. Blood spurted upward, blinding Ludwig as the hands around his throat released their iron grip. He collapsed to the floor, his head spinning.

26

DIPLOMACY
SPRING 1104 SR

Someone rolled him over and sat him up, wiping the blood away from his eyes.

"Are you all right?" called out Kandam.

"I'm fine," said Ludwig, his voice hoarse. He looked at Reylar's warriors, strewn motionless around the room. Two had fallen to Ludwig's men while Sindra's magic dispatched the rest.

Ludwig got to his feet with the help of Kandam. He took two steps, then more Elven warriors burst into the room, rushing towards him. He briefly wondered if they might be part of Reylar's Elves, but then Sindra raised her hand, stopping them. The familiar tingle denoting the spell of tongues washed over him as Elonin used her magic.

"*These Humans,*" Sindra was saying, "*slew my father's murderers. Remove the bodies and give them the treatment due all traitors.*" Her gaze came to rest on the bloodied countenance of Gustavo. "*And send for Master Galrandir. We have need of his healing.*"

She moved to stand before Ludwig. "*I owe you a tremendous debt, Ludwig of Hadenfeld. Tell me how I can repay it.*"

"*You can release me and my men.*"

"*Consider it done. I shall grant you the freedom of the city.*"

"*But not the freedom to go home?*"

"*Not yet. Elonin tells me you have certain ideas where the future is concerned. I would hear more of them.*"

"*Then allow me to extend an invitation for you to visit. Come see us in Eisen, where we would welcome you as guests of honour.*"

"I would be hard-pressed to convince my advisors of my safety within the halls of men."

"Then bring an escort—as many warriors as you please."

"How is it you, who was our prisoner until a moment ago, are now extending the hand of friendship?"

"He is not," said Elonin. *"He presented this same idea to me last night before your father's brazen murder. His actions here prove he truly desires our friendship."*

Having disarmed the bodies, the guards dragged them from the room. Other warriors entered, reporting directly to the talon.

"Conduct these Humans to a place of rest," she ordered. *"They are to be considered honoured guests."*

A gaunt Elf entered the room, his black robes standing out against the guards' white and silver.

"Ah, Master Galrandir," said Sindra. *"Your timing could not be any better."*

"What has happened here, Lady Sindra?"

"That is High Lord Sindra now," said Elonin. *"Her father lays slain at the hand of Lord Reylar."*

"And these... Humans?"

"They came to our rescue," offered Sindra. *"I would have you attend to their wounds."*

The Elf healer bowed. *"Of course, Your Eminence. I shall see to it at once."*

"Just how many mages have you, Eminence?" asked Ludwig.

"That is a discussion for another day. Go and rest. We shall talk again come daylight."

Ludwig awoke with a start, covered in sweat, a victim of the humidity so pervasive in their new quarters. An Elf entered, throwing open the shutters, the sun flooding the room.

"What time is it?" he asked before realizing he could not be understood. He waited for the Elf to leave, then got out of bed and went to the window.

Outside, a walled garden blocked his view of the rest of the city, save for the giant tree atop the hill that dominated the entire area. As the sun caught the leaves, he held his breath at the sheer majesty of it. The door behind him opened.

"Feeling better?" Elonin asked, using the Human tongue.

"Much. Thank you." His hands instinctively went to his throat.

"Do not worry," she soothed. "Master Galrandir treated your injuries."

"And my men?"

"They are well, all of them."

"Where are they?"

"I thought they would appreciate a tour of the city."

"I would have liked to see that myself."

"And you shall have your chance, but there are more pressing matters needing your attention. High Lord Sindra wishes to see you."

"In the great hall?"

"No," replied the talon. "I am to conduct you to her home. I hope that is acceptable?"

"I'm afraid I have little to wear for such an auspicious occasion."

"Then it is fortunate we arranged for more suitable attire." She clapped her hands, and a trio of Elves entered, bearing elegant robes of green and gold along with a water-filled basin.

"I shall give you a chance to dress," Elonin continued, "but do not take long. There is much to discuss."

"I will heed your words," replied Ludwig.

He dressed quickly, meeting Elonin outside. She guided him through the city to Sindra's house, located on the opposite side of the hill from the great hall. This building, too, was of wooden construction, although the wood here was paler, while its shingles were stained green.

Guards stood outside but issued no challenge at their approach and opened the doors for them. Sindra waited inside, sitting on a wide chair that could easily accommodate three. Opposite her were two other seats, and she beckoned them both to take one.

Ludwig sat, unsure of how to proceed, but the new High Lord of Nethendril held no such qualms. "Greetings," she said, using the Human tongue. "No doubt you are wondering what I have decided regarding your fate."

"The thought had crossed my mind," he replied. "Have you decided to accept the hand of friendship?"

"Not yet. Instead, I propose a journey to your land."

"You would be welcome in Eisen."

"I doubt our arrival there would be greeted with enthusiasm without preparation."

"What are you proposing?"

"That Elonin escorts you to the forest's edge. She will then accompany you back to your city to ensure you keep your word."

"Just Elonin?"

"Well, her and a handful of her warriors. Do you accept this offer?"

"I do," replied Ludwig.

"You surprise me. I expected negotiations would be needed. Were I in your place, I would have asked for much more."

"I am earnest in my desire for peace. I assure you we have no territorial ambitions in this region."

"That is not what I heard," said Sindra. "My informants tell me you plan to expand your baronies eastward into the very land we claim as our own."

"How do you know that?"

"We have kept your people under observation since the attack on my father. It is amazing what one can learn with a spell of scrying and of tongues."

"I must speak with my men."

"Do not blame them. They had no way of knowing we were observing them. What concerns me is what you have to say on the matter."

"My king indeed wishes us to push eastward, but now that we know you're here, I'll put an end to such plans."

"And how will you do that? He is your king. Are you not, therefore, forced to follow his wishes in this regard?"

"I believe he'll see reason in the matter. The land itself is of little consequence to us, and having a friendly realm on our borders only makes us safer. If we sign an agreement, he will have no choice but to honour it."

"What kind of agreement are you suggesting?"

"A non-aggression pact to begin with," replied Ludwig. "I propose we agree to respect each other's borders and allow the free exchange of trade goods."

"And how exactly would this trade occur?"

"We'd use the river, provided you agree not to kill us on sight. Perhaps we could set up a trading hub at the source of the Erlen?"

"Erlen? Is that your name for the river we captured you on?"

"It is."

"That would be acceptable, although I will need time to make the necessary arrangements."

"She needs to alert the other cities," explained Elonin, "and that alone could take weeks."

"Then let us start slowly," said Ludwig. "If you provide quill and parchment, I shall draft a proclamation recognizing your borders. Of course, you'll need your own copy written in your language."

"That should not present a problem. The spell of tongues allows us to read and speak your language."

"Does it? I had no idea."

Sindra chuckled. "You Humans are still so naïve when it comes to magic."

"Don't look at me," said Ludwig. "I'm a warrior, not a mage."

"And are you typical of your countrymen?"

"In what way?"

"Are all Humans taught the art of war?"

"No. Only those tasked with defending the realm."

"Interesting," said Elonin. "I would like to learn more about how a Human army functions."

"I shall be happy to show you, though it will prove difficult without my captains."

"Your captains?"

"Yes. You slew them when you attacked our boats. You might remember them: a tall man with a beard and a short woman."

"They are not dead," said Elonin.

A sense of elation bubbled up within Ludwig. "They're not?"

"No. They fled westward. Our border sentinels have watched for their return but saw nothing of them."

"That's a great relief."

"It does, however, raise an important issue. We must get Lord Ludwig back to his lands before an army descends upon our home."

"I agree," said Sindra. "Let us draft this document you spoke of, and then you can leave."

"And my men?"

"I will have them assembled," said Elonin. "We should have you on your way before midday."

Elonin and two hundred Elven warriors led the five Humans through the narrow forest paths. Unlike Ludwig's first trip across the Goldenwood, their pace was much more relaxed. They planned to part at the forest's edge near Eisen, at which time the talon would continue with an honour guard, the intent being for them to remain in Eisen until further notice.

The sun's rays peeked through the thick canopy of leaves for most of the trip, but then a torrential downpour threatened to overwhelm them on the third day. The Elves led them deeper into the forest, constructing shelters to protect them from the rain, a task completed with such speed it astounded Ludwig. They soon sat beneath the trees, watching the rain form into a thick mist.

"Is it always like this?" asked Ludwig.

Elonin, who had taken to casting her spell of tongues each day, simply shrugged. "Tauril can be a fickle mistress at times. One day, she wishes you well: the next, she tests you."

"Tauril is the Goddess of the Woods, isn't she?"

"She is much more than that. She gave life to the Elves."

"And what does she look like?"

"She is all around you, in every tree, plant, even the stones scattered across the forest floor. She lives through the animals native to the region. In a word, she is the balance of all things."

"I'm not sure I understand the concept. Are you suggesting she is everything?"

"No, but she is the caretaker of all things natural. We believe she created the animals and plants that feed us."

"I notice you referred to animals native to the region. Was that an intentional remark or merely a turn of phrase?"

She smiled, an action becoming more common of late. "You pay attention. Many animals live in the forest: bears, wolves, and a host of others you would be familiar with. They are not, however, the only things found beneath the boughs of the Goldenwood."

"Go on."

"Two other types of creatures exist, what we refer to as aberrations and animated constructs. Aberrations are creatures manipulated by some form of intent, such as magic or exposure to intense deposits of ithilium."

"I don't know what that is."

"It is a rare metal, often found in stones that fall from the sky. The metal is prized for its use in constructing weapons, for it can store great magic. In its unrefined state, however, it can cause sickness or even death, but more commonly, it warps that which grows around it."

"And such creatures live in this forest?"

"Yes, though you need not worry. There are none in this particular region." She drew her sword, holding the blade out for him to inspect. "If you look closely, the metal exhibits a remarkable brightness, almost as if it captures light and reflects it back. This is what we call ithilium, though I imagine Humans have a different name for it."

"And is Tauril responsible for that as well?"

"No. That gift comes from Gundar, the God of the Earth and, incidentally, the creator of the Dwarven race."

"How many Gods have you?"

"Dozens, though only seven are greater Gods, the rest we pray to on special occasions. Do your own people not worship the same gods?"

"Some do, but it's more common these days to worship the Saints."

"Yes," said Elonin. "You mentioned them previously. They were Human, were they not?"

"They were, and we don't worship them like we did the Gods. Rather, we take their teachings as guidance to help us make our way through life."

"You are a curious people, made more so by your strange religious practices. All races in the world of Eiddenwerthe used to worship the Gods, even the Orcs, but now Humans have invented their own deities."

"As I said, they're not deities, merely mortal men and women who led by example."

"Perhaps it would be better for my own people to do the same."

"Why do you say that?" asked Ludwig. "Do you not believe in Tauril?"

"There is no denying the existence of the Gods," she replied, "but sometimes I wonder if their message has been diluted through the ages."

"In what way?"

"Our belief tells us we must live in harmony with nature, yet our people suffer. We are now a dwindling race, while Humans expand across the Continent. Perhaps, if we adopted your methods, we, too, would prosper."

"I'm afraid that without children, little would change. One reason we Humans have spread so far is our ability to procreate. Tell me, when was the last time an Elven child was born?"

"Not for more than a thousand years."

"Do your people not..." He blushed.

"Not what?"

"You know, attempt to create babies?"

"Of course, but it only ends in failure."

"Is it some sort of sickness?"

"Determining that has proven difficult for us. Our healers tried all manner of things, but nothing worked. It is a commonly held belief it is the punishment of Erylor, the Goddess of Fertility."

"Why would she punish your people?"

"For past misdeeds. I cannot tell you more without breaking the confidence of my people. I hope you understand?"

"Fear not. I shall not press you on the matter."

"You have a child, have you not?"

"I do," replied Ludwig. "Frederick, named after my late father. I shall introduce you to him once we reach Eisen."

"I look forward to meeting him."

27

RETURN TO EISEN

SPRING 1104 SR

Three days later, they reached the forest's edge to find an army encamped in the fields east of Eisen. It appeared to Ludwig they were preparing to move, for wagons were hitched, and men formed up, ready to march. Elonin halted her warriors, unsure of how to proceed.

"Let me go ahead," said Ludwig. "I don't want there to be any misunderstanding."

"Very well," she replied, "but your men will wait here with us."

"Agreed." He stepped out into the open, half expecting someone to notice him, but the army was so busy, he escaped their attention. The gathered warriors were a mixed bunch, consisting primarily of footmen with a smattering of archers. Horsemen were also present, although he couldn't distinguish whose colours they wore, from his current position. He walked towards them, keeping his gaze on the encampment.

An alert sentry called out an alarm when he was about two hundred paces away. A trio of horsemen galloped towards him, and at any other time, Ludwig would have drawn his sword, but it quickly became obvious who approached.

"Ludwig?" called out Sigwulf. "We thought you dead!"

"I assure you I am in good health."

The northerner slowed, pulling up beside him while his two companions, both warriors, rode slightly past, watching the forest's edge.

"Did anyone else survive?" asked Sigwulf.

"Yes, four others. Yourself?"

"Cyn's back at the camp, as is Father Vernan."

"And the rest?"

"Four made it, though two were badly wounded. They're recovering at the Mathewite mission."

Ludwig nodded towards the camp. "What's all this about?"

"We gathered an army to come seeking retribution, but it appears unnecessary. Or is it?"

"No, it's not. In fact, I'd like you to meet someone." He turned towards the forest and nodded.

Elonin strode forth, the other Human survivors accompanying her. Her warriors moved to the edge of the treeline, their armour glinting in the mid-morning sun. Sigwulf's hand instinctively went to the hilt of his sword.

"Don't worry," said Ludwig. "They're friendly." He waited as the Elf approached. "Allow me to introduce Elonin, Talon of Nethendril, the Kingdom of the Goldenwood. At least, I think that's her full title."

"Greetings," she called out.

"An Elf who speaks our language?" said Sigwulf.

"Only when she casts her spell," said Ludwig. "Elonin is an Enchanter and a warrior. She comes to us as a representative of High Lord Sindra."

"In that case, greetings. I am Sigwulf Marhaven, Captain to His Highness Prince Ludwig."

"Pleased to meet you," said the Elf.

They both stood there, looking uncomfortable.

"This will never do," said Ludwig. "Let's bring everyone back into the city, shall we?"

"What about the army?" asked Sigwulf.

"There's no need for it now. Send them back to their quarters."

"And those Elves at the treeline?"

"They will be our guests."

"You must excuse our display of strength," said Elonin, "but my High Lord thought it best I come with an escort."

"And how many are your escort?"

"Only fifty. The rest will travel back to Nethendril."

"Fifty?" said Sigwulf. "Might I ask why so many?"

"My people are distrustful of Humans. I wanted to bring less, but the High Lord overruled me."

"She is to be our guest at the Royal Keep," said Ludwig. "I'll leave it to you and Cyn to work out where to billet the Elven warriors."

"My people's needs are simple," said Elonin. "The bulk will camp near the woods, with only ten in the keep at any one time, aside from the changing of the guard."

"Are you certain that's all you want?"

"You said it yourself. If we are to gain your trust, then we, in turn, must learn to be trusting of others."

Sigwulf grinned. "Wait till Cyn gets word of this."

"Cyn?"

"Yes," said Ludwig. "She's one of my captains. Now, if you would be so kind as to collect your warriors, we'll escort you to the keep."

"I would be delighted to do so." Elonin turned, walking back to the trees.

"I've been busy," said Ludwig.

"Clearly," replied Sigwulf. "Are you confident we can trust them? They did kill some of our expedition."

"Regrettably, yes, but if we don't move towards peace, then we are no better than they were."

"Peace. I like the sound of that. I'm not sure the king will, though."

"Why wouldn't he?"

"He wants to prove the might of his army, remember? What better way than to launch a campaign against a bunch of Elves?"

"That would be a mistake," said Ludwig. "From what I've seen, they're more than capable of holding us at bay, not to mention they appear to have a lot of mages amongst their numbers."

"Mages? What kinds of mages?"

"Elonin is an Enchanter, and I've witnessed an Earth Mage in action, not to mention a Life Mage. There was also talk of Fire Mages."

"That certainly puts a single Sartellian to shame."

"If we get them on our side, we can guarantee the security of the eastern baronies."

"I'm with you, Ludwig, but I hope you're not taking on more than you can handle."

"And if I am?"

"Then I guess we'll all deal with it together. Cyn and I are with you, whatever you get up to."

"Thank you. I appreciate it. Now, let's see to our guests, shall we?"

Looks of disbelief abounded at the sight of Elves in the city of Eisen. Before they travelled more than a few streets, the townsfolk had gathered in droves to witness the historic event.

Ludwig walked beside Elonin to show everyone they were on the same side. Ten Elven warriors followed, with a corresponding number of Ludwig's men bringing up the rear. Word spread quickly, and by the time they reached the Royal Keep, Cyn had assembled an honour guard to welcome them.

Charlotte stood waiting, young Frederick at her side. Once his father came through the gate, the four-year-old tore himself from his mother's hand, rushing across the courtyard, yelling, "Papa!"

Ludwig stooped to pick him up and was engulfed in a tremendous hug. Elonin halted to stare.

"This," said Ludwig, "is my son, Frederick. Say hello to Elonin, Freddy."

"Elo-nin," he said, then giggled. "She's got pointed ears."

"She's an Elf, which is normal for her people."

The child reached out, and Elonin took his hand in hers. "His skin is so soft. Is that normal for Human children?"

"As far as I know."

"Sorry," called out Charlotte, huffing to catch up.

"My wife, Lady Charlotte," explained Ludwig.

"Greetings, Princess," said Elonin.

"Oh, I'm not a princess, merely a baroness."

"Is your husband not a prince?"

"He is, but I am not of Royal Birth. My father was only a baron."

"Your customs once again confuse me. My pardon if I caused offence."

"None taken. Might I ask how we address you?"

"Elonin will do, or you could address me as my rank, Talon, or, if you prefer, you can use the Human equivalent, which I'm told is captain."

"Then Elonin will do, and you must call me Charlotte. Come inside, and I'll show you around the keep."

Frederick squirmed in his father's arms, so Ludwig put him down. The boy squealed and raced off to catch up to his mother.

"I see someone's excited," said Sigwulf, coming up to stand at Ludwig's side. "He must take after his mother in that regard."

"Are you suggesting I never get excited?"

"I've seen you in battle, Ludwig. You're possibly the calmest person I've ever met."

"Only on the outside, Sig. Only on the outside."

They spent the evening sitting in the great hall, the table laden with food. Elonin picked at the meat as they chatted, making no complaint but clearly not enjoying it. Ludwig made a mental note to speak with the keep's cook about menu options.

"So," said Charlotte. "Tell me about your home, Elonin. Is it much like Eisen?"

"In some ways," replied the Elf. "Our buildings are similar in design to those found here, although we prefer wood to stone."

"I suspect that has more to do with the building materials you have at hand."

"I must admit I am surprised at your acceptance. I was not expecting you to welcome an Elf into your home."

"I was born and raised in a place called Reinwick. A few Elves live in the cities there, primarily merchants."

"But none here?"

"None that I know of," said Charlotte.

"I was aware some of our cousins took up lives in Human cities, but I never met one myself."

"We have this in common. How long do you plan on staying in Eisen?"

"My intent," replied Elonin, "was to remain here for several months, thus allowing me to learn your ways. Your husband thinks the more we understand each other, the more valuable our relationship will become."

"My husband is a wise man."

"I would tend to agree."

"Tell me," said Cyn, "is it true you're an Enchanter?"

"I am," said Elonin. "Why do you ask?"

"Just curiosity. I've never met an Enchanter before. What does your magic do?"

"Enchantment spells enhance something already present. I can make a person stronger or more dexterous for a short period or use my magic to make a weapon deadlier in battle."

"How does that work?"

"There are a variety of ways. I can sharpen the blade to inflict more damage or harden it to penetrate armour better. I can even use magic to make a weapon seem lighter, making it faster in battle. Of course, many of my spells would not necessarily be considered battle spells."

"Such as?"

"The spell of tongues, which I'm currently using to speak your language, or there is far scrye, which allows me to observe things at a distance."

"Are there no limitations to your magic?"

"Magic is limited by the magical energy contained within the caster. Exceed that, and you risk permanent injury."

"I had no idea," said Cyn. "But to be fair, the only mage I ever met was an Earth Mage, and even then, the visit was short."

"Sindra is an Earth Mage. She learned it from her mother."

"Sindra is a woman?" said Charlotte.

"She is, although I fail to see why that surprises you. Do you not have female rulers in Human lands?"

"We do, but they're rare. It's her title that confused me—you called her the High Lord. In our society, we would call her... Actually, I'm not sure what we would call her, perhaps High Lady?"

"We Elves do not differentiate genders in such a manner."

"I'm not suggesting it's wrong," said Charlotte, "merely different from what we're used to."

"We'll all need to adapt in the coming months," said Ludwig, "so I hope you'll forgive us if we make the occasional mistake."

"Will you be meeting the king?" asked Charlotte.

"That was not my intent," replied Elonin.

"Why is that? He is the ruler, after all."

"The High Lord has formed a personal connection with Prince Ludwig, and we prefer to deal with those we trust. Your king is unknown to us, and we do not care to meet him until we learn more about your people."

"A sensible approach. I wish more Humans did the same. The Continent would be far better for it."

"Have you had any dealings with Elven realms in the north?"

"No, but Ludwig might be able to tell you more," replied Charlotte.

"Yes, Commander Charlaine spoke of an Elf named Bethiel."

"I do not know that name," said Elonin, "but I am not the one who maintains contact."

"Who is?"

"You met the Lords of Nethendril. They have a variety of duties they perform in the service of the Goldenwood, one being maintaining contact with our fellow Elves."

"How many kingdoms are there?"

"I am not at liberty to say. It is Sindra's decision whether or not to reveal that information."

"But you're fine with telling us you know about them?"

"That is a simple statement of fact and has no bearing on our relationship."

"Spoken like a true diplomat," said Charlotte. "I can see why your High Lord chose you for this."

"I'm curious," said Ludwig. "Why do you think Bethiel was willing to assist those in the north?"

"She had no choice," said Elonin. "I am unfamiliar with the details, but I would surmise her lands were in danger of being overrun."

"Would an invasion of Hadenfeld be seen as a threat to Nethendril?"

"Most likely, although it is not my decision to make. Are you expecting a war?"

"Eventually. The empire that attacked in the north has been expanding into the Petty Kingdoms for centuries. It's only a matter of time before they attempt the same with us. That's why I support the king's desire to build a bigger army."

"How large is your army?" asked Elonin.

"Theoretically, in the thousands, but only assuming we have time to prepare."

"Prepare?"

"Yes. We have to call up the men. In Hadenfeld, each baron is responsible for fielding four hundred warriors, although that number is substantially reduced in times of peace. We are still required, however, to maintain the arms and armour necessary to equip our assigned complement of men."

"And how many barons have you?"

"Fifteen. Then there's the Royal Army, which falls directly under the king's command. The plan calls for them to number one thousand, although we are yet to reach that."

"I am surprised you talk so openly about your numbers."

"There is nothing to hide," said Ludwig. "Our army is easily the largest in the region; its very size helps keep us safe."

"We Elves have not fought a battle in over two thousand years. I would be interested to see how your army trains."

"Then I will arrange a little demonstration. Perhaps, in return, you might allow your warriors to give us a display of how they fight?"

"That would be most agreeable."

"Excellent. I shall place you into the care of Sigwulf and Cyn, my most trusted captains."

"Captains? I was led to believe they commanded the army massed outside the walls of this very city."

"So they did," said Ludwig. "I suppose that makes them commanders, then."

"Oh goody," said Cyn. "A promotion. Does that come with a raise?"

"We'll discuss the details later."

Elonin turned pale.

"Is something wrong?" asked Charlotte.

"I am afraid I may have eaten too much meat," replied the Elf. "With your permission, I would like to retire to my room."

"By all means. I'll show you there myself." She stood and then came to stand beside Elonin. "This way, if you please." They exited the room.

"Well?" said Ludwig. "What are your impressions, everyone?"

"I like her," said Cyn. "She seems to have an open quality about her."

"I don't agree," said Sigwulf. "I think she's hiding something."

"You think everyone's hiding something."

"Because they usually are."

Ludwig smiled at their banter. "What of you, Father Vernan? You've been particularly quiet since we returned."

"I'll admit I have been. The arrival of these Elves is most curious, but I'm still undecided if their presence here is problematic or beneficial. Their leader, Elonin, speaks quite eloquently of friendship and peace, yet, like Sigwulf, I can't help but feel she's holding something back. A secret, if you will."

"I'd be surprised if they didn't have their own plans," replied Ludwig, "but the challenge for us is ensuring theirs align with ours. They haven't the numbers to attack us, if that's what you're worried about."

"With all due respect," said Sigwulf, "how would you know if they did? It's not as if they'd simply tell us."

"Bollocks," said Cyn. "I can't believe Elonin has any ulterior motives here. I'm good at reading people, and I see no signs of deception."

"Ah," said Father Vernan, "but that's just it, don't you see? You may be good at reading people, but she is an Elf. Putting Human emotions and thoughts into such a race could be a mistake. We have no way of knowing what lurks behind those eyes."

28

BORDER TROUBLE

SUMMER 1104 SR

The heat of summer arrived in full force, and while Eisen sat astride a lake, it did little to cool the keep. Ludwig stood on the battlements, overlooking the calm waters and enjoying the faint breeze that offered a slight reprieve from the oppressive temperature.

Footsteps announced the arrival of a servant. "Your Highness," the man said. "Lord Anson Meier, the Baron of Zwieken, has arrived and seeks an audience. He told me to inform you it is a matter of great import."

Ludwig stared back silently. Ordinarily, he would meet with a baron in his office or the great hall, but he preferred a cooler venue today. "Bring him to me here," he said at last.

"Here, Highness?"

"It's preferable to be cooled by a breeze than forced to sweat in an oven, don't you think?"

"Yes, of course, Highness." The fellow ran off.

Ludwig stared out at the lake, but his mind turned elsewhere. Lord Anson was an older baron who'd stood firmly behind the King of Neuhafen during the last war. Despite those leanings, Ludwig found him to be a straight-talking individual who took his responsibilities as baron seriously. If Anson claimed it a matter of some import, then Ludwig was inclined to believe him.

He pictured a map of the area in his head. Zwieken lay to the north, on the border of Zowenbruch, which, in all probability, meant their northern neighbour was somehow involved.

"Your Highness," came the voice of Lord Anson.

Ludwig turned as the man bowed. "Good to see you again, Baron. I'm told you bring an important matter to discuss?"

"Indeed, Highness." Anson paused, shifting his feet, not meeting Ludwig's gaze.

"Let's dispense with formalities, shall we? Tell me what's on your mind and be blunt. I sense we haven't time for frivolities."

"I was approached, Highness."

"By?"

"Agents of Konrad the Fourth, King of Zowenbruch."

"I feared as much when I heard you were here. Go on."

"His Majesty wishes me to talk to the other barons of Neuhafen and convince them to swear allegiance to him."

"He knows Neuhafen is no longer a kingdom, doesn't he?"

"Most certainly, but those were the words his agent used. He obviously believes we are in a weakened state after our recent war."

"And so he seeks to drive a wedge between us," said Ludwig. "How did you respond to this request?"

"I sought to buy us some time by pretending to agree. In the guise of seeking the other barons' opinions, I came straight here to give you fair warning."

"You think he intends to invade?"

"There can be little doubt, Highness. I have received reports of him massing an army across the river, although I have no exact numbers concerning their strength."

"There has always been tension between Hadenfeld and Zowenbruch."

"Might I ask why the animosity? I know Neuhafen had its share of disagreements; we even went to war, but why Hadenfeld?"

"It all comes down to politics," said Ludwig. "As you know, the Petty Kingdoms comprise a complex web of alliances. We are allied with Deisenbach, which lies west of Zowenbruch, but more importantly, we are also allied with Erlingen on their northern border. In their mind, they are surrounded by potential enemies."

"Would it not make more sense for them to seek peace?"

"Perhaps, but if they claimed our eastern baronies, it would severely weaken us." It suddenly occurred to him there might be another reason. "What do you know of Konrad's court?"

"Very little, I'm afraid. Why?"

"There's a good chance these notions of expansion result from outside influence."

"Who? The empire?"

"No, at least not directly, but it would certainly serve their interests to see us weakened."

"Then who?"

"Have you ever heard of anyone named Stormwind or Sartellian?"

"Of course. They're influential members of courts across the Petty Kingdoms." Lord Anson hesitated. "Are you implying they are involved somehow?"

"I have it on good authority they serve the interests of Halvaria."

"Are you certain? Perhaps your source is mistaken?"

"No," said Ludwig. "It comes directly from a Temple Commander."

"Ah, well. If you can't trust a Cunar, who can you?"

"Not a Cunar—a Temple Commander of Saint Agnes."

"Then I shall take her at her word, as you clearly have. My question to you, Highness, is how we respond?"

"I will meet with my advisors and see if we can't devise a plan of action."

"And King Morgan?"

"I'll send word to him, but I fear the matter will be resolved one way or the other long before he sends men to aid us. I'm afraid we're on our own as far as the immediate threat is concerned."

"What can I do to help?"

"Return to Zwieken and stall for as long as possible."

"And how do I do that?"

"By delaying your response to King Konrad's overtures."

"And if he should march?"

"Then you must do all you can to slow down his advance."

Lord Anson smiled. "You intend to use the same strategy they did in eighty-five."

"It's the most logical course of action."

"It is, but I doubt Zowenbruch will be as unprepared as the last time."

"Nor do I. If you'll excuse me, Lord Anson, I must call together my advisors."

Ludwig looked around the table. Charlotte sat on his right, with Cyn and Siggy beside her. Opposite them was Father Vernan, along with Elonin. Since her arrival, the Elf had spent most of her time at the Royal Keep. When she wasn't observing the training of Ludwig's men, she read all she could find on Human history. Her visit had been uplifting, with as much curiosity from the Humans as the Elves.

"Well?" said Ludwig. "Your thoughts?"

Father Vernan cleared his throat. "You outlined your concerns, Highness, but couldn't this be a diplomatic offensive trying to capitalize on our unrest?"

"Then why mass an army near our border?"

"You make a good point. If what you say is true, it bears a remarkable similarity to the eighty-five incursion. Konrad has little choice but to capture Zwieken and Valksburg before marching to Eisen. What is your plan to counter that?"

"That's precisely why I asked all of you here," said Ludwig. "Let's start with you, Sigwulf."

"I say we gather our forces and march directly for Zwieken. It's better to mass there and oppose the river crossing than meet them in an open field. Hopefully, the few companies here, combined with the garrison of Zwieken, can hold them off indefinitely."

"I disagree," said Cyn. "We don't have much in Eisen, so we'll need to gather our forces. By the time that's done, they'll already be across the river. It's best if we mass here, then march up the road to intercept them."

"That's what they did in eighty-five," said Father Vernan. "They attacked at night and, in the confusion, captured the enemy's king. It was called the Battle of Shadows. Their king's ransom gave a hefty boost to the coffers of Neuhafen. Without those coins, the recent war of reunification would never have been funded."

"All this is interesting," said Charlotte, "but let's begin with the fundamentals, being exactly how many warriors are at our disposal?"

"Well," said Ludwig, tapping his fingers on his chin. "I think we can safely assume the forces of Zwieken and Valksburg will be busy in the north, leaving us with the men of Dornbruck, Langeven, and Eisen."

"You forget Tongrin and Ramfelden," added Cyn. "They might be small, but they don't want to see us overrun any more than you do. Then there's the barons of Arnsbach and Udenacht, not to mention those west of the river."

"I take your point concerning Tongrin and Ramfelden, but I doubt the others will deign to send help."

"Why is that?"

"If you recall, they were part of the baron's alliance in the south, which tried to incite a war with Hollenbeck. The same campaign, I might add, that was overseen by a Sartellian. Even if they did send men, I'm not sure we could trust them."

"So what does that leave us?"

"Dornbruck and Langeven will form the backbone, each supplying three hundred and fifty men, to which we'll add the Royal Garrison here in Eisen, along with my own three companies. I'll send word to Verfeld for additional men, but I doubt they'll arrive in time."

"There is also the cavalry we're training," said Sigwulf, "giving us another hundred men. Let's see—that brings our total in Eisen to…"

"Three hundred," said Cyn.

"Three hundred and fifty," added Father Vernan. "You're forgetting about the Temple Knights of Saint Mathew."

"They agreed to train our horsemen, not go to war."

"True, but things are changing in the north, and the order's new Temple Captain is most eager to play his part."

"New Temple Captain?" said Ludwig.

"Yes. I believe you know Temple Captain Hamelyn, the same fellow who accompanied you north to Reinwick, although he was only a Temple Knight then."

"When did he arrive?"

"A week ago. It all makes perfect sense when you think about it. You offered to let them set up a commandery in Eisen, and you can't have that many Temple Knights without someone to command them."

"Of course, I should have realized. I know they've dedicated knights to help train our cavalry, but how many men have they in total?"

"A full company, which, if I'm not mistaken, numbers fifty."

"That's a nice addition," said Ludwig, "but still leaves us short."

"That gives us over a thousand men," said Sigwulf.

"It does, but Konrad is no fool. He wouldn't invade without twice that, perhaps more."

"You forgot to include Tongrin and Ramfelden," said Cyn. "That's no more than a few companies, but every little bit makes a difference."

"What if I found you more?" asked Elonin.

Everyone looked at the Elf in surprise.

"I thought you were here as an observer," said Father Vernan.

"Your realm is threatened. If you fail, so does our hope of everlasting peace."

"Even if you could help," said Ludwig, "you'd have to travel back to Nethendril, raise the required troops, then return to us. The invasion would be over by then."

"You fail to consider my magic. Since arriving here, I have contacted High Lord Sindra daily. Providing she agrees, warriors could be marching by sunrise tomorrow."

"IF she agrees," said Father Vernan. "There's no guarantee she will, and why would there be? It's not as if the Elves are in danger of invasion."

"What you say is true," replied Elonin, "yet you neglect to consider the ramifications of your defeat. If this foreign king accomplishes his objectives, we will again find a potential threat on our borders. We have expended considerable effort to understand your people. The last thing we want is to be forced to start again."

"How do we know we can trust you?" asked Sigwulf. "Your people attacked when we last entered the Goldenwood. They could easily turn on us at a critical moment."

"Trust goes both ways. By your own logic, you Humans could turn on us."

"She's right," said Charlotte, "but we need them. Without their assistance, we face the prospect of almost certain defeat. With their help, we stand a chance of actually winning."

"Well," said Father Vernan, "that largely depends on how many warriors they send."

"I pledge my own company right now," said Elonin, "and hope to have an answer about the rest this evening."

"And if your High Lord agrees, how long will it take them to march to Eisen?"

"I suspect they would be here before your barons of Dornbruck or Langeven arrive."

"I assume you would command them?"

"Most likely."

"That would be greatly appreciated," said Ludwig. "If you need anything to convince the High Lord, please don't hesitate to ask."

Elonin rose. "With your permission, I will retire to my quarters. I shall seek you out once I learn her response."

With that, she departed, leaving the others to carry on.

"What do we know of Zowenbruch?" asked Sigwulf. "Have we any idea what their army consists of?"

"I suspect it's very similar to the Army of Hadenfeld," replied Ludwig. "Father Vernan has read extensively on the subject. Perhaps he'd care to add more?"

"I should be delighted," said the Holy Father, sitting up in his chair. "As His Highness suggested, it is similar to that found in Morgan's army. During the invasion of eighty-five, Zowenbruch's army was structured around the barons, each providing similar numbers to what we see here."

"That being?"

"Somewhere in the region of three to four hundred apiece, the difference being Zowenbruch has more baronies than us."

"How many more?" asked Cyn.

"I'm afraid I have no definite numbers, but I should think twenty or so is a reasonable assumption, giving Konrad six to eight thousand men. Even if he left a significant portion back home to guard his borders, we're still looking at three to four thousand men. The odds are not in our favour."

"You forget," said Charlotte, "they will be forced to garrison Zwieken and Valksburg, reducing their numbers."

"What do you think a suitable garrison for those towns?" Cyn asked.

"One hundred each, or slightly more, but I'm afraid, even with that further reduction, they still outnumber us by a wide margin."

"Then we must rely on superior tactics," said Ludwig.

"Which are?" asked Charlotte.

"I wish I could say, but until I've seen our army assembled, I won't know what we're capable of. We must also trouble ourselves with the possibility that some of our barons might decide to accept Konrad as their king."

"Surely you don't think Emmett would turn?"

"No," replied Ludwig. "I have no fears where he's concerned. It's the barons of Zwieken and Valksburg which worry me."

"They have given you no reason to think they're disloyal," said Father Vernan.

"True, but their towns will likely be put to the torch if they don't surrender. Were I in their shoes, I'd have difficulty sacrificing my people for a distant king. Saints know, Morgan hasn't exactly endeared himself to them."

"Where do we proceed from here?" asked the Holy Father.

"I'll send word today for the barons to gather their forces and march for Eisen. We'll hold off on any further plans till they arrive. Until then, we'll dispatch scouts north to watch for the Army of Zowenbruch."

"Perhaps they will reconsider invading?" offered Sig.

"I hope you're right," said Ludwig, "but I shan't gamble away lives on hope. We'll prepare for war and pray it won't prove necessary."

Ludwig lay awake, staring into nothingness. War was coming, and he was ill-prepared to fight. If he were farther west, the Army of Hadenfeld could have held off the enemy, but being in the east meant he was forced to deal with under-manned garrisons and barons whose loyalty was in question. His own insecurity added to his problems. He'd fought in battle, even commanded his own companies at the Battle of Harlingen, but that was completely different from commanding an entire army. Was his legacy to be remembered as the man who lost half the kingdom?

His wife gently placed her hand on his chest. "You're worried."

"Can you blame me? We are on the knife edge of history; one false move, and we shall be ruined."

"You must have faith, Ludwig. The Saints saw fit to place you here in this moment. Surely you can see that?"

"I'm here because I ruined Morgan's plans in the south."

"No. You prevented a war, one that would have killed hundreds of innocents. I see the work of the Saints in you, even if you do not."

"Would that it were so."

Charlotte sat up. "Charlaine kept the empire's forces at bay, did she not?"

"She did. What of it?"

"She'd be the first person to tell you it was the will of Saint Agnes. She was where she was meant to be at that exact moment. That's far more than mere coincidence."

"I am no Temple Commander."

"No, you are not. You're a prince, and like a Temple Commander, you take your responsibilities seriously. Just as Charlaine was, you are in the right place at the right time to save this land and hopefully gain a valuable ally. Did you not say the Elves helped in the north?"

"I did."

"Then what more proof is necessary for you to recognize this is an act of divine providence?"

"When did you become so smart?"

"When I married you. Now, stop worrying and go to sleep. It's getting late."

29

INVASION
SUMMER 1104 SR

Ludwig fretted throughout the two weeks that the army assembled. With the news that Zwieken was under attack, the invasion was no longer only a threat. A messenger had taken four days to reach Eisen, meaning the town had already fallen when he walked into the Royal Keep.

The barons responded quickly, with Lord Emmett's men first to arrive. Next came the people of Langeven, followed by two companies of foot from Tongrin and Udenacht.

Elonin had promised the Elves' support, but Sindra did not specify how many warriors they were sending. The Elven talon led a well-armoured and experienced company, but more were needed.

The forces of the Goldenwood arrived just as Ludwig had decided to march without them. In addition to those of Elonin, the High Lord of Nethendril supplied a further company of foot, two companies of cavalry, and two of archers armed with armour-piercing Elven bows. Even more welcome was the arrival of Galrandir, the Elven Life Mage. He, along with Elonin, gave them access to magic, which could well tip the balance when it came to battle.

With the army assembled, Ludwig rode through the lines, looking them over. Most were nervous, which was to be expected, but the seasoned veterans remained calm and collected, their example soon spreading amongst the rest.

He occasionally stopped and chatted with the men, knowing these small gestures inspired confidence. By the time he reached the Temple Knights, his foot soldiers were eager to meet the enemy.

Unlike their Cunar brothers, the Temple Knights of Saint Mathew eschewed plate armour, wearing simple mail shirts and using axes. Their brown surcoats stood out amongst the other men's sea of colour, but there was no doubt as to their effectiveness, for they were well-disciplined, their horses well-trained. Ludwig was proud to call them part of his command.

He moved on to inspect the Elven cavalry, whose slender, snow-white horses hid a keen intelligence behind their eyes. Armed with spears and swords, the riders wore the silver scale armour he'd first seen in the Goldenwood.

The Elven warriors on foot bore swords and shields, but instead of the lighter silver scales of their brethren, the chain links they wore shone as bright as the sun reflecting off the lake. They stood rigidly as Ludwig passed, and then he was amongst the Elven archers, whose blank expressions stared back at him. While their foot soldiers wore helmets covering their faces, these bowmen wore no such protection, going bareheaded.

Once finished his inspection, Ludwig rode to the head of the army. The order of march had been decided long before today, so he told Sigwulf and Cyn to carry on.

The Elven horse led, their mounts well-suited to screening an army, spreading out once underway, keeping watch for any sign of the enemy, ready to raise the alert if necessary.

Ludwig had divided his army into four parts. The men of Dornbruck, following in the cavalry screen's wake, formed the vanguard, ready to fight at a moment's notice. Next came the main guard, consisting of the men under the direct command of Ludwig: his own baronial troops, the garrison of Eisen, and his mounted troops, including the Temple Knights. Just behind them, the remaining Elves followed at fifty paces. The men of Langeven led the rearguard, joined by those from Tongrin and Udenacht.

In addition, Father Vernan had organized a second army of wagons and horses loaded with provisions to feed everyone.

As they marched past, Ludwig felt a mix of pride and foreboding. How many would die in the coming battle? How many would never see their loved ones again? Would he himself be doomed to fall in a field in the middle of nowhere, his passing a mere footnote to history?

He tried to shake off his dire thoughts, but it was difficult. Desperate, he reached into his pouch, pulling forth the soft, worn book Lady Rosalyn had given him. It was not the complete Book of Saint Mathew but a collection of his writings, yet he found it comforting in times of need.

Today, it caused him to think of Charlotte, and that, in turn, reminded him of her words. Was he destined to be here at this particular moment? He believed it of Charlaine; why not himself? Was he merely a tool of the Saints? The thought made him want to scream in frustration, but then reason took hold. His actions led him here, not the machinations of a long-dead Saint. If that was considered fate, then so be it. He would embrace it with all his heart, doing his utmost to save his people.

He stared down at the book clutched in his hand. He called them his people, but he was a prince, not a king, having sworn to serve Morgan. What right did he have to claim otherwise?

A horseman approached, and he looked up to see Temple Captain Hamelyn.

"Greetings, Highness. I trust all is well?"

"As well as can be expected," replied Ludwig.

The knight's gaze wandered to the book. "Is that the Book of Mathew?"

"Merely some of his writings."

"You say 'merely' as if they are of no consequence. In my experience, everything our precious Saint wrote holds profound truths."

"And what does he say about war?"

"Quite a bit. He was a modest man but certainly saw more than his fair share of battles."

"I find that surprising," said Ludwig. "I was under the impression Cunar Marthune was the more experienced warrior."

"His followers want you to believe that, but there's far more to the story than what is found in the Holy texts."

"Is it not his order that commands the Holy Army?"

"It is," replied Hamelyn, "and I'm not trying to diminish the accomplishments of another Saint. By all accounts, Cunar was a master of strategy and tactics, but the individual fighting ability of Mathew was second only to Ragnar."

"I don't know much about Saint Ragnar. I know his name, and that he's one of the six Saints, but the Church is not very forthcoming regarding the details of his life."

"His was a life of pain, for his sister succumbed to the lure of Necromancy. He tracked down her group and wiped them out but could not cleanse her. He dedicated the rest of his life to eliminating those who practiced the dark arts. They were actually the first Temple Knights."

"I had no idea. Why is it I've never heard about their battles?"

"They wage their battles on a smaller scale, hidden from sight of the common man. One-on-one, they are the finest warriors on the Continent, but few remain these days."

"Because they defeated Necromancy?"

"No, because only a few choose this calling. Everyone knows the empire is at our door; those joining the Temple Knights these days primarily wish to join the Cunars."

"Your order appears to have done all right for itself."

"That's because more people pray to Saint Mathew than any other Saint. That doesn't, however, mean our Temple Knights are more numerous."

"But you're not the smallest, surely?"

"No. If you were to rank us by numbers, it would put us in third place, below the Temple Knights of Saint Agnes. There is always hope our fortunes will improve."

"Fortunes?" said Ludwig with a grin. "Don't your people take a vow of poverty?"

"We do, as you well know, which makes it hard to compete with the Cunars, what with their fancy armour and large warhorses."

"I, for one, am glad you're with us, though I am surprised."

"How so?" said Hamelyn.

"In the past, your order refrained from getting involved in politics."

"True, and the Church itself still follows that particular belief, but our order has come to realize if we don't fight to protect what's right, we are all doomed. If permitted a victory, the empire certainly wouldn't allow our continued existence. We've fought them twice now."

"Twice?"

"Yes, once in Reinwick and again in Arnsfeld. We may not be a large order, but we stand arm in arm with the Temple Knights of Saint Agnes."

"But not the Cunars?" Ludwig noted Hamelyn's mild look of annoyance. Charlaine had hinted the Cunars actively tried interfering with the campaign up north. Could the same happen here? It suddenly occurred to him there might be Cunars amongst the enemy warriors. He noticed the Temple Captain staring at him as if waiting for a reply.

"I'm sorry," said Ludwig. "Did you say something?"

"I wondered why you would ask that. Have you heard something?"

"Nothing, really. Just rumours."

"What kinds of rumours?"

"The Temple Knights of Saint Cunar were causing some friction up north."

"I know nothing of that," said Hamelyn, "and if I did, I would not repeat it here."

"Understood. I shall speak no more on the subject."

"That is most kind of you." The knight lowered his voice. "If you run across any Cunars, though, you might refrain from telling them of our participation in this campaign."

Ludwig chuckled. "It seems the Church has its secrets just like the rest of us."

. . .

They camped twenty miles outside Eisen that night. From Ludwig's point of view, it was a decent accomplishment, especially considering they'd arranged it all on relatively short notice. Campfires were lit, sentries posted, and everyone settled in for a restful night.

The Elven cavalry returned with the news the enemy marched in force. They had taken Zwieken and proceeded without delay, putting them well within a day's march of Ludwig's present position.

With orders given, and the captains assembled, Ludwig faced the decision he had been avoiding. The army would fight tomorrow, and he had to determine how to position it.

They gathered at midnight: Ludwig, Cyn, Sigwulf, Elonin, Temple Captain Hamelyn, and Father Vernan, and by the light of a single lantern, they plotted.

Father Vernan had quickly sketched the area, Ludwig using this as a reference. "Neither the hills to the west nor the forest to the right guarantees us much safety."

"Allow us to guard the woods," offered Elonin. "Our archers are most effective when loosing from the cover of trees."

"I'm more concerned with those hills." Temple Captain Hamelyn pointed at the map. "If they get horsemen in there, they'll outflank us."

An image crystallized in Ludwig's mind. "These hills may be just what we need." He turned to Elonin. "What did your scouts discover about the enemy?"

"They march in three large formations, much like us, but their numbers are greater."

"And have they many horsemen?"

"They had some heavily armoured riders they kept to the rear of their formation."

"Probably knights," said Hamelyn. "I believe they call them the Knights of the Golden Chalice, a reference to the cup of wine shared the first time the Saints met."

"The Saints?" said Elonin. "Does that make them a religious order?"

"No. They serve King Konrad, not the Church. I doubt they possess the discipline required of an order of Temple Knights."

"How many knights do they have?" asked Ludwig.

Hamelyn thought it over. "The entire order hovers around a hundred and fifty. Of course, the numbers fluctuate, so I can't give you an accurate count."

"My riders counted no more than a hundred," offered Elonin.

Ludwig recognized an opportunity. "And you saw no other horsemen?"

"Only their leaders. Of these, the largest group gathered around King

Konrad. At least, I assume that was who he was. Shall I use my magic to confirm it?"

"You can do that?"

"Yes, but it will take time. I do not know the king personally, so I must begin by looking down on ourselves, then move my point of view."

"How long will that take?"

"That largely depends on how far away they are."

"What do you need?"

"Merely a reflecting surface," said Elonin.

"Let me know what you see."

The Elf left them to cast her spell.

"What is it you're thinking?" asked Cyn.

"They significantly outnumber us, but we can try using subterfuge to even out the odds."

"How, exactly?"

"I want them to think the bulk of our cavalry is in those hills, but instead, they'll be hidden in the forest on our eastern flank. The aim is to draw them in, past those woods, then hit them from behind. We must somehow lure their knights to those hills to the west."

"Allow us the honour," said Hamelyn. "I shall take the Temple Knights and carry out this ruse while you mass your horsemen to the east. Will that suffice?"

"It should," said Ludwig. "With the knights distracted, they'll have nothing to counter our cavalry. It's a gamble, but if our horse reach Konrad, we might end this battle with minimal bloodshed."

"And if we don't?"

"They take Eisen, and then Morgan turns his full attention on reclaiming his land. He'd eventually succeed, but I shudder at how many lives would be lost."

"It's a risky plan," said Sigwulf, "but it's not the first time we've taken a great risk, nor the first time we've tried to capture a king."

"Truly?" said Hamelyn.

"Has Ludwig never told you about the King of Andover?"

"He has not."

"Another time," said Ludwig. "We should focus on more important matters."

"I assume," said Cyn, "you want the archers stationed to the rear of the footmen?"

"I do, but before we start, I wonder if you might ask Lord Emmett and Lord Merten to join me. There are matters I need to discuss with them.

"I'll send them right over."

"The rest of you had best get moving. The men must be in position by morning.

Ludwig fretted. Fighting a battle involved so much risk. What if the enemy anticipated his strategy? What if his plan failed to fool them? What if Konrad's strategy was superior to their own? Despite feeling overwhelmed, he also felt alive. The fate of Hadenfeld lay on his shoulders, the lives of hundreds affected by his choices. Would he be remembered as a butcher of men or the saviour of Hadenfeld?

He thought back to the battlefield in Erlingen—a desperate affair, but in the end, he'd won through to the King of Andover and ended the invasion. It was a great victory, yet the faces of the dead still haunted him.

The same sort of thing happened at the Battle of Harlingen. A moment of clarity amidst the carnage of war was all he'd needed to save the day. Looking back, he saw it for what it was—reckless abandon. How many of those men would still be alive if they'd remained in place? His thoughts darkened as he imagined himself standing in the Underworld surrounded by those he'd lost in battle. The vision threatened to overwhelm him.

Lord Emmett cleared his throat. "You wanted to see us?"

Ludwig shook off the gloom. Lords Emmett and Merten stood waiting before him, but it took him a moment to gather his thoughts.

"We shall see battle tomorrow," he began, "and I must ensure everyone does their part." Ludwig held up his hand to forestall any argument. "I'm confident you'll both do what's necessary, but in every battle, there's always the possibility a commander might fall. If that happens, command falls to Temple Captain Hamelyn."

"Are you certain?" asked Lord Merten. "It's highly unusual to name a Temple Knight as an army commander."

"It is, but Temple Knights train for this sort of thing. I want your promise you will support him in this, should it prove necessary."

Lord Merten bowed. "Of course, Highness. I give you my word."

Ludwig waited on Emmett, yet the fellow was hesitant to speak.

"Please, Emmett. If I am to have a clear head tomorrow, I need to know you support my decision."

"I do," he said at last, "and I'll make sure Charlotte and Frederick are taken care of. You have my promise."

"Thank you, both of you. It is an honour to serve with you."

30

BATTLE

SUMMER 1104 SR

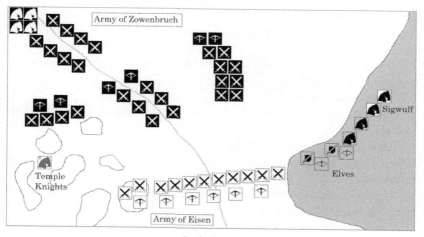

Battle of Eisen

Dawn came far too early for Ludwig. He'd barely gotten his troops in order as the rising sun revealed a line of red heading directly towards them.

Elonin had confirmed the enemy was short of cavalry, but they still outnumbered his meagre force. He fought down the impulse to turn and run. The Royal Keep at Eisen would hold this army at bay, but the city had no wall to protect it. If he were to do that, he'd abandon the people to the enemy's mercy.

He noted the unease of those around him. The men formed a line, anchored on the east by the woods where the Elves and his cavalry were concealed. He took a terrible gamble, for the horses were almost useless amongst the thick foliage, yet he saw no other way to outmanoeuvre his enemy.

In the hills to the west, he'd placed three companies of men to anchor that end of his line, but he knew the Temple Knights were out there somewhere, ready to lure the enemy onto the uneven ground. It wasn't the best terrain for cavalry, but Temple Captain Hamelyn understood the risks. Now Ludwig must do his part to prevent the line from collapsing under the press of the enemy foot.

At first, he thought the Army of Zowenbruch advanced in one solid mass, but as they drew closer, he realized they'd broken into four columns. Two led, with a third following close behind, while the last, barely in sight, advanced on the hills.

"Frightening, isn't it?" said Father Vernan.

"Is this your first battle?"

"I was at the Battle of Harlingen, but I was too busy preparing for the wounded to see anything."

"What do you make of it?"

"They are an impressive force. Are you certain we'll be able to stand up to them?"

"That's my intention." Ludwig turned to Elonin, standing ten paces behind him, her attention fixed on a small mirror. "Any news?" he called out.

"He has committed almost a quarter of his foot to clearing the hills. I fear your Temple Knights will be hard-pressed to hold them back."

"And King Konrad?"

"At the rear, along with his reserve. His knights are stationary."

"I doubt he'll commit them till he sees the chance of a breakthrough. The die is cast. It's only a matter of waiting for its inevitable conclusion."

"You sound as though you know exactly how this will unfold."

"No, only that we have reached the point where we are fully committed. We cannot change plans now, even if we wanted to. We must see it through and hope we outsmart our adversary."

"Then, with your permission, I shall join my warriors. Good luck, Highness. I hope we meet again."

He watched her leave, then turned to Father Vernan. "A prayer, Father?"

The Holy Father closed his eyes, gathering his thoughts. "Oh, gracious

Saint," he began. "Look down upon us with favour this day as we strive to help those who cannot help themselves. Guide us in our time of need so that we might see our way to victory in your name. Saints be with us."

"Saints be with us all," replied Ludwig.

The enemy advance continued, the columns drawing inevitably closer until Ludwig could discern the faces of individual soldiers. Konrad had placed his lighter troops in front, armed with throwing spears and axes, an ancient tactic most armies had abandoned centuries ago. They appeared young, with a thirst for battle and a sense of invulnerability that often came with men their age.

Ludwig could see nothing of what transpired to the west, for the very hills giving his Temple Knights their advantage also hid them from view.

Arrows flew from the forest, drawing first blood. The Elves poured volley after volley into the enemy's easternmost column to significant effect. Zowenbruch's screening force broke, leaving their mailed warriors to continue the advance.

Ludwig tore his gaze away from the assault as Cyn prepared her archers. They might not have the range of the mighty Elven bows, but were ready to tear into the enemy before they reached Ludwig's footmen.

The western column loosed axes and spears, doing little damage, and then the lighter skirmishers parted, allowing the Zowenbruch footmen to emerge unscathed.

Cyn gave the command, and arrows flew, but the effect was negligible. Ludwig held his breath as the armies met, and then the melee was in full swing.

The battle devolved into one mass of warriors pressing against the other, spears jabbing out as swords swung back. The clash of metal on metal grew louder, drowning out voices as they fought for their very lives.

Ludwig wanted to be there with his men, swinging his sword in defence of his home, but as a commander, he must suppress his own desires for the greater good. He needed to keep a clear head, not get lost in the moment.

The enemy advanced in two columns, but instead of spreading out along the line after contact, they remained in formation, exposing their flanks. He thought it to be a trap, but the more he watched, the more he became convinced it was bad planning on their part. They were disciplined but lacked initiative, a quality his troops were willing to demonstrate.

There was the risk that the Temple Knights couldn't halt the advance on the western flank, but trusting them to do their duty, he ordered his footmen to advance, overlapping the enemy column's flank.

The melee expanded, and Ludwig wished he'd kept Elonin close by if only to monitor the progress of his Temple Knights. He kept glancing west, sure hordes of red-clad warriors would sweep into his rear at any moment, yet he saw nothing.

His thoughts turned to the east, and he worried about his cavalry advance. Sigwulf commanded them, waiting to move out when Elonin informed him the enemy knights were committed, but he found the wait unbearable.

His view of the immediate area from atop his mount was excellent. His own line held, even advancing to envelop one flank, but the enemy still held the numerical advantage. He spotted white amongst the red of Konrad's forces as Elven warriors broke from the trees, hitting them on the eastern flank. Elven archers soon joined them, lining up in the open, loosing volley after volley into the unsuspecting enemy.

His footmen thinned. It was a simple matter of attrition, yet he knew they couldn't trade casualties. He'd kept two companies in reserve but now ordered them forward, his last attempt to stop the invaders from breaking through.

Trumpets blared in the distance, and then a colourful mix of enemy knights raced towards the hills. Temple Captain Hamelyn had done his job, and now it was up to Sigwulf to carry out his before it was too late.

Sigwulf moved his horsemen to the forest edge while, in the distance, the enemy columns struggled to push back Ludwig's army. Off to his left, Elonin sat astride her horse, her Elven cavalry ready to leap into action. Staring into a small mirror, she used magic to observe the battle from above. Then, she put it away, looked at him, and nodded.

The cavalry of Hadenfeld advanced out of the trees, forming into lines. Elonin led her riders westward, striking towards the rear of the enemy column and ignoring Zowenbruch's reserve, but if Konrad committed the remainder of his army, he might still win the day. Sigwulf followed her example, leading his small command in the same direction.

Ludwig watched in horror as his line began to crumble. He cast around, looking for someone to plug the gap, but no one remained unengaged. Then he spotted Cyn, leading the archers forward into the vicious hand-to-hand conflict raging along the line. This was their last gamble—they faced certain disaster if it failed.

Banners appeared behind the men of Zowenbruch, and he realized what was happening. The Elvish cavalry had charged into the mass of red-coated footmen, their swords rising and falling with great precision. Blood splattered their silver armour, staining their white cloaks, but the blades continued. Sigwulf's horsemen joined them, carving into the rear of the enemy's columns and cutting off any chance of escape.

With nothing left to direct, Ludwig rode westward, hoping for a sign of his knights. As he topped a rise, he spotted the Temple Knights of Saint Mathew between two hills, their horses drawn up in a line. Opposite them, to the west, were Konrad's knights, but rather than advancing to attack, they remained stationary.

He struggled to understand why when what looked to be their commander rode forward and bowed to the Temple Knights. Ludwig couldn't believe his eyes—the Knights of the Golden Chalice refused to engage. Their leader returned to his brethren, and then the Knights of Zowenbruch turned, retreating north to their king.

Ludwig rode back to his men, but little was left to do. The massive enemy army marching to destroy him was now in tatters. Men of Zowenbruch threw down their arms while others cried out for mercy. The stench of death hung heavy in the air, and he struggled to keep the contents of his stomach from heaving. The thought of having to bury all the dead overwhelmed him.

Covered in blood, Cyn made her way towards him. "The victory is yours," she yelled, though her voice was hoarse.

"Another like this, and we'll have no army left," he replied.

Only the screams of the wounded pierced the silence hanging over the battlefield. It was as if every single person involved had simply run out of strength. Men threw themselves on the ground, too exhausted to continue, their horses seeming just as affected.

Ludwig spotted a solitary figure galloping towards him. "Father Vernan," he called out. "I was wondering where you got to."

"They've given up, Highness. King Konrad asks for a parley."

"Then I'd best see what he wants."

Ludwig let Vernan lead as they rode past what remained of the enemy columns, the survivors' faces wearing a look of utter defeat. Just past the bloodied field where the road ran northwest, King Konrad sat on his horse, accompanied by a single knight and a herald.

Ludwig halted ten paces away, saying nothing as he eyed the King of

Zowenbruch, trying to take the measure of the man. He appeared of a similar age to Ludwig, though perhaps a little taller. His ornate armour, from his golden spurs to the battle crown worn atop his helmet, glowed in the sunlight. Considering the magnitude of his defeat, he was surprisingly composed.

"Who are you?" asked Konrad.

"Ludwig Altenburg, Prince of Hadenfeld."

"I am here to discuss terms."

"You agree to surrender?"

Konrad laughed. "Surrender? I think you overestimate your success."

"We crushed your army," replied Ludwig.

"I still have my reserve."

"You asked for this parley. What do you want?"

"Allow me to retrieve my wounded. In return, I shall march back across the border and agree never to return."

"And if I refuse?"

"Then my men and I will make a stand with whatever forces remain. You might defeat us, but your losses will be so great you'll cripple your king's plans for expansion."

"How do I know you're a man of your word?"

"You don't, just as I don't know if you can be trusted not to turn on me as I gather my wounded."

Ludwig urged his mount forward, stopped beside Konrad, removed his glove, and held out his hand. "I accept your offer, provided you will take my hand in friendship."

"Friendship? Why would you seek such a thing from an invader?"

"It is my belief someone coerced you into this invasion."

"Why would you think that?"

"We narrowly avoided the same fate a short while ago. Have you a mage at court advising you by the name of Sartellian? Or perhaps Stormwind?"

Konrad did not even try to hide his surprise. "How in the name of the Saints did you know that?"

"They work on behalf of Halvaria and are not to be trusted."

"Surely you jest. They are the most influential mages on the Continent."

"Then it is time we banish them from our courts. I will not demand this of you, Majesty, but I would seriously consider sending them away if I were you."

Konrad stared off to where the dead were being collected. His face looked drawn as if all his strength had left him. He held out his hand, shaking Ludwig's. "I shall heed your advice, Highness, though it may cost me allies."

"Then let us start fresh. You and Morgan are both new rulers. It's time to set aside past differences and work together for the betterment of our people."

"What are you suggesting?"

"Hadenfeld is an old kingdom, thriving after the defeat of Therengia, but we, too, have experienced struggles. Alliances aside, our people are not so different."

"Easy for you to say; your kingdom has allies everywhere."

"As do you, or at least you did."

"It's true, I won't deny it, but our failure here puts us in a bad position. I fear our enemies will be tearing at our flesh within the decade."

"I will speak to my king," said Ludwig, "and convince him we are better served by extending the hand of friendship."

"Truly?"

"The time is coming when the Petty Kingdoms must stand shoulder to shoulder. It stands to reason we learn to do so before the war commences."

"You speak of Halvaria?"

"I do."

Konrad nodded again. "I heard what happened in the north. These are perilous times. What you propose makes sense." He stopped talking, staring open mouthed at something. Ludwig twisted in the saddle to see Elonin approaching.

"Is that an Elf?" asked Konrad.

"It is. Allow me to introduce Talon Elonin of the Goldenwood."

"The Goldenwood?"

"Yes, an Elven realm."

"An entire kingdom? Where in the name of the Saints did you discover them?"

"Within the very land my king claims. We shall adjust our borders to accommodate them, but you must admit they were very effective as warriors."

"Astounding."

"Greetings," said Elonin. "I am here to insist on behalf of my High Lord that you recognize our lands as part of your agreement."

"Most certainly."

She turned to Ludwig. "What are the terms of his surrender?"

"He is not surrendering; he is gathering his wounded and going home. In return, he promises not to cross our border again in anger."

"You surprise me. Amongst my own people, we would not consider such a request. He would pay with his head."

Konrad gasped as all the colour fled his face.

"There's been enough bloodshed this day," said Ludwig. "If we were to execute King Konrad, it would only build more anger and loathing amongst his subjects. If we wish for a lasting peace, we must find a way to coexist."

"As you did with us," said Elonin. "I understand now. You possess the foresight to secure the future rather than perpetuate the problems of the present. You surprise me yet again."

"As he does me," added Konrad. "Though I'm unsure how King Morgan will receive this agreement of yours. I fear your dreams may be your undoing, Highness."

"That is a risk I'm willing to take," replied Ludwig.

"Spoken like a true statesman. Like the Elf here, I am impressed with you. Perhaps you will do me the honour of visiting me back in Kurslingen someday."

"I would like that, although I fear it will take time to convince my king of the wisdom of such a move."

"As is often the way with kings. Now, may I send my men forward to collect the wounded?"

"By all means, though I insist your knights remain with you during this unpleasant task."

"Understood."

31

ROOM TO BREATHE

SUMMER 1104 SR

Father Vernan cleared his throat. "Might I ask what you intend to do about Esmerelda Boesch?"

Ludwig set down his drink. They sat in the great hall in the middle of a meeting with the eastern barons, and this question had come out of nowhere. "Remind me again why she is of concern?"

"She arrived in Eisen seeking a husband, if you recall."

"Yes, I remember now. I assume her search proved unsuccessful?"

"That's putting it mildly."

"I sense you have a solution in mind."

"I do," said the Holy Father. "Providing her father, Lord Merten, has no objection."

"Go on," replied Merten. "I'm curious to learn what you're proposing."

"We stand at a crossroads in history. The path we choose greatly affects our future."

"Are you purposely being cryptic, or is this your natural way of being obtuse?"

"Both," offered Ludwig. "If you would get to the point, Father, we would appreciate it."

"I propose," said Father Vernan, "we send Lady Esmerelda to Kurslingen, the capital of Zowenbruch. We would provide a suitable escort, not to mention a chaperone."

"Are you mad?" said Lord Merten. "We only just pushed back an invasion, and now you suggest we send my daughter to Konrad's court?"

"What better way to show we are serious about mending our relationship?"

"He has a point," Ludwig noted. "There are far more prospects there than Eisen."

"I took the liberty of speaking with her at length on the subject, and she assures me she's willing to try."

"I'm not certain," said the baron. "How do we know she'd be safe?"

"What if Temple Knights accompanied her?"

"This isn't a matter for the Church."

"But it is, don't you see? The Church's duty is to bring peace and harmony to the Petty Kingdoms. What better way to encourage greater cooperation than through marriage?"

"Very well," said Ludwig, glancing around the table as the other barons nodded.

"Excellent," said Father Vernan. "I shall let those concerned know you both agreed to this arrangement."

"Good. What's next on the agenda?"

Charlotte had assumed the responsibility of keeping notes of the meetings, but she was a victim of her illness this day. In her absence, Cyn had taken over. "Patrolling the roads," she said. "Some time ago, you mentioned we need to be more active in clearing them."

"Yes," said Ludwig. "We must also prevent bandits from operating in the area."

"Do you really think that necessary?" asked Lord Anson. "It's not as if anyone has been robbed recently."

"True, but as the eastern baronies prosper, it will attract the more undesirable elements of society. I'd like to deter that by creating a system of road patrols who'd report hazards on the road and act as the king's representatives in matters of justice."

"So, a roving magistrate of sorts?"

"No. They'd be empowered to arrest, but we'd leave the actual punishment up to the courts."

"Who would want to take on such a task?"

"I can think of many," offered Sigwulf. "Plenty of old soldiers would welcome the steady income, and they require little training."

"I agree," said Ludwig. "My question to you, my lords, is what should we call these individuals?"

"In the north, they're road wardens."

"Sounds good to me," said Lord Anson.

All the barons were in agreement.

"Then that's another matter settled," said Ludwig. "We're making good progress today." He looked at Cyn as she consulted Charlotte's notes.

"There's the issue of the army," continued Cyn. "With the invasion repelled, do we send them home or maintain them in Eisen?"

"We should keep some, but I doubt we need them all. Let's send half home. I'll leave it up to each baron to decide which ones." He looked around the table. "My lords, while I value your advice on these matters, my true intent in inviting you was to answer any questions you might have. Please feel free to speak freely."

"I have a question," said Lord Rikart. "How has the king reacted to recent events?"

"I wish I knew," replied Ludwig. "I sent word when we marched north and again after defeating King Konrad, but I've not received a reply. The distance to Harlingen is significant, but I expected news of this magnitude would warrant some response."

"He's upset," said Lord Emmett.

"Why would you say that?"

"You won a great victory. I doubt that endeared you to him."

"I think not," said Rikart. "Surely he'd be pleased we defeated the invasion?"

"To some extent, he likely is, but His Highness made a name for himself, so it'll be difficult for the king to punish him."

"Why in the name of the Saints would he wish to punish him?"

"Because to Morgan's mind," replied Emmett, "he's a rival. Morgan craves acceptance. You were there when he spoke about making Hadenfeld the greatest amongst the Petty Kingdoms. He wants a war, one where he can boast of his greatness. Ludwig stole that from him." He paused, turning to Ludwig. "No offence, Highness. I mean no disrespect, but I'm trying to explain this from the king's perspective."

"You make a good point," said Ludwig. "I didn't consider the ramifications of my actions. I strove to bring peace, not glory, to King Morgan."

"You had little choice," said Lord Emmett. "If you hadn't acted, Eisen would be under siege, or worse, under the control of Zowenbruch. You saved the kingdom from an external threat, but we must now deal with the repercussions."

"What if you travel to Harlingen?" suggested Lord Merten. "Meeting directly with His Majesty would surely settle the matter?"

"I can't," replied Ludwig. "The king banished me to Eisen. I cannot return without his leave."

"You could write to him about your concerns?"

"I already did so, yet he sends no reply."

"There might be a valid reason for that," offered Lord Jonas. "The king may be ill or out of the capital, or maybe he needs time to decide on his response. For all we know, he's travelling here in person to thank you for your service."

"I agree," said Lord Werner. "It's better to wait than take action that might be construed as antagonistic. After all, it wasn't so long ago we were at war with Harlingen. We don't want the king to think we are at odds with him yet again."

"I'll heed your advice," said Ludwig, "leastways for the present. I'll have to reconsider my options if I hear naught by month's end." He glanced at Cyn. "What's next?"

"A few minor issues, nothing that can't wait."

Ludwig stood. "Thank you for your thoughts today, my lords. We are adjourned until tomorrow, but as always, if there's anything of a pressing nature, feel free to send word, and I shall arrange a private audience."

The others stood, filing from the room.

"That was remarkably easy," said Ludwig. "I expected more arguing."

"You fought for them," said Cyn. "That earned you their respect."

"Agreed," added Sigwulf. "Now, how about something to eat?"

"Sounds good to me, but let's move somewhere more comfortable."

"An excellent idea," said Ludwig. "My backside is a mite sore from sitting in this chair. Why not outside? It's a pleasant enough day."

They had only taken a few steps when Liesel descended the stairs. "Highness, a moment if you would?"

"Of course," said Ludwig. "What's on your mind?"

"It's Lady Charlotte. I'm afraid she's in a particularly dark place today."

A fist closed over Ludwig's heart. Few things made him fearful these days, but his wife's health was always his priority. "Has Kandam seen her?"

"He has, but I'm afraid his knowledge of such things is limited. I wondered if we might ask the Elf healer to look at her?"

"Galrandir? It's worth a try, but I must speak to Elonin first. I shouldn't like to offer insult. Despite her being here for months, we still know little about their customs."

"Thank you, Highness."

"No. Thank you for suggesting this. I should have thought of it myself."

"I'll find Elonin," offered Cyn.

"You say she's worse today than normal?"

"Indeed," said Liesel. "She lacks even the strength to get out of bed and has no desire to eat."

"She's been like this before. This is my fault. I've been so busy that I've not spent enough time alone with her. I shall be more attentive in future. I promise."

"You are a Prince of the Realm. You cannot simply abandon your responsibilities."

"I am also her husband, and my vows to her take precedence over being a prince. A role, I might add, I never asked for."

"Yet here you are. Whether you wanted it or not, you've accepted your responsibilities as the prince. Without you, the kingdom would still be at war. It is the Saints' calling."

"Just as I married my wife with the blessings of the Saints. Are you suggesting one is more important than the other?"

"I meant no offence," said Liesel, "but you are destined for great things, and great things often demand sacrifice."

"I would give my life for this realm, but I will not lose that which is most precious to me. I refuse to abandon my wife in her moment of need."

"Good. Then we are agreed."

Ludwig stared back, not understanding her sudden change of attitude. "Agreed?"

"My pardon, Highness, but I needed to gauge the depth of your commitment. Were you any other man, you might send Lady Charlotte away, confining her to the care of lay sisters, but you show genuine compassion in the best tradition of Saint Mathew."

"I am here," announced Galrandir.

"I expected Elonin," said Ludwig.

"So Lady Cynthia informed me, but I was nearby and felt it best not to wait on the good talon. I understand Lady Charlotte is ill?"

"She is. A malady that has afflicted her for years."

"Can you be more specific?"

"She will be full of strength one day only to be weak the next, as if the darkness of the Underworld envelopes her from within, paralyzing her."

"I have heard of this before."

"Then you can help her?"

"I will try. However, I cannot guarantee success."

"But isn't Life Magic able to heal flesh?"

"It is," replied Galrandir, "yet the mind is different. I will understand her situation better once I examine her, but I do not wish to give you false hope. Who cares for her health at present?"

"A fellow named Kandam, skilled at treating the wounded."

"Do you think he would be willing to expand his knowledge?"

"Expand?" said Ludwig. "What are you suggesting?"

"That I take him under my tutelage, teaching him the ways of Life Magic. I cannot guarantee he is capable of mastering the art, for a potential mage must possess magic within them to contemplate such a thing."

"Why do you believe he is a suitable candidate?"

"You describe him as having a gift for treating others. This is often a sign of an innate affinity for Life Magic. I will know more once I speak with him, providing you approve."

"How long would this process take?"

"That is difficult to gauge. It depends on the student's willingness to learn and the strength of their potential. I would say three or four years, assuming he has the latent power within him."

"Then I give you my blessing to train Kandam, so long as he agrees."

"In that case, I will take my leave of you and examine Lady Charlotte. Once done, I shall chat with your man, Kandam."

Late in the evening, Ludwig stood once again on the battlements, gazing out over the distant waters of Lake Eisen.

"Ludwig?"

He turned, surprised at Gita's voice. "When did you get here?"

"I just arrived," she replied.

"Is Merrick with you?"

"No. Only Kenley and a few servants."

Something about her gave him pause. "What's wrong?"

"We came directly from Harlingen. I'm afraid the news is dire."

"Go on," said Ludwig.

"I've come to warn you. The king is in a foul mood due to your bad news."

"I would think defeating an invader is considered good, not bad."

"Had our previous king still been on the Throne, it would. Morgan, however, is no Otto. He expressed his displeasure most vociferously to those who cared to listen and several who did not."

"Meaning?"

"Morgan feels you wasted an opportunity to display our military prowess."

"We defeated Konrad's army. How much more could we have done?"

"He expected you to march into Zowenbruch."

"We didn't have enough men for that. Morgan, of all people, should realize that."

"He is a man driven by his passions, and I fear the words of others have tipped him over the edge. Lord Meinhard tried to present your side of the argument but was shouted down."

"Shouted?"

"Yes. The king was in a frightful temper. I suggested Merrick and I come here directly, but he felt it best to remain in Harlingen to monitor the situation."

"This is ill news indeed," said Ludwig.

"And likely to get worse. It's been suggested Morgan dispatch an agent here to let his displeasure be known."

"Any guesses whom he might send?"

"Sir Emril, I would imagine. According to rumours, he planted the idea into the king's ear."

"Oh, perfect," said Ludwig. "Yet another problem to occupy my time. Is there no end to it?"

"I'm sorry to be the bearer of bad news, but we considered it best to warn you rather than let you be surprised."

"And for that, I am thankful."

"How is Charlotte?"

"Not well, I'm afraid. She's taken to her bed."

"Not an unusual development," said Gita.

"True, but she is despondent. I've tried to devote more attention to her, but I'm overburdened by crisis after crisis."

"I shall go visit her. Perhaps that will help."

"That would be most appreciated."

As she turned to leave, she came face to face with Elonin. Gita froze, the appearance of the Elf transfixing her.

"This," said Ludwig, "is Elonin, a captain in service to the High Lord of the Goldenwood."

"Goldenwood?"

"Yes. The Elven realm that lies to our east. I wrote about this to King Morgan. Did he not see fit to inform his court?"

"He most certainly did not."

"They helped us defeat the invasion from Zowenbruch."

"Then we are blessed to have such friends."

"Greetings," said Elonin. "To whom do I have the honour of addressing?"

"Lady Gita Sternhassen, Baroness of Drakenfeld. I come from our capital, Harlingen."

"And from your king, from what I overheard."

"Indeed, Captain."

"You say he mentioned nothing of our aid?" Elonin looked at Ludwig.

"I wrote extensively on the matter," he replied, "but it appears Morgan kept that from his court."

"Have you an explanation for why?"

"If I had to guess, he doesn't wish to share the credit for the victory."

"While he complains about you not marching into the invader's lands?"

"He is a complex man," replied Ludwig, "but I suspect he is not himself of late. I fear outside forces are influencing him."

"Those being?"

"A Fire Mage, Koldan Sartellian, may have wormed his way into the Royal court."

"Koldan?" said Gita. "He is the talk of Harlingen."

"And what does that talk say?"

"Far be it for me to repeat idle gossip."

"This may be important," said Ludwig, "especially in light of recent events."

"Meaning?"

"A Sartellian was instrumental in convincing Zowenbruch to invade."

"I don't understand. Why would they support both sides in a war?"

"They mean to destroy us. A campaign taking us into Zowenbruch would deplete our army and trigger our allies to intervene."

"But that could lead to a Continent-wide war."

"I think that's their intention. Last spring, I learned the Stormwinds and Sartellians are in league with Halvaria. It serves the empire's needs to see us weakened."

"Halvaria only attacks once every decade," said Gita, "and we're far from its border."

"Perhaps," said Ludwig. "But their recent loss in Arnsbach gave the Petty Kingdoms hope. What better way to crush it than by engineering a Continent-wide war."

"Is it that bad?" asked Elonin.

He nodded. "The alliances and twisted loyalties of the Petty Kingdoms are ripe for conflict. One spark, and the entire Continent will be engulfed by the flames of war."

32

HIGH LORD
SUMMER 1104 SR

Ludwig waited as High Lord Sindra entered the field, escorted by Elven warriors clad not in silver scale armour but Elven mail, brighter than the Human chainmail commonplace amongst the warriors of Hadenfeld.

The men of Eisen stood before him, the garrison having turned out in full to welcome the High Lord of the Goldenwood. It was a momentous occasion, for never before had a foreign ruler visited Eisen, let alone an Elven one.

She rode up to Ludwig, then halted, her guards spreading out on either side, their lances held high in tribute.

"Prince Ludwig," she said, using the Human tongue. "I bring greetings from the people of the Goldenwood." She let her gaze wander over the assembled warriors. "Your men are most impressive. Word of their courage in defeating the invaders has spread across our lands."

"You are most gracious," said Ludwig. "Do you wish to inspect them?"

"I shall decline the invitation. The sun is hot, and these heroes have remained standing far too long. I invite them to partake of the Elven wine I bring from Nethendril." She nodded towards a cart being wheeled onto the field.

Ludwig smiled. It had all been arranged, but he thought it best his warriors were surprised. He nodded to Sigwulf. "Dismiss the men."

He waited as the giant of a northman shouted out the orders. Within moments, they flooded towards the offering.

"Your warriors are enthusiastic," said Sindra. "I hope they know how to handle their wine."

"I dispatched people to keep an eye on them. I wouldn't want them to get carried away. Tell me, do Elves have such difficulties?"

"They do, although most become morose rather than boisterous when overindulging. It is what comes of being immortal."

"I'm afraid I don't follow?"

"They grow bored with life. In some ways, I envy you Humans with your brief lives. It gives a much greater urgency to living. In contrast, we often postpone things, thinking there will be ample time later."

"I see how that might cause problems," said Ludwig. "Elonin tells me she's kept you abreast of recent events. Is there something specific you'd like to discuss?"

"Yes, but your keep would be a more suitable location to speak."

"Then we shall travel there directly."

A sumptuous feast was being prepared to welcome Sindra to Eisen, but she insisted on a private venue for a meeting beforehand. Thus, while the cooks worked their fingers to the bone preparing food, Ludwig sat in his study with Sindra, Elonin, Sigwulf, and Cyn. Drinks were passed out, then the servants left them to carry on.

"Elonin's reports are most interesting," began Sindra. "Admittedly, before this, we had no meaningful contact with your people, yet we find your culture surprisingly well-developed."

"I shall take that as a compliment," said Ludwig.

"As it was meant to be. I spent much time reading over accounts of your recent battle."

"And your conclusions?"

"Your actions show a remarkable flair for tactics and strategy. Few leaders would risk a double envelopment with enemy warriors on their flank. Have you studied battles from the past?"

"Extensively, although I haven't had time of late for reading."

"Your duties keep you that busy?"

"They do. I thought a baron's life a constant struggle, but a prince's is even more challenging."

"I, too, find the responsibilities of a leader tiresome in some respects."

"Might I ask where this is heading?" asked Ludwig. "You insisted on a private meeting before the feast yet have brought up nothing besides pleasantries? At the risk of being blunt, what do you wish to discuss?"

"We provided you warriors when invasion threatened you. I only seek you to return the favour."

"Are you under attack?"

"No, not currently, but one must always prepare for the future. After a discussion with my advisors, we concluded it is time to take our place amongst the Human kingdoms of the Continent."

"And you need our help to stave off would-be attackers?"

"Precisely."

"Were it up to me, I would agree, but I'm afraid my king may see things differently."

"Would your king be amenable to meeting with us?"

"I can ask, but now doesn't seem the right time."

Sindra wore a knowing smile. "You do not trust your king."

"I recently received news he is upset with my... choices."

"And what is the custom of displeased Human kings?"

"That's just it. I've yet to receive word."

"Then how is it possible you know he is upset?"

"A friend at his court brought the matter to my attention."

"Hearing this, I seek an agreement with you, Prince Ludwig. In exchange for the protection we provided Eisen and your baronies, I ask your promise to come to our aid should the need arise."

"I am no king."

"True," said Sindra, "yet do you not rule this part of the kingdom as a governor?"

"I suppose, but only because I perceived that to be my duty."

"Then, in the absence of a formal acknowledgement of your king's approval, I accept your promise to come to our aid should it prove necessary."

"I shall do all in my power," said Ludwig. "You have my word."

"Good. Now let us discuss the details."

"What numbers are you looking for?"

"Our support consisted of three hundred warriors. I expect the same to come to our aid if needed."

"Have you particular types of warriors in mind?"

"Your horsemen would be next to useless in the Goldenwood, and your bows are inferior to ours. Your foot soldiers, however, are of exceptional quality. Shall we say three hundred of those?"

"Just to clarify, are we talking about sending them when needed or making them a permanent part of your city garrison?"

"The former, although I would be open to discussing a permanent solution in the future."

"I see no reason not to agree," said Ludwig.

"Except for the opinion of your king?"

"My task here is to encourage growth and secure the borders of Hadenfeld. If this agreement contributes to that, then so be it. I'll take care of presenting this to King Morgan."

"Good," said Sindra. She rose from her chair. "Let us join the feast."

"By all means."

The tables in the great hall were arranged in a 'U' shape, with Ludwig and Sindra at the head. On the High Lord's left sat Elonin, while on Ludwig's right was Charlotte, who, despite her melancholy, insisted on taking her place at his side.

In preparation for the event, Elonin brought Elven cooks to the keep, and they, along with their Human counterparts, produced a feast for the ages. Sumptuous meats were piled high on plates while exotic bowls of roots and tubers sat beside them. The more adventurous of those present sampled both cuisines, but the vast majority stuck to the familiar dishes of their youth.

Ludwig kept a close eye on Charlotte, trying to include her in the conversation, but it was difficult given the noise level in the great hall. Part of him wanted to ease her suffering and insist she retreat to their room, but that meant losing her company.

He leaned in close, whispering, "Are you certain this isn't too much for you?"

Her pale face stared back at him. "It is my duty as your wife to share hosting the High Lord." She reached out, placing her hand on his forearm. "I shall endure. I promise you."

He stared into her eyes, bathing in her love. Despite Galrandir's best efforts, there was little improvement, and he worried she might not fully recover this time.

"Tell me," said Sindra, interrupting his thoughts. "Do you customarily invite this many attendees to an event of this nature?"

"These are only the local barons and their families, Eminence. We wanted to match their numbers to your own, but we didn't want to offer insult to anyone by not inviting them."

"Ah, politics. Yet another thing our people have in common."

"Being an immortal race, I would think you'd have settled your differences years ago."

"That is a logical conclusion, but we have had far too long to harden our opinions on almost every matter."

"Yet here you are, feasting with Humans."

"Yes, but my father would never have agreed to something like this in the past. He was a staunch traditionalist for millennia, dedicated to keeping us isolated from the rest of Eiddenwerthe."

"Might I ask why?"

"We were once a great people, but the shame of our misdeeds proved too much to bear."

"You speak of destroying the Orcs?"

"I hold no affection for Orcs," said Sindra, "and the Gods know I killed many, but the very war that cleansed the land of them nearly destroyed us. My father's isolationism was designed to protect those who remained."

"Then why come forward now?"

"My people always viewed outsiders as deceitful, but you showed us some Humans should be trusted. A necessary trait if we are to live amongst you. As Elonin has said repeatedly, we can no longer remain hidden. Your people expand with every century, and one day, they shall inevitably come to the forest we call home, demanding room to enlarge their kingdoms."

"So you aim to keep them at bay by forging an alliance now?"

"Precisely. You already have alliances all across the Petty Kingdoms. Why not one more?"

"You make a compelling argument," said Ludwig, "but it's not me you'll need to convince—it's King Morgan."

At the very mention of the name, the doors flew open to Sir Emril, his boots covered in dirt, evidence of his hasty arrival. He rushed in, looking as if he expected a fight, but the sight of a banquet caused him to pause. He visibly composed himself, then proceeded at a more sedate pace, standing before the head table.

"Highness," he said. "I come at the bidding of His Majesty, King Morgan." His gaze rested on Sindra, then snapped back to Ludwig. "What's going on here?"

"A feast," replied Ludwig, "in honour of Sindra, High Lord of the Goldenwood."

Emril held his tongue, but the sudden flush to his cheeks revealed his anger. "Might we speak in private, Highness?"

"I am presently entertaining a foreign dignitary."

"And I am here at the behest of our king. Which relationship do you value more?"

"You dare to challenge me at a feast?"

"I am carrying out my orders. Had you done the same, we wouldn't be in this position."

"And what position is that, precisely?"

"Perhaps," said Sindra, "this is a matter best discussed elsewhere before words are spoken that cannot be unsaid."

"Yes, of course," said Ludwig. "My pardon, Eminence." He glanced at his wife, who nodded her approval. "In my absence, Lady Charlotte shall play host."

Although he wanted to lash out at the knight, he realized it would be sheer folly. The man had the ear of the king, making him a dangerous foe. Ludwig must watch his words.

"If you'll come with me, Sir Emril, we shall seek a more suitable place to discuss matters."

He left the great hall via the stairs, two guards falling in behind. He entertained no desire to argue Morgan's policies but knew he could no longer ignore the king's erratic behaviour. Would the coming confrontation with Sir Emril prove his undoing?

They walked to the study in silence, and then Ludwig took up his customary place behind his desk, inviting his unwanted guest to sit, but it looked as though the knight held no desire to do so. "Can I offer you a drink, Sir Emril?"

"I am not here to celebrate."

"Then you best tell me why you're here."

"His Majesty is most irate."

"In general, or over something specific?"

"Do not mock me, Highness. Your fate hangs in the balance."

"So," said Ludwig, "you've gone from talking to threatening now. What's next, outright violence?"

"I'm attempting to be diplomatic, Highness, but your recent actions made things incredibly difficult for the king."

"How? I defeated an invader with minimal loss of life. Is that not cause for celebration?"

"You failed to take advantage of your victory. If you'd attacked Zowenbruch, he might have forgiven you, but to release King Konrad without a ransom is unconscionable."

"You weren't there," said Ludwig, "so I'll forgive your ignorance. We defeated his army, but he held reserves in Zowenbruch. If, as you suggested, we crossed his border, we'd be inviting disaster. As it stands, I secured a treaty guaranteeing our borders for years to come."

"Your actions made us appear weak."

"Weak? We beat an army twice our size. If anything, that shows strength."

"The details matter not. To the outside world, we looked so weakened we couldn't press our advantage. The king is not happy our reputation has been called into question."

"Our reputation? I might remind you that until recently, we were a divided kingdom. Now, we've demonstrated the ability to repulse an invader, which reveals our resiliency."

"The king doesn't feel the same."

"That is his prerogative."

"And another thing," said Sir Emril. "Why in the name of the Saints would you be hosting Elves? Have you completely lost your mind?"

"Whether the king likes it or not, the Elves have an entire kingdom hidden in the forest to the east of us."

"So your letters indicated. King Morgan wants to know why you didn't raise an army to wipe them out? That is our land, Highness, and if we don't defend our right to it, we invite our enemies to claim what is ours, making us appear even weaker!"

"Are you so blind that you would willingly plunge the realm into a devastating war? Do you have any understanding of how difficult that would be?"

"It is not your place to question your king."

"So you keep saying, but I am a Prince of the Realm, and it's my duty to bring these matters to His Majesty's attention."

Sir Emril shook his head. "I tried talking sense to you, Highness, but you are not receptive to the king's words." He took a deep breath to calm himself. "I am not here to punish you; I'm here to help you. Come, stand alongside Morgan, and be welcomed back into his embrace. Not only will it further your influence, but the kingdom's as well."

"And to achieve that, what is he asking me to do? Go to war with the Elves?"

"If His Majesty wishes, yes."

Ludwig sat back, taking the measure of the man. Emril came to express the king's displeasure, but did the knight genuinely want him and Morgan to reconcile? He had a hard time believing it. "Let me reassure His Majesty that I have only the best interests of Hadenfeld at heart."

"So you'll do the king's bidding?"

"When have I ever refused a Royal Command?"

"Don't play games with me," said Sir Emril. "You know as well as I that he sent you here specifically to punish the eastern barons."

"Interesting you should say that," replied Ludwig, "because it seems clear the Crown has embraced Arnsbach and Udenacht. Then again, they participated in that scheme to force a war on Hollenbeck. Why are only the barons here being punished?"

"They were traitors."

"As were Arnsbach and Udenacht, yet they're not facing the king's wrath."

"The king ordered you to punish them!"

"No. He ordered me to deal with disloyalty, but I found none."

"He also commanded you to begin clearing the great forest."

"I arrived here last fall, and it's hardly something that can be done in the dead of winter."

"It's summer now. Why haven't you begun?"

"Who says we haven't? You came directly to the Royal Keep, didn't you? How could you possibly know what we've done?"

"Don't play games with me. Have you begun clearing the forest or not?"

"We haven't, but we had an invasion to deal with. Surely the king understands that?"

Sir Emril shook his head. "The king gave you far too much leeway. If I were in charge, things would've turned out differently here."

"You are not a prince."

"No, and you won't be for much longer. He's already arrested Meinhard. You'll end up in the same dungeon with him if you don't follow the king's commands."

"He arrested Meinhard?"

Sir Emril smiled. "Ah. I see I surprised you after all. Yes. They placed him in irons before I left Harlingen."

"On what charge?"

"Treason. He was too vocal in his support of you. Let this serve as a warning, Highness. Even the mightiest of heroes can be labelled a traitor."

33

ILL TIDINGS

SUMMER 1104 SR

L udwig stood on the battlements, staring down into the courtyard as Sir Emril and his escort climbed onto their horses to return to Harlingen. No doubt, the knight's report would paint the Prince of Hadenfeld in a poor light.

He chuckled at that, for he'd never wanted to be a prince. His barony was just beginning to prosper, yet he'd answered the king's call, doing what he thought best for the realm. Now, it was all coming back to haunt him.

"Troubled?" asked Charlotte, moving closer to wrap her arms around his waist from behind.

"The king is displeased. He's arrested Lord Meinhard under a charge of treason."

She broke the embrace, moving to stand beside him. "Surely not?"

"I'm afraid it's true, and I can't help but believe Emril is behind it."

"What makes you say that?"

"Something tells me he wants to claim Luwen as his own."

"So he trumped up charges of treason? Isn't that a little far-fetched?"

"Ordinarily, I'd agree, but if there's one thing the last few years have taught me, it's anything can happen." He turned to face her. "I'm afraid I've not become a very good prince. I ruined Morgan's plans, failed to press the King of Zowenbruch for ransom, made peace with the Elves, and, worst of all, neglected you. You must hate me for that."

"I could never hate you, Ludwig. I knew what I was agreeing to when I married you, and you've kept up your side of the agreement admirably."

"Would it be better if I renounced my claim to the Throne? That would certainly make Morgan happy."

"It might, but at what cost?"

"What do you mean?"

"Morgan is no King Otto. Since his ascension to the Throne, all he's done is divide the realm and court war. Without your intervention in Eisen, we would've been dragged into a war of attrition, something we can ill-afford with the empire breathing down our necks. I've said it before, and I'll keep saying it—you are where you're needed most. If Morgan can't accept that, then to the Underworld with him."

"He is the king," said Ludwig.

"Is he? Then he should begin acting like one."

Ludwig paused, looking down on the now empty courtyard, Sir Emril and his escort having departed. "I shall go to Harlingen. If I plead my case in person, I might get through to His Majesty."

"Are you certain that's wise? He's already arrested Meinhard; you may be next."

"I have difficulty believing he'd go that far."

"I've read many books," said Charlotte, "and the history of the Petty Kingdoms is rife with similar situations. It starts with a single arrest, then another, and before long, escalates into a bloodbath. Morgan won't be happy until he eliminates anyone who opposes his views."

"Making it all the more imperative I stop him while I can."

"At the risk of your own life? We have a wonderful life together, Ludwig. I don't want to jeopardize losing that."

"If I stand by and do nothing, it will only get worse."

She nodded, a tear coming to her eye. "You must do what you believe best."

Once again, Ludwig's advisors surrounded him, this time to ensure they carried on with his wishes during his absence.

"I don't like this," said Sigwulf. "If you go to Harlingen, you seal your fate."

"I agree," added Cyn. "That toad Emril will have nothing nice to say about you. He'll poison the king with his words."

"What other choice is there?" asked Ludwig.

"Let me send warriors after him. We'll cut him down before he crosses the river."

"That will solve nothing, and I won't condone murder."

Cyn looked at Sigwulf. "I tried."

"You'd have a hard time anyway," added Charlotte. "The man's been travelling for a couple of days, and you don't know his route."

"There's only two to choose from."

"Enough!" said Ludwig. "Let's move on to other matters. Where do we stand on the road wardens?"

"We've recruited the men," replied Sigwulf, "but face the same problem we had with the cavalry—a lack of horses. Unless you want them wandering around on foot, I'm afraid we'll need to wait. Could you ask the Elves if they have any to spare?"

"That's not a bad idea," added Cyn. "They're smaller than our cavalry mounts but would be fine for patrolling the roads."

"I'll speak with Sindra about it before her return to Nethendril. What about the army?"

"We disbanded half the men we brought to war. I've considered reducing our numbers even more, just not all at once."

"Hold off on that for now," said Ludwig.

"Are you expecting trouble?"

"Nothing I can name, only a feeling more bad news is coming."

"Then we'll trust your instincts. The remaining men will be stationed here in Eisen."

"When do we leave?" asked Sigwulf.

"Who said anything about 'we'?" replied Ludwig. "I got us into this mess. I'll be the one to humble myself before the king."

Clutching a scroll, a pale Father Vernan came through the door. "Highness," he said. "Word just arrived from Harlingen."

"So soon? Sir Emril left only two days ago."

"Sir Emril? I had no idea he was here. My news came through the Church. The king has arrested Lord Meinhard."

"Yes," said Ludwig. "For treason."

"Did you also hear he's under sentence of death?"

"Death? Are you certain?"

"I'm afraid there can be no doubt. The Prior of Harlingen reports performing the last rites himself."

"Why would he send word here?"

"He and Prior Hieronymus are good friends. They met at the seminary in Eidenburg."

"That's near the Forge, isn't it?"

Father Vernan smiled. "I wasn't aware you were familiar with that name. Officially, it's known as the training commandery for the Temple Knights of Saint Agnes."

Ludwig smiled, a rare occurrence these days. "If you recall, I have a contact amongst their order."

"You speak of Temple Commander Charlaine?"

"I do. She trained there."

"Interesting, but I fear it has little bearing on this news. If the king is going to execute Meinhard for treason, things must be dire indeed in Harlingen."

"Then I should make amends before it gets worse."

"What are you proposing?"

"I intend to go there myself."

"You can't!" said Father Vernan. "In this current climate, the king would lock you up."

"It wouldn't be the first time I was a prisoner. Come to think of it, that happens a lot to me."

"Meaning?"

"There was Lord Wulfram, the Baron of Regnitz, then I was locked up here in Eisen during the war, and most recently, the Elves in Nethendril. Perhaps I was born to suffer?"

"Nonsense. You endured imprisonment, and you came out stronger for it, your faith renewed. Now is the time for you to sit back and let others do your bidding. Allow me to travel to Harlingen on your behalf."

"And leave you to face the king's wrath alone?"

"I am a Holy Father. Even a king wouldn't dare imprison a member of the Church."

"It's my fault this all came to pass."

"You did what you believed right," said Father Vernan. "Look at all you've accomplished. The kingdom is reunited, the Elves are on friendly terms, and we secured the border with Zowenbruch. What more evidence do you need to prove you're working in the kingdom's best interest?"

"Yet somehow, the king remains displeased."

"That he may be, but I assure you he will come around to your way of thinking once I explain your reasoning."

"I concede. You may travel to Harlingen on my behalf, but I must compose a letter detailing the reasons for my decisions."

"A wise choice, Highness."

"Any advice on how I should word it?"

"Adopt a conciliatory tone," said Father Vernan, "but be resolute in your conviction that you chose the right course of action."

"And if that isn't enough?"

"If the king doesn't forgive you, you might want to consider alternatives."

"Such as?"

"Flight would be my first instinct. All indications reveal the capital is in turmoil. I fear it wouldn't take much for your enemies to call for your head."

Father Vernan left early the following day, riding a fast horse with four men to guarantee his safety on the road. Admittedly, it was unheard of for bandits to target a Holy Father, but in the current political climate, other enemies might be out there, particularly if the Stormwinds or Sartellians found out he was aware of their plans.

The next few days were nerve-wracking for Ludwig. He knew his letters wouldn't reach Harlingen for some time, yet he couldn't throw off the sense of disaster waiting at his doorstep.

His experiences in the north convinced him to return home, and he'd done this, assuming the mantle of responsibility as Baron of Verfeld. He would've happily continued in that role for the rest of his life, but then Otto died, leaving Morgan as the new king.

Now, the politics of court worked against him, and he feared not so much for himself but for those around him, particularly Charlotte and Frederick. Had it not been for them, he might've fled already, seeking life as a mercenary in the north. No, even without his family, his sense of duty remained too strong. He'd made mistakes, and now he must face the king's wrath.

A full week after Vernan left, a courier arrived bearing missives from the king. Ludwig sat in the great hall, discussing matters with Sigwulf and Cyn, their meals largely uneaten, a rare occurrence, especially for the huge northman.

"Your Highness," the messenger said, bowing deeply. "I bring news from King Morgan." He stepped forward and handed Ludwig three sealed letters.

Ludwig took them, examining the seal. They were definitely from the king, yet he wondered who was manipulating His Majesty.

He broke the seal of the largest, carefully unfolding the parchment. "A Royal Proclamation," he said after reading its contents. "It's now official: He executed Lord Meinhard for treason."

"Unfortunate," said Sigwulf, "but hardly unexpected. What's in the others?"

Ludwig picked up the next letter, staring at the front where his name was inscribed in a different hand than the previous one. He opened it, scanning its contents before turning to Sigwulf.

"Your past has caught up with you, my friend. The king accuses me of harbouring a rebel from Abelard. I'm ordered to send you to Harlingen in chains so he can ship you off for punishment." He tossed the letter on the table.

"Perhaps it would be best if I left," said Sigwulf.

"No," said Cyn. "We're not running."

"Who said anything about 'we'?"

"Don't you dare talk of leaving without me!"

"No one's going anywhere," said Ludwig.

"The letter is clear," said the courier. "The king's words leave no room for misinterpretation."

"You are aware of the contents of these?"

"I am," the fellow replied. "I must warn you, though, the third letter is the most disturbing."

"And if I choose not to open it?"

"Then you force me to explain your actions to His Majesty."

Ludwig broke the last seal, rereading the letter's contents to ensure he had not mistaken the words. "This is unconscionable."

"It is the king's command. To refuse is an act of treason."

"What is it?" asked Cyn.

Ludwig shook the letter. "This is a warrant ordering the execution of every member of Meinhard's family, including Lady Alexandra."

The courier smiled, obviously pleased at the response. "May I inform His Majesty you will comply with his demands?"

Ludwig ignored the fellow, speaking instead to Sigwulf. "Send word to Dornbruck. Lord Emmett and Lady Alexandra are summoned to Eisen, and be sure to invite Evangeline and her sister as well."

Sigwulf rose to object, opening his mouth to speak. Cyn reached out, grabbing his forearm. "Do as he says, Siggy. Let's not create a scene in front of the king's man."

The courier's smirk could not be missed. "A wise decision, Highness. His Majesty will be most pleased. I shall happily escort the rebel back to Harlingen on your behalf. When do you want us to leave?"

Ludwig felt as if the walls were closing in on him. "Let's give you a few days to recover from your trip here, shall we? I shouldn't like you to wear yourself out with all this riding. Might I enquire how you intend to transport the prisoner?"

"I thought we'd find ourselves a cage and wagon, Highness, providing you could spare them."

Something about the man bothered Ludwig. "Have we met before?"

"No," the fellow replied, "although I know all about you. One could hardly live in Hadenfeld without knowing of your exploits."

"Then perhaps you'd indulge me by introducing yourself?"

"My pardon for neglecting to do so upon my arrival. My name is Sir Reisen Forst. I believe you know my cousin, the Baron of Glosneke."

"I am trapped," said Ludwig, throwing himself into a chair. As if sensing his mood, Frederick ran over and climbed into his lap.

"What will you do?" asked Charlotte. "You can't execute Alexandra or hand over Sigwulf."

"Don't you think I know that?" He took a breath. "Sorry. I didn't mean to take my anger out on you." He looked at Frederick, and everything fell into place. "I'm sending you both north," he said, "to Erlingen. The Baron of Regnitz will keep you safe."

"No," said Charlotte. "My place is here with you. I refuse to abandon you in your time of greatest need."

"I appreciate that, but I fear this will end badly."

"Then we shall face it together, regardless of the outcome."

"What of Frederick?"

"I'll make arrangements."

"Those being?"

"If they come to arrest us, I'll place him in the Church's care. Not even Morgan can reach him there." She rose, crossing the room and placing her hands upon his shoulders. Keenly aware that something was wrong, Frederick put his head against his father's chest, wrapping his small arms around him.

That evening, Ludwig met with Sindra and Elonin, his mood heavy, yet he was determined at least some of his accomplishments would stand the test of time.

"I heard disturbing news," said the High Lord. "Is it true your king demands you arrest your friends?"

"Yes," replied Ludwig. "I shan't deny it."

"What will you do?"

"For now, I'll wait in the hope King Morgan might realize the error of his ways."

"That is foolish," replied Elonin. "Once a king commits to such an act, he cannot afford to back down. It would be his ruin."

"There is no choice but to hold tight and weather the storm. In any case, that's not the reason I asked to meet. Regardless of my own fate, I wanted to ensure amicable relations still exist between Hadenfeld and the Goldenwood."

"That is something I cannot guarantee," said Sindra. "Our agreements thus far have been with you, Ludwig. A bond forged on mutual respect. How can I trust the word of a king who removes you from the position of prince?"

"Peace is more important than personal connections."

"Ah, but the personal connection is what allows us to work together so well. If they remove you from your position, we have no choice but to withdraw back into isolation."

"I fear that could lead to war with Hadenfeld."

"We cannot worry over what the future might bring; I must concern myself with the present."

"Meaning?"

"Let me ask you this," replied Sindra. "What will you do if the king orders your arrest?"

"Yes," added Elonin. "We discussed this at length. Sindra believes you would surrender yourself to your king, but I think you would fight back."

"Fight back? With what? I have no army."

"Don't you? I would not be so quick to dismiss your influence here in the east."

"Meet with your barons," suggested Sindra, "and discuss this with them. What you discover might surprise you."

"I am not ready to go to war!" insisted Ludwig.

"Is one ever truly ready for war? Our advice to you is, if war comes to your doorstep, do not shirk your duty to the people of this land. Fight with every fibre of your being."

34

STRIPPED

AUTUMN 1104 SR

For weeks, no further messages came from Harlingen. Autumn arrived, and with it, the hope Morgan might have reconsidered. Father Vernan had yet to return, and Ludwig had sent Sir Reisen on his way weeks ago without Sigwulf. He'd even brought Emmett, Alexandra, and their daughters to Eisen to safeguard them from the king, an act that could only be seen as confrontational, yet still, he heard nothing.

The cooler days of autumn blew in, and the waiting unnerved Ludwig. He fretted and paced, second-guessing himself until he was worried sick. Charlotte tried to calm him, but with every passing day, he grew more distressed.

Throughout it all, though, he kept up the training of his men. The cavalry companies grew to four, their training at the hands of the Temple Knights proving most successful. The barons prospered, Frederick became more entertaining, and even the remaining Elves appeared in a good mood despite High Lord Sindra returning home.

On a typical autumn day, with the leaves gathering in the streets, Ludwig walked the battlements, surveying the city. Spotting a rider racing towards the keep, he returned to the great hall, hoping the messenger was from the king. The rider, covered in dirt, stood wringing his hands, and Ludwig recognized the man by his manner, not his face.

"Pelton?" said Ludwig. "What in the name of the Saints are you doing here?"

"Highness," he said, uncharacteristically nervous. "I didn't know where else to turn."

"Why? What's happened?"

"Verfeld is gone."

"What do you mean, gone?"

"King Morgan gave it to another, Highness—a man named Lord Emril. There was nothing I could do. He showed up with a band of warriors and a writ from the king, saying you forfeited all claim to your ancestral home."

Ludwig sat down, too stunned to speak.

"That's not all," continued Pelton. "I tried to argue the point, but another one conjured fire, threatening to burn down the keep if we didn't capitulate."

"Let me guess—his name was Koldan Sartellian?"

"I'm afraid no one introduced him."

"Are you sure Emril came at the behest of the king?"

"There can be no doubt, Highness. I saw His Majesty's proclamation with my own eyes. What am I to do now?"

"You shall stay here in Eisen, assuming you have no objection." Ludwig addressed a nearby guard stationed at the door. "Edwig. Find Sigwulf and Cyn, will you? I need their council, and while you're at it, have someone bring some food."

"Yes, sir." The grey-eyed warrior left the room.

"Come, Pelton. Sit down. You must be exhausted." He waited while his castellan took a seat. "When did this all happen?"

"A week ago, Highness."

"And you say he brought his own men?"

"He did, along with the man with hands of fire."

"How many did he bring?"

"Only a company."

"Is there anything else you remember?"

"He took up immediate residence in the keep. I remained long enough to see if I could ascertain their intentions before I fled here, bringing you the news."

"And I'm grateful you did."

"What is happening, Highness? Has the king gone mad?"

Ludwig gritted his teeth. It appeared that was precisely what was happening, yet he clung to the hope Morgan's advisors were leading him astray. The door opened, revealing his closest companions.

"What's up, Boss?" said Cyn, smiling until her gaze came to rest on the castellan. "What's happened?"

"The king gave Verfeld to Sir Emril," said Ludwig. "Or should I say, LORD Emril."

"That's not even legal, is it?"

Sigwulf snorted. "Legal? Don't expect a king to follow the laws of the land. The only law they respect is their own commands."

"We can't sit here and do nothing."

"We won't," said Ludwig, "but there is little I can do by myself."

"How can we help?"

"We must gather the eastern barons. I'll meet with them in Eisen at month's end. That should give them plenty of time to respond to my summons."

"Do you mean to fight?" asked Sigwulf.

"I'd be lying if I said I hadn't considered the possibility, but I haven't the numbers."

"Nonsense," said Cyn. "You know the barons support you."

"And what if they did? The barons of Udenacht and Arnsbach are unlikely to heed my summons, and the rest won't be able to call up anywhere near the numbers they did in the last war. I'm afraid the chance of victory is slim."

"Better to die trying than give up, surely?"

"Might I suggest something?" asked Sigwulf.

"By all means."

"Let me arrest the Warden of Eisen. We know he reports everything to Morgan."

Ludwig nodded, too overwhelmed to voice the command. He felt a pang of guilt, for, in one order, he'd gone from doing his duty to taking an active hand against the king. He fought down the impulse to scream in frustration. "Has Father Vernan returned?"

"You know he hasn't," said Cyn. "If he had, he'd come straight to the keep."

"He may be a prisoner of the king," suggested Sigwulf. "We could ask Temple Captain Hamelyn to enquire about the good father's situation in Harlingen."

"Let's do that," said Ludwig. "Now, take care of the warden before he causes any more mischief."

Sigwulf left, rushing from the room.

"I haven't seen him this energetic for months," said Cyn.

"This is no laughing matter."

"I didn't mean to imply it was, but Siggy always does better with something to keep him busy. Now, what can I do?"

"I'm not sure. This is all so overwhelming. What would you suggest?"

"We start by ensuring the loyalty of our captains."

"And if they swear to support the king?"

"Then strip them of their rank and send them on their way. The last thing we can afford is leaders with questionable loyalties. Not that your men are, but the new horsemen are a different story."

"While you're at it, remove the Eisen guards from the outer walls of the keep."

"Will do, Boss."

She left, almost bumping into Gustavo, who bore a tray of food.

"You wanted something to eat, Highness?"

"Couldn't the servants have brought that?"

"Aye, they could have, but we all heard there was news from Verfeld." His gaze rested on Pelton. "So it's true?"

Ludwig sighed. "I'm afraid so."

Gustavo placed the tray before the castellan. "We're all with you, Highness, right to the very end, no matter what may come of it."

"Thank you. I appreciate it."

"What can we do to help?"

"Find me Talon Elonin. I must speak with her."

"Here?"

"No, in my study. I'll need some privacy."

"Certainly, Highness. Shall I increase Lady Charlotte's guards?"

"You really think that necessary?"

"I might remind you, Highness, except for Lady Liesel, the servants are all in the king's employ."

"I hadn't considered that. Please take care of it. If the men give you any trouble, tell them you outrank them."

"But I don't," said Gustavo.

"You do now, Sergeant."

"Sergeant?"

"You've more than earned it. Get going before I change my mind."

The distance between Eisen and Harlingen on the old road through Hasdorf exceeded three hundred miles. The new route linking Dornbruck and Verfeld cut that by almost a third, making it possible to get a message to the capital in just over a week, assuming a fast horse and weather permitting. That also required a rider to cover nearly thirty-five miles a day without considering the wear and tear on both rider and mount. A more conservative estimate would be a trip of two weeks, four if it was meant to include a return.

There was still no word from Father Vernan when the barons arrived in Eisen. They'd gathered in the great hall as usual, but the mood was sombre, and Ludwig couldn't blame them. War clouds gathered, and while he hoped conflict might be avoided, it grew less plausible each day.

"The news is not good," he began. "As some of you know, I received word of Lord Meinhard's execution on a charge of treason. In addition, the king sentenced his family to death, including his daughter, Lady Alexandra Kuhn."

"Outrageous!" said Lord Merten. "Who does Morgan think he is?"

Ludwig ignored the outburst. "He also ordered me to arrest Sigwulf Marhaven as a rebel and intends to send him back to Abelard to stand trial for his part in an insurrection." He looked up at Sigwulf. "I should point out that at the time, he was merely a boy and had no involvement in the fighting."

"What are you not telling us?" asked Lord Anson.

"I received word that Morgan stripped me of my barony and gave Verfeld into the care of Sir Emril, or rather, Lord Emril, as he is now known."

"And where do we stand regarding the king's favour?"

"I refused his orders to arrest Sigwulf, as well as ignored the warrant for Lady Alexandra's death. It's safe to assume the king and I are no longer on speaking terms."

"Your arrest will be next," warned Werner. "We should act before he sends troops."

"I agree," said Lord Jonas. "If we wait, it only gives the king time to muster his men. War has returned to the east, and if we don't resist, we shall be the ones to suffer this time."

"That brings me to a rather delicate matter," said Ludwig. "If we resist the king's orders, it is treason. There's no coming back from that."

"Then so be it," said Lord Anson, pushing his chair behind him as he stood. "I stand with Prince Ludwig."

Merten rose next. "As do I."

The rest followed suit, pledging their loyalty, save for one.

"You're all mad," said Lord Rikart. "We lost the last time we took on Harlingen and have even fewer men at our disposal now."

"Aye," said Merten. "That's true, but we possess the one thing Morgan doesn't—Prince Ludwig."

"And you believe that's enough?"

"As long as we stick together."

"Then count me in as well."

Ludwig let out a sigh of relief. He'd gambled they would support him without knowing how it would turn out. To see them all on his side overwhelmed him.

"What is our strategy?" asked Emmett.

"We secured the leadership of our companies and put the Warden of Eisen under lock and key, halting his reports to the king. It will be weeks before Morgan catches on, giving us time to go on the offensive."

"But we don't have an army?" said Rikart. "At least nothing big enough to challenge the king's."

"On the contrary," said Emmett. "We have the seasoned force which defeated Zowenbruch."

"The Elves helped us then," said Merten. "Would they consider doing so again?"

"This is not their fight," replied Ludwig. "Though I might be able to convince them to play a passive role."

"Meaning?"

"I considered asking them to provide the garrison for Eisen, freeing up our men to march."

"Are you mad?" said Rikart. "You'd hand over our largest city to a bunch of foreigners?"

"Foreigners who helped us defend our land. I know it's not ideal, but we're already short of men. The more we free up for the offensive, the better."

"That works," said Lord Jonas, "but let's talk strategy, shall we? Assuming we get our army assembled, what's the next step? Do we march south, taking the traditional road to Harlingen?"

"No. We head west, through Dornbruck to Verfeld. We have no friends in the south, but if we capture Verfeld and Glosnecke, we may convince others to join us."

"Those others being?"

"Drakenfeld," said Lord Emmett. "I'm sure, given the circumstances, Merrick would support us."

"Is that enough to capture the capital?"

"Likely not," said Ludwig. "At least not using conventional tactics."

"I don't understand," said Lord Anson. "What are you proposing?"

"The bulk of the king's strength comes from the southern barons, but they won't march if their lands are in danger."

"Didn't you just say we're marching west through Dornbruck? Are you now proposing we go south instead?"

"I'm suggesting we use the king's tactics against him." Ludwig sat back, mulling things over. "Before he sent me here, I uncovered a plot to foment a war with Hollenbeck. They planned to stage raids and make it look like the duke ordered them. Let's turn this idea around and raid the southern barons' lands. A small number of men would do, but they'd have to avoid getting caught."

"A sound idea," said Rikart, "but that weakens our numbers. How many do we send?"

"No more than a company."

"Who would lead them?"

"I hoped Sigwulf might take on that responsibility."

The northerner standing near the door grinned. "I like the sound of that, and I have nothing to lose now that Morgan's ordered my arrest."

"I have a better idea," said Cyn. All eyes turned on her.

"You're no baron," said Rikart. "What are you even doing here?"

"She is one of my trusted commanders," said Ludwig. "Go ahead, Cyn. What were you about to suggest?"

"Siggy spent time with the Duke of Hollenbeck. Perhaps he might convince him to help? After all, Morgan nearly invaded him. He may wish revenge."

"There's a big difference between seeking revenge for a war that never happened and invading a country. I doubt the duke is willing to cross that line. You know him better than us, Sig. Do you think he'd be interested in aiding our cause?"

"I doubt it. His kingdom isn't anywhere near the size of ours, and he lacks any real allies. He'd likely see crossing the border tantamount to suicide."

"A good point," said Ludwig. "You'd best confine yourselves to simply harrying the southern barons. The more you can tie them down, the better."

"What about the rest of us?" asked Rikart. "Are we to send all our men to Eisen?"

"No. We'll concentrate at Dornbruck, but we must act quickly. For all we know, the Royal Army may already be coming."

"I'll send men to watch the road," offered Lord Jonas. "If they see anyone moving out of Arnsbach or Udenacht, we'll know within days."

"You need to speak to the Temple Knights," said Lord Emmett. "They stood with us against Zowenbruch, but that's no guarantee they'll march against King Morgan. Even if they don't join us, knowing they'd remain neutral would be comforting."

"What are our numbers?"

"Just over one thousand men," said Ludwig. "In theory, we'll have more from Zwieken and Valksburg, but we need them to man the keeps in our absence, providing that's agreeable?"

Both Rikart and Anson nodded.

"We were successful against Zowenbruch's invasion, so we'll keep the same command structure for this campaign. Emmett, I'd like you to return to Dornbruck. You need to make arrangements for the army to assemble there. The rest of you should gather what wagons and horses you can, for we'll require plenty of food if we're taking this army on the march."

"I'll send men to watch the ferry," said Lord Emmett. "I shouldn't like to be caught unawares. What about Verfeld?"

"What about it?"

"Shall I send some men to spy on it?"

"Not yet," said Ludwig. "I don't want them to know which direction we're heading."

"You're assuming they're aware we've rebelled."

"It's only a matter of time before they reach that conclusion." Ludwig scanned the table. The barons appeared nervous but determined to see this through.

"What we do is dangerous," he continued, "but we can no longer sit back in idleness. It's time for this kingdom to be truly united, not divided by factions of nobles. Succeed in this, and we build a better future. Fail, and we forfeit our lives as well as our lands."

"Well said, Highness," said Lord Merten. "Once again, your words inspire us. The odds of successfully removing Morgan from the Throne are slim, but if we lose this campaign, rest assured it will not be due to the quality of our resolve."

35

REBELLION
AUTUMN 1104 SR

Ludwig watched Cyn and Sigwulf ride south with fifty archers, bringing the war to the southern barons. Their orders were simple—keep the enemy busy but avoid bloodshed wherever possible. Tomorrow, he'd assemble his men and march them to Dornbruck, joining the other barons who'd pledged their support.

He was taking a terrible gamble, for their combined strength was barely a third of what Morgan could muster. Recent events kept replaying in his mind. Could he have avoided all this? Should he have come to Eisen and done what Morgan bid? It would have improved his situation, but what about the people here?

He knew he'd made the right decisions, yet part of him yearned for a simple life free from strife. Charlotte stood in the doorway, silently watching him as he returned to the keep. The ministrations of Master Galrandir had soothed her moods of late, and she no longer experienced bouts of melancholy, but neither did she exhibit the zest for life that so often followed such things. Instead, she was in a moderate mood, neither happy nor sad, stuck between the extremes as if sleepwalking. He questioned if she might not be better off without the Life Mage's ministrations. He made his way over to her, and they embraced.

"How are you feeling?" he asked.

"Adequate," she replied. "Cyn and Sig are on their way?"

"They are."

"You doubt yourself?"

"I do. I'm sending fifty archers to face off against the combined might of the southern barons. Am I ordering their deaths?"

"This is but one element of your plan," she replied. "Most assuredly an important one, but nothing more than a distraction. The real fight will be when we retake Verfeld."

"IF we retake it. It's a keep, and we have no siege engines."

"True, but you possess the one thing Emril lacks—the loyalty of your men."

"It's possible Emril saw fit to replace the garrison with his own men."

"Where would he find them?" she asked. "Only Malburg has enough people to recruit, and I can't see them turning against you."

"He could have petitioned Harlingen for more."

"It's possible," replied Charlotte, "but unlikely. Until he became a baron, he was a simple knight, which suggests he lacked means."

"He has the ear of the king."

"Yes. That allowed him to rise in station, but he needs coins to equip men. Look how long you took to raise men in Verfeld?"

He took her hands in his. "Do you think it would be better if we left Hadenfeld forever? We could travel north where I could take service with Lord Haas."

Charlotte forced a smile. "I can't deny that suggestion comforts me, but we are victims of fate, Ludwig." She squeezed his hands. "The kingdom is suffering. You are the only person who can heal that wound."

"I am nothing but a traitor. I defied the orders of my king and now take up arms against him."

"No! Morgan is the traitor by turning his back on you when you revealed his plan to invade Hollenbeck. Now, the likes of Emril and Darrian have poisoned his mind."

"Then perhaps we can still save him?"

"It is too late for that, my love. You know as well as I, he'd rather die than admit defeat."

Ludwig swallowed, the weight of responsibility growing ever heavier. He nodded, too overwhelmed to voice his fears.

"I've decided to accompany you," announced Charlotte.

"You can't. The Elves will not participate in this war, which means Galrandir remains here."

"True, but Kandam has made significant progress in his training."

"So soon? I thought it would take years?"

"As did Master Galrandir, but Kandam has greater potential than he realized."

"How is that possible?"

"It's difficult to say. The most likely explanation is that one of his ancestors was a mage. I've read magic can sometimes skip a generation or two.

Perhaps that's the situation here? In any case, he's already mastered his first few spells."

"And does one keep you from your..."

"Moods? Yes, he holds them at bay but lacks the skill to cure me—that is much more complicated. Galrandir says it's a long and arduous process, taking months, perhaps even years. In time, Kandam will master it, but the war won't wait, and my place is at your side."

"And Frederick?"

"Alexandra offered to help me look after him. You'll be far too busy."

"She's marching with us as well?"

"You did name Emmett as one of your commanders, did you not?"

"I did."

"Good. Then, I'll brook no further argument on the matter. Now, when do we leave?"

"Tomorrow. The men will assemble at dawn, but it will take time to get underway. It's not that they can't march fast, but we must wait for the supply wagons. I intend to keep to a slower pace so they can match our speed."

"And the order of march?"

"The horsemen will scout ahead, though I doubt we'll encounter any trouble in these parts. However, it's an entirely different matter after we cross the river."

"When do you expect the king to march?"

"I imagine he's already started gathering his forces. The fact he gave Verfeld to Emril indicates he suspects we're planning something."

"And once Morgan's assembled his army, what will he do?"

"That depends on whether he's got enough foresight to anticipate our strategy. If he does, we'll meet him on our way. If not, he'll march through Hasdorf, cross the river in the south, and continue up through Langeven."

"And do we respond to that?"

"No. We threaten Harlingen, drawing him westward. He doesn't impress me as a king willing to sacrifice his capital. Of course, I have no idea if he'll insist on leading his army himself or if he'll delegate that responsibility."

"I think he'd want the glory for himself."

"Perhaps," said Ludwig, "but he originally wanted me to lead the army, which suggests he knows he's not up to it."

"Then come, let us go to the chapel where the Saints can hear our prayers and help guide us towards victory."

. . .

Five hundred men stood waiting to march. The cavalry led, accounting for nearly half their number, a screening force spreading out to the front and sides as they got underway. They were a fine body of horsemen trained in the traditions of the Temple Knights. Behind them came four companies of footmen and two of archers who'd eventually be parcelled out to the barons of Dornbruck and Langeven, but for now, they protected the supply wagons, along with the carriage carrying Charlotte and Frederick.

Ludwig rode towards the head of the army, ready to lead them westward, but as he took up his position at the front of the column, a group of horsemen approached the assembly field. No one could mistake who they were, for they wore distinctive brown surcoats emblazoned with a white axe, the mark of the Temple Knights of Saint Mathew. The knights drew closer, then halted, their leader advancing to come within hailing distance.

"Temple Captain Hamelyn," called out Ludwig. "This is unexpected. Are you here to stop us or help us?"

"Help, if you'll have us."

"I must admit to some surprise. I know you helped us defeat Zowenbruch, but this rebellion is a far different situation."

"Agreed, but we all understand the real threat is Halvaria. My superiors believe the best way to prepare to face the empire is to ensure strong leadership of this realm."

"And so the Church now interferes in local politics?"

"Let me be clear about this," said Hamelyn. "This is not the will of the Church. Prior Hieronymus was most definite on that, despite his affection for you. No, this comes from our regional commander based in Agran, which, as you are no doubt aware, is the capital of Deisenbach. The recent events in Arnsfeld demonstrated the empire's readiness for war. The only way to counter them is by ensuring a quick conclusion here."

"I'm flattered," said Ludwig, "but most would consider this an uprising, not a war."

"Uprising, rebellion, war—it matters little which name you use. To survive the empire's inevitable invasion, we must end the internal strife plaguing Hadenfeld these last few years."

"Why don't you support King Morgan? He is the rightful ruler."

"I shall not lie; they considered it, or so I was told. In the end, however, they felt you were more capable of defeating Halvaria. Thus, we've committed to throwing our full weight behind you." He turned to glance at his knights. "You'll note we replaced our losses from the recent invasion."

"So you have."

Hamelyn grinned. "There is more."

"Do tell."

"The Temple Knights in Agran will soon be joined by their brethren from the bordering realms. Succeed in reclaiming Verfeld, and they will join you."

"I appreciate the support. Would you like the honour of leading us to Dornbruck?"

"I'd be delighted."

Ludwig waited until the Temple Knights took up their position before giving the order to march.

Under normal circumstances, they could make the journey to Dornbruck in three or four days, but the addition of supply wagons slowed their pace considerably. Ludwig rode at the back of the column to speed things along, keeping an eye on the slower members of his supply train, as well as spending some time with Charlotte.

Three days out of Eisen, news arrived that the Temple Knights had encountered two travellers. Ordinarily, Ludwig would think nothing of it, but Temple Captain Hamelyn felt it important enough to send word they'd detained the individuals. He rode to the head of the column, where the Temple Knights had paused for a rest. Sitting at a campfire were a couple of familiar faces.

"Sir Petrus," said Ludwig. "I'm surprised to find you here in the east."

The knight stood, offering a bow. "When we heard about the recent events, we decided to offer our services to you. You remember Sir Heston?"

Ludwig regarded the fellow's companion. "The last I saw of you, you fell off your horse at the Verfeld tourney."

Heston's cheeks turned crimson. "Not my finest moment, I'll grant you, but I assure you I am a knight of considerable skill, jousting aside."

"You both came from Harlingen?"

"We did," replied Petrus. "The king called for all his knights to assemble. I'm afraid he's coming for your head, Highness. He's already thrown your confessor into the dungeons."

"I feared as much, but I doubt he'll be the last to suffer the king's wrath."

"I'm sorry to be the one to bear such ill news, Highness."

"What made you decide to join us?"

"Morgan has lost his mind. Things only got worse once he made Lord Darrian his marshal."

"Got worse, how?"

"Far be it for me to speak ill of a baron, but the fellow couldn't organize an army if his life depended on it. He has no concept of supplies, insisting the men will find food along the way."

"What can you tell us of his army?"

"It's taking a long time to assemble. He can't count on Luwen, not since the king executed Lord Meinhard, and Bruggendorf is yet to send any men, nor Hasdorf. The results of Morgan's summons to the northern barons were equally as disappointing. It seems they are not eager to confront you."

"But he must have some men, surely?"

"He has the Royal troops, and Grienwald sent some, but that's to be expected, considering they're his own lands. Hasdorf sent a token force, as did Glosnecke, but no one is overly enthusiastic about it."

Sir Heston glanced at Temple Captain Hamelyn. "How is it you have Temple Knights with you?"

"They are supporting my cause," replied Ludwig.

"Which is?"

"To secure the Throne of Hadenfeld once and for all."

"And declare yourself king?"

"I hoped we might convince Morgan to back down by removing the outside influence."

"You mean to make him a puppet king?"

The label made Ludwig uncomfortable. Was that what he intended? Part of him still hoped Morgan might be saved, but was that in the realm's best interests? A king in name only cannot make decisions, begging the question of why he should be on the Throne at all.

"Morgan would never allow that," offered Sir Petrus. "He's too stubborn to admit when he's wrong and too convinced of his destiny to take a proposal like that seriously."

"What can you tell me about his recent behaviour?"

"What do you want to know?"

"I am of two minds," said Ludwig. "Either someone is controlling him, or he's convinced himself he's incapable of making mistakes."

"Perhaps a little of both? I know Sir Emril has become indispensable to him, though whether that's because of Emril's influence on the king or him taking advantage of the king's weakness, I couldn't say."

"I think it's the latter," offered Sir Heston. "I've known Morgan for years, and even as a baron, the man was strong-willed. I can't imagine him succumbing to the influence of others."

"That being said," said Petrus, "will you take us into your service?"

Ludwig mulled it over. They were both experienced knights. Their acceptance into his ranks would be a blow to Morgan, but how did it benefit him? None other than the Temple Knights trained his cavalry; what could these two add to that?

"I am pleased to do so," he said at last, "although I have no idea how I might employ you."

"Where would you like us to ride?"

"At the back of the column with me."

"I thought you'd be leading," said Sir Petrus.

"I will once we're in enemy territory, but right now, we're headed to Dornbruck, where we'll rendezvous with the rest of the army. We might find something suitable for your talents once we've gathered our forces."

"Thank you," said Sir Heston. "You won't regret it."

"I'm sure I won't."

They left, heading down the road. Having observed the interview, Temple Captain Hamelyn wandered closer.

"What do you make of those two?"

"I harbour no fears where Sir Petrus is concerned. Sir Heston, however, is a hard man to read."

"You've heard of him?"

"I have," said Ludwig. "He competed at a tournament I held back in ninety-eight."

"Did he do well?"

"No. Another knight knocked him off his horse, but that doesn't reflect on his loyalty."

"Naturally, yet I sense you're nervous about him."

"I can't dismiss the idea Morgan might've sent him here."

"To kill you?"

"I was thinking more along the lines of him spying on our numbers and then riding off to inform the king. Whatever gave you the idea he was out for blood?"

"He claimed to know Morgan for years, casting His Majesty in a disparaging light, the exact thing that would endear him to you."

"You surprise me," said Ludwig. "Doesn't being a Temple Knight make you more trusting in nature."

Hamelyn laughed. "You mistake me for a lay brother. Temple Knights are far more judgmental, though if you ever suggest I said that, I'll deny it."

"I'll bear that in mind."

"In any case, we've both travelled with Petrus. I doubt he's colluding with the king. I wish I felt as comfortable with Heston. I'd keep a close eye on him if I were you."

"And I shall, I promise you. Now, you'd best get your men on the road. I'd like to make a few extra miles on today's march."

"Of course, Highness, but might I ask you a question before I go?"

"By all means."

"If you were offered the Crown of Hadenfeld, would you accept it?"

"That's difficult to answer."

"Because you gave your oath to Morgan?"

"No, because I don't know if I'm qualified to be a king."

"You fought for your country twice, Highness, and both times displayed generosity to the defeated. Some would consider those very actions mark you as a great man."

"I've helped win battles," said Ludwig. "I won't deny that, but that's far different from ruling a kingdom."

36

THE ARMY GATHERS

AUTUMN 1104 SR

The Army of Eisen, twelve hundred strong, assembled in Dornbruck. Lord Emmett had the men camp east of the keep in the only available field with enough space to hold everyone.

Ludwig was suitably impressed, for he'd expected such a gathering to take weeks, yet here they were, ready to carry the fight to the enemy. The thought brought up mixed emotions. Part of him still considered himself a loyal servant of the king, but circumstances now forced him to make war on his own countrymen.

"You are troubled," said Hamelyn. "A burden shared is halved."

"Yes. I suppose it is." He paused to gather his thoughts, but the Temple Captain spoke first. "You're wondering if this is all worth it."

"How did you know?"

"I see the conflict in your face, Highness. It is not an easy decision to overthrow a tyrant, but that choice, once taken, must be pursued to its inevitable conclusion. History will thank you."

"History? Is that the only reason we fight?"

"Think of it another way. Yes, there will be loss of life, but how many more would die if Morgan remained king?"

"Is that supposed to justify my betrayal?"

"Do not think of it as betrayal. If a ship out at sea starts taking on water, would you let it sink or do all you could to keep it afloat?"

"I'd keep it afloat, but by that reasoning, I should do all I can to correct Morgan's mistakes."

"That is where you are mistaken. The ship is not Morgan—it's Haden-feld. In this instance, Morgan represents the captain heading the ship towards the rocks. It now falls upon you to do everything in your power to correct course."

"Even at the risk of more death?"

"Even so," said Hamelyn. "There's much more at stake here than just Hadenfeld. If Morgan continues, it weakens the kingdom, which would have repercussions across the Petty Kingdoms. What mayhem would result without the intricate web of alliances keeping the Continent from war?"

"Hadenfeld is but one kingdom," replied Ludwig.

"Yet it is important, even more so given the recent incursions of Halvaria. Mark my words, Highness. War is coming on a scale never before seen, and this realm will play an integral part."

"How can you possibly know that?"

"The very fact a Temple Commander helped defend Arnsbach reveals the final war draws nigh. The empire will not accept their losses for long. They'll attempt it again with even more numbers. When that time comes, the Petty Kingdoms need every warrior they can get their hands on."

"How long do you think we have?"

"That's not my area of expertise, but my superiors believe a decade at most."

"That soon?"

"I'm afraid so," replied Hamelyn.

"And might I ask where they think the enemy will strike?"

"That's not something they've chosen to share with a mere Temple Captain." He paused. "I hope you don't think me impertinent for bringing this to your attention. I know there is much on your mind, and I shouldn't like to add to your burden."

"As you said earlier," replied Ludwig, "a burden shared is halved. Now, come. Let us seek out the others. There's a campaign to plan."

Ludwig would have hosted the meeting inside the keep, but the pleasant weather outside beckoned. Lords Emmett and Merten were in attendance, as were Sir Petrus and Sir Heston. Temple Captain Hamelyn joined them, along with Charlotte, whose advice Ludwig relied on more and more.

"The first step," said Hamelyn, "is to march to the river and cross it. I assume we'll be taking the ferry?"

"We shall," replied Ludwig. "There is a fording point farther north, but both banks are heavily wooded, making the terrain impossible for our supply wagons."

"I agree," admitted Emmett, "but the ferry's biggest issue is that it can only carry so many at once. It'll take days."

"The men could build rafts," offered Charlotte. "That might speed things up."

"I disagree," said Sir Petrus. "Just building the rafts would consume precious time."

"Nonsense," said Hamelyn. "All we need do is cut down trees and lash together the logs. We certainly have the men for it."

"Good," said Ludwig. "Then that's how we'll proceed. Have the cavalry cross first so they can ride ahead to Freiburg and discover what's happening with Lord Emril. We'll follow with footmen to secure the western side of the ferry."

"Might I suggest the Temple Knights cross first?"

"Why?" said Petrus. "Doesn't your order preach humility?"

"We do not seek glory," replied Hamelyn. "It is merely common sense. If Royal troops are in the area, they'd think twice before attacking Temple Knights."

"Excellent," said Ludwig. "We'll put our archers on the east bank, ready to protect us in case the enemy attacks as we cross."

"I admire your strategy," said Emmett, "but I doubt it would come to that. They'll likely choose to take refuge in Verfeld Keep."

"Even so, it won't harm us to take precautions. We face the dilemma of not knowing how many men the king has in the vicinity. There was the garrison at Verfeld, but how many remained there?"

"You should know your own garrison," said Petrus.

"I did, but I have no knowledge of any changes Emril made or how many more troops came from the capital."

"I suspect he will dismiss many of Verfeld's garrison," said Charlotte. "He wouldn't want people under his command with divided loyalties."

"We're overthinking this," said Sir Heston. "There's no way King Morgan can raise a large enough force to oppose us, particularly with his troubles regarding his summons. That's not to say he doesn't have men in the area, but I doubt they'd provide much opposition, considering the size of our army."

"Six barons are on our side," said Charlotte. "Seven, with Ludwig, and that's not including Lord Merrick. I can't imagine him taking up arms against us. By my reckoning, that leaves seven barons against us, plus the men under the king's direct command. I should also remind you that all the barons were present at the Battle of Harlingen, giving everyone experience. Admittedly, it would surprise me if any were as skilled as my husband."

"I would second that," said Hamelyn. "Now, what is our next step once we cross the river? March to Verfeld?"

"Most definitely," replied Ludwig.

"And if they refuse to yield?"

"Then we assault the place, but it's not something I care to undertake unless completely necessary."

"What if we surrounded them?" asked Lord Merten. "No one in or out, that sort of thing?"

"No," said Ludwig. "That ties down too many of our men. Our strategy is to get to the capital as quickly as possible."

"What if we choose to ignore the keep completely?"

"That's a terrible gamble; they could sortie out and attack us from behind."

"Well," said Hamelyn, "we have one advantage—it's your home, Highness. If I were a betting man, I'd say you are intimately familiar with Verfeld Keep's defences."

"That I am."

"Then you would know the keep's weaknesses."

"Also true, though that doesn't mean it'll be any easier to capture."

"It's a keep, not a castle. A battering ram should be sufficient to bring down the door."

"True," said Ludwig, "but the doors are thick, and there's the matter of the portcullis. We'd win through eventually, but I fear the losses would cripple our chances of taking the capital."

"We won't find the answer here," said Hamelyn. "It's best to concentrate on crossing the river. Then, a solution might reveal itself once we're within sight of the place."

"Then let's get this army moving."

It took a further two days to march to the river, but building on Charlotte's idea, Ludwig sent riders ahead, their task to cut down trees to make rafts. The rest of the army arrived to find logs floating with men lashing them together.

The first group went under the cover of darkness. Half the Temple Knights were across by dawn, along with a full company of footmen, who secured the western bank while more crossed.

In a move that surprised everyone, Ludwig accompanied Hamelyn's cavalry to Freiburg. Villagers were out in the fields as they'd arrived mid-morning, but at the sight of armed riders, they fled into the safety of their homes. Once within hailing distance, Ludwig reassured them he and his men meant no harm. Many emerged from hiding at this news, though a few remained wary of the Temple Knights.

Ludwig headed straight for the tavern, a rundown place called the

Lucky Crow. He dismounted, then entered, Hamelyn at his side. Those within fell silent, staring open-mouthed at the pair of armoured warriors.

"You know me," said Ludwig. "I am the rightful Baron of Verfeld."

"That's not what we were told," replied an older fellow.

Ludwig moved closer, keeping his hands well away from his sword. "What's your name?"

"They call me Bernardo, Lord, as you well know. You've collected taxes from me for years."

Ludwig smiled. "I have. I believe raiders from Neuhafen killed one of your cows back in the winter of ninety-five."

"Aye, it was." The man stared down at his drink. "It's not that I have anything against you, Lord, but King Morgan made Lord Emril the Baron of Verfeld. Who are we to speak out against the command of a king?"

Ludwig tossed some coins on the table. "Barkeep," he said. "A round of ale for all present." He focused his attention on Bernardo. "What can you tell me about Lord Emril?"

"He hasn't shown his face," the old man replied, "but there's a new tax draining our purses."

"Have you any news from Verfeld?"

"Aye, a little. Most of the garrison fled to Malburg, not that it seems to matter. Apparently, Lord Emril brought his own men."

"Anything else I should know?"

"Not that I recall. As I said, the new baron hasn't set foot in our village."

"Who collects this new tax?"

"A trio of men dressed in armour like yours, though I daresay theirs wasn't as fancy."

"Knights," said Hamelyn. "Were they mounted?"

"They were, and on large horses too."

"Unusual that knights are carrying out such duties."

"That tells me Emril is nervous," said Ludwig. "He can't trust his garrison to collect on his behalf, so he sent the king's knights."

"Rather an extravagance, if you ask me."

"Desperate men are prone to do desperate things. If this means what I think it does, we may be in luck."

"Meaning?"

"First, Emril has a reduced garrison."

"And second?"

"Many of my former warriors are in Malburg, which may give us additional men."

. . .

By the day's end, one-third of his army had successfully crossed. More would follow throughout the night, but darkness slowed their progress considerably. Ludwig watched the ferry bump up against the dock, disembark its load, then pole back across the river.

"This is too slow," he said.

Charlotte joined him. "You need a drawbridge," she said. "That way, it could be raised to allow boats passage. They have them in the north."

"In Reinwick?"

"Saints, no. There's no need—those rivers are far too shallow for water traffic. I was thinking of Abelard. I went there as a child."

"I had no idea you travelled."

"My father hoped to make a match for me, but I proved unsuitable."

"How old were you at the time?"

"Twelve."

"A bit young for marriage, don't you think?"

"Nonsense," she replied. "In the north, it is customary to arrange marriages of convenience at an early age." She looked at her husband, noting the disgust on his face. "They consummate such unions when the individuals come of age." She chuckled. "You need to be more accepting of such practices, for you'll soon be arranging a bride for Frederick."

"I will?"

"Once you're king, you will."

"I haven't decided on that. I still hold out hope for Morgan's salvation."

"You must let that go. We've come too far for the king to pardon us. I'm afraid the only option is for you to take the Crown."

"I never wanted the Throne."

"Yet, if we are successful, that's precisely where you'll end up. It's also why you'll make a good king."

"I'm afraid I don't follow."

"Those seeking power often abuse it. The fact you'd prefer not to rule indicates you'll do what's best for the realm rather than seek personal gain."

"They say power corrupts."

"I've watched you grow into the role of baron, then settle comfortably into that of prince."

"I'd hardly say comfortable."

"Yet you wear it as a mantle," said Charlotte. "They see you as I do, a caring leader who wants only the best for his people."

"I wish I possessed your confidence."

"You'll gain it in time."

"How can you be so certain?"

"When I first met you, you were doing your duty. Your king ordered this marriage, yet you took it upon yourself to promise me that, though you couldn't guarantee me love, you'd treat me with dignity and respect, and you honoured that."

"But I do love you."

She smiled. "Yes, and I, you, but that came later. What I meant is you're still that caring, thoughtful individual, which is why people look up to you. What more could a kingdom want than a ruler who truly cares about his people's welfare?"

"Highness?" came a voice.

A flicker of annoyance flashed across Ludwig's face. He was enjoying Charlotte's company, but the arrival of Sir Petrus felt like an intrusion. "What is it?" he snapped.

"My pardon, Highness, but I suggest we send footmen to Verfeld at first light. We don't want any of Emril's men causing trouble."

"The army is still crossing."

"And will continue to, but there's ample to surround the keep. The rest can follow once they cross."

"No. I'll not risk splitting our numbers. No one advances until we're all across."

Petrus bowed. "As you wish, Highness."

"Any reports from our scouts?"

"No contact with the enemy yet, but I doubt they'd march in darkness."

"How many knights does Morgan have?"

"You'd know better than I, Highness. Your plan defined the updating of the Royal Army."

"At the Battle of Harlingen, Otto brought a hundred and fifty knights. Morgan's proclamation increased that to two hundred, but that was to be spread over several years. You're a knight; were any more inducted into the order?"

"Not while I was in Harlingen," replied Petrus, "and I've heard no word of plans for expansion, but it's hardly something you need worry about here. The king's army is likely hundreds of miles away."

"Three knights are already in Verfeld, possibly more."

"I sincerely doubt there'd be more, Highness. After all, where would they stable their horses? There's not room in the keep."

"Nothing is stopping them from stabling them in the village."

"I hadn't considered that possibility. Still, it's more likely the king would keep his knights close. They're the most important part of his army."

"I'll grant you they're important, but an army is more than its cavalry. Foot soldiers are as valuable as are the archers."

"I don't mean to imply they're not, Highness, only that from the king's point of view, he considers his knights indispensable."

"He has you there," said Charlotte. "Knights are frequently seen as the most vital part of an army, particularly amongst the higher-ranking nobles, and you can't get much higher than a king."

37

VERFELD

AUTUMN 1104 SR

F rom afar, it was hard to tell Verfeld Keep was in enemy hands. The flag presumably flew the coat of arms of Lord Emril, but with no breeze, it hung limply, making it impossible to identify.

Ludwig ordered the cavalry to advance first, their job to chase away any resistance, but the tactic proved unnecessary, for none of the new baron's men waited outside the keep's walls.

The village of Verfeld welcomed their former baron with open arms, and he soon found many from his old garrison had taken up residence and were eager to help upon their master's return.

He ordered his foot soldiers to surround the keep, then waited as Temple Captain Hamelyn strode up the steps and demanded Sir Emril's surrender. Words were exchanged, though Ludwig heard none of it, and then Hamelyn returned.

"They refuse to surrender," said the Temple Captain.

"Did you speak to Emril directly?"

"No, Highness. He sent a sergeant to talk with me. He impressed me as sensible enough but was unwilling to open the door and surrender. Given his position, I can hardly fault him for his defiance."

Ludwig was about to reply, but a shout from Lord Emmett caught his attention. He pointed towards the top of the keep, where a man in armour bearing an unknown coat of arms stared down at them. At first, this confused Ludwig, for he prided himself on recognizing such things, but then it occurred to him that Emril had a new design, more befitting his status as the realm's newest baron.

Emril shouted something, but it was inaudible from this distance. Ludwig stared as the former knight held his hand up in a rude gesture.

"He's decided to remain safe in the keep," said Ludwig. "Now we'll have to devise a way of prying him out."

"I'd suggest starving them out," said Hamelyn, "but there's not enough time, which means our only choice is assaulting the front door. What is the likelihood of it succumbing to a battering ram?"

"The keep's design makes it a difficult proposition. Men must haul a ram up the steps, then turn right, all while archers rain arrows down on them. The platform outside the door is specifically designed to be narrow, making using a ram even more problematic."

"We must do something."

"We'll meet with the others and see if they have any ideas."

They came together in Verfeld village, out of range of the keep's bowmen. Emmett and Merten were there, as was Temple Captain Hamelyn. Ludwig had invited Charlotte, but she had her hands full with Frederick. In her place were the two knights, Sir Petrus and Sir Heston.

"Well?" said Ludwig. "Any ideas?"

"We can't scale the walls," noted Sir Petrus. "We didn't bring ladders, and even if we built some, they'd be too short to reach the top."

"What about a window?" asked Heston.

"They're too narrow," replied Ludwig, "and far too easy to defend. It would be a slaughter."

"Have we any magic we might employ?"

"Kandam can knit flesh, but that won't help us against the stone walls of the keep."

"Surely we could convince them to surrender?" said Emmett.

"We tried that, and they refused."

"Then we must apply more pressure."

"I'm open to ideas."

Lord Merten cleared his throat. "I hate to even suggest this, but what if we burned them out?"

"A definite possibility," said Ludwig, "but I'd prefer not to destroy my own property."

"What if we set fire to the main door?"

"That's an option, but there's still the matter of the portcullis beyond."

"Perhaps," said Emmett, "we should come at this from a different direction."

"What are you proposing?"

"What are our strengths as an army?"

"It's simple," said Hamelyn. "We outnumber the enemy and have the people of Verfeld on our side. We also have the garrison locked up tightly in their keep."

"How many defenders are there?"

"That's an excellent question, but I doubt Lord Emril will tell us."

"Ah," said Emmett, "but as you already said, we have the villagers on our side. They'd likely know how many men reside in that keep. They might also be able to tell us if their new baron stockpiled supplies for a siege. After all, he'd need food from somewhere, and the villages hereabouts are the logical place."

"Even if we know how many defenders he has, how does that help us?"

"I see where he's headed," said Ludwig. "If Emril's garrison is small, we can create a diversion and then attack the main door."

"He has at least three knights," noted Merten. "You said so yourself. I don't need to tell anyone how dangerous those are. Why, with their armour, they could hold off an assault indefinitely."

"Not so," insisted Ludwig. "Even knights tire."

"Yes, but the entrance is a narrow corridor designed to be defensible like most keeps. Tell me, Highness, are there murder holes?"

"I'm afraid there are."

"There. You see? The very model of a keep. Getting in will take more than simple numbers."

"Perhaps a ruse?" said Lord Emmett.

This intrigued Ludwig. "How do you propose that would work?"

"We stage a mock fight against some of our men dressed as Royal troops. They escape our clutches, then run for the keep, begging for entry."

"It just might work. We'd need to sort out the details, but you're onto something." Ludwig noticed Paran approaching in a hurry. "What's wrong?" he called out.

"The king comes with an army, Highness."

"Where?"

The footman, halting to catch his breath, pointed. "They're coming from the west, beyond Malburg."

"By the Saints," said Temple Captain Hamelyn. "How is this even possible?" He turned to the two knights, but they'd backed up with swords drawn.

"Surrender!" demanded Sir Heston, staring at Ludwig. "Give up, and the king will grant you a merciful death. Refuse, and you'll suffer the fate of a traitor."

Emmett and Merten drew their weapons while Hamelyn remained

calm, moving to place himself between the two betrayers and Ludwig. He held up his hands, keeping them well away from his axe. "Our troops surround you. It is you who should surrender."

Heston lunged, his blade striking the Temple Captain in the chest, the tip catching on the mail, and though the impact pushed Hamelyn back, it didn't penetrate.

Emmett rushed forward to engage Sir Petrus, but the knight was quick, far quicker than the baron, his blade scraping up Emmett's arm, drawing blood but failing to incapacitate him.

Ludwig was in shock, unable to accept the treachery of the two knights. Though willing to admit he mistrusted Heston, he'd never seen Sir Petrus as a man who'd turn on him. A hand tugged him backwards a few steps.

"Better stay here," said Lord Merten. "Let the others fight it out."

Ludwig's gaze flew to the fight. Hamelyn had somehow gotten his axe out and was now pressing in on Sir Heston, attacking with such ferocity that the traitorous knight could do little but weakly block. The axe head struck out again and again, clanging against his opponent's sword, Heston retreating, desperate to avoid the onslaught.

Petrus's sword flew out in a wide arc, slicing into Emmett's left shoulder, soaking the arm in blood. Emmett staggered back, white-faced, then fell to the ground.

Ludwig had the presence of mind to draw his own blade, and then Petrus was there, a whirlwind of blows forcing him back, his strength threatening to overwhelm the prince. With no immediate battle in sight, Ludwig had neglected to don his armour. Now, that mistake might well cost him his life.

He raised his sword in time to block another blow, stopping his opponent's blade scarcely a finger's width away from his face. Petrus's next swing came faster than Ludwig could defend, and had he not tripped on a tuft of grass and tumbled to the ground, the knight's attack would've ended his life then and there.

Ludwig could only raise his weapon, warding off the continued blows. Then, Sir Petrus went rigid, blood pouring from his mouth as he pitched forward, landing to one side.

Paran placed his foot on the dead man's back, pulling his sword from the fellow's neck. He looked down on Ludwig. "Are you all right, Highness?" he asked, offering a hand.

"Yes. Thank you." Ludwig accepted the offer and rose. Looking around, he saw Hamelyn standing over a prone Sir Heston. Drawn by the sounds of fighting, his men appeared in great numbers. Within moments, loyal footmen surrounded Ludwig.

"Let me pass," he shouted. He knelt by Sir Petrus, only to see blood gurgling from the knight's mouth. "He's alive!"

He was trying to say something, so Ludwig leaned closer.

"Traitor!" spat out Petrus, then his eyes rolled up into his head, and he went limp.

Before he knew it, Charlotte was there, her face unusually pale. "Ludwig? Are you injured?"

"I'm fine," he replied, rising to his feet. He hugged her, then turned, scanning his surroundings. He remembered Lord Emmett taking a wound and spotted him lying in an expanding pool of blood. "Get Kandam," he called out. "And someone see to Sir Heston."

"I've got him," said Hamelyn. "He's not going anywhere."

Charlotte held Ludwig's hand until the healer arrived, then she pointed at Lord Emmett. The Kurathian quickly examined his wounds.

"He'll live, Highness, though I doubt he'll be doing much for the next few days." He bound the man's shoulder before tending to Sir Heston. The knight was kneeling now, his surcoat soaked in blood, Temple Captain Hamelyn standing over him with a bloodied axe.

"What's the prisoner's condition?" asked Ludwig.

"He's badly wounded, Highness. Shall I treat him?"

"No," said Charlotte, her voice remarkably calm. "This man is a traitor and deserves death."

Kandam looked at his prince. "Highness?"

Ludwig stared back, his mind in turmoil.

"Let him live," said Charlotte, "and it encourages others to betray you."

"Mercy," begged Heston.

"Mercy? Did you offer mercy to my husband?"

The knight turned away.

Ludwig nodded at Kandam, who took out his knife, drawing it across the knight's neck. Blood poured forth, and then Heston pitched forward, gurgling as he died.

"It is a hard lesson," said Hamelyn, "but you did what was necessary."

"I did not expect to hear that from a Temple Knight."

"I wouldn't say it under normal circumstances, but we are at war for the very soul of the kingdom. King Morgan will stop at nothing to see you in the grave. Will you now renounce your oath to him?"

"Yes."

Kandam wiped the blade of his knife on the body. "What should be done with the bodies, Highness?"

"The normal procedure is to hang them for all to see," said Lord Merten. "It sends the message we will punish all traitors."

"No," said Ludwig. "Let the forest have them. They are now nothing more than putrefying flesh. Their very presence will be erased from the history books."

"And what about the king's army?"

Ludwig shook his head, overwhelmed. First, there was the betrayal, and then the unexpected news of being led into a trap. "Send men to scout out the enemy. If we are to fight, we need a better idea of their numbers."

"Fight?" replied Merten. "Are you mad? They're bound to outnumber us. Can't you see this was a trap?"

"Where would you have us retreat? Safety lies across the river, but they would overwhelm our army long before we could reach the ferry. No, we shall fight, even if it be the end of us."

"And the keep?"

"Ignore it. Withdraw the men to the south. We'll make our stand there." He paused, thinking things over. "On second thought, we'll make our stand on Erhard's Folly."

"Which is?"

"A group of hills to the north. According to local legends, Therengians made their last stand there before the founding of Hadenfeld." His mind drifted back to ninety-four, the last time he'd been near the place. Life was simpler in those days, when his only goal was to impress Charlaine. He marvelled at the strange twists of fate that led him there today.

"Use the cavalry to screen our advance. Temple Captain Hamelyn, if you don't mind, I'd like your knights to lead the way. Head due north from the keep until you see a group of hills. I'll send the archers and the foot to follow you."

"How would you like the men deployed once we arrive, Highness?"

"Archers on the top of the largest hill, footmen in front of them."

"And the cavalry?"

"Behind, where they're out of sight. It's not the perfect strategy, but it'll serve until we know what we're up against."

"Yes, Highness."

"Paran, did you see this army yourself?"

"No, Lord. Word came from Malburg. The Royal Army is massing north of there. I doubt we'll meet them till morning. Does that give us enough time to prepare?"

"Let's hope so. Pass the word throughout Verfeld that the villagers are to evacuate. Tell them to head east, to Freiburg. They'll be safe there, at least in the short term."

"Shall we send word to Malburg?"

"No. It's too late for that. If the enemy is north of the city, their advance scouts could be anywhere." His gaze rested on Charlotte. "Get the carriage. Lord Emmett will need help. Where are the children?"

"In the village with Alexandra."

"Then find them and follow the army north."

"What of you?"

"I will come soon, I promise, but I have something to deal with first."

"Be careful, Ludwig."

"I shall."

"Where would you like me, Highness?"

"With me, Paran. And wipe that smirk off your face. This isn't a game."

"If you say so, sire."

"I'm not the king."

"Maybe you aren't, but you might as well be."

"Let's just stick with Highness for now, shall we?"

"As you wish, Highness. Where are we going?"

"I want to examine the terrain the Royal Army needs to cross."

"Didn't you grow up here?"

"I did," said Ludwig, "but although I'm familiar with the area, I don't claim to know every blade of grass. I spent a good deal of my youth riding north and east, not so much to the west."

"And when you came of age?"

"Malburg was a frequent haunt of mine due more to the availability of women than any interest in culture. That feels like ages ago now."

"Any regrets, Highness?"

"Plenty," said Ludwig, "but we can't undo the past. And despite the difficulties I've faced these last few months, I'm happy with my life. What about you? Any regrets about becoming a soldier?"

"Only in the beginning when I lay in bed with sore muscles. The training is a blur, but the same could be said of anything repetitive."

"Repetitive," said Ludwig. "An interesting turn of phrase. Perhaps that's what we should serve up to the Royal Army. You may have given me a way to hold them off."

"I have?"

"Yes. You pointed out that an army entails a great deal of repetition. Soldiers are taught to react in certain ways, as are their leaders."

"I'm not sure I follow?" said Paran.

"Try to imagine you're in charge of an army."

"That's stretching it a bit, don't you think?"

Ludwig laughed. "It's not so far-fetched. Cyn is common-born, and she led men at Harlingen."

"Yes, but not an entire army."

"Dream big, Paran. It's the only way to live. Now, where was I?"

"Suggesting I was in charge of an army?"

"Yes, that's right. Now, you march to Verfeld and catch your enemy between your army and the keep. They can't easily retreat, so their only option is to make a stand somewhere."

"Yes, up by Erhard's Folly. But isn't that exactly what we're doing?"

"It is, but to them, it's only a few hills, whereas I've ridden through that same terrain many times."

"I thought it was haunted?"

"It is, but that's a story for another day."

"I'm still not seeing it, Highness. According to you, we're doing exactly what the enemy thinks we'd do."

"We are, but that doesn't require us to behave as they want us to. Granted, I haven't worked all the issues out yet, and we still don't know the king's numbers, but at least we'll have a fighting chance."

38

ERHARD'S FOLLY

AUTUMN 1104 SR

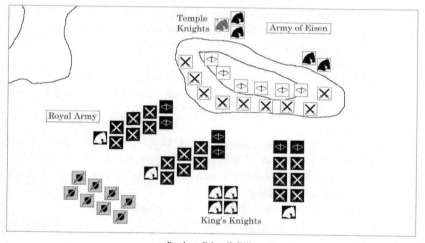

Battle at Erhard's Folly

The mist dissipated, unveiling the blue-clad troops of Morgan's army advancing at a slow, steady pace. It would be mid-morning before anyone came close enough to pose a threat, but it allowed Ludwig a first look at his enemy.

Like the Battle of Harlingen, the army was divided into groups of a few hundred men, each presumably commanded by a baron. Without a wind, flags hung limply, making it impossible to identify which Lords of Hadenfeld had answered the king's call, but by their formation, only three were present.

Ludwig gave a silent thanks to Sig and Cyn. Their efforts in the south must have yielded results, or he'd be facing an even graver threat.

Surprisingly, each baron fielded their own cavalry, a tactic in direct opposition to the king's proposed changes. This might work in his favour, for there was no central threat from massed horsemen, then the last of the army came into view, dashing his hopes.

Beyond the barons were the king's personal warriors, and from what he could see from atop the hill, that included a mass of knights, nearly two hundred. Ludwig's plan for the army was to raise two hundred knights, and it appeared Morgan committed them all to this engagement. Perhaps the king sought to end the uprising in one fell stroke.

Ludwig's army positioned itself on a hill with his horsemen concealed behind, hidden from the enemy's sight. Though there were hills on either side, they were too distant to offer any advantage to his bowmen and would only complicate his defence. Instead, he kept everyone close by, allowing him to form a small reserve he could deploy where needed.

Lord Emmett rode up beside him.

"You should be resting," said Ludwig. "You took a nasty wound."

"Nonsense. That healer of yours proved capable of caring for my injuries."

"You're still pale."

"Well, he did say I'd lost a lot of blood. Don't worry. I'll refrain from swinging a sword, but I should be here to oversee my men." He looked at the distant army and sighed. "I hoped there'd be less of them. I don't suppose you have an accurate count?"

Ludwig raised his thumb and finger, then paused.

Emmett looked at him, then back at the king's army. "What in the name of the Saints are you doing?"

"I'm trying to estimate their numbers."

Emmett waited patiently for the answer.

"No more than two thousand unless I miss my guess."

"Remarkable! How did you do that?"

"I used my fingers to divide them into roughly a tenth and then counted. They're marching in columns of ten, making estimating that much easier."

"That's not as bad as I imagined," said Emmett. "Our own forces number, what was it? Twelve hundred?"

"Very good. I see your wound hasn't affected your memory."

"If I recall, those are almost the same odds we faced against Zowenbruch."

"They are, but we don't have the Elves with us or a conveniently placed set of trees to guard our flank. Our one advantage lies in our ability to hide our reserves."

"At least the king isn't here in person."

Ludwig was taken aback. "What makes you say that?"

"The Royal troops are easy to see; their surcoats are dark blue, but no Royal Pennant marks the king's location, only a green flag amongst them. It looks familiar, but I can't quite place it."

Even as he spoke, a gust of wind blew in, displaying the banner in all its glory.

"No," said Emmett. "It can't be."

"Who is it?"

"Lord Emril."

"Are you certain? Wasn't he in Verfeld Keep?"

"It appears that was a ruse."

"Saint's alive," said Ludwig. "That's twice Morgan's fooled me. No wonder the fellow atop the keep didn't say much. He was playing a part to distract us."

"Yes," said Emmett, "and it bought Emril time to get his army into position. Where do you suppose the king is?"

"Likely back in Harlingen. He doesn't impress me as the type to seek personal glory on the battlefield."

"But didn't he want the mightiest army on the Continent?"

"Yes," replied Ludwig, "but not at the risk of endangering himself. The presence of Emril confirms that."

"So what do we do?"

"At the most basic level, it's simple. We beat Emril, then march to Harlingen and depose the king."

"The basics don't worry me," said Emmett, "it's the details."

"You and me both," said Ludwig, "but we must take things one at a time. As far as this battle goes, it largely depends on what strategy Emril employs."

"Have you any idea of his competency in leading an army?"

"I'm afraid not. As a knight, he would have training in leading men, but I've never gotten to know the fellow."

"Not surprising," said Emmett. "He's never been approachable, and his recent actions in service to the king haven't exactly endeared him to the rest of us. Still, he must've been competent enough to convince Morgan to give him command of the army, so we can't rule out the possibility he may have some skill."

"A valid deduction. I'll be certain not to underestimate him." Ludwig gazed up at a clear sky, but the wind was picking up, bringing dark clouds from the west. "This weather won't last," he mused. "There'll be rain come nightfall, perhaps even sooner."

"Will that delay their attack?"

"I doubt it. Emril will be eager to close his trap. I suspect he'll attack sooner rather than later, attempting to wrap things up before the weather turns." He smiled.

"And that makes you happy?"

"A rushed attack plays into our strengths," said Ludwig. "It means a greater likelihood of them charging in without considering the consequences."

"Rain would muddy the field."

"Yes," replied Ludwig, "and wet bowstrings make for poor volleys. Which means this fight will come down to the footmen."

"Of which they have considerably more than us."

"Now, now. Let's look at this with favourable eyes, shall we? It will slow their cavalry."

"As it will ours."

"True, but ours are already close, whereas theirs are at the rear of their formation. With a little faith, we might scrape through this with a victory."

As the morning wore on, the enemy slowed their pace. Ludwig hoped Emril might reconsider attacking due to the increasingly dark clouds, but even at their reduced speed, they'd make contact well before noon.

He arranged the men into three groups, much as he'd done against Zowenbruch. Those of Dornbruck were on his right, while Merton's stood to his left. Ludwig's men, including those from Tongrin and Ramfelden, took the centre of the line. The archers waited behind the footmen, the hill's added height allowing them to see the enemy beyond. They were to strike out with volleys before they made contact. However, the weather showed signs it wouldn't be cooperating.

Ludwig paced, eager to confront the enemy, yet fearful of the impending battle. He'd seized an opportunity at Eisen, yet he detected no mistake in Emril's strategy here. The king's army marched directly for his position, intending to win through with superior numbers. And at this precise moment, it seemed they might actually do that.

Drums sounded from across the field, the constant beat encouraging the Army of Hadenfeld to advance at a steady pace. It was strange watching them draw closer and closer, but then he realized it wasn't just drums he heard, there was thunder, too. Feeling a drop of rain on his cheek, he looked up as the clouds burst wide open, a torrential downpour commencing.

Ludwig panicked as his archers were no longer effective, yet the same could be said about the enemy. Earlier in the day, he'd told Emmett the rain would help them more, but that had largely been bravado meant to reassure his friend.

Doubts crept in, the urge to change his plan overwhelming him. He almost gave the order to move but came to his senses, knowing that doing so when the enemy was about to make contact was foolhardy. The die was cast, and the plan set in motion. All he could do now was pray.

He closed his eyes, seeking inner peace, anything to calm his nerves. He did not fear battle once he was in amongst the enemy, but the waiting was almost too much to bear.

Someone threw a cloak over his shoulders, and he turned to see Charlotte wearing her own cloak with the hood thrown back, letting the rain soak her hair.

"You should stay in the carriage," he said.

"My place is here, with you," she replied. Something drew her attention, and she used her hand to shield her eyes from the rain. "It looks like knights are moving to oppose Lord Merten."

"That's possible, although I suspect he intends a flanking manoeuvre. Should that be the case, I'll redeploy our cavalry."

She shouted to be heard in the rain. "Will the weather slow them?"

"It already is. Look!" He pointed.

The archers at the front of the enemy advance withdrew to either side of the columns, the rain having spoiled their original tactic.

"Is that good or bad?"

"A little bit of both," admitted Ludwig. "Our archers will be less effective, but the king's men are advancing uphill through mud and heavy rain, not the most secure footing." He noticed her shivering. "Are you scared?"

"At present, I'm incapable of fear, just as I am incapable of joy."

"I'm not sure I understand?"

"Before undergoing treatment, I experienced intense periods of melancholy, but once they passed, the moments of pure bliss made them bearable. Now, my life is one of constant mediocrity. I cannot continue to live this way, Ludwig. I want to enjoy life again."

He took her hand. "Then we shall discontinue the treatment."

"I'm sorry," she said. "Now is not the time to speak of such things."

"Nonsense. I can do nothing else while I wait for their advance, so what better time to talk?"

She shifted her gaze back to the enemy struggling to make progress, the runoff from the hill turning the field to mud. "The Saints have blessed us. This rain will be our salvation."

"I admire your faith, but battles are not won by it alone. The courage of our men will bring us victory today, not prayers."

"Is it not prayers that inspire men to stand when all else appears lost?"

"That's a quote from Saint Mathew," said Ludwig. "You've been reading my book again."

"Can you blame me?"

"No, of course not. Tell me, what do you make of the enemy?"

"They are numerous," she replied. "My guess is they have more men than we do."

"My thoughts as well, though not enough to overwhelm us. The central advance will make contact shortly, but Emril's reserve worries me. By my estimation, he has several hundred spare footmen. I'd give up my claim to the Throne to know where he'll use them."

"That will become apparent soon enough," said Charlotte, "but what concerns me more are the men behind his reserve."

"What men?"

She pointed, but the rain made it difficult to see. Desperately, he shielded his eyes, much as his wife had. Sure enough, additional warriors marched behind the king's personal troops. "Who are they?" he said, more to himself than anything.

"Could it be another baron coming to his aid?"

"If that's true, it doesn't bode well for us."

"What will you do?"

"There's nothing I can do," said Ludwig. "It's too late to change our plan. We have to wait it out and pray we survive until nightfall." He fell silent, feeling a terrible burden descend on his shoulders. He'd been overconfident, believing his small army could defeat Morgan. Now, his people would pay the price. He should have known the king would send everyone he could to crush the rebellion. What had he been thinking? Was he so obsessed with his reputation that he believed himself unbeatable?

"You mustn't worry," said Charlotte, interrupting his thoughts. "We will win through."

"How can you be so certain?"

"My faith guides me."

"The Saints can't help us now."

"I'm not talking about the Saints. I meant I have faith in you."

Ludwig stared at the approaching army. "Let us hope it's not misplaced."

. . .

The rain took its toll, turning the field into a gigantic mud pit. As the enemy advance continued, their pace slowed considerably. They were close enough now that Ludwig could pick out individuals struggling to pull their boots from the muck, their attention on the ground rather than those before them, but they'd soon ascend the hill, and then his army would strike.

Lord Emril had planned the battle well, for all three columns simultaneously hit the defender's line. The exhausted king's men did not back down despite having marched through the mud.

Ludwig's archers let off a weak volley while his footmen prepared to repel the attack. The sky lit up with lightning, and then a peel of thunder rumbled through the air as if the ancient Gods had been unleashed upon the Continent once more.

Keeping track of battle on a sunny day was one thing, but rain coming in droves made it almost impossible to recognize friend from foe. Ludwig could only put his faith in his men, hoping they held their positions.

Rain dampened the sounds of battle, but there was no mistaking the clash of arms as men fought and died for possession of the hill. Ludwig spotted the king's personal footmen moving farther west, likely to attempt a flanking attack against Emmett's position. He looked behind him to where Paran and Edwig waited to deliver his orders, and waved over the Therengian.

"Go find Temple Captain Hamelyn," said Ludwig. "Tell him to take his reserve and come around the western end of the hill to threaten the footmen."

"Are they to engage?" asked Edwig.

"I leave it to him to make that decision. Once you've passed that on, return here. I shall have further need of you."

"Yes, Highness." The fellow ran off, making excellent speed despite the muddy conditions.

"He's a good man," said Charlotte. "You should make him a sergeant or a captain."

"I haven't enough men for him to command."

"One day, you'll be king, and all that will be yours." She pointed, indicating the Royal Army. "Of course, it will probably be much smaller after the battle."

He hesitated, taking time to really look at her. He was torn between telling her to get out of the rain and return to the carriage and wanting her to stay with him. She watched the battle with an air of detachment when all around them was fear and aggression, and then he realized how much she'd lost thanks to magic.

The fighting to the west intensified, and he noted the Royal troops gained a foothold. He thought to send help, but then Emmett's small reserve moved up, pushing the enemy back down the hill.

Ludwig breathed a sigh of relief but knew it was short-lived. In the distance, he spotted the other men Charlotte had noticed. They were armed with long spears, and although the rain made it impossible to identify their flag, their intent was unmistakable, for they followed along in the wake of the king's personal guard. Were even more troops coming from farther west? He'd been confident he faced the entire Royal Army but now wondered if they'd outmanoeuvred him yet again. Was another army about to appear?

39

BATTLE

AUTUMN 1104 SR

I n the east, Merten held on, reinforced by two companies of cavalry. To the west, however, the king's guard pushed hard against Ludwig's flank while the men under the command of Morgan's barons pinned them in place. The entire rebel position hung by a thread, and then the Temple Knights led the rest of Ludwig's cavalry around the hill and charged directly into the flanking manoeuvre.

Had the weather been clear, it would've been a simple matter to track the battle's progress, but both sides were thoroughly soaked and coated in mud, making it difficult to distinguish friend from foe. The entire front of the hill had become a giant mass of men, fighting in some macabre parody of the Underworld, their bodies packed so closely together it was a wonder the dead could even fall to the ground.

Ludwig wanted to join them, to feel his sword bite into his foes, but he recognized his place was here, where he could direct and inspire his army.

A man covered in mud and blood ran up to him. "Highness," he said. "Lord Merten sends his regards and wishes to inform you the enemy's flank is collapsing."

Ludwig gazed eastward but saw little save for a massive press of men. Somewhere down there, the king's knights waited to be unleashed. Could this be a ruse to gain them an advantage?

"There," said Charlotte, pointing due south as if reading his mind. "The banner of the king's knights. They're coming straight for you, Ludwig."

"They'll have difficulty climbing the hill after all those footmen have churned up the mud." He risked a glance skyward but found no sign the weather might lighten up. "Our bigger challenge is the western flank where we haven't the manpower to stop them."

"What will you do?"

He called for Paran. "My regards to Lord Emmett, and ask if he can spare some men to move farther west. He's in danger of being flanked."

"And if he can't?"

"Then pray, for I fear he is our only salvation."

Paran ran off, slipping as he went.

Ludwig closed his eyes. "Heed my prayers, oh, blessed Saint, and watch over us this day. Bless our swords that we may defeat our enemies and guide those who fall to the Afterlife." He opened his eyes to see a trio of men coming towards him. Two footmen, encased in mud-soaked mail, held a man wearing mud-encrusted plate armour between them. Blood seeped down his cheek from a long gash across his forehead, but there was no mistaking his identity.

"Lord Wilbur," called out Ludwig. "It seems we meet again."

The Baron of Hasdorf attempted to straighten himself but lacked the strength, barely able to remain upright. "I appear to be your prisoner, Highness. I throw myself at your feet and beg for mercy."

"Mercy? Was it mercy you intended to show the people of Hollenbeck when you planned to invade them?"

Lord Wilbur bowed his head, a look of utter defeat flooding his face. "I will not lie, Highness. I was involved in that, but we were assured of the king's blessing."

"The same king who sent you here to die?"

"I can offer you ransom, Highness. Name your price!"

"I have no interest in ransom," said Ludwig, "although there is something that could save your life."

"Anything."

"Instruct your men to lay down their weapons and surrender."

"That would be suicide!"

"Would it? Then order them to retreat down the hill and leave the battle."

"The king would crucify me."

"Your life is in my hands now, not Morgan's. I'll make this offer once. Refuse, and I have no option but to put you in irons."

"You should execute him," said Charlotte. "He waged war on the people of Hadenfeld and is no longer worthy of his barony."

"He is a man in his prime," replied Ludwig. "Perhaps his actions can be explained away by his inexperience in the role of baron."

"Yes." Wilbur nodded vehemently. "That's it, precisely. I was misled, Highness. I swear it. I will do whatever I can to place you on the Throne."

Ludwig looked at his wife, but her eyes held no compassion, only a cool, detached gaze unfazed by the baron's pleas. "I'll be merciful," he finally replied, "providing you order your men to stop. They will withdraw down the hill and refuse to continue fighting immediately."

"I shall do so. I promise you."

"You gave me your word, Lord Wilbur. If you refuse to honour it, you'll be damned to spend eternity in the Underworld."

The baron appeared distressed, for he broke his oath to serve King Morgan by taking Ludwig's offer. Would he honour this agreement, or was he saying whatever was needed to save his skin?

"What do you think, Charlotte? Can we trust him?"

"It is your decision, Majesty."

Ludwig felt as though a great weight was lifted from his shoulders. He'd denied it as long as he could, but now was time to embrace the role of king. He had neither sought nor conspired to place himself on the Throne, but he would strive to rule the kingdom in a just and honest manner.

"Renounce your allegiance to King Morgan," he said, "and I will swear you into my service."

"You would do that, Majesty? After all I've done for King Morgan?"

"I would."

"Then I pledge myself to you, Majesty. My sword is yours, to do with as you will until my dying day."

"And King Morgan?"

"I renounce my oath to him and promise to do all in my power to overthrow his corrupt and loathsome rule." He bowed, a difficult thing to do with his arms held fast by his captors.

"I accept your service," said Ludwig, turning to the two footmen holding the baron. "Take him back to his men, then release him."

They stared in shock, then did his bidding.

"He might betray you," warned Charlotte.

"True, but it makes little difference. The battle's outcome will be determined on our western flank, beyond the reach of his men."

He watched Lord Wilbur being escorted to where the fighting was thickest. As the baron approached the mud-soaked warriors, the battle slowed, and then a gap opened up through which he rejoined his troops.

Ludwig half expected Wilbur to betray him, but as he walked amongst his men, they drifted down the hill, leaving behind their dead and wounded. Ludwig's warriors gave a cheer as the enemy retreated. It was a small victory on this bloody day, but a victory nonetheless.

The rain slackened, revealing the entire battlefield to Ludwig for the first time since the storm began. Noticing Wilbur's command retreating, the king's knights attempted to take their place, but the hillside was too muddy, and their horses struggled to make progress. The few knights who reached Ludwig's footmen were greeted by set spears and soon gave up, appearing to have no stomach for an uneven fight.

The west troubled him, though, for the king's retinue pressed north in overwhelming numbers, with reinforcements still arriving. It appeared the enemy would break through the valiant Temple Knights.

All seemed lost, and then he beheld a sight he never imagined possible—the reinforcements from the enemy's rear falling upon the king's own men.

Ludwig stood in his stirrups, eager to get a better view, but it was impossible. Whoever these newcomers were, they'd timed their attack perfectly and were now slicing through the Royal Ranks with ease. Confronted with enemies to the front and rear, the Royal Army disintegrated.

Ludwig picked his way through the dead and dying. The enemy had withdrawn with only a portion of their forces but had a long retreat in their future. Had he fresh troops, he would've sent cavalry to pursue, but the fighting had drained everyone's strength. Some men collapsed on the mud-soaked hill, sleeping where they'd fought, while other, more adventurous souls moved through the bodies littering the field, searching for plunder.

He ignored them, his attention focused on a group of blue-coated warriors to the south who numbered close to two hundred, including a company of horsemen. Having surrendered their weapons, they waited silently as Ludwig's men watched them. True to his word, Lord Wilbur stood amongst his men, awaiting Ludwig's pleasure.

He paused, considering their fate, but something about his new, unexpected allies pulled his gaze westward.

Lord Emmett rode over, coming from that very direction. "A great victory, Ludwig! Who would have believed it?"

"Who are those men?"

"They are from Malburg. They came to support you." He drew closer, a grim look on his face.

"What's wrong?"

"I'm afraid their leader is gravely injured. Come. I'll take you to him."

They rode through the battlefield, the grass, trampled by hundreds of feet, now more of a lake than a field. They went in amongst their new allies to find the man who'd saved them propped up against a discarded saddle in an attempt to make him more comfortable, but his blood-soaked stomach gave no illusions as to his fate.

"Find Kandam," ordered Ludwig. He dismounted, knelt by the man's side and grasped his hand. "Tomas," he said, tears falling freely. "You saved us all."

Tomas deShandria squeezed back weakly. "Promise me you'll make a good king," he said through rasping breaths.

"I shall. I promise you."

"They are coming," the old man added. "Though it might not happen for a few years, you must be ready when it does." A spasm of pain lanced through him.

"We already won," said Emmett.

"No," replied Ludwig. "He refers to Halvaria. Morgan's forces pale in comparison to what they're capable of." He patted Tomas's shoulder. "Sleep well, my friend, and know the Saints embrace you."

"I was never a religious man, and now my daughter serves the Saints themselves. Will there be a place for me in the Afterlife?"

"I know there will." Ludwig felt the grip go limp, and then Tomas deShandria passed.

"He saved us all," said Ludwig. "We shall reserve a place of honour for him in the history of Hadenfeld."

"Who was he?" asked Emmett.

Ludwig stood. "Tomas deShandria, Master smith and one of the Electors of Malburg. His daughter is Temple Commander Charlaine of the Temple Knights of Saint Agnes. He had a wife, Estelle, though it's been some time since I set foot in his smithy."

"She lives," replied a nearby warrior. "Shall I send word of his death?"

"No. I will undertake that burden myself. For now, find a wagon to carry his body to the Temple of Saint Mathew in Malburg."

Emmett climbed out of the saddle and moved closer, placing a consoling hand on Ludwig's shoulder. "His sacrifice shall be honoured."

"As it will for all who died today. These people sacrificed much, and I refuse to see their efforts forgotten." He looked around at the carnage. "How many gave their lives today?"

"We won't have a full accounting till tomorrow, but we fared better than Morgan's men."

"And Lord Emril?"

"He managed to escape and was last spotted heading west surrounded by knights."

"How many got away?"

"Upwards of two hundred, maybe three, but we'll have a better idea once we've counted the dead."

"Make way," came the voice of Temple Captain Hamelyn, pushing through the men of Malburg who'd gathered to pay their respects to their beloved leader. He saw the body and knelt to offer a silent prayer. Once done, he stood, turning to face Ludwig. "You won the battle, Highness, but there are matters needing your attention."

"Such as?"

"Lord Wilbur must be dealt with, along with the fate of Lord Jurgen."

"Jurgen was here?"

"Yes. He led the attack against Merten's position on the eastern flank. Even though his men were surrounded, they refused to surrender, leaving most dead. Somehow, he survived, likely because of that expensive armour of his. He is in irons awaiting your pleasure."

"I'll deal with the barons in the morning. Anything else?"

"Yes. It's been suggested we move the wounded to Malburg, but it'll take time to sort them out from the dead. My men are combing through the battlefield, but it'll be dark soon, making the search even harder, and we'll need additional wagons before we can consider moving the wounded to safety."

"Send riders to Malburg to inform the electors of what transpired here. They'll be anxious to learn the fate of their army."

Ludwig climbed the hilltop, staring at the carnage below as the sun rose over Erhard's Folly. The blood-soaked fields were dry, but bodies littered the ground, the survivors too exhausted to bury them. Even here, the nauseating stench of death nearly overwhelmed him as crows circled overhead. He spotted Lord Merten heading towards him and waved. "Still alive, I see."

"Indeed, Highness, despite the best efforts of Lord Jurgen to finish me off." He moved closer, then halted to catch his breath. "No offence, but it was a fearsome battle. I hope to never witness such slaughter again."

"I'd like to say our victory ended all the fighting, but I'm afraid that's not my decision—it's Morgan's."

"Perhaps he'll surrender now we've crushed his army."

"We dealt him a heavy blow," said Ludwig, "but I fear we're far from winning the war."

"What will Morgan do now?"

"The only thing he can—take refuge behind the walls of Harlingen."

"Then we starve him out."

"I'm afraid it's not that simple. As you know, Hadenfeld has allies, and Morgan will call on them to lend him aid."

"Perhaps," said Merten, "but how likely is a foreign king to interfere in a civil war?"

"I have no idea. I would've guessed the likelihood of him getting help was slim, but we can't dismiss the fact a Sartellian is in his court."

"Doesn't Koldan serve Lord Jurgen?"

"Yes, who is in Morgan's service. You'll also note he was absent during the battle, which means he's still selling his lies in Harlingen."

"He is but one man."

"But one who represents a powerful family of mages. Do not underestimate their influence. One word from them could convince the King of Deisenbach to come to Morgan's aid. If that happens, our victory here becomes meaningless."

"Then we must hurry to Harlingen."

"Not so fast, my friend. Show me to Lord Jurgen. I'd like to speak with him."

"Good luck with that," said Merten. "The man's stubborn as a mule. I doubt he'll tell you anything."

"Still, we must give him a chance."

"Follow me, then, and I'll take you to him."

Lord Jurgen Voltz, the Baron of Bruggendorf, sat in the mud, his armour removed, his hands and feet in irons, which were tied to the wheel of a large wagon. He glared at Ludwig as he approached but said nothing.

Ludwig stared down at the baron. He found it hard to pity the man, especially when his defiance was taken to such extremes, but Ludwig knew if he ruled Hadenfeld, he must make an attempt.

"What have you to say for yourself?" he asked.

"I don't speak to traitors," said Jurgen.

Ludwig couldn't help himself. "You just did, so that's a lie. Now, shall we talk, or do I order my men to execute you."

"You wouldn't dare!"

"Wouldn't I? You fight for the very king I've come to dethrone. My advisors suggest that execution is the only way to ensure a smooth transition of power to a new king."

"You are not king."

"No, I'm not," said Ludwig, "and I never intended to be, but I am left with no other choice." He knelt before the baron, their eyes at the same level. "Make no mistake, Jurgen. I will be king. What happens to your lands after that is entirely in your hands."

"Or what, you'll murder me and my family?"

"Saints know there's reason enough to see you hanged, but I have no quarrel with your family." He noted the smile of satisfaction on Jurgen's face. "However, I can't allow them to live in Bruggendorf anymore, so your former lands will be ceded to a new baron."

"You can't do that; they belong to me."

"No. They belong to the King of Hadenfeld and are held by you in the king's name. A new king means a new distribution of wealth. Need I say more?"

"What do you want?"

"Swear an oath to never raise arms against me again, and I will release you."

"And my men?"

"They will also be spared, provided they take a similar oath."

"You would free us just like that?"

"Once the war ends. Until then, they'll be held in Malburg. I'll be leading the army, so I won't be there in person to ensure their well-being, but I believe Prior Yannick is willing to oversee their internment."

"You won't win," declared Jurgen. "You still need to retake your precious Verfeld, which will keep you busy for weeks."

"No, it won't," said Charlotte, coming around the end of the wagon. "We've just received word it surrendered. Apparently, news of your defeat made them reconsider their situation."

Ludwig smiled. "What do you say now, Baron?"

40

AFTERMATH

AUTUMN 1104 SR

On a typical day, Malburg's streets would be flooded with noise, everything from labourers working to people talking, yet today, all was quiet. War had arrived, bringing the inevitable loss of life, and the city grieved, its citizens staying in their homes and praying.

Ludwig rode through the streets with a heavy heart. As a youth, coming here had been one of his greatest pleasures, but today, he came to deliver bad news.

As a child, he'd learned of Tomas deShandria's reputation as the maker of the finest swords in all of Hadenfeld. Indeed, the commissioning of such a blade led to meeting the smith's daughter, Charlaine, which, in turn, changed his life.

His father was furious that his son fell in love with a tradesman's daughter, made even worse by the discovery she was a smith in her own right. Yet through it all, Tomas deShandria kept a level head.

Now, his shop sat empty. Charlaine had left, forced to join the Church by Ludwig's father. She'd found her true calling there, but the guilt still plagued Ludwig, for his love for her cost her family dearly.

He'd visited the smithy occasionally over the last few years but never bearing such terrible news. How does one approach the subject of a loved one's death? Tomas had become a strong ally, giving his life to help Ludwig's cause. He owed it to the man to bring word in person.

He slowed his horse as he entered the Artisan District. Finding what he was looking for, he dismounted, tying off the reins to a nearby post.

The workshop doors loomed before him, yet an ominous silence issued forth instead of the familiar pounding of steel. Ludwig pondered whether to knock, then decided against it. He pushed the door open, stepping into the workshop.

The absence of the Calabrian smith made the room feel smaller. The cold forge taunted him with its silence. Ludwig stood there, grappling with his role in all of this. He could still imagine the sights and sounds of the smithy, the old man hammering away on a blade or sitting at a small table, carving a new wooden handle for a customer.

Ludwig's thoughts went to his sword, and he pulled it out, marvelling at its finery. His father had commissioned it, but Charlaine completed it rather than Tomas, yet it bore the characteristics of a deShandria blade. Tomas's legacy was now passed down to his daughter.

Did Charlaine continue to work a forge? Somehow, he doubted it, yet he knew, deep down, Tomas lived on in her through his sense of honour and fairness, making her the person she was today.

The opening of a door interrupted his musings. Ludwig turned at the sight of a shadowy figure in the doorway.

"Who's there?" called out a woman.

"Ludwig Altenburg," he replied, not deigning to use titles.

She stepped from the doorway, her tear-stained face in full evidence. "He's dead, isn't he?"

"I'm afraid so."

"It's all your fault."

"He died fighting the king's army."

"You nobles are all alike, trading the lives of innocents in your unholy quest for power. Why couldn't you leave us alone?"

"I never asked for his help."

"But he gave it all the same. That guilt is yours, Highness, and shall be till the end of your days."

"I'm sorry for your loss." The words sounded hollow, but Ludwig could think of nothing else to say. A great sadness welled up within him, and he struggled to breathe.

"Sorry?" she said. "Don't you dare tell me you're sorry! You're a plague on civilized folks, as was that father of yours. Begone from my property, or I'll have the town watch remove you!"

"I shall trouble you no more." He turned, exiting the smithy, closing the door behind him.

Ludwig's heart went out to Estelle. He watched her through the window, slowly wandering around, looking lost. What would happen to her? Had Tomas saved enough to keep her the rest of her days? Feeling responsible for her well-being, he resolved to ensure she was cared for. She would always hate him, of that he was sure, but that did not absolve him of the guilt over her husband's death.

He wanted desperately to talk to Father Vernan, but he languished in Morgan's dungeon. It took a particularly arrogant king to imprison a member of the Church. It occurred to Ludwig the circumstances of the Holy Father's arrest might be the reason for the recent support of the Temple Knights of Saint Mathew. Hamelyn hadn't discussed the matter, only indicating his superiors in Agran made such decisions. Could they have caught wind of Vernan's imprisonment?

To Ludwig, the most important question was whether Vernan's life was in danger. Before his time in Eisen, he never had concerns for Morgan's sanity. He was opinionated; that was a fair observation, but never in his wildest imaginings could Ludwig have predicted Morgan would execute Lord Meinhard and then order the man's entire family to suffer the same fate. The king had clearly lost his mind and could no longer be trusted to care for his subjects. He must be removed, and the sooner, the better.

Ludwig climbed into the saddle and then headed down the street. A woman stepped from a nearby building and paused, looking at his armour. She appeared fearful, then noticed the coat of arms on his surcoat. "Saints bless you," she said, placing three fingers on her chest and making a wave pattern, the blessing of Saint Agnes.

"And to you," he replied.

It was nothing more than a momentary interaction, yet it helped lighten his mood, reminding him he fought this war not for his own glorification but for the common folk. They were the ones who suffered. No statues commemorated their deaths or histories written of their sacrifice, but people like this allowed the nobles to live their lives of luxury and power. He made himself a solemn vow. When the time came for him to ascend to the Throne, his reign would be dedicated to bettering the lives of all his subjects, be they rich or poor, noble or commoner.

He returned to camp, his reflection bringing his intentions into sharp focus. Charlotte waited, but rather than say anything, she moved closer and embraced him, holding him tightly. It felt endless, but to Ludwig, it would never be long enough. They separated at last, Charlotte locking eyes with him.

"I'm proud of you," she said. "It couldn't have been easy to tell Tomas's wife of his death. How did she take the news?"

"Not well. She blames me for his demise, and I can't blame her."

"More deaths are coming before this is over."

"I know, but that doesn't make the burden any easier to bear."

"This is a curse that faces all leaders, but your compassion will make you a great king."

"And observations like that will make you a great queen."

"You mean king's consort, don't you?"

"No, I mean queen. If we win through this, I want you by my side as my closest advisor."

"I can do that without taking the role of queen."

"True," said Ludwig, "but I won't always be available to make decisions, so I will rely on you to fulfil that role in my absence."

She cast her gaze down. "I'm not worthy. My illness—"

"Your illness is part of who you are, but it does not define you. Your intellect is greater than anyone I know, and when combined with your compassion, there's no one I'd rather have by my side."

"And when I have one of my bouts?"

He placed his fingers beneath her chin and raised her head to meet his gaze. "You have friends you can lean on when needed. Tell me you'll be my queen."

"I accept."

He couldn't help but smile. "You've made me very happy."

"I sense you're still mourning."

"I am. I'll not deny it. Today's loss of life was tremendous, and I must still inform Charlaine of her father's death."

"Let me help you put words to paper."

"That would be greatly appreciated, although it surprises me you'd be willing to assist."

"Why? Because you were intimate with her many years ago? Let me put your mind at ease. She is a Temple Commander now, far beyond the effect of your charm."

"Does that mean you think me charming?"

"Since the moment we met," she replied, "and you've always treated me with dignity and respect despite my ailment. Now, let us fetch ink and quill and, together, compose a letter of condolence."

The next day, Ludwig called a meeting of his closest advisors at the Willow in Malburg, an inn with which he was intimately acquainted. Typically where the wealthy celebrated, the recent death toll had put a damper on such festivities.

The usual suspects were present, including Lords Emmett and Merten, as well as Temple Captain Hamelyn. In addition, Ludwig asked that Lord Wilbur be in attendance despite his recent allegiance to Morgan.

Ludwig and Charlotte arrived last, entering to find the Willow's common room rearranged to accommodate the meeting, a pair of tables placed end to end with the rest moved aside.

Everyone rose as they made their way to the end of the table. "Thank you all," said Ludwig, then sat, Charlotte taking the seat to his right. He looked at all in attendance. "We are waiting on one more, and then we'll start."

The announcement caught them by surprise.

"Might I enquire who?" asked Emmett.

"I invited Prior Yannick to attend. His opinion on recent events might prove beneficial."

"He shall be here shortly," added Charlotte. "He was scheduled to conduct a prayer of mourning at the Temple of Saint Mathew."

"While we wait," said Ludwig, "let's go over a few basics, shall we? What are our losses?"

"I lost two hundred," replied Emmett. "Fortunately, only a third of those died. I hope fifty of the injured can return to duty in the next few days. The rest will either be invalided or require more time to recover."

"I find myself in a similar situation," added Merten. "I'm led to understand the men of Eisen fared considerably worse."

"You are correct," said Temple Captain Hamelyn. "The cavalry suffered greatly, though it held off the king's personal troops. As a result, they're reduced to a single company of horse, not including the Temple Knights, but replacements from Deisenbach are months away. Thanks to your masterful deployment, the footmen sustained a much lower loss of life, though the number of casualties was significant. Your healer, Kandam, has been working to restore the health of the lightly wounded, but even with magic, they still require rest to recover their vitality."

"Interesting," said Ludwig. "Can you give me some idea of actual numbers?"

"If we wait till week's end, an additional company of foot will be ready to march."

"Is that all?"

"I'm afraid so. The archers came out of it relatively unscathed, so we'll have no difficulties fielding bowmen."

The door opened to a Temple Knight, who looked around before stepping aside, allowing the prior to enter.

"I hope I'm not interrupting," said Prior Yannick.

"Not at all," replied Ludwig. "Please take a seat. We are discussing the current state of our army."

"And what might that be?"

"We have less than what we started with, but more than I expected after that battle."

"I might be able to help you there."

"In what way?"

"The Electors of Malburg wish to ingratiate themselves with you, Highness. Despite their losses, they want to see you on the Throne. My question to you is, what are your intentions? Assuming your campaign is successful, will you crown yourself king?"

"Given the current circumstances, I fear there is little choice. I know of no other way to prevent my head from being separated from the rest of my body."

"I thought as much."

"I'm sorry to disappoint you, Your Grace. I know the Church doesn't look favourably on such matters."

"Morgan openly defied the Church when he imprisoned Father Vernan. We cannot let that stand. I sent a strongly worded letter to the Archprior in Harlingen, but it did nothing to secure the good father's release. Given those circumstances, our best course of action is to support your claim to the Throne. Although not an easy decision, I feel it's in the people of Hadenfeld's best interests."

"Thank you, Your Grace. I appreciate your support."

"Might I ask your intentions with Morgan?"

"I hadn't given that much thought," replied Ludwig. "Until recently, I hoped to bring him to his senses, but that's unlikely."

"It would be better if he died," declared Charlotte.

They all looked at her in shock.

"You know as well as I that his continued existence threatens the Crown. To achieve any semblance of peace in the kingdom, Morgan must die. The sooner everyone accepts that, the better it will be."

"I hate to say it," said Emmett, "but she's right. If Morgan survived, he'd become the rallying point for any disaffected nobles."

"It stands to reason," added Temple Captain Hamelyn. "Removing any possible rivals to the Throne is the best way forward."

Yannick's gaze fell on the Baron of Langeven. "What think you, Lord Merten?"

"I fully support Ludwig's claim to the Throne. If that means the death of Morgan, then so be it."

"Then we are all in agreement. My next question is how we continue with the campaign."

"We?" said Emmett. "Are you suggesting you will march with us?"

"It makes sense. After all, the Saint we take our name from did something similar."

"That is good news indeed," said Ludwig. "Now, let's discuss strategy, shall we? I debated marching on Glosnecke and capturing the keep there, but that would slow us down considerably. Instead, I propose we march directly to the capital before Morgan can reconstitute his army."

"A bold move," said Merten, "but our numbers are significantly reduced."

"I sent word to Lord Merrick. I'm hoping he'll come to our aid."

"I doubt he'd refuse," said Emmett. "The only question he'll have is where to march."

"To the crossroads," replied Ludwig, "where the Drakenfeld and Verfeld roads converge. That will put us a few days from the capital."

"How many men does Merrick have?" enquired the prior.

"I expect him to march with two or three hundred. He'll have more but can't leave his keep defenceless."

"What of you, Lord Wilbur? Will your men fight in service to Prince Ludwig?"

"I gave my word," the fellow replied, "although I cannot speak to the zeal with which they'll fight."

"And how many men have you?"

"Three companies, of which two are foot."

"That helps," said Merten, "but Morgan won't make a stand north of the city, not after the loss he suffered. No, he'll take refuge within Harlingen, forcing us to siege the place."

"Then we shall need to devise an alternate plan," said Emmett.

"I've taken care of that," replied Ludwig, "although I admit there are a few details to work out."

"Care to share?"

"Not yet, but I'll need volunteers when I'm ready."

"How many?"

"About a company's worth. It'll be dangerous, and a good deal may die, but if they succeed, it will save hundreds."

41

THE CROSSROADS

AUTUMN 1104 SR

The rebel army marched out of Malburg at first light. Ludwig let Hamelyn watch over them, for he'd other matters on his mind. They'd won a great victory over Morgan's army, yet Harlingen would be much more challenging.

He'd spent a good portion of his time trying to devise a way to gain entry into the city. The traditional methods of starving them out or using siege equipment were proven ways to force a surrender, but Ludwig feared the delay could cost him the war. Even now, Morgan would be asking his allies to come to his aid. Ensuring victory relied on capturing the capital as quickly as possible.

He'd formed a plan, but it was so unorthodox he was reluctant to bring it to his closest advisors. Instead, he sat in a rundown tavern, staring across the table at Paran, Gustavo, and Edwig.

"Any luck?" he began.

"Aye," replied Gustavo. "Though I'm confused about how any of this will win us the capital."

"You're going to become king's men, mingling with the prisoners we took at Erhard's Folly and finding out everything you can about the gates of Harlingen. You've got two days, and then you'll need to rejoin the army. I'll have horses standing by, and the guards will be prepared to extract you at the first hint of trouble."

"And the others?"

"No need to worry. They'll be with the rest of the army. You'll be back amongst them before we reach the capital." Ludwig hesitated. "Listen, this is dangerous. You don't have to go through with it if you feel it's too risky, but it's the only solution I can think of that ends this war sooner."

"We've talked it over," said Gustavo, "and we understand the risks. We're all in."

"Have you any concerns that the other prisoners might turn on you?"

"No," replied Edwig. "It's the assault on Harlingen that has us worried. What if our information proves false?"

"Then you'll abandon the attempt and seek safety. There's no sense in throwing your lives away on something doomed to fail. This idea of pretending to be prisoners is risky, but I must face facts. I've passed through those gates numerous times, yet I couldn't tell you the first thing about how they're manned. There's no guarantee any prisoners have information we can use, but it's worth investigating."

"When do we start?"

"This morning. I had the men of Malburg rounding up stragglers throughout the night. A few more added into the mix won't raise any suspicions." He handed a note to Gustavo. "This is the name and address of a man called Hartwin Bengle. He commands the men of Malburg now that Master Tomas is dead. He'll get you in amongst the prisoners and ensure you're pulled out once you're done. He'll also provide you with horses when you're ready to rejoin the army. Any questions?"

"Is this truly our only hope?" asked Paran.

"Unless something else presents itself, yes. I'd commit additional men to this endeavour if I believed it would help, but they'd only get in your way. There's also the matter of trust. I trust you three to do everything possible to succeed in this."

"We won't let you down, Highness."

"I'm sure you won't. Now, you'd best head out, gentlemen."

He watched his men leave, his thoughts turning to the future. Would this madcap plan of his get them into the capital? He hoped so but must make alternate arrangements to draw attention away from them.

The crossroads lay almost a hundred miles from Malburg. In good weather, a rider could cover the distance in three to four days, but an army cannot move as fast. Ludwig's calculations had them marching ten miles a day. The cavalry would go farther afield, searching for signs of the enemy, but the wagons supplying food to his men slowed down the entire army.

His losses were substantial, but adding three companies from Malburg and Lord Wilbur's remaining men helped mitigate the loss. Ludwig's chief worry, however, was how reliable Wilbur's would be, for they'd initially taken up arms in service to King Morgan.

He was pondering this very point when his carriage hit a rut, almost knocking him from his seat. Frederick thought this most entertaining, and Ludwig couldn't help but grin. He let his gaze drift to Charlotte, who watched them with emotionless eyes.

"How are you feeling?" he asked.

"Numb. A result of my treatments."

"Didn't we agree you'd stop undergoing them?"

"We are in the middle of a war," she replied. "You can't afford the distraction of my natural state. Therefore, I shall continue as I am until you are properly enthroned as king."

"That will take time. We still have the capital to capture, which may be months."

"I have complete faith you will devise a way to hasten their surrender, for the blessings of the Saints are with you."

"Perhaps they might be willing to inform us how to win this war?"

"You know as well as I that they don't work that way. They guide us by their teachings, not through direct action."

"Sometimes I wonder if the old Gods were a better choice."

"Despite what you may have read, the old Gods did no better."

"Oh? Are you an expert in religion now?"

"As you know, I am well-read, and the old religion is still common in the north. I'm unsure if you are aware, but even the Temple Fleet sees fit to bless their ships in the name of Akosia."

"Yes. I recall Akosia's blessing during our marriage ceremony. Is it that widespread?"

"It is, especially amongst rural folk. In many ways, the worship of the Saints is only a thin layer on top of centuries of ancient worship. Several of our holidays have their roots in pagan rites, which makes sense if you read about the Saints. They didn't aim to start a new religion, merely define acceptable rules for people to live by."

"You would've made an outstanding prioress."

"I doubt my condition or my noble birth would allow that."

"I don't know," said Ludwig. "Plenty of nobles join the Church."

"True, but very few are the only child of a baron."

"Their loss is my gain."

"There it is again, the Ludwig charm."

"A charm reserved for your exclusive use."

"Tell me, and be honest now, what are our chances of winning this war?"

"It all hinges on Morgan. Even if we fight our way into the capital, we must still track him down. If he escapes, the war will drag on."

"And do you have a plan for that?"

"I hope so," said Ludwig. "I have a way into Harlingen, but there's no guarantee Morgan remains there. He wasn't with his army at Erhard's Folly, and for all we know, he's already fled Hadenfeld to raise additional men."

"Then why take the capital at all?"

"Mostly because it sends a message to the other barons that we are in control. If we prove Morgan fled, it also weakens his position."

"But the war isn't necessarily over at that point?"

"I'm afraid not."

"In that case," said Charlotte, "I shall pray for your success."

"It's not my success, it's ours, but praying is still appreciated."

They arrived at the crossroads to find Lord Merrick waiting for them with two hundred footmen, fifty archers, and another company of Temple Knights of Saint Mathew.

Ludwig greeted his friend with an embrace. He'd returned to Hadenfeld nine years ago, and Merrick had remained a staunch ally ever since. Gita accompanied him, along with young Kenley and a veritable horde of servants to look after the lad.

Rather than waste time, the army continued south towards Harlingen, and by nightfall, they covered another five miles. That evening, they sat by the fire, reminiscing about old times and how much their children had grown. It wasn't until after Gita and Charlotte put their sons to bed that they talked about the war.

"I must admit," said Merrick, "I was taken aback when the Temple Knights showed up. I wondered if I'd done something to upset the Church, but then Temple Captain Henfrey explained things. It appears you've made quite the impression on his superiors."

"I believe that's more due to the efforts of Prior Hieronymus."

"Who is?"

"The Prior of Eisen."

"Captain Henfrey said something about events in the north. Do you know anything about that?"

"Yes. An army led by Temple Commander Charlaine defeated the Halvarian's attempted invasion of Arnsfeld."

"Is she the same Charlaine you're familiar with?"

"She is, and Temple Knights of both Saint Agnes and Saint Mathew were present at the battle."

"Doesn't the Church follow a strict policy of neutrality?"

"Not anymore, it would seem."

"Remarkable," said Merrick. "Dare we hope that the Cunars were present?"

"I'm afraid that's an entirely different matter," replied Ludwig. "Their order not only withdrew from the frontier, thus creating the crisis in the first place, but actively tried to prevent the Agnesites from marching to assist. I'm told it very nearly came to blows."

"But their presence held back the empire!"

"Unfortunately, that's no longer the case."

"Do you think they'll side with Morgan?"

"I doubt it. Even if they did, they don't maintain a commandery in Harlingen, making it very difficult to intervene. I don't suppose Temple Captain Henfrey said anything about additional men?"

"Not in the short term," replied Merrick. "I'm told there are more in nearby kingdoms, but it'll be weeks before they converge on Agran. Of course, if the war drags on, they might play a role, provided you still want them. Speaking of the war, how did you defeat the Royal Army? Didn't they outnumber you?"

"I sent Cyn and Sigwulf south with some archers to keep the southern barons from sending reinforcements."

"And did it work?"

"It must have," replied Ludwig. "The army we faced wasn't nearly as numerous as we'd feared."

"Now you're just being humble. I heard they brought more than you."

"Yes, until the men of Malburg came to our rescue."

"Are you suggesting it was close?"

"We were on the very brink of destruction. Not something I'd care to repeat."

"What did you do about Glosnecke?"

"We ignored it."

"What of its garrison?" asked Merrick.

"If they were coming for us, they would have already done so. It's more likely Lord Darrian is in Harlingen."

"And Emril?"

"He commanded the Royal Army at Erhard's Folly, but I'm afraid he eluded us. Right now, he's probably explaining to Morgan how he lost the battle and a good portion of the king's army."

"What will you offer them once this war's over? Death or forgiveness?"

"I shan't devote any energy to considering that until I'm in Harlingen."

"Have you given any thoughts about how you'll rule?"

"No," said Ludwig. "I've only just come to accept I will be king. Up until now, I had hoped to bring Morgan to his senses."

"You're a better man than me. I'd execute them both."

"As would be your right, as king, but I'd prefer not to begin my rule with a bloodbath."

"So you'll let them off with only an apology?"

"As I said, I haven't decided, but when I sit down to deal with them, I promise I shall consult with my advisors, which includes you. Speaking of advisors, have you heard anything about Father Vernan?"

"The last I knew, he was under lock and key in Morgan's dungeons. I wouldn't worry. It's not as if he's likely to execute a Holy Father."

"I wish I could be certain of that," said Ludwig. "The king increasingly sounds like his emotions are ruling him, and he knows Vernan and I are friends."

"Even so, he'd incur the Church's wrath, which would be the end of him."

"And imprisoning a Holy Father isn't?"

"I know how you feel," said Merrick, "but Vernan is strong of character. He'll survive."

"It's not his character I'm worried about—it's Morgan's temper. Were you there when he executed Meinhard?"

"I was in Harlingen but wasn't at court that particular day. We all heard about it, though. They say the king lost his temper and ranted about you most of the morning."

"It's my fault he killed Meinhard."

"Don't blame yourself for the king's madness."

"Is he mad, though?"

"Are you suggesting he's not?"

"I know he's angry," said Ludwig, "and he thinks highly of his accomplishments, but has he truly lost his mind, or are we using madness as an excuse for his behaviour?"

"I don't know if there's a simple answer to that. Certainly, he's not the same man we met at the coronation. His reign has made him question everyone's loyalty, and you'd eventually earn his wrath even if you hadn't enraged him."

"What makes you say that?"

"Morgan was always a solitary individual. He rarely attended court, and though present for your elevation to baron, he didn't mingle with the other nobles. I think that contributed to his self-reliance and, in turn, his belief in his destiny. Gita tells me it's common for new kings to let their heads expand too quickly."

Ludwig laughed. "All I can do now is picture Morgan with a massive head."

"That's good. It means he has become an object of derision rather than fear. If only the war were so simple."

Ludwig was up before dawn, wandering the camp, deep in thought. All was quiet, but they would arrive at the capital by the end of their march, and the fighting would begin anew. Could he defy all odds and defeat Morgan, or was this his death knell?

"Highness?"

He turned to see Gustavo and grinned. "I was beginning to worry something had happened to you."

"Sorry, Highness, but things took slightly longer than expected."

"Were you successful?"

"We were. We learned the strength of the gate guard, along with the layout of the gatehouse itself. Getting in there will be a tough fight, but I believe it's doable."

"And the other two?"

"They're well, Highness. We only just arrived, so Paran and Edwig went to see the others."

"You've picked your men?"

"I have. Two dozen are prepared to move on your word. Do we break out the surcoats now, or would you rather we wait?"

"Wait," said Ludwig. "Act too soon, and we risk the enemy getting wind of our plan."

"Couldn't we take more men?"

"No. A small force won't appear suspicious, especially when the entire army is in retreat. Bring too many, and you're likely to be put under the command of a captain."

"We could eliminate the captain."

"While I admire your determination, let's not lose sight of what we're trying to accomplish."

"Understood, Highness. We're ready. Just say the word."

Ludwig nodded. "Very well. Stand by, and if anyone gives you any trouble, tell them you're here to guard Lady Charlotte."

"And if they try to confirm that with her?"

"She knows the plan, so she'll cover for you. Remember, this must be kept quiet. Its very success depends on secrecy."

"Aye, Highness. Anything else?"

"Yes. If you manage to do this, I'll promote the three of you to captain."

The man visibly brightened. "Captain? I like the sound of that. What if we fail?"

"Then it won't matter since no one will be left for you to command."

"Understood."

"Send Edwig to me once you've gathered your men. I'll send him back when it's time for you to act."

"We're that close?"

Ludwig pointed south. "Harlingen lies thirty miles in that direction. If we push, we'll arrive in a day and a half. You'll only have one chance, so you have to be convincing."

"We won't let you down, Highness."

"I know you won't."

He waited as the Calabrian disappeared into the darkness. The sun would soon rise, perhaps the last before the fighting commenced. How many more men would die putting him on the Throne?

42

SKIRMISH

AUTUMN 1104 SR

T he messenger rode right up to Ludwig, then halted. "Highness, Lord Merten sends his regards and wishes to inform you he encountered the enemy."

"How many?"

"Our estimates place their numbers somewhere close to two hundred, but we can't be sure. They've fortified a roadside inn, so getting an exact count is difficult. His Lordship wants to know if you wish him to engage."

"Not quite yet," replied Ludwig. "I want to see this myself."

"I assure you, Highness, Lord Merten has more than enough men to deal with them."

"The last time I looked, I commanded this army. Are you now suggesting otherwise?"

"No, Highness. Sorry. I was overcome with excitement."

"Understandable given the circumstances, but if we are to win this war, we must maintain our discipline. Are you familiar with Temple Captain Hamelyn?"

"I am, Highness."

"Then find him and ask him to meet us farther up the road. I assume that's where Lord Merten is?"

"Indeed."

"Then off with you." Ludwig looked around, pausing on Edwig. "Come with me," he said. "Your time is almost upon us."

The Therengian urged his horse forward. Not the most confident of riders, but he managed to keep the beast under control. "You think they'll fall for this?"

"We'll know soon enough."

They galloped off, eager to find Lord Merten before they missed their opportunity. The Baron of Langeven was perched on a slight rise overlooking the road. He bowed his head as Ludwig approached, then nodded at a distant building. "That's it, the Dove. You've likely stayed at it once or twice yourself."

The Dove consisted of two buildings—the inn and a stable, with a large courtyard surrounded by a stone wall to keep wild animals, or bandits, at bay.

"It won't take much to rout them out," said Merten. "I'll send some horsemen south to cut off their retreat. With luck, this entire affair will finish by noon, then we can continue marching."

"Leave your cavalry here," replied Ludwig. "I don't want a slaughter."

"If we don't fight them now, we'll face them on the walls of Harlingen."

"Perhaps, but there's no need to risk additional casualties, especially when there's a city to assault."

"That's your prerogative," said Merten, lapsing into thought. "What if we could force them to surrender without fighting?"

"While I admire the idea, I have other plans."

"Which are?"

Ludwig smiled. "I'll discuss that when the time is right. For now, assemble your men north of the inn, keeping them out of bow range but prepared to advance on my orders."

"Yes, Highness."

Ludwig spotted Temple Captain Hamelyn trotting up the hill. "Get your men into position, Lord Merten. It won't be a long wait."

Merten nodded, then galloped off, eager to begin the fight.

"You wanted to see me, Highness?" said Hamelyn.

"Yes. I have an important task for you and your men, one for which Temple Knights are particularly well-suited."

"I'm all ears."

"Shortly, Lord Merten's going to attack that inn. I'm certain the garrison will resist, but, outnumbered as they are, they'll decide retreat is their only option."

"And you wish my men to chase them down?"

"No, in fact, quite the opposite." Ludwig waved Edwig forward. "Do you see this man here? He and his companions will be dressed in Royal Colours. When the enemy breaks, I want you to pursue, but I need your men to resist the temptation to kill. The object is to drive them back towards the city in a panic. Edwig and the others will join that exodus, but you must make it appear you are chasing them, understand?"

"A ruse? Very clever, Highness."

"Only if it works. My regular cavalry lacks the discipline for this. They'd likely get carried away and kill the enemy, not realizing they're our own men."

"You can count on the Temple Knights, Highness. They won't let you down."

"Edwig, show Temple Captain Hamelyn to the rest of your band. You'll need to coordinate where best to introduce your pack of miscreants into their retreat."

"Yes, Highness."

"And be quick about it. Lord Merten is champing at the bit to get into the fight."

Ludwig turned, looking south as they headed to the army. Harlingen remained out of view, but he knew it was close. This evening, once his scouts were in sight of the walls, the battle for the capital would commence. Was Morgan inside the Royal Keep, plotting Ludwig's demise, or waiting for the inevitable showdown?

A laugh interrupted his thoughts, and he turned to see Frederick running towards him at full speed. Ludwig dismounted, scooped up his son and held him tight. Liesel pursued, huffing and puffing to catch up to the youngster while Charlotte followed at a more sedate pace, focused on Merten's men.

"Sorry, Highness. He's far faster than I am these days."

"Quite all right, Liesel. He can sit here with me and watch the battle unfold."

"So?" called out Charlotte. "Are things about to unfold?"

"They are. I only hope we haven't made a colossal mistake. I'd hate for this to go awry."

"The Saints will protect them."

Lord Merten was now amongst his men, and Ludwig watched them begin the attack. Archers moved to the flanks, raining arrows down on the defenders. They did no visible damage, but it kept the king's men from manning the defences.

Whoever readied the defenders had done an admirable job. Barrels and boxes lined the wall, providing them means to watch the attackers advance. A six-foot-high wall did not supply much in the way of obstacles, for it was easily climbed over, but spearing a man from atop was just as easy. The main gate was the most likely point of attack. A set of double doors barred entry to the courtyard, but a smaller door along the southern wall would likely be their escape route once the time finally came.

Merten's footmen advanced, most having discarded their spears in favour of swords and axes, better weapons for the coming fight. As Ludwig predicted, they headed straight for the main gate. Crossbowmen appeared from behind the wall, loosing bolt after bolt towards the advancing men, doing little damage, but it slowed the advance, leading Ludwig to wonder what other surprises lay in store for them.

They reached the main gate, and axes chopped away at the door. Spearmen moved up on either flank, stabbing at anyone who appeared from the top of the wall.

The axe blows echoed across the field to where Ludwig stood, enthralled. The cries of men were mingled in, some full of bravado, others of fear. He could well imagine the horrors of being packed into that confined space, ready to bring down the door and face prepared defenders.

In an instant, the mob at the gate burst the door open, flooding into the courtyard. Ludwig briefly panicked as Merten's warriors poured in, fearful they'd trapped the defenders, but then a group of the king's men rushed out from the inn, repelling the attack and regaining half the courtyard.

The wild melee continued, and then he noted a stream of men issuing from that southern door, desperate to escape the carnage. They ran towards a nearby copse of trees, fleeing as if the very denizens of the Underworld nipped at their heels. One by one, they disappeared beneath the boughs even as their compatriots still fought for control of the inn.

"There," said Charlotte, pointing.

Ludwig gazed farther south, where a group of men emerged from the safety of the trees, running for all they were worth. Moments later, a horseman wearing the Temple Knight's distinctive brown surcoat burst forth, and then more footmen, followed by horsemen, urging them on in their flight.

Ludwig smiled, for though the Temple Knights were amongst the enemy, not a single one fell. Terrified, these men were oblivious to the restraint shown by their pursuers, nor would any take the time to conclude enemy warriors disguised as fellow soldiers fled with them.

"It worked," said Charlotte. "All thanks to the discipline of the Temple Knights."

"Agreed," he replied, "but let us hope the rest of this wild idea works equally as well."

"It will, for it's both reckless and daring."

"Daring? Or foolhardy?"

"Can it not be both?"

"I should've led them myself."

"You're too easily recognized. Your presence would put them in greater danger."

He fell silent.

"I know you," she said. "You're worried you've thrown these men to their deaths. They volunteered for this, Ludwig. They knew what they were getting into."

"Did they? Or are they trying to impress their future king?"

"You honestly don't see it, do you?"

"See what?"

"The way you affect others. You're a natural leader, Ludwig. You care for your people, and in return, they offer you undying loyalty. You will make a great king."

"How can I rule when I am so full of doubts?"

"It is precisely because of those doubts you will rule wisely. Only a fool rushes into the unknown. Your decisions are tempered by reason. Were more rulers amongst the Petty Kingdoms like you, we'd be the better for it."

"Yet I fight against the very king I swore to serve."

"What else could you have done, handed over Alexandra to be executed? And what about Sigwulf? Without you, he'd be heading to Abelard to face a hangman. You chose to make a stand against tyranny. No one will fault you for that."

"Perhaps, but other rulers don't like usurpers. It sends a message any king might be toppled with the right incentive."

"Then that's a message they all need to hear," said Charlotte. "Too many sit back in wealth and comfort, watching their people suffer. It's time they learned how to govern properly."

"And you think they'll accept me?"

"Hadenfeld has alliances with many places, chief amongst them Erlingen and Reinwick. Do you believe the dukes from the north care one whit about who actually sits on the Throne? They only want you to come to their aid should war break out. I doubt half even know who the King of Hadenfeld is."

"You're right. I worry too much about what I have no control over. I shall try to remain more positive in future."

"Good, and as for the rulers of Erlingen and Reinwick, I'll write to them on your behalf, praising your virtues."

"You know considerably more about this than I do. I'm happy to leave the matter in your hands."

"As you should. You are as wise as you are charming."

"Charming," said Frederick, leading them both to laugh.

. . .

The mist burned off slowly, revealing an army ready to march. Harlingen lay fifteen miles away; by this evening, its walls would be within range of his archers. The very idea both amazed and terrified Ludwig.

In theory, he fielded an army of nearly sixteen hundred men, but nowhere near what he needed to siege the capital. His one hope was that Gustavo's group would do the impossible and seize the city's northern gate.

He noted the approach of Temple Captain Hamelyn, whose horse looked exhausted.

"It is done, Highness," the knight called out. "We kept at them until they were within bow range of the city. I saw your men enter the gate. It's in the hands of the Saints now."

Ludwig let out a breath of air. He hadn't realized how much he feared disaster. This entire plan was fraught with potential problems, yet somehow, they'd pulled it off.

"I assume only we Temple Knights are aware of this?"

"Along with Lady Charlotte, yes, and I think it best we keep it that way."

"You fear the enemy might be amongst us?"

"It's definitely a possibility. A civil war like this splits families and causes people to question their loyalties. The last thing I need is a disgruntled warrior bringing this information to Morgan."

"I swore my men to secrecy, Highness."

"And for that, I thank you."

A shout announced the army was about to march. Hamelyn regarded the distant troops. "They're eager, but I fear they have no idea what they're up against."

"You've been in a siege?"

"I have, although that was before I joined the order. In fact, you might say it's the reason I became a Temple Knight."

"When did this happen?"

"Seems like a lifetime ago. I was barely a man, yet the horrors I witnessed still haunt me. What about you? Have you experienced assaulting city walls?"

"A city, no, but I was once involved in a castle siege in Regnitz, up in Erlingen. Well, I say castle, but it was a keep with an outer courtyard."

"And what was that like?"

"I remember my heart pounding as I climbed the wall only to find myself badly outnumbered. Rather than risk capture, I withdrew with the remainder of the army." He pictured it in his mind. "We used ladders to scale the wall, but there weren't enough of us."

"Did you eventually get in?"

"We did," said Ludwig, "but that's a story in itself. The besieging baron hired an Earth Mage, a decent fellow by the name of Linden Herzog. I don't suppose you know him?"

"I'm afraid not, but then again, practitioners of magic tend to shun Temple Knights."

"Why is that?"

"I'm told they carry a deep-seated fear that the Church disapproves of magic. It's not true; they're merely stories handed down from days long past. I suppose that's due to the mystique of the Ragnarites."

"You said they're dedicated to tracking down and destroying practitioners of dark magic, didn't you?"

"Yes," replied Hamelyn. "The Temple Knights of Saint Ragnar don't operate as other orders do. They have no commanderies in the traditional sense, operating as individuals instead of in companies. They occasionally collaborate with mages, but the average commoner is ignorant of their activities."

"And are there any Ragnarites in Hadenfeld?"

"I couldn't say. They only wear their surcoats for official ceremonies. They usually dress as commoners, the better to blend in and search for signs of trouble."

"Would there be any in Morgan's court?"

"It's a possibility, but it makes little difference. Ragnarites possess no interest in politics; their sole focus is eradicating the forbidden arts."

"Yet your own order is now involved in politics?"

"True, but even if the Ragnarites got involved, their training does not include battlefield tactics. There is a common misconception regarding the fighting orders of Temple Knights. Certainly, some are skilled in swordplay, but our discipline is what makes us so effective on the battlefield. One-on-one, any knight of the Petty Kingdoms might outfight us, but what we lack in individual prowess, we more than make up for with our battlefield awareness and formations."

"Even the Cunars?"

"The Cunars recruit the most able knights on the Continent, but once again, their rigorous adherence to order makes them the most feared fighting order on the Continent."

"I'm told they didn't fight in Arnsfeld."

"Yes, a most disturbing development. I can only surmise the Grand Master of the Order has some grander scheme in mind."

"Let us hope it's a strategy benefiting all the Petty Kingdoms." Ludwig paused, considering his next words carefully. "Might I ask you a question?"

"Of course, Highness."

"Temple Knights fought in Arnsfeld, but why has it taken so long for them to actively resist the empire?"

"I'm afraid I understand little of Church politics, but perhaps it has more to do with gold than belief. Though I am loathe to admit it, it takes coins to run the Church, and if they chose sides in regional conflicts, they might find donations coming to a standstill."

"Yet your own order is helping here."

"As did the sister knights in Arnsfeld. As I've said, times are changing, and we must change with them."

43

HARLINGEN
AUTUMN 1104 SR

After raiding their way through Arnsbach, Hasdorf, and Grienwald, Cyn and Sig had turned their attention towards the lands of Lord Jurgen. They soon discovered they were too late, for the baron had already marched to Morgan's aid.

They'd halted astride the Harlingen-Bruggendorf road, considering their next course of action, when the sound of horses interrupted them. Sigwulf ordered everyone into the bushes, where the archers stood in readiness, poised to shower the enemy with arrows, awaiting the command to commence their deadly work.

The horsemen came into view, four men leading the way, their armour gleaming in the noonday sun, but the flag they carried wasn't that of Hadenfeld.

Sigwulf grinned. "Lower your weapons," he commanded his men, then stepped from the treeline. The knights slowed, drawing their swords. Behind them came a carriage, followed by another four knights.

"Greetings," said Sigwulf. "I trust His Grace is well this day?"

The lead knight halted his men and sheathed his sword. "I know you. You attended the duke's court last year."

"That I did. The name's Sigwulf Marhaven."

Cyn emerged from the woods. "Are you going to introduce us?"

"Aye. This is Captain Cynthia Hoffman, commander of Prince Ludwig's archers."

"Greetings," the knight replied. "My name is Sir Roderick of Tollingsbruck. I have the honour of commanding the escort of Lord Ulfric Sternhassen, Duke of Hollenbeck."

"What's going on here?" called a voice from the carriage.

"We have company, Your Grace."

The door opened, and a tall man, around forty years of age with a mane of red hair and a matching bushy beard, stepped out. Lord Ulfric grinned as he set eyes on Sigwulf. "You're the last person I expected to find in the middle of nowhere."

"Might I ask where you're headed?" said Sigwulf.

"Isn't it obvious? To Harlingen. Unless you mean to suggest I'm on the wrong road?"

"Not at all, Your Grace. I'm just struggling to understand why you're here in Hadenfeld?"

"After last year's unfortunate events, I decided I should meet this King Morgan of yours. My hope is that we can come to some sort of peaceful resolution. Many issues still lie unresolved as a result of those circumstances."

"I assume you passed through Bruggendorf on the way north?"

"I did. It looks like war has come to Hadenfeld. Might that have something to do with your presence here?"

"It might," said Sigwulf. "But before I continue, you could save me some time by sharing what you already know."

"The locals informed me Prince Ludwig has taken up arms against his rightful king. Is that correct?"

"It is, though there's a lot more to the story."

"Which you are about to explain?"

"I already told you about the plot to invade Hollenbeck. What you don't know is that King Morgan was behind it."

"You said naught of this when you came to my court in Klermacht."

"I didn't hear about it until well after the fact, Your Grace."

"You give me pause," said the duke. "In light of this information, I should reconsider my visit."

"Did you send word you were coming?"

"No. I didn't know who to trust to ensure it reached the king."

"What would be the point?" piped in Cyn. "You know how court works; notes are passed off to someone at the Palace. That's likely what he was worried about."

"You are perceptive," said the duke. "And yes, that was exactly my concern. Hollenbeck is not an influential kingdom, and, as such, it's unlikely to attract attention from a powerful ruler like Morgan. Going in person, however, makes it impossible to ignore us. Your news has me reconsidering the wisdom of it."

"Perhaps I can suggest an alternative?" said Cyn.

"What would you have me do?"

"Allow us to escort you. We'll ensure your safety while within Harlingen's walls."

"With all due respect, I fail to see how the pair of you could guarantee my safety."

Cyn whistled, and two-score of archers stepped from the woods. The duke's knights looked ready to fight, but His Grace raised his hand. "Hold!" he called out. "Sheath your weapons. They are not your enemy." His gaze flicked to Cyn. "Remarkable. I never imagined so many could hide in there."

"It is their stock-in-trade, Your Grace. These men are rural folk used to living in the wild. I propose we march with you to Harlingen. Consider us servants of the king, escorting you to court if you wish."

"But you serve Prince Ludwig, do you not?"

"We do," replied Sigwulf. "But I promise you, we bear you no ill will."

"I'm afraid you've confused me. While I appreciate the extra men to keep me safe, what do you hope to gain by this?"

"It will put us within the city of Harlingen," said Cyn.

"How does that aid your prince?"

"Sooner or later, he'll come to take the Throne. If we're in the capital, we can help."

"I'm afraid cooperating in this manner wouldn't endear me to King Morgan."

"King Morgan will fall," insisted Sigwulf, "and Ludwig will become king in his place, which puts a friendly face on your border."

"How do I know he would honour your promise?"

"Because he sent me to warn you about the impending invasion last year."

"And he suffered for that," added Cyn, "all the while refusing to compromise his principles."

"Whatever do you mean?" asked the duke.

"When he exposed the plot to King Morgan, the king banished him to a place called Eisen, with orders to punish the eastern barons for their part in the recent war."

"And did he?"

"He did not. Instead, he helped them rebuild, earning their loyalty and respect."

"Yet he chose to rise against King Morgan."

"One of the barons, Lord Meinhard, spoke on his behalf, and the king executed him for his temerity. He later extended the death sentence to include the baron's entire family. If that weren't enough, he seized Ludwig's barony, giving the title to someone else."

"Astounding. I had no idea. I see now why he rebelled."

"So you'll help us?"

"I only have eight knights here at present. Much as I sympathize with your circumstances, I can do little."

"But you could allow us to escort you into the city," said Cyn. "Call us an honour guard from Bruggendorf if you like. It's not as if our archers wear surcoats identifying who they serve."

"I could do that, but I'm afraid you and Sigwulf are distinctive individuals. Wouldn't someone recognize you?"

Sir Roderick cleared his throat. "I might have a solution of my own, Your Grace, though it requires a little more active participation on our part."

"Go on."

"If I understand correctly, your archers could pass for Royal Troops, yes?"

"Most certainly," said Cyn.

"But it's you and Sigwulf who risk discovery?"

"Yes."

He smiled. "Here's what I'm proposing…"

A line of people sought entry at Harlingen's southern gate, for word had spread that a rebel army was closing in on the capital. Now, every farmer from the surrounding area hastened to the safety of its walls, flooding the streets with all their worldly belongings.

Upon seeing the Duke of Hollenbeck's carriage, the guards pushed the commoners off the road, mistaking the duke's arrival for reinforcements. The archers of Verfeld halted as they reached the gates, their 'captain' presenting himself to the guards.

"I am Captain Roderick," he said. "We've brought reinforcements for His Majesty. What news have you of the rebels?"

"They're north of the city," replied the guard. "Word is they'll be here by the end of the week." His gaze wandered down the road. "You have knights?"

"Yes. They were down in Bruggendorf selecting replacement mounts." He lowered his voice. "Had they not been so particular, we would've arrived sooner, but you know how knights can be."

The fellow grinned. "Aye, I do. You'd best get inside before we're ordered to close the gates." He was about to wave him through when he remembered the carriage. "Wait. Who's in there?"

"The baron, of course."

"Lord Jurgen marched through here weeks ago."

Roderick smiled. "I never claimed it was Jurgen."

"Who else would be coming from Bruggendorf?"

"Who do you think His Majesty trusts to gather more knights?"

"Lord Nikolaus?"

"Ah. I can't fool you, Sergeant."

The guard's chest puffed up. "Very well, on your way."

Roderick gave the command, and the archers continued into the city. Sigwulf passed through the gatehouse, dressed as a common archer, while Cyn rode on the back of the duke's carriage, hoping to pass for a servant. The condition of her clothing was the only disadvantage, for she'd used her dress repeatedly to infiltrate the towns and villages of the southern barons. The information she'd gleaned was well worth the risk, but as it now stood, her clothes were covered in filth, hardly the type of thing a baron's servant might wear.

Thankfully, the guards took no notice. The entire group was soon in amongst the streets of Harlingen, halting once they'd gone a few blocks, and then Sir Roderick surrendered his temporary command.

"You impress me," said Cyn. "You managed that situation well."

"A little improvisation on my part," replied the knight. "I once considered a career in the theatre."

"And you became a knight instead?"

"I'm afraid I have expensive tastes, and it doesn't pay well. It was much easier finding service as a knight."

"Doesn't that require years of training?"

Roderick smiled. "Being the second son of a baron, it was more of a birthright for me than any particular calling."

The duke stepped from his carriage, walking over to Sigwulf. "Your little ruse was successful. Now that you're in Harlingen, what's your plan?"

"Disappear into the city streets and learn more about recent events. What about you?"

"I shall find somewhere nice to stay and then send word to King Morgan that I am here. After that, I'll await his pleasure."

"I wish you well, Your Grace."

"And I, you, Sigwulf. I hope we meet again."

Cyn joined them, now back in her armour. "It was nice meeting you, Your Grace."

"The pleasure was all mine. I wish both of you well in your future endeavours, but I hope you'll understand when I deny knowing you should things turn out for the worse.

"We wouldn't have it any other way."

"And if Ludwig does seize the Crown, I shall happily pay my respects."

"I'm sure he'd appreciate that," said Sigwulf. "Now, if you will excuse us, Your Grace, we have men to look after."

It was a cold evening as they stepped from the Lucky Duck, a rundown place, not typically the spot one might expect to find well-dressed clientele, but it served the needs of the warriors who manned the walls.

"Winter is coming," said Cyn, her breath visible. "If Ludwig doesn't attack soon, he'll be too late."

"It won't be long now." Sig thumbed over his shoulder towards a building. "Those folks came from Verfeld, and I heard them say the rebels weren't far behind. You?"

"I heard similar. They're expecting an attack in the next day or two." She looked at him and grinned. "We have a knack for arriving just at the right time."

"You're the tactician; what's our next move?"

She nodded eastward. "The north gate is over there. How about we wander down there and take a gander?"

"I thought you'd never ask."

They sauntered down the street so as to not attract undue attention. At this time of night, only guards were about, either returning home or reporting to their posts. None paid any mind to the duo as they advanced towards their objective.

The walls of Harlingen rose higher than any single-storey building nestled in behind them. The gatehouse was even larger, with two massive towers standing on either side. They couldn't see the bases, for the intervening building blocked their view, but it soon became apparent they weren't the only ones interested in viewing the king's defences.

Cyn spotted a pair of men peering around the corner of a building, watching the gate. Their backs were to Cyn and Sig, but the bright moonlight glinted off their armour.

"What's this now?" she said, stopping abruptly.

Sigwulf followed her gaze. "What is it?"

"Can't you see those men?"

"Men? I thought one was a woman, and they were just enjoying each other's company."

"By peering around the corner of a building while wearing armour? I think not."

"What else could they be? We told our men to stay away. Besides, they don't wear metal armour."

"Perhaps we should investigate?"

"How do you want to proceed?"

"I'll go ahead," replied Cyn. "After all, I'm the quiet one. You be prepared to charge in if things go bad." She moved up, keeping to the shadows. As she got closer, she heard the men whispering.

"I don't like this," came a familiar voice. "There are too many."

"We knew the risk when we took it on," replied another, tinged with an accent of some type.

"Gustavo?" called out Cyn. "Is that you?"

Both figures whirled around, hands dropping to sword hilts. Paran was the first to recognize her. "Captain Hoffman? What are you doing here?"

"I could ask you the same."

Gustavo looked around, noting the presence of Sigwulf. "We are discovered!"

"That's just Siggy," said Cyn. "Why are you here?"

"We're spying out the north gate. His Highness intends to attack tomorrow night, and we're supposed to seize it."

"Just the two of you?"

"No. We've got some men hidden away."

"How did you manage that?"

Gustavo grinned, the white of his teeth standing out in the moonlight. "It was Ludwig's idea, Saints love him. We dressed in captured surcoats, joining what remained of the Royal Army as it retreated into Harlingen."

"How long ago was that?"

"Just last night. Weren't you two in the south?"

"We were," said Cyn. "We tied down some of the enemy but then learned Lord Jurgen made it north with his men. We reckoned it best to come here ourselves in the hope we could be of use."

"How many did you bring?"

"Forty archers, ourselves included." She waved over Sigwulf. "It looks as though the Saints brought us here for a reason."

"Nonsense," replied Sig. "I've got a hard time believing the Saints had anything to do with it. Are you proposing they brought us here to take the gate because, if so, their timing is off. We've seen no sign of Ludwig's army."

"Until now," said Cyn. "Don't you recognize Gustavo and Paran?"

Sigwulf rubbed his eyes. "I have a hard time seeing in the dark, as you well know."

She giggled. "That's how the badger got into the tent."

"This is not the place to discuss that!"

"Why don't we combine forces? Our archers can help protect your men as they advance on the gate."

"A wonderful idea," replied Gustavo, "although I fear it'll still be a tough fight."

"Then allow Siggy to lend a more direct hand. I'd offer to join the melee myself, but I'm needed to organize the archers. Don't worry. If the fighting gets too fierce, we'll charge in and help."

"I can't thank you enough."

"Nonsense," said Cyn. "We're all on the same side."

"How did you get into the city?"

"We had some help from an outsider."

"Who?"

"Let's just say the guards at the gate were happy for reinforcements, and leave it at that, shall we? I shouldn't like to name names."

"This is grand," said Sigwulf, "but if we're going to succeed, we'll need to know when the attack is coming."

"I doubt that'll be difficult to discover," said Gustavo. "Word will spread rapidly, and every available soldier will be called to defend the walls."

"True, but we have forty men scattered throughout the city. Alerting them they're needed could take precious time."

"We need to mass them somewhere nearby," suggested Cyn. "That way, they'll be available on short notice." She looked back up the street. "We'll place them all within a block of the Lucky Duck and send word once the siege commences."

"That works," replied Gustavo. "I'll send someone there to inform you when the attack on the gate is ready."

44

ASSAULT

AUTUMN 1104 SR

Ludwig stood on the hilltop, gazing at the distant walls of the capital. The assault commenced tonight; one way or the other, this would end his rebellion. There was no turning back. Either he would sit on the Throne of Hadenfeld come morning or lie rotting on the battlefield.

Below, to the south, the rebel army was preparing to attack. A nighttime affair allowed his men to get close to the wall before the king's archers could begin picking their targets. Ladders had been prepared to assist them in their endeavours, but Ludwig hoped they'd prove unnecessary.

Lord Merrick wandered up to stand beside him. "The men are nervous, Highness."

"Please," he replied. "Call me Ludwig. We're not exactly at court here."

"Are you certain a direct assault is our best course of action?"

Ludwig smiled. "I've been keeping a secret, but it's time I shared it."

"Whatever do you mean?"

"I smuggled two dozen men into Harlingen posed as Royal Troops. They'll attempt to seize the north gate once the assault begins."

"How will they know when to strike?"

"They can't miss our men advancing, but just to be safe, I have archers standing by to send up a signal."

"That being?"

"Flaming arrows."

"How will they spot those from within the city?"

"The plan is to aim nearly vertical. It would be easier with a Fire Mage, but I hear they're in short supply these days."

"Speaking of which," said Merrick, "what do we do if Koldan Sartellian shows up?"

"We kill him. You can't negotiate with someone hurling flames at you."

"But he's a Fire Mage? Surely his power could wipe out our army?"

"No. Even a powerful mage is weak against numbers. I have no doubt he could kill any of us with a single fire streak, but we have nearly fifteen hundred warriors at our disposal. It only takes one arrow in the right location to down someone like that."

"Wouldn't that make an enemy of his family?"

"Likely," said Ludwig, "but they're in league with the Halvarians, so they're already against us."

"I wish I saw the Continent's politics as clearly as you."

"It's not difficult. You need only think with your heart. If something seems morally wrong, then it is." When Ludwig returned to Hadenfeld, Merrick welcomed him with open arms, and the two had been firm friends ever since. Now Ludwig worried this war might cost the baron his life. "Be careful today," he warned. "I know leading men in battle isn't your area of expertise."

"Don't worry. I will do my duty."

"I never doubted that for a moment."

"Any advice for my first battle?"

"Yes. Spend some time with Gita before we start. You need a clear head once the assault begins, and you can't do that when you're worried about her and Kenley."

"When are we to start?"

Ludwig glanced west at the sun low on the horizon, but there was still time before darkness enveloped them. "We won't attack till well after dark. I want to lure the defenders into a false sense of safety." He pointed to a hill farther to the east. "The group of archers waits over there. When they send up flaming arrows, the attack commences. Your men have their orders?"

"Indeed. They shall form up as the sun sets."

"It might be wise to get them into position earlier if possible. Things become a little confusing once we lose the light."

"Might I ask who will lead the attack on the gate?"

"I shall do that myself."

"Surely not. You're the prince. Without you, there is no rebellion."

"We waged this entire campaign against overwhelming odds, yet we now stand at the gates of Harlingen itself. I cannot allow my warriors to sacrifice their lives without me leading them."

"And if you die?"

"My life matters not in the grand scheme of things. The most important outcome of this battle is to remove Morgan from the Throne. Do that, and the realm will prosper."

"Can it, though? It feels like the last few years have brought nothing but turmoil. First, it was Neuhafen, then this rebellion. Will we ever see true peace?"

"Peace is fleeting," said Ludwig. "This war is only the beginning of our troubles, not just for Hadenfeld but the Continent as a whole."

Merrick nodded his head. "Yes. It was only a matter of time before alliances broke down and the Petty Kingdoms started fighting amongst themselves."

"It's not the Petty Kingdoms I fear—it's the Halvarians. They and their allies have been planning the complete conquest of the Continent for centuries."

"But we beat them in Arnsfeld, didn't we?"

"We defeated one army," said Ludwig, "but I fear they have many more. The next time they cross the border, they'll come in numbers too great to count."

"I suppose that makes it even more important we defeat Morgan?"

Ludwig smiled. "If I am to rule Hadenfeld, I must demonstrate I'm not afraid to take chances. Don't worry. I won't throw my life away on a whim, but I can't oversee this one from a distant hilltop, particularly at night. I need to be up close to react to changing developments while you're creating a nice distraction."

"By threatening to scale the walls with a ladder assault?"

"Precisely."

"I can do that."

"I'm glad to hear that. Now, you'd best find Gita while you still have time."

Merrick regarded him once more before holding out his hand. "Let us part now, Ludwig, with a promise to meet again in the morning."

Ludwig shook his friend's hand. "So be it."

By the time darkness had covered the city, Ludwig stood amongst his warriors. The assault was being carried out on a broad front, with eight hundred footmen advancing on the walls of Harlingen simultaneously. Behind them, four hundred bowmen would send volley after volley over their heads, the barrage continuing until they would deploy the ladders, then the footmen were on their own.

Under the command of Lord Emmett, the cavalry remained in reserve, prepared to charge forward once Ludwig's group seized the gate, all save for the Temple Knights. Hamelyn's dismounted knights accompanied Ludwig in his mad rush to the gate. The Temple Captain proposed that the presence of Holy warriors amongst the attackers might give the defenders second thoughts about their loyalty to the king. Even without a guarantee it would work, Ludwig accepted the idea, for it allowed his army's most well-trained men through the gate first, assuming those inside secured it in time.

Ludwig gazed off to the east, waiting for the signal to attack. He closed his eyes, reflecting on what had brought him to this day. When he'd returned to Hadenfeld, he expected to live out the rest of his days as Baron of Verfeld, but it was not to be. There was his arranged marriage, and though he loved Charlotte, it still stung that he had no choice.

After that came the civil war and the Second Battle of Harlingen, a close-run thing so intense it could've easily ended in disaster. On that day, he killed the King of Neuhafen and, by his actions, brought the eastern barons back under the King of Hadenfeld's banner.

After the war, he was content to spend his time with his wife and child, but then Morgan was crowned, creating new problems. Would there be no end to this? Was he to seize the Throne only to be beset by more troubles? This wasn't the life he sought, but by the Saints, if he became king, he'd do his best to avoid the mistakes of his predecessors.

A dozen fiery arrows flew into the sky, signalling the beginning of the assault. Ludwig turned back to the gate, only to find Temple Captain Hamelyn watching him.

"We are ready to advance on your command, Highness."

"Then let it begin."

Orders echoed along the line, and the footmen advanced. Behind them came the archers, accompanying them until they reached their designated positions, and then they'd start their barrage of arrows.

The Temple Knights of Saint Mathew marched in step, the entire line advancing in perfect harmony. Voices rose from the darkness, and Ludwig realized they sang a hymn to their Saint.

They passed a series of stakes set into the ground, marking the farthest advance of the archers, the knights continuing, their voices growing louder in praise of blessed Saint Mathew.

Ludwig glanced skyward, knowing the volleys would soon begin, but in the darkness, he saw little save for the flicker of embers drifting up from torches.

The walls grew closer, the enemy archers gathering atop them. With the gatehouse so well-lit, even from this distance, he spotted men manhandling large pots close to the battlements, ready to topple boiling liquid down upon the attackers. He suddenly imagined himself screaming with the agony of scalded flesh, and then the hymn reached its chorus.

Be not afraid. In thy service, thou does do the will of the Saints. A surge of calm washed away his fears, his steps grew more determined, and he felt as if his destiny guided him. The thought would have horrified him at one time, but now it comforted him. He was the servant of Saint Mathew, guided by his hand. No, that wasn't quite right. The Saints led by example, not through direct intervention. A hard reality, yet it still comforted him.

An arrow flew in amongst the Temple Knights, then another. Soon, dozens were hurtling towards them, though few did any damage. Ludwig heard one career off Hamelyn's helmet, and then one dug into his cloak, lodging there, reminding him of his mortality.

A noise arose ahead, and he assumed the enemy was organizing their defences, but then someone fell from the wall.

"It's the assault on the gate," he called out. "We need to reach the gate-house as quickly as possible."

Hamelyn gave the order, and the knights surged forward. It was a strange sight—fifty Temple Knights running at the same speed, refusing to break formation even in their haste.

Ludwig struggled to keep up, amazed at the pace these men managed while fully armoured. They pressed up against the great doors of Harlingen, battering away with their axes.

He glanced up and saw liquid pouring from an embrasure. "Back!" he shouted.

Five men were struck, soaking them with boiling water. Steam sprayed everywhere, and though the knights received burns, for the most part, their armour protected them.

Those he'd warned surged forward again, their axes hacking away at the great doors of the city. Another body toppled over the battlements, and then a bearded face peered down, waving a hand.

"Cease!" called out Ludwig.

The Temple Knights halted their assault. A rattle was heard as the drop bar was lifted, and then the doors opened wide, and Hamelyn ordered his men to help seize the tower.

Inside the gatehouse, the short tunnel led to an open door at the farther end, the city beckoning.

"I need to reach the Royal Keep," Ludwig shouted, straining to be heard above the din of battle.

"Follow me," said Hamelyn. "I know it well."

They rushed into the streets of Harlingen, a score of knights following.

"This way!" a voice called out, and Ludwig grinned in response.

A group of archers with a strip of green tied to their arms paused just inside the gate. Cyn stood to one side, looking pleased with herself, waiting until they neared before continuing. "You certainly took your time getting here."

"Where's Sigwulf?"

She nodded at the gatehouse. "Over there, keeping the enemy busy."

"I don't suppose you have any idea where Morgan is?"

"At the keep, but if you want to catch him, you'll need to move quickly. He has a carriage waiting for a quick escape."

"What makes you say that?"

She grinned. "We took a look around before we lost the light."

"Then lead on. I'm eager to pay him a visit."

"Good," said Cyn. "I hoped you'd say that. Let's go. I know a shortcut." She tore off down a side street, her archers rushing after her.

Ludwig and Hamelyn followed in their wake, the Temple Knights setting a more measured pace. The path twisted and turned, and Ludwig soon lost his bearings. Cyn, however, didn't lead them astray, emerging from an alleyway next to the side of the Royal Keep. She waited until the others caught up, then brought them around the front of the building.

A trio of guards stood ready, weapons drawn, fear etched on their faces. Ludwig slowed, trying to project an air of calm. "Throw down your arms," he called out. "It's over. The city is ours."

Cyn spread the archers out and had them nock arrows. Despite this, the guards stood firm.

"Leave now, in the name of the king."

"I can't do that," replied Ludwig. "Lay down your arms, or I'll be forced to order your deaths."

The Temple Knights joined them, and given the now overwhelming odds, the king's men threw down their weapons. Hamelyn moved up, taking them into custody.

"Where is the king?" he demanded.

"Inside," one replied.

"Something's wrong," said Cyn. "There should be a carriage waiting for him."

"Has he already fled?" asked Ludwig.

The guard met his gaze. "No, Highness, not while we've been on duty."

"How long have you been here?"

"We took our posts just before dark."

"There was a carriage," offered one of his compatriots.

"Where is it now?"

"It was ordered to move around behind the keep."

"By whom?"

"A tall, long-haired fellow."

"Blond?"

"Yes, that's him. Do you know him?"

"Koldan Sartellian," said Ludwig. "Cyn, take the archers and secure that carriage, but be careful. We're dealing with a Fire Mage."

"How can my men help?" asked Hamelyn.

"You'd best come with me. We've got a king to find and plenty more Royal Guards to deal with."

They rushed into the keep, finding Lord Emril pacing in the great hall, wearing the plate armour favoured by knights, but his helmet was nowhere to be seen.

"So," Emril snarled, "the traitor finally appears."

"Stand aside," said Hamelyn. "This doesn't concern you."

"Doesn't it? I swore myself to the service of the true King of Hadenfeld. If necessary, I will give my life."

"My knights will cut you down where you stand."

"No," said Ludwig. "He's my problem. I'll deal with him." He stepped forward, his sword at the ready. "Block the doors. I don't want him getting away."

"As you wish, Majesty."

"Majesty?" said Emril. "Don't make me laugh. You're no more royal than a rat."

"Even a rat has teeth."

"Spoken like the cur you are."

"Your words do not frighten me," said Ludwig. "Give up this useless charade while you still live."

"You forget, I was a king's knight. I've spent my entire life training for war."

"And I've spent years fighting them. You're not the only one in Hadenfeld who received such training."

They circled each other, both hesitant to attack first.

"Whatever happened to you, Ludwig. You could have stayed in Eisen and done the king's bidding, and no one would've thought ill of you."

"Who says they do now?"

"You and I both know you schemed to usurp your rightful king."

"I didn't turn on my king—he turned on me."

Emril lunged, the tip of his sword scraping across Ludwig's chest plate, doing no damage, then followed up with another strike.

Ludwig was ready for him, parrying the blow and letting Emril's sword slide up to his cross-guard before he twisted his blade, his tip digging into

Emril's gauntlet. The former knight shrank back, his blade still in hand, blood dripping down its handle.

"I learned a few things in the north," said Ludwig. "One of which is to invest in a good pair of gauntlets." He lashed out with his fist, slamming into his opponent's face, his cross-guard digging into the man's cheek.

As Emril backed up to gather courage for a strike, Ludwig lunged, ramming his blade into Emril's face, penetrating the skull. The weight of Emril's body tore Ludwig's weapon from his grasp as the knight fell.

Hamelyn advanced, looking down at the body. "Well," he said, "at least you've saved us the trouble of a trial."

"He wouldn't see reason," replied Ludwig.

"True, but the fight's not over yet. There's a king waiting to be vanquished."

45

CONFRONTATION
AUTUMN 1104 SR

They spread out, searching the keep room by room, determined to end Morgan's reign. The few Royal Guards remaining fled rather than face the Temple Knights' fury. The longer the search went on, the emptier the keep became.

A trio of servants rushed past Ludwig, eager to escape, and then a familiar face entered the corridor.

"Darrian," said Ludwig. "What are you doing here? I expected you to stay in Glosnecke."

The baron sneered. "You'd like that, wouldn't you? Save you the trouble of facing my steel."

"I have no desire to kill you."

"It's a bit late for that, don't you think?"

Ludwig glanced behind him, but the Temple Knights were busy clearing other rooms.

Darrian noticed the glance. "What's the matter, Highness? Worried your allies abandoned you?"

"Stand aside. I'm after Morgan, not you."

"And you believe I'll hand him over?" Darrian drew his sword, but instead of advancing towards Ludwig, he ducked through a nearby door.

Ludwig rushed after him into an unfamiliar room, likely a private dining area for the king. Someone had gone to the trouble of pushing the table and chairs to one side, freeing up a large, open space. Ludwig realized his mistake as the door slammed shut behind him, and six knights surrounded him.

"Kill him!" screamed Darrian, fleeing through a door on the other side of the room.

The attacks came in a rush. A blade hit Ludwig in the back, his armour preventing any damage. Another struck out, and he raised his weapon just in time to block it, even as a third scraped off one of his greaves. He remembered the training of his former sword master, Kurt Wasser, and embarked on a series of whirlwind strikes designed to keep multiple enemies at a distance. It partially worked as he now faced only three men, the others backing away to allow their comrades space to fight.

Ludwig blocked another blow, forcing the tip of the knight's sword into the floor, and then he stomped down, breaking the blade. Before his foe recovered, he swung his sword with all his strength, smashing it into the fellow's gauntlet. The metal held, but the knight grunted in pain, dropping his weapon.

Another stepped forward, his attack a feeble thrust at Ludwig's chest. He let the blow deflect off his armour, then hit the fellow's helmet with such strength it rang out, echoing off the walls.

He kept up his defence with a flurry of blows, forcing his foes at bay, but he was so busy protecting himself that he had little chance to launch a counterattack.

He thought he was a dead man when the door behind him flew open, but then Temple Knights rushed to his aid. The attacks against Ludwig subsided, with two of Darrian's men dead on the floor, the rest nursing wounds of varying degrees.

"This way," shouted Ludwig, sprinting towards the other door. He was about to rush in, but that had nearly led to disaster. Pausing, he readied his weapon before opening the door to a small room. Against the far wall stood a statue of a Saint. This was obviously a chapel, adorned as it was with a stained-glass window that would have been bathed in light if it weren't for the late hour. The statue and its pedestal caught his attention, for someone had shifted it to the side.

A Temple Knight peered over his shoulder. "Where did they go?"

Ludwig moved to the window, then dropped to his knees, examining the floor. "There must be a hatch here somewhere."

"In a chapel?"

"It's an escape route." He pulled forth his dagger, prying at a floorboard to no avail.

The Temple Knight examined the statue. "Something looks out of place here."

Ludwig rose, moving closer to look. "This is Saint Mathew, or so says the plaque."

"Then it's a poor sculptor who created it." The knight pointed to the sword at the Saint's side. "There are several reasons why Temple Knights use axes, one being we emulate Mathew's practices."

Ludwig looked closer. The statue was carved from a single block of stone with the pommel added after the fact. He removed a gauntlet and reached out, grabbing it. Nothing more than a stone disk, but the pommel rotated with a resounding click, and a portion of the floor sprang up slightly, revealing a trap door hinged on one side.

The knight lifted it up, exposing a set of spiral stairs. Ludwig peered down, straining to listen, but more Temple Knights entered the tiny room, making such efforts impractical.

"Let me go first, Highness," said one. Ludwig nodded despite his desire to lead. The steep stairs left no space to wield anything other than a dagger. The knight ahead of him descended at a reasonable pace, but dressed as he was in bulky plate armour, Ludwig's arms scraped the walls.

With light sconces every ten steps, the smoke they produced had nowhere to go, lingering in layers, burning his eyes. They reached the bottom and found a tunnel heading in a straight line.

Onward, they went until the floor slowly began to rise, indicating the tunnel was nearing its exit. The Temple Knight in front yelled a warning as flames flew towards them, taking the brunt of it, falling face down to lie motionless.

Ludwig struggled to breathe. The flames, the work of a Fire Mage, burned away the air, leaving the tunnel full of smoke and the grotesque stench of burned flesh. A Temple Knight pushed past him, intent on seeking revenge for his brother's demise.

Ludwig collapsed to his knees, gasping for air. Another knight took hold of his arms, tugging him to his feet as a flash of light exploded down the corridor. Then, just as suddenly, the fire abated, and a dull thud echoed towards him. As his eyes adjusted, he observed an axe being pulled from the dead Fire Mage.

He staggered forward, aided by his allies. At the end of the corridor, a ladder led up towards another trap door thrown open to the night sky. Someone helped him get his feet on the rungs, and it didn't take long before he inhaled fresh air.

Ludwig looked around, trying to determine where he was. The back of the keep overshadowed him while a carriage and horses stood in front, waiting. Between them, bodies littered the street. A warrior leaned over a body filled with arrows.

"Rikal? Is that you?"

The archer grinned. "It is, Highness, or should I say, sire?" He rolled the body over, revealing King Morgan with even more arrows protruding from his chest.

"It couldn't be helped," came Cyn's voice as she examined three more corpses, all warriors.

"Where's Darrian?" asked Ludwig.

She pointed. "Over there."

A scowling Baron of Glosnecke sat beside the carriage, blood dripping from an arrow embedded in his shoulder. Ludwig approached the man, quickly noticing he was tied to the carriage wheel. "I surrender," Darrian said. "Morgan is dead, and you are now the rightful King of Hadenfeld."

Ludwig ignored him, turning to Cyn. "What happened here?"

"I brought the archers round back and found the carriage. We took the driver into custody, then hid men amongst the shadows. This lot didn't waste any time showing up."

Ludwig wandered over to Morgan's body. "Twelve arrows. A mite extreme, don't you think?"

"Sorry," replied Cyn. "When they realized it was the king, the men got a little carried away."

"Yet Darrian received only one?"

She shrugged. "What can I say? The man's a coward and begged us to let him surrender."

More knights exited the escape tunnel, and then Temple Captain Hamelyn emerged, scanning the area until his gaze fell on Ludwig. "Majesty. The keep is yours."

"Thank you," replied Ludwig. "I'd be obliged if you would garrison it until I can make alternate arrangements."

"Of course, sire."

"And send someone to release everyone in the dungeon."

"Everyone?"

"Keep them close at hand till we sort them out, but somewhere amongst them is Father Vernan." As soon as he said the words, panic rushed through him. Was Vernan still alive, or had the king executed him? He looked at Darrian.

"Don't worry," replied the baron. "He's alive, although I daresay he's lost some weight." He chuckled at his jibe, but then his wound caused him to grimace in pain.

"Cyn, spread the word that Morgan is dead. That should end any remaining fighting."

"And then?" she asked.

"Find Sig and get both your arses to the keep. We'll have plenty of work come morning."

"Yes, Majesty." She made an exaggerated bow.

Hamelyn was not amused. "You should show proper respect to your king."

"No," said Ludwig. "She's reminding me I'm only a man to keep me humble."

Dawn arrived, and with it, Lord Merrick brought his men to the keep, replacing the Temple Knights. A thin, frail-looking Father Vernan insisted on being at Ludwig's side.

Charlotte and a full cavalry escort arrived by mid-morning. She stepped from the carriage, holding Frederick's hand as he jumped out. Ludwig grinned from ear to ear, and though the coming months would be difficult, he knew he could endure them with her by his side.

Late that afternoon, they gathered in the great hall. At Ludwig's insistence, the room was cleared of furnishings to accommodate the participation of commoners. He stepped onto a chair to address everyone. Admittedly, it was not the most dignified way to go about this, but it allowed one and all to see him.

"Morgan is dead," he announced. "And with him dies the petty jealousies and scheming that has plagued our kingdom. I cannot promise you my rule will be perfect, for I am but a mortal man. However, I will strive to fulfil the sacred vow all kings should make, that of protecting the welfare of the good people of Hadenfeld."

He paused to take a breath. The crowd watched, expectation on their faces, and suddenly, he was at a loss for words. Struggling to think what to say, he felt Charlotte's hand slip into his. He looked down at her, their eyes met, and it calmed him.

"Let it be known, all men who fought for King Morgan are granted amnesty if they present themselves at this keep within a week to swear an oath of loyalty." He paused, letting the words sink in. "Those who defy this edict are considered outlaws and will feel the full weight of the king's justice."

He raised his voice to address the commoners in the back. "The fighting has ceased, and while I cannot guarantee that war will never return to this fair land, I promise we will be prepared if it does."

The words felt inadequate, yet they had the desired effect as cheering broke out, drowning out any possibility of anything further. Ludwig stepped down from the chair, still gripping his wife's hand.

"Let's find you a little peace and quiet." Merrick led them from the room.

They hosted a small, celebratory dinner with their closest friends that evening. The mood wasn't so much festive as relief that it was finally over.

Ludwig sat at the head of the table, Charlotte on his right. Beyond her was Cyn and Sig, whom he'd met years ago as a mercenary. Then Merrick and Gita, who'd welcomed him home, along with Emmett and Alexandra, who'd been such a great help in Eisen. Father Vernan attended, though he ate little and spoke even less. The Holy Father's face wore a blank expression, and Ludwig could only guess what he'd endured. The children joined them for the meal but remained quiet, somehow sensing the mood.

He'd invited Temple Captain Hamelyn, but the fellow insisted his order should have no say in the running of the realm. Ludwig respected his opinion but convinced him to maintain a presence here in Harlingen, ostensibly to help keep the peace during the transition of power.

The conversations felt forced, as nobody wanted to talk about the horrors of war. Once the children went to bed, Lord Emmett was the first to speak. "I think the question on everyone's mind is, what's next? It's one thing to seize the Crown but quite another to decide how to rule."

"I agree," said Ludwig. "Which is why I shall move slowly. I must ensure each baron takes an oath to serve the Crown, even those who fought against us. We can't have a united kingdom without shedding our past differences."

"Are you sure that's wise?"

"If we are to avoid the mistakes of the past, yes. Considering all that has happened, this won't be easy, but it's my hope we can bring everyone together for the betterment of all. To that end, I shall call each baron here to pledge their allegiance. I'd also like to invite the Elves of Nethendril to send a delegation, not to swear allegiance, but to demonstrate we are earnest in our desire to keep our promise to them."

"What of Verfeld?" asked Merrick. "I expect your duties here in Harlingen will keep you too busy to manage a barony."

"Pelton can oversee the day-to-day management, but perhaps it's time to create a new baron or two?" He let his gaze wander to Sigwulf and Cyn.

"Don't look at me," replied Cyn. "I'm happy being a captain. Make Siggy one, if you want, and I'll lend him a hand."

"Me, a baron?" said Sigwulf. "Seriously?"

"I can think of no one more deserving," replied Ludwig.

"Go on, Siggy. You know you want it."

"I accept, as long as you agree to be my baroness."

Cyn adopted the personality of a young maid, gushing her answer. "I thought you'd never ask."

"Good," said Ludwig. "I promised a few people some captaincies, but I'm afraid I'll be stealing them from the Verfeld garrison, so you'll need to do without them."

Sigwulf grinned. "I think I can manage."

"There's still the matter of the neighbouring realms," said Merrick. "I imagine it'll take some effort to convince them we mean them no harm."

Ludwig pondered how to achieve this. Deisenbach had been an ally of Otto, but would they recognize his reign? Then there was the matter of Grislagen.

"We'll start small," he finally said. "Cyn tells me the Duke of Hollenbeck is here in Harlingen. I'll meet with him tomorrow and assure him we'll come to his aid should he be invaded."

"And what do we get in reply?" asked Emmett.

"A friendly duchy on our border. He can also inform others we mean to help those in need."

"We already have people in Zowenbruch," said Charlotte. "We could send more to assist in diplomatic arrangements if needed?"

"An excellent idea. We'll also need to inform our allies in the north, assuring them we'll honour all existing agreements. Merrick, I wonder if I might impose on you and Gita to visit Deisenbach on our behalf?"

"We would be delighted," replied Merrick. "When would you like us to travel?"

"In the spring, but don't worry, we'll send word before your trip informing them you're coming."

"And Grislagen?"

"I considered sending Alexandra if she's willing." He turned to her. "I understand King Sagarus was friendly with your father. Speaking of which, your ancestral lands are restored to you, Alexandra, as is your name."

Father Vernan coughed. "If I may, Majesty, might I ask when we can expect your coronation?"

"Let's wait for winter so we can give some consideration to organizing things in the wake of this war."

"Might I suggest Midwinter Day?"

"That's a marvellous idea," replied Charlotte.

"Agreed," said Ludwig, "but I want no spectacle. If we are to be crowned, then let it be with humility. Father Vernan, could you convince the Archprior to forego the traditional extravagant trappings of his office?"

Vernan smiled. "I shall do what I can, Majesty."

EPILOGUE
WINTER 1104 SR

S igwulf and Cyn led the procession, riding in front of the king's archers, who were followed by a contingent of Temple Knights of Saint Mathew in their distinctive brown surcoats. The Royal Carriage came next, with Ludwig, Charlotte, and Frederick inside. Once they reached the Cathedral, Liesel would be waiting for their son, allowing the new king and queen to take their pledges as rulers of Hadenfeld. The men of Malburg, who'd risked so much during the rebellion, marched in their wake.

The procession halted as it reached the Cathedral of Saint Mathew. Servants rushed forth, depositing a step for their new sovereigns to exit, while warriors formed up on either side of the carpet, keeping the crowds at bay.

Ludwig stepped from the carriage, holding out his hand. Charlotte descended next, followed by Frederick. Father Vernan appeared out of nowhere to guide them towards the great doors of the Cathedral. He looked much better these days, having regained his previous weight, but his eyes still held a haunted look.

They reached the entrance, where Liesel waited along with Gita and young Kenley. The young prince was handed into Liesel's care, and then the Royal Couple entered.

Here, Merrick waited, along with more escorts. Traditionally, they would've been the king's knights, but with the war in everyone's thoughts and loyalties still in question, the Temple Knights stepped in to perform the duty.

In a move that surprised even Ludwig, half a dozen Temple Knights of Saint Agnes attended, including one wearing the distinctive sash of a

Temple Captain. These took up station on Charlotte's right while their brothers stood on Ludwig's left.

Everyone waited until the choir broke into song, then they walked down the nave towards the Archprior. This day, a new age for Hadenfeld was ushered in with the crowning of a new king and queen.

<<<<>>>>

REVIEW WARRIOR PRINCE

ONTO BOOK SEVEN: TEMPLE GENERAL

If you liked *Warrior Prince*, then *Servant of the Crown*, the first book in the *Heir to the Crown* series awaits with a sample chapter after the Cast of Characters or
START SERVANT OF THE CROWN

CAST OF CHARACTERS FOR WARRIOR LORD

MAIN CHARACTERS

Alexandra Kuhn – Baroness of Dornbruck, wife of Emmett
Charlotte Altenburg - Baroness of Verfeld, wife of Ludwig
Cynthia 'Cyn' Hoffman – Mercenary, good friend of Ludwig
Emmett Kuhn - Baron of Dornbruck
Gita Sternhassen - Baroness of Drakenfeld
Ludwig Altenburg - Baron of Verfeld
Merrick Sternhassen - Baron of Drakenfeld
Sigwulf 'Siggy' Marhaven - Mercenary and good friend of Ludwig
Vernan - Holy Father of Saint Mathew

BARONS OF HADENFELD

Arnsbach - Heiden Bohm
Bruggendorf - Jurgen Voltz
Dornbruck - Emmett Kuhn
Drakenfeld - Merrick Sternhassen
Glosnecke - Darrian Forst
Grienwald - Morgan Bahn
Hasdorf - Wilbur Kohl
Langeven - Merten Boesch
Luwen - Meinhard Schafenburg
Ramfeldon - Jonas Goswald
Tongrin - Werner Zimmer
Udenacht - Nikolaus Wendt
Valksburg - Rikart Schriener

Verfeld - Ludwig Altenburg
Zwieken - Anson Meier

NOBLES OF HADENFELD

Amalric Schafenburg (Deceased) - Younger brother of Alexandra Kuhn
Egan Kohl (Deceased) - Former Baron of Hasdorf
Emril - Knight of Hadenfeld, in service to Morgan
Erisella Zimmer - Baroness, wife of Werner
Esmerelda Boesch - Daughter of Merten
Evangeline Kuhn - Daughter of Emmett and Alexandra
Frederick Altenburg - Son of Ludwig and Charlotte
Frederick Altenburg (Deceased) - Baron of Verfeld, Father of Ludwig
Gowan Forst - Son of Lord Harvald and younger brother of Darrian
Harvald Forst (Deceased) - Former Baron of Glosnecke
Heston - Knight of Hadenfeld
Kasper (Deceased) - Cousin to Otto
Kenley Sternhassen - Son of Merrick and Gita
Luther (Deceased) - Cousin to Otto
Morgan II - Present King of Hadenfeld
Otto (Deceased) - Previous King of Hadenfeld
Petrus - Knight of Hadenfeld
Reisen Forst - Knight, cousin to Darrian Forst

PEOPLE OF THE BARONY OF VERFELD

Bernardo - Villager, Freiburg
Brother Hamelyn - Temple Knight of Saint Mathew, Malburg
Carson - Manservant, Verfeld Keep
Dolf Macken - Villager, son of Deiter Macken, Eramon
Edwig - Warrior from Roshlag, Therengian descent, Verfeld Garrison
Estelle deShandria - Charlaine's mother, Malburg
Gustavo - Warrior from Roshlag, Calabrian descent, Verfeld Garrison
Hartwin Bengle - Elector, Malburg
Kalen Hasrich - Archer from Roshlag, Verfeld Garrison
Kandam - Warrior, Kurathian descent, Verfeld Garrison
Kenmar - Foot soldier, Verfeld Garrison
Kurt Wasser - Expert swordsman, Verfeld
Marjorie Macken - Villager, wife of Dolf Macken, Eramon
Paran - Warrior from Roshlag, Verfeld Garrison
Pelton Wakefield - Castellan, Verfeld
Rikal - Archer from Roshlag, Verfeld Garrison
Tomas deShandria - Charlaine's father, Master Swordsmith, Elector,

Malburg
    Yannick, Brother of Saint Mathew, Malburg

PEOPLE OF NETHENDRIL
    Elonin - Elf Talon (Captain), Enchanter
    Falandril - Elf High Lord of Nethendril
    Galrandir - Elf Life Mage
    Reylar - Elf Lord, Brother to Falandril
    Sindra - Elf Lord, Earth Mage, Daughter of High Lord

OTHERS
    Berath Yorian - Warden of Eisen
    Bethiel - Elf Lord, Arnsfeld
    Charlaine deShandria - Temple Commander of Saint Agnes
    Danica Meer - Temple Captain of Saint Agnes
    Diedrich (Deceased)- King of Neuhafen
    Graxion Stormwind - Advisor, King Konrad
    Hamelyn - Temple Captain of Saint Mathew, Eisen
    Henfrey - Temple Captain of Saint Mathew, Agran
    Hieronymus - Prior of Saint Mathew, Eisen
    Jochen Frei - Scholar, Eisen
    Koldan Sartellian - Fire Mage, in service to Jurgen, Harlingen
    Konrad- King of Zowenbruch
    Liesel - Wife of Emmet's cousin, Eisen
    Mina Stormwind - Water Mage, Neuhafen
    Rascalian - Bard, visiting Harlingen
    Roderick of Tollingsbruck - Knight, Hollenbeck
    Rosalyn Haas - Daughter, Baron of Regnitz, Erlingen
    Rurlan - Dwarf courier, smiths guild
    Sagarus - King of Grislagen
    Ulfric Sternhassen - Duke of Hollenbeck
    Willy Stoltz - Crossed Swords mercenary company
    Wulfram Haas - Baron of Regnitz, Erlingen

PLACES
HADENFELD
    Eisen - Old capital, Neuhafen
    Eramon - Village, Barony of Verfeld
    Erhard's Folly - Hills north of Verfeld
    Erlen River - River fed by Lake Eisen
    Freiburg - Village, Barony of Verfeld

Harlingen - Capital, Hadenfeld
Hollen River - River forming the southern border of Hadenfeld
Lake Eisen - Beside the City of Eisen
Lucky Duck - Tavern, Harlingen
Malburg - Free city, Barony of Verfeld
Roshlag - Village, Barony of Verfeld
The Badger – Tavern, Glosnecke
The Cygnet - Tavern, Harlingen
The Dove - Roadside Inn, north of Harlingen
The Ragged Dog - Inn, Village of Roshlag
The Willow - Well-to-do Inn/Tavern, Malburg
Thorncraft - Abandoned village, east of Eisen
Verfeld - Village, Barony of Verfeld
Volsund - Village, Barony of Verfeld

PETTY KINGDOMS

Abelard - Northern kingdom
Ardosa - Kingdom, east of Hadenfeld
Arnsfeld - Northern Kingdom, borders Halvaria
Deisenbach - Kingdom, north of Hadenfeld
Erlingen - Duchy, north of Zowenbruch
Grislagen - Kingdom, west of Hadenfeld
Hollenbeck - Duchy, south of Hadenfeld
Kingshaven - Kingdom, east of Hadenfeld
Menzen – Kingdom, east of Hadenfeld
Neuhafen (Dissolved) - Former Kingdom, eastern Hadenfeld
Reinwick - Duchy, north coast
Talstadt - Duchy
Zowenbruch - Kingdom, north of Hadenfeld

OTHER PLACES

Agran - Capital, Deisenbach
Blunden - Charlotte's birthplace, town, Reinwick
Calabria – Former Kingdom, occupied by Halvaria
Eiddenwerthe - The known lands
Eidenburg - City, Duchy of Talstadt
Great Northern Sea - Large body of water, north
Halvaria – Empire, west of the Petty Kingdoms
Harlingen Hills - Hills east and north of Harlingen
Herani - Holy City, western coast, Shimmering Sea
Klermacht - Capital, Hollenbeck

Korascajan - Training academy for Fire Mages
Kurslingen - Capital, Zowenbruch
Lucky Crow - Tavern in Freiburg
Nethendril - Elven city, The Goldenwood
Regnitz - Village/Barony, Erlingen
Rosenbruck - City, Zowenbruch
Stormtop Mountains - Between Halvaria and the Petty Kingdoms
The Forge - Training academy, Temple Knights, Eidenburg
The Goldenwood - Elf name for the forest in East Hadenfeld
The Greenwood - Forest, Barony of Verfeld
Therengia – Realm, east of the Petty Kingdoms
Volstrum - Training academy, Water Mages, Karslev, Ruzhina

GODS AND SAINTS

Agnes - Saint
Akosia - Goddess of Water
Cunar Marthune - Saint
Erylor - Goddess of Fertility
Gundar - God of earth, creator of the Dwarves
Mathew - Saint
Ragnar - Saint

BATTLES

Second Battle of Harlingen (1100 SR) - Hadenfeld defeats Neuhafen
Battle of Shadows (1085 SR) - Neuhafen defeats Zowenbruch's invasion
The Great War - Between Orcs and Elves, 2000 years ago

THINGS

Barn bread - slices of old bread fried in bacon fat
Book of Saint Mathew - Tome of the teachings of Saint Mathew
Grim Defenders - Mercenary company, former employer of Ludwig
High Elves - One of the Elder Races
Ithilium(godstone or sky metal) - Metal from the sky
Knights of the Golden Chalice - Order of Chivalry, Zowenbruch
Old Gods - gods worshipped before the coming of the Saints
Sartellians - Fire Mages, trained in Korascajan
Stormwinds - Water Mages, trained at the Volstrum
Temple Knight - Member of a religious fighting order
The Crossed Swords - Mercenary company run by Cyn's father
Underworld - Where people go after they die if they are not virtuous
Valiant - Temple warship serving in the north

A FEW WORDS FROM PAUL

Ludwig is evolving. After beginning life as the spoiled son of a wealthy baron in Warrior Knight, he learned humility and the value of friendship. Returning home in Warrior Lord, he discovers his father has died, forcing him into the role of baron. In the beginning, he struggles but comes to accept his role as a noble of the realm.

In Warrior Prince, he is once more thrust into an unexpected life, that of heir to the crown. In a sense, he's a reluctant prince, but he takes his responsibilities seriously and does what he believes is best for the people of Hadenfeld. This very characteristic is what leads to conflict with his king.

Charlotte's evolution is almost as striking as Ludwig's. When Warrior Prince begins, we see her struggling to fit in, much like her husband. Her illness requires patience and understanding, which Ludwig strives to give her. As events unfold, however, their roles reverse, with her providing Ludwig emotional and intellectual support in his time of greatest need.

By the end of the story, they stand as equals, shoulder to shoulder, ready to take the oath of King and Queen of Hadenfeld, a fitting ending to this particular story arc, but their tale is far from over. The Halvarian Empire will soon rear its ugly head once more, and this time, they'll ensure there's no more interference from the meddlesome Temple Knights.

The story continues in the next Power Ascending Book, Temple General. Ludwig will return in Warrior King.

I want to thank my wife, Carol, whose tireless encouragement and editing led to the completion of this tale. Without her support, this series would never have seen the light of day, let alone eventually reach eight books. I want to express my appreciation of Christie Bennett, Stephanie Sandrock, and Amanda Bennett for their love and support, along with our gaming friends, Brad Aitkin, Stephen Brown, and the late Jeffrey Parker.

My BETA team, as always, has provided valuable feedback leading to a better novel, so let me give a special shout-out to: Rachel Deibler, Michael Rhew, Phyllis Simpson, Don Hinckley, Charles Mohapel, Debra Reeves, Susan Young, Anna Ostberg, Joanna Smith, James McGinnis, Jim Burke, Lisa Hanika, Lisa Hunt, and Keven Hutchinson.

I also want to acknowledge the outpouring of support from readers like you, who encourage me to continue these stories through your emails and online reviews. I hope you enjoy Ludwig's newest adventures.

ABOUT THE AUTHOR

Paul J Bennett (b. 1961) emigrated from England to Canada in 1967. His father served in the British Royal Navy, and his mother worked for the BBC in London. As a young man, Paul followed in his father's footsteps, joining the Canadian Armed Forces in 1983. He is married to Carol Bennett and has three daughters who are all creative in their own right.

Paul's interest in writing started in his teen years when he discovered the roleplaying game, Dungeons & Dragons (D & D). What attracted him to this new hobby was the creativity it required; the need to create realms, worlds and adventures that pulled the gamers into his stories.

In his 30's, Paul started to dabble in designing his own roleplaying system, using the Peninsular War in Portugal as his backdrop. His regular gaming group were willing victims, er, participants in helping to playtest this new system. A few years later, he added additional settings to his game, including Science Fiction, Post-Apocalyptic, World War II, and the all-important Fantasy Realm where his stories take place.

The beginnings of his first book 'Servant to the Crown' originated over five years ago when he began running a new fantasy campaign. For the world that the Kingdom of Merceria is in, he ran his adventures like a TV show, with seasons that each had twelve episodes, and an overarching plot. When the campaign ended, he knew all the characters, what they had to accomplish, what needed to happen to move the plot along, and it was this that inspired to sit down to write his first novel.

Paul now has four series based in his fantasy world of Eiddenwerthe, and is looking forward to sharing many more books with his readers over the coming years.

Printed in Great Britain
by Amazon

41321494R00219